Perseverance Street

Ken McCoy

2 7 / 7 / 13

piatkus

PIATKUS

First published in Great Britain in 2013 by Piatkus

Copyright © 2013 by Ken McCoy

The moral right of the author has been asserted.

*All characters and events in this publication, other than those clearly in
the public domain, are fictitious and any resemblance to real persons,
living or dead, is purely coincidental.*

All rights reserved. No part of this publication may be reproduced,
stored in a retrieval system, or transmitted in any form or by any means,
without the prior permission in writing of the publisher, nor be otherwise
circulated in any form of binding or cover other than that in which it
is published and without a similar condition including this condition
being imposed on the subsequent purchaser.

A CIP catalogue record for this book is available from the British Library.

ISBN 978-0-7499-5847-3

Typeset in Bembo by Hewer Text UK Ltd, Edinburgh
Printed and bound by CPI Group (UK) Ltd, Croydon, CR0 4YY

Papers used by Piatkus are from well-managed forests
and other responsible sources.

MIX
Paper from
responsible sources
FSC® C104740
www.fsc.org

Piatkus
An imprint of
Little, Brown Book Group
100 Victoria Embankment
London EC4Y 0DY

An Hachette UK Company
www.hachette.co.uk
www.piatkus.co.uk

To my daughter-in-law Gemma Louise Myers

Chapter 1

Leeds. Saturday 21st April 1945

'Hey, cloth ears! I said 'ow old are yer? If yer don't tell us, we'll do yer.'

Michael looked up at the two boys towering over him. They were quite old, possibly as old as six. Everyone said how he looked older than his age, which was a problem right now. He screwed up his face in deep thought. What to say for the best? If he told them he was four they'd most probably think he was telling lies and *do him*, whatever that meant – it didn't sound good. Then he thought of a great answer and looked down at his boots, which could do with a good polish.

'Allus look at yer boots when yer tellin' fibs,' was what Tony Lafferty had once told him. 'If yer look at yer boots they can't tell if yer fibbin'.'

'Five.'

One of them grabbed a handful of his jumper and snarled at him.

'Yer little liar!'

Michael was a bit shocked that they knew he was fibbing. He'd been looking at his boots, so how did they know? He was now considering a second option

– running away. He was a good runner, nearly as fast as Tony Lafferty who had something called rickets which gave him bow legs. 'Poor lad wouldn't stop a pig in a passage,' Michael's dad once said. 'Never drank his milk, that's his trouble. Drink your milk, son, or you'll end up with bendy bones like Lafferty's lad.'

If only this big kid would let go of his jumper. Michael was wishing he *was* five. But if he was five he'd most probably look six. If they didn't believe he was five they'd never believe he was four, which was how old he was. Four and a quarter, according to his mam. What should he tell them?

He felt a cuff to the side of his head that sent him spinning to the ground. He grazed his knee but he wasn't going to cry. If they thought they could make him cry they had another think coming. His dad was a soldier and he wouldn't think much of his son if he started crying just because he'd grazed his knee. It was just one more scab to go with the others that decorated both of his knees. At least no one was holding on to his jumper now. They were both standing over him and laughing, which wasn't fair. His dad had told him it was rude to laugh at people. It wasn't the sort of laughing that might make him laugh along with them. This was bad laughing because they were bad boys.

Tears arrived, despite his determination not to cry. In a fit of petulance he lashed out with the heel of his right boot, which was reinforced with brand-new steel segs. Great for kicking up sparks. He caught one of the boys on his bare shin. The boy let out an agonised howl.

Michael sprang to his feet and set off running. He'd gone no more than half a dozen steps when the other boy caught him up and grabbed his jumper again.

'Right, yer little bugger! Yer've proper 'ad it now!'

Michael wiped away the tears with the back of his hand. 'Leave us alone. I've done nowt!' A low hum sounded in the distance, giving Michael a germ of an idea.

'Yer've just broke me mate's leg. That means yer'll go ter jail.'

The low hum gradually built up to an echoing whine as the man winding the handle that worked the air-raid siren picked up speed. Michael knew there weren't any German bombers coming because his mam had told him about them testing out the siren just before teatime, and he was due in for his tea any time now. He'd been standing at the end of Perseverance Street waiting for it to start when the two bullies arrived. He was wondering if they knew it was only a test. He pointed at the sky.

'Look. There's a load o' German bombers over there.'

'Where?'

'Oh, they've just gone behind a cloud.'

It was a brilliant fib, one he was quite proud of. He'd tell Tony Lafferty about this. It'd make him laugh. The siren whined on. The bully looked up, uncertainly. His crony was staggering to his feet, hobbling on his injured shin.

'This kid reckons he can see German bombers.'

'I can,' said Michael. 'Up there, look. Oh heck! They've gone again.'

The siren's whine grew to a crescendo as the man winding it got up to full speed. The siren was on the

3

roof of Kershawe's factory about a quarter of a mile away from the boys. A woman was hurrying down the road. The bigger boys looked around. Everyone seemed to be hurrying.

'Me mam said I've got ter go home, when t' siren starts,' said Michael. 'We've got a shelter in our cellar. Me dad made it.' He was backing away as he said it. His finger was pointing upwards once again.

'Look, it's a Messyshit.'

It was the only German plane he knew. Tony Lafferty had taught him the name. Tony was five and knew all sorts of stuff. Michael's mam didn't like him playing with Tony because he was a rough lad but Michael thought he was great. He turned and ran, as did the bigger boys, only in opposite directions.

Michael arrived home just as the siren was winding down. He had a grazed knee and a big smile on his face. He'd tricked the big boys. He'd tell Tony all about it tomorrow, but he wouldn't mention it to his mam. If she knew what had happened she wouldn't let him play out on his own again. She'd only let him if she was watching and he wasn't a baby any more.

The door to number 13 was open and Michael shot straight into his house. His mother was in the scullery boiling eggs. They'd have two eggs each followed by an Eccles cake, with bread and jam to fill up any empty spaces plus a glass of milk for Michael. Michael always managed to have an empty space and, not wanting to end up with bendy bones like Tony, he liked his milk. Lily Robinson preferred a nice cup of tea. She turned and revealed the bump that housed the next addition to their family. Michael knew it was a baby brother or a sister but he wasn't sure how it had got in there, or how it would get out. He smiled up at his mam. She smiled down at him.

'Hello, cheeky face. Hey, have you been crying?'

'I fell on me knee.'

He showed her his injury.

'That's with running too fast. I've told you about that. Come in the scullery, I'll have to get all that muck off before I stick a plaster on.'

'What's for tea?'

'Boiled eggs and Eccles cakes.'

'Ugh! Fly pie.'

'I thought you liked Eccles cake.'

Tony Lafferty had told him that Eccles cake was really fly pie and Michael couldn't understand why a pie made with flies should taste so good. He was a happy boy who knew no better than the circumstances in which he lived. Dad away at war; mam scraping to make ends meet; fly pie for tea.

Chapter 2

Tuesday 24th April 1945

The telegraph boy wasn't whistling as he pedalled his red bicycle over the cobbles of Perseverance Street. Far from it. His chain needed oiling, but he usually whistled, creaking chain or not, as telegraph boys did back then. It was their way of heralding their arrival, followed by a cheerful knock. Any telegraph boy who wasn't whistling had nothing to whistle about. At times like this he thought his was the worst job of the war – apart from being a soldier and being shot at by Germans. His first delivery was a notification of death and he was not to hang around. His instructions were to deliver it with politeness, respect, *and no whistling*.

'And clear off sharpish before she starts moaning.'

His dispatcher wasn't a heartless man, just practical. When the residents of Perseverance Street heard the creaking bike they glanced through their windows to see where he was heading; praying that he wasn't going to slow down and dismount outside their house. Him and his bad tidings. Well-off people living in the more northern suburbs wouldn't have been quite so worried, as they used the telegram service to exchange urgent

6

messages. Not so the people of Perseverance Street whose messages were never so urgent as to waste good money on their delivery. The telegraph boy would be a guaranteed messenger of doom at any of these doors.

Had it been a doctor at a Perseverance Street door it would have been a sure-fire way of knowing someone inside was on their last legs; the same went for a priest or a minister of any church. The watchers at the windows breathed sighs of relief that the boy had passed them by; relief that turned to morbid curiosity which took them to their doors where they stood with folded arms. He dismounted outside number 13 and propped his bike up by resting a pedal on the kerb.

'Oh heck! It's young Lily – it'll be 'er Larry.'

'And 'er over eight months gone an' all.'

The watchers saw Lily standing at her window.

'Oh, heck! She can see 'im!'

There were small bay windows in each house from where the occupant had a good sideways view of the street. Lily Robinson heard the creaking bike and glanced out of the window at the approaching boy. Her heart sank like a stone when she saw him swing his leg over the bike to dismount and cruise to a stop outside her house. He looked inside his bag, took out a brown envelope and double-checked the address against the house number. His knock was loud enough for anyone inside to hear but not so loud as to be disrespectful. Across the street the morbid watchers watched from beneath furrowed brows. Inside the house an icy dread rushed through Lily's body, freezing all movement. On the doorstep the boy's concentration was on the unpleasant job in hand. Glancing neither right or left, just at the door, waiting for it to open. Half hoping the lady wasn't in.

Lily managed to move to the door and stood behind it, a hand on her mouth, paralysed with dread. It might well be that she was worrying for nothing, but deep down she knew she wasn't.

Half a minute went by without the door opening. The boy was about to knock again. If no one answered after two knocks he'd leave it for someone else to deliver later in the day.

'She *is* in, love,' called out one of the watchers helpfully.

He knocked again and waited. The door opened, very slowly. The boy held out the envelope and announced, 'Telegram for Mrs Lilian Robinson.'

'W – what is it?' Lily asked him, making no attempt to take it.

The fourteen-year-old-boy had met with many reactions, none of which he was ever prepared for.

'Are you Mrs Lilian Robinson . . . Mrs?'

His arm was still outstretched, holding the envelope to which her eyes were glued with dread.

'Er . . . yes, yes, I am.'

Her quivering hand went to her mouth. The neighbours were glancing at each other, not quite knowing what to do. Should they go across and give her their support? Eventually, with an effort, Lily took the envelope and disappeared inside the house.

The boy got on his bike and pedalled off to deliver a *Missing In Action* to a house on Perseverance Mount. He really hated this part of the job but his mam had told him the war would be over soon and he wouldn't have too many more to deliver. The neighbours gathered round in a circle and discussed what to do for the best. Jobs were being assigned.

'Give her five minutes then a couple of us go over – make her a cup o' tea. That's allus good fer shock.'

'That's her washin' on t' line. I'll take it in – it looks like rain. Someone'll need ter keep an eye on 'er Michael.'

'I'll do that. I'll bring him over here fer 'is tea, poor little beggar.'

They were being good neighbours in a time of crisis. But good neighbours can be capricious creatures, as Lily would soon find out.

Chapter 3

[faint show-through text from previous page, illegible]

Friday 27th April 1945

The Austin 7 rattled over the cobbles with its wipers fighting a losing battle against the pouring rain. The street was deserted because the rain had washed all the residents indoors. The small car slowed down to walking pace and the large man inside peered out through the windscreen to try and identify Lily's house from the numbers neatly painted on the bricks beside each door. The rain was washing chalk graffiti off the walls. One of them was a streaked and fading HITLER IS A TWERP, alongside a blurred drawing of the ubiquitous Chad saying WOT, NO BANANAS? Washing lines were strung out across the street, all empty except for two sparrows sitting side by side and taking it in turn to disappear inside a flurry of feathers and spray, then reappear, as calm as you like. Beside the large man sat his wife who had wiped a hole in the condensation on her side window with her gloved hand. Her eyes were scanning the doors.

'The odd numbers are on my side,' she was saying. 'Nineteen . . . seventeen . . . fifteen . . . Here we are.'

She looked at the dark red door of number 13 which

stood out from its drab, paint-peeling neighbours. Even through the rain she could tell that the front steps had been donkey-stoned, leaving a neat, rust-brown line around the edges. It was the doorway of someone who usually tried to make the best of things. The man stopped the car outside the house and turned off the engine, which shuddered to an eventual halt. He pulled on the handbrake and turned off the windscreen wipers. He glanced through the side window to where his wife was pointing, then from the back seat picked up a grey trilby which he jammed on his balding head and checked his appearance in the driver's mirror. His wife took out a powder compact and gave her cheeks a liberal dusting. The man set his hat straight, tweaked his military moustache into place, stepped out of his car and stretched the cramp from his legs. Then he walked round to the passenger side to open the door for his wife who was quite diminutive and fitted the tiny car a lot better than he did.

'Pity you didn't think to bring an umbrella,' she said brusquely.

High in the sky several barrage balloons swayed in the wind, anchored to the ground by steel cables; two of them disappeared into the rain clouds, up there to prevent German aircraft flying too low. Surplus to requirements really; as much use as party balloons, some people said, but the Home Guard needed something to do and guarding the barrage balloons was the only job available at this end of the war. The man glanced up at them, then winked at his wife.

'Just what the doctor ordered,' he said.

The street doorway offered little protection from the rain and they stood on the top step as close to the door as they could. Their knock was answered almost immediately and the man removed his hat, partly out of politeness and partly so that she might immediately identify him and invite them in out of the rain.

'Mr and Mrs Oldroyd . . . I didn't . . . Oh, please come in out of this awful weather.'

The couple stepped through the door, gratefully, and wiped their feet in turn on the door mat. At Lily's behest Mr Oldroyd took a seat in the chair that he guessed had once been her husband's and his wife sat down on a two-seater settee. A small boy was playing on the floor with a brightly painted wooden giraffe.

'Hello, Michael. I wonder if you remember us?' said Oldroyd.

'Of course you remember Mr and Mrs Oldroyd, don't you, Michael?' said Lily. 'You'll remember feeding the horses in the field at the back of their lovely house in the country.'

Michael looked up at the man and nodded, slowly, to indicate that he did remember – if not Mr and Mrs Oldroyd, then at least the horses. Lily turned off the radio which had been tuned in to the Light Programme and playing *Music While You Work*. She was wearing a pinafore that hung down from her bump like a curtain in a bay window. She pushed away a loose strand of dark hair which she'd hurriedly tied back when she'd heard the knock at the door. She'd looked outside and seen the car, and recognised it as the Oldroyds'.

She wore no make-up and looked older then her

twenty-five years. Her red-rimmed eyes were under-lined by the dark shadows of sleepless nights. Her skin was pale and drawn and her mouth slightly turned down at the edges. Not for Lily the bloom of a pregnant mother; such a bloom tends to pale when your soldier husband is killed in action, but beneath it all lay the evidence of a good-looking young woman. That was the one thing Oldroyd remembered about her.

She looked to have been busy around the house. It was probably all she had to keep the pain of bereavement at bay.

Three days had passed since Lily had heard the news; ten days since Larry's death. He would have most prob-ably been buried by now, with whatever military honours were available, so she'd been told. That didn't help. To lose her Larry and not have the chance to say a proper goodbye was hard.

He'd just been an ordinary man, a twenty-eight-year-old bank clerk who given the chance would probably have risen to bank manager after the war. Unremarkable but decent, Larry was never a fighting man but he'd been called up along with two million others and he'd had to go. Given the choice he'd have stayed at home with Lily and Michael and the new baby and let some-one else do the fighting.

'Keep your head down, Larry,' she'd told him often enough.

'No need to tell me that, love. Them Nazzies won't get me in their sights. No two ways about that, love.'

The day after she received the telegram, a man from the War Office had called on her, offering his condolences and giving her details of the help she could receive, including her war widow's pension. He told her that Larry had been killed in action, apparently by a German shell as he was helping a wounded comrade to safety under heavy fire. It sounded quite heroic. She'd tried to conjure up pictures of her Larry springing into action against the enemy, but her imagination wouldn't stretch that far. The violent manner of his death had seemed so much at odds with the gentle manner of his pre-war life.

Oldroyd sat scrunching the brim of his trilby in both hands, his face in mourning. 'We read about Larry in the *Yorkshire Post* this morning. Edith insisted that we come as soon as I could. We're ever so sorry. We both are. Edith cried buckets when she heard, didn't you, love?'

'Heartbroken,' confirmed Edith.

She glanced at Lily's bump. 'This should be such a happy time for you. What a cruel world we live in. Such awful people, them damned Germans. Why they should want to do this beats me. Bernard'd join up in a flash but he's too old to go fighting wars.'

'Well, I'm pushin' fifty now,' Bernard told her. 'Mind you, I did me bit in the first lot. Lucky to come home unscathed.'

He smiled down at Michael then placed a contrite hand over his mouth and looked at his wife, wondering if they'd spoken out of turn about Larry's death.

'It's all right, I've told him,' said Lily, running a crook'd finger under her left eye to remove a tear – something she'd done so often in the last three days that she scarcely knew she was doing it. 'He knows his daddy has gone to heaven where all the really brave soldiers go.'

There was a silence. Edith looked around the room which smelled of pine furniture polish and looked spotless, with pristine white lace curtains and a generous square of patterned Axminster over gleaming linoleum.

'You keep a good house, Lily. A house to be proud of.'

'I have to keep myself busy or I'll go mad.' Lily paused and added, 'You always know it can happen, but nothing prepares you for it. It's usually something that happens to other folk.'

'I know,' Bernard said. 'I lost a brother in 1917.'

'I didn't know that. I'm ever so sorry.'

'Don't really know how he died. Missing presumed dead was all we were ever told.' He looked out of the window. 'Yer'll have heard of Passchendaele, I suppose?'

'I have,' said Lily.

'Foul weather – ten times worse than this. July and absolutely bucketing down. Heaviest rain in thirty years. Went on for weeks. Absolute quagmire. Mud so deep a man could drown in it, and a lot did. Horses as well. If our Stuart was killed outright it'll have been a mercy. The odds were that he was probably wounded and drowned in the mud.'

Then he added, sadly, 'I was in Flanders meself as matter of fact – different regiment. Didn't find out about our Stuart for nearly two months and I can't have been above five miles away from him when he died. The whole thing was a right bloody mess. A waste of good men's lives. At the end of it all there was nowt left worth winning.'

'My Larry was killed outright by a German shell.'

'He won't have suffered, then.'

'No, I don't imagine he did.'

'I have to say, this is a war worth winning – not like the first bloody lot. What I'm trying to say is that your husband won't have died for nowt like our Stuart – if that's of any comfort.'

'Well, I wouldn't like to think he'd died for nothing, Mr Oldroyd.'

'It's Bernard and Edith. No need for us to be formal. We are old friends, after all.'

Lily wouldn't have classed them as old friends, but it would have been impolite to point that out. They were sitting in a wine-coloured three-piece lounge suite in uncut moquette. Also in the room was a drop-leaf dining table with four chairs, an oak side board on which was a wedding photograph, a Bush radio and three vases of flowers representing, Mrs Oldroyd guessed, the condolences of well-wishers. The wedding photo showed Lily looking her best in a white wedding gown and Larry beaming. He was looking at her from the corner of his eyes, as if unable to believe his luck at having won himself such a beautiful bride.

One wall was dominated by a cast-iron range that was a fireplace, an oven and a water heater. Above it was a mantelpiece on which stood a grinning toby jug, an old tobacco tin containing money for the milkman and other sundry requirements, a slender glass vase full of multi-coloured wooden spills (to light the fire, a cigarette or the gas ring in the scullery) and a framed photo of Larry in his army uniform. He wore a beret set at a rakish angle and a moustache that he'd grown since he'd been called up. The beret was a bit too big and the moustache didn't really suit him. It wasn't Lily's favourite photo of him but it was the most recent and it had been done in a studio so she'd given it pride of place.

It was a modest dwelling of which the most had been made. Larry had been buying the house on a bank mortgage which, since his call-up, was being paid by the army in exchange for Larry fighting for his country. It would now be paid off in full by the bank, something Lily hadn't even thought about until a letter of condolence had arrived from the bank that morning. She was a property-owning war widow. It was little consolation.

'Would er . . . would you like a cup of tea?'

Her voice was hesitant and devoid of all the life and charm he remembered in this young woman, but it was no more than he expected. An antique wallclock that looked to have come from a much grander house than this began to chime the hour, which was five p.m.

'Tea would be lovely, thanks,' said Bernard.

'Edith?'

'Please. Milk, one sugar.'

'Just milk for me, please.'

Lily gave him a wan smile. 'That's right. I remember. You say you're sweet enough, or something like that, don't you.'

He returned her smile and said, 'Something like that.'

She went into the scullery with Michael clinging on

17

to her skirt, not really remembering these people who had come to see his mam. After a couple of minutes she came back with two cups of tea, rattling in their saucers; so much were her hands shaking.

'Are you not having one?' Bernard asked, taking the tea from her.

'What? Oh, no. I've just had one. This is what was left in the pot. It should be all right.'

He took out a packet of Churchmans from his pocket and offered one to Lily, who declined.

'No thanks very much. I've given up until the baby's born. I've been told it's harmful to the baby to smoke during pregnancy.'

'Really? Well, I've never heard that. They blame cigs for most things nowadays, even cancer. Rubbish to that is what I say. Cigarette smoke purges the lungs – I've read that. That's why footballers smoke.'

'Pity it doesn't purge the brain of foolishness,' said Edith. 'As far as I'm concerned you can't be too careful as far as babies are concerned. We were never blessed, as you know.'

'Do you mind if I –?' asked Bernard, holding a ciga-rette in one hand and a lighter in the other.

'Not at all. I'll get you an ashtray.'

'I don't indulge,' said Edith piously. 'I don't think smoking does anyone any good. His fags cost half a crown for twenty and he smokes forty a day. Every four days it's a pound note gone up in smoke. Daylight robbery if you ask me.'

'Nay, lass, it's the only vice I've got,' grinned Oldroyd. 'I'm not a big drinker and I don't gamble, apart from a few bob on t' Grand National once a year.' He lit his cigarette and looked down at Michael, giving the boy an avuncular smile. 'Now then young feller, you look to me like a lad who likes Dinky Toys. Am I right, Michael?'

Michael, who didn't know what a Dinky Toy was, stared up at him, saying nothing, just clutching his wooden giraffe. Bernard stuck his cigarette in the side of his mouth and patted either side of his coat with both hands before reaching inside the right-hand pocket. He brought out a model car, which he placed in the boy's hand.

'It an American Cadillac. I thought you might like it. All the Hollywood film stars have 'em so I thought you might as well have one.'

Michael's eyes widened in wonder as he took the gift and examined it closely.

'Say, "Thank You",' said Lily.

'Thank you,' Michael said, without taking his eyes off the car.

'We've got a lot more of those at home,' the man said. 'If you ever come to visit me you can play with them as long as you like.' He winked at Lily and added, 'I never did grow up.'

'Like a big kid sometimes,' confirmed Edith, smiling. She reached out and placed a hand on Lily's. 'How're you coping, love – honestly?'

Lily felt Bernard's eyes on her as well. She ran her hands through her hair and began to cry.

'Oh, I'm sorry, love,' said Edith. 'I didn't mean to set you off.'

'No, it's not you – it's just that . . . well, apart from neighbours I really haven't got anybody.'

'What about Larry's family?' asked Bernard.

Lily shook her head. 'Them? I might as well be dead as well as far as they're concerned. I was never good enough for their Larry. They probably blame me for him being killed, knowing them.' There was unashamed bitterness in her voice.

'Oh dear,' said Edith. 'I wish we lived nearer so we could help.'

'Maybe we can,' said Bernard.

Edith looked at him querulously.

'I do have a car, Edith. We can pop over from time to time. Tell you what, here's an idea. Why don't we take Michael off your hands for a couple of days? Give him a bit of a treat and give you a bit of a breather.'

Edith answered for Lily. 'No, Bernard. She'll want the lad with her at a time like this. You men, you just don't understand stuff.'

'Sorry. It was just an idea.'

'It was a very nice idea, Bernard,' said Lily, 'but Edith's right. Michael's a great comfort to me right now.'

'Of course there's all that stuff about the bombing,' Edith said. 'I couldn't help but notice the barrage balloons are all up, so there must be some truth in it.'

'What stuff about bombs?' said Lily.

Bernard gave his wife a reproachful glance that Lily noticed. 'Look,' he said, 'we don't want to scare you, Lily, but there's been stuff in the papers recently saying that the Luftwaffe's going to make one last big effort to come up to Leeds here and bomb our munitions factories.'

'But I thought the war was nearly over.'

'Try telling that to them daft German beggars. Fight to the last man, some of 'em. Bloody fanatics!'

'When's all this supposed to happen?'

'I don't know, love,' Bernard said. 'Probably never, but the papers say any time now. They evidently invented some new type of planes called jets – Messerschmitts or something. They're supposed to be twice as fast as anything we've got. It could be that Edith's right about the barrage balloons.'

'What? But they're always up . . . aren't they?'

Edith jabbed a thumb in the direction of the window. 'Are they really? As many as that?'

'Oh, I don't really know. I never look up at them, nowadays.'

'They're after that Royal Ordnance Factory at Barnbow,' said Bernard, 'and all them engineering works down in Hunslet. It what they were after when they bombed Leeds in 1941 – and you know where the bombs landed then.'

Lily nodded. 'Not far from here. There were bombs two streets away, quite a few killed.'

'I know – that's what bothers us. The problem is when they fly up to Yorkshire they've only got just enough fuel left to get back to Germany, and there's always a mucky cloud over Leeds from all these factory chimneys and they can't see where to drop their bombs so they just drop 'em anywhere to get rid and bugger off back home. Yer all targets, love.'

Edith looked at Lily and shrugged. 'We've already got my sister from Hunslet and her two boys living with us but we could squeeze another small boy in at a pinch.' She looked down at Michael, now running his new toy across the lino and making a car engine noise, then back up at Lily. 'Anyway, it's up to you, love. I fully understand if you can't bear to be parted from him, it's just that he'd probably be a bit safer with us – if only over the weekend. I'd ask you to come as well, but I expect you don't want to be too far from the hospital right now.'

Lily patted her stomach and nodded ruefully. 'How old are your sister's boys?' she asked Edith.

'One's six, the other's younger – about Michael's age. Nice lads, although they're a bit lively at times. Most boys are. I expect Michael'd get along with them like a house on fire. This is very nice tea, I must say. Is it Rington's?'

'Yes, a man comes in a van round every week.'

'What, a little Rington's van pulled by a pony?'

'No, it's just a van.'

'Ours is pulled by a pony. You're obviously much more up to date in the big city.'

The conversation stuttered along with Lily not in the mood for polite chat, nor conversation of any kind. After a while Bernard got to his feet.

'Look,' he said. 'I think we might have jumped the gun a bit here about having young Michael come over for a couple of days because you might get bombed. We're scaremongering where we shouldn't be. I blame Edith, I'm afraid.'

'What!' exclaimed his wife angrily. 'It was you who was doing all the damned scaremongering!'

Bernard ignored her and turned his attention to Lily. 'She would insist that I come straight here and mention the bombing. It wasn't my idea. You know what she's like. Prone to exaggeration is my Edith. To listen to her you'd think Hitler was going to bomb us all this very minute.'

'I am not prone to exaggeration!' protested Edith. 'I was only thinking of Lily. She's a young widow woman on her own who needs a bit of respite – and they *are* going to be bombing Leeds, according to you! You've been prattling on about it all the way here!' She turned to Lily. 'I'm sorry love but he gets me so mad at times.'

'It's all right,' said Lily. 'His heart's in the right place, so's yours.'

'Well, you know where we are, Lily,' said Bernard.

'I do,' said Lily. 'I noticed you have a phone in your house, could you let me have the number?'

Oldroyd looked questioningly at his wife who raised her eyebrows at him. He turned and smiled at Lily.

'Course I can, love. Have you got a pen or something?'

Lily produced a pen and a writing pad for Bernard to write down his number. He showed it to Edith for her to check.

'That's it, isn't it, love?'

'If you say so,' she snapped.

Lily felt slightly guilty at being the indirect cause of bad feeling between these two friends of hers. On top of which the threat of more bombs was a bit worrying.

23

'Do they actually say *when* the Germans are going to bomb us?' she asked.

Bernard shrugged. 'Well, I don't suppose Mr Hitler telephones Mr Churchill to let him know these things. It could be tonight for all I know. Maybe never. Maybe it's all propaganda. But I couldn't help notice there's a lot of barrage balloons up there, despite Leeds not being bombed for four years. Is there an air raid shelter handy?'

'My Larry reinforced the cellar ceiling. There's a proper one in the next street.'

'Anyway, it's all a question of whether you want to take the risk,' Oldroyd said. 'I do know that children tend to be more vulnerable to bombs than adults. It's frightening how many kiddies've been killed compared to adults.'

'Really?'

He nodded, sadly. 'I'm afraid so.' He looked down at Michael, still playing with his new toy. 'If you change your mind I can come and pick him up. If he gets homesick I'll run him straight back here. And when you ring you must tell the operator to reverse charges, then you're not forever sticking pennies in.'

'That's very kind of you.'

'Lily, it's the least I can do. We all need to do our bit during these troubled times and you've done more than your share.'

Lily walked to the window and remembered the view from the Oldroyds' house up in the Dales. Green hills, peppered with grazing sheep and a paddock backing on to the huge garden, with three horses in it. The paddock dipped down into a shallow stream where

Michael had paddled and tried to catch tiny fish with his bare hands. The memory had her smiling. The foul weather outside helped to emphasise the contrast between here and the beautiful Yorkshire Dales village. How much fun would her son have with two friends to share it with, and no bombs threatening to end his life before it had really begun?

'The weather forecast's good for the weekend,' said Bernard. 'This rain's supposed to clear up overnight.'

'Are the horses still in the field at the back?' asked Lily, without taking her gaze from the dismal street.

'They are, lass,' said Oldroyd, 'and there's a couple o' ponies come ter join 'em. Cute little beggars.'

'I think they're Shetlands,' added Edith.

Lily smiled at the image as a rag-and-bone cart passed the window accompanied by a familiar cry.

'Raggabone!'

The horse looked as miserable as Lily felt. Its master was huddled under a cheap raincoat. Not much on his cart to have made it worthwhile coming out today. He had little enthusiasm for his job as he called out.

'Any owd rags?'

'It should be nice weather to be out and about in the Dales,' said Oldroyd. 'They'll have a right old time, playing with the horses and ponies and mucking about in that stream.' He laughed. 'It'll be a struggle to get the young devils in for their meals. There's a fair in t' village on Sunday as well. We could take him to that.'

'What, with roundabouts and things?' Lily asked.

'Well, it's a proper country fair,' said Edith. 'All sorts goes on, but there'll be roundabouts, coconuts shies,

25

helter skelter and all that stuff. It'd be like a little holiday for the lad.'

'Hook-a-Duck?' asked Lily. 'I always liked Hook-a-Duck because you always win.'

'Oh, yes,' said Oldfield. 'It's not a proper fair without Hook-a-Duck.'

Lily stared out at the street trying to make up her mind. If she was able to go with Michael she'd jump at the offer, but at her late stage in her pregnancy she didn't want to be too far away from her midwife, who only lived in the next street. Eventually she looked down at her son.

'Michael, would you like to go for a ride in Mr Oldroyd's car out to the house where you fed the horses and played in the stream? There are two boys living with him about your age who you'd be able to play with.'

Michael looked up and studied her intently. The offer was enormously tempting. He'd never been in Oldroyd's car.

'Will you be coming, Mam?'

'No, love. I have to stay here because of the baby.'

Michael gave the matter more thought, then asked, 'Will I be allowed to sleep there?'

'If you like.'

'How many sleeps?'

It was Michael's way of measuring time.

'Two, if you're good.' She looked at Oldroyd. 'Would you be able to bring him back after the fair on Sunday?'

'Not a problem, love. I bet he'll be so tired he'll sleep all the way back.'

Lily smiled down at her son, one of the two most precious things in her life, and she knew it was her duty to protect him to the best of her ability. 'It depends how good a boy you are.'

'Can I sit in the front of the car?'

'So long as you don't want to drive,' laughed Bernard.

And so it was settled that Michael would go that very evening to stay at the Oldroyds' for a couple of days while Hitler dropped the last of his bombs.

Chapter 4

Saturday 28th April

'Is your Mickey playin' out, Mrs Robinson? We're playin' 'opscotch an' I thowt he'd like ter learn how ter play like.'

Lily looked down at the boy standing on her step. His hair was shaved way up past his ears in a basin cut. His nose was running and there were many holes in his grey pullover. His short trousers were torn and his socks flopped around the tops of his black pumps, each of which had a hole in the toe to give his feet room to grow. Michael was turned out better, but not much. It crossed her mind to tell young Tony Lafferty that her son's name was Michael. He'd been named after Michael Wilding, not Mickey Rooney.

'He's not here, Tony. He's gone to stay with his er, his uncle and auntie over the weekend.'

Tony hesitated, then galloped away at full speed, slapping his backside with his hand in the manner of all five-year-old Yorkshire cowboys. Lily watched him leave and, not for the first time, wondered if she'd done the right thing in letting Michael go off with the Oldroyds. It was four days since she'd heard the news about Larry. Her heart was still leaden, her tears not far away, but she knew she had to get through it. She wasn't the only war widow in Perseverance Street. Ethel Baskind from number 38 had lost her husband at Dunkirk, leaving her with three children to bring up and Joyce Allison from number 7 had a husband who'd been in a POW camp in Burma since 1939; she wasn't sure if he was still alive.

But as she watched Tony gallop off it suddenly hit her just how much she missed her Michael. He'd been gone for a less than a day and the house felt wrong without him. The absence of her darling son was too much to bear. Michael was the first, and maybe the only, person in the whole world who had shown her what real love was. From the instant he'd been placed in her arms she'd been completely besotted by him. Often in the middle of the night she'd creep into his room and sit by his bed just to watch him. The sheer magnificence of having given birth to this tiny but perfect creature had overwhelmed her. Losing Larry she would cope with, she knew that; she felt guilty about it but it was a fact.

She went back into the house to get Oldroyd's phone number. All she wanted at that moment was to hold her boy. On her way to the public phone box she passed the lavvie yard which housed eight lavatories and as many dustbins. Mr Pilkington, who was in his sixties and worked on the buses, was just emerging, still adjusting his braces. He was carrying a *Yorkshire Evening News* and she guessed he'd spent a comfortable half hour perusing it away from Mrs

Pilkington, who rarely gave him a minute's peace. A thought struck her.

'Hello, Albert.'

'Hello, love. Ee, I er, I were fair saddened to hear about your Larry. If there's owt we can do. The missis would've been round, but yer never know what ter do for t' best in these things. Never know when yer gonna be in t' road, like.'

'It's all right, Albert.'

Lily looked down at his newspaper. She usually picked one up from the local newsagents, but not in the past week.

'Is there anything in the paper about this bombing we're supposed to be getting?'

'What bombing's that, love?'

'I'm told there's been a lot in the papers and on the news that the Germans are planning to bomb Leeds about now. Barnbow and Hunslet's what I heard.'

He shook his head. 'Well, I've never heard nowt about it. What I've heard is that Jerry's air force is just about knackered. If there was any notion of an air raid we'd have had them ARP fellers comin' round ter warn us. Who told yer, love?'

'Just someone I know, that's all.'

'Well I never read nowt o' the sort an' I like ter keep abreast o' things.'

'If they're not going to bomb us,' said Lily, looking up at the sky, 'why have we still got barrage balloons?'

He scratched what little hair he had. 'Hey, yer've got me there, luv. It gives t' Home Guard summat ter do, standin' guard over 'em. They let one get loose last week. Word is they'd been sittin' round drinkin'. Dozy beggars. I reckon it'll be somewhere over Russia by now.' He gave her a toothless smile and placed a hand on her shoulder. Anyroad, I wish yer the best o' luck, an' as I said, if there's owt we can do . . .'

'Thanks, Albert.'

She walked on, wondering how the Oldroyds could have made such a mistake. There again, they lived out in the country and would have got a different newspaper. All Albert ever read was the *Yorkshire Evening News* – but if Leeds was going to be bombed surely the local paper would know about it. It made up her mind. She'd ask Mr Oldroyd to bring Michael back and if that wasn't convenient she'd get the bus out there and bring him back herself. It wasn't fair to rely too much on the man's good nature. Because of this she decided not to reverse the charges.

'Hello, could you put me through to Grassington three two eight, please?'

Pause.

'Is that Grassington in Yorkshire?'

'Yes.'

'Are you sure it's Grassington? You see, there's no exchange in Grassington. The nearest exchange is Skipton.'

'Oh, maybe it's Skipton three two eight, then.'

'I'm afraid that's not a valid number. There are four digits in the Skipton area numbers. Do you have a name and address? I can try and get it for you.'

'Yes, of course. The name is Bernard Oldroyd and the address is er, Lark House, seventy-four High Bank Lane, Grassington.'

'One moment please . . .' There was a long pause and a rustling of pages. 'I'm sorry. We have no number against that name and address.'

'Oh, I see . . . right.'

'Thank you, caller.'

The line went back to dial tone. Lily looked at the receiver for a long moment. She realised that she'd have to go to Grassington herself, tomorrow. On her way home she called in to Scrimshaw's fish and chip shop. Three women and a man were already queueing up. They all recognised Lily and stood to one side so she could be served first.

'Too right,' said Nelly Scrimshaw as she shovelled chips out of the fryer. 'Heroes' wives'll never have ter queue in my shop.'

Lily was slightly embarrassed by this preferential treatment.

'A fish and two pennyworth please.'

'Would yer like some scraps fer your young lad?'

'He's er, he's not at home at the moment. He's visiting his uncle and aunt for the weekend. Thanks anyway.' She was hoping Nelly wouldn't enquire further. What would people think about her sending her son away with people she didn't know all that well and who had given her a wrong telephone number? She might find herself at the back of the queue very quickly if they found out.

'I've no doubt yer've enough ter cope with,' said Nelly, wrapping up the fish and chips and waving away Lily's offer of money.

'Oh, thank you very much.'

'Don't mention it, Lily – and if there's owt we can do yer've only to ask—'

'That's goes fer me as well, Lily,' said one of the woman customers. The others, not to be outdone, made the same offer.

Chapter 5

Sunday 29th April

Lily had just about had enough after the two-and-a-half-hour bus journey from Leeds. It had stopped a good dozen times before it got to Skipton where she had to get off and wait half an hour for a connection to Grassington. The last stretch had been an extremely bumpy journey and she was more than conscious of the small person inside her, due to make an appearance in a couple of weeks; it felt more like two minutes at times. When she and Michael had travelled there a few weeks ago it had been on a comfortable coach that had taken them straight there, without stopping, in an hour and twenty minutes.

She stepped off the bus and rubbed her back, looking around, not entirely sure which direction to take. She'd know the house when she saw it. An elderly man, who looked like a native of the village, was sitting on a wooden bench smoking a pipe.

'Excuse me,' she asked him, 'could you point me towards High Bank Lane?'

The man jabbed over his shoulder with his pipe then looked at her stomach and gave her an ancient smile. He had teeth like a row of bombed houses but he looked friendly enough. 'Down there, lass. When yer get ter t' end o' t' lane turn right. Hey, it's a fair old hike an' yon babby looks as if he's ready ter drop.'

'I'll manage.' A thought struck her. 'Isn't there a fair here today?'

The old man shook his head. 'Fair? Not today, love. If there were a fair on I'd know about it.'

'Right.'

She assumed the Oldroyds had made a mistake about the fair and set off walking, wondering how the old man knew she was having a boy. It was more than she knew. She recognised certain landmarks that told her it was a good mile to the Oldroyds' house. Please God let them be in. The mile turned out to be nearer two and she breathed a sigh of relief when she recognised the hawthorn hedge that ran along the front boundary of the property, which was set back from the road. Her relief was short-lived – there was nobody home. Worse still, it looked uninhabited. She walked around the old, stone house and peered through the windows. The furniture was gone and the house had an air of neglect. She became suddenly very scared. What was this? She'd been speaking to the Oldroyds two days ago. Where was Michael? What had they done with him?

The house stood on its own, a couple of hundred yards from its nearest neighbour. Lily hurried up the road and knocked on the neighbour's door. A middle-aged woman answered.

'I was wondering if you knew where Mr and Mrs Oldroyd are. I've come up from Leeds to see them but they're not in.'

'I'm sorry, I don't know any Mr and Mrs Oldroyd. Where do they live?'

'Just down there at number seventy-four.'

The woman shook her head, mystified. 'I don't think so, love. There's been no one livin' there since old Mrs Ramsden died four years back. Never heard of any Mr and Mrs Oldroyd.'

What blood there was in Lily's face drained away. She stood there, shocked and scared by what she'd just heard. Not knowing what to do or to say. Her mouth opened and closed, causing the neighbour some consternation.

'Look, love, yer best come inside. Have yer walked from the village?'

Lily nodded and began to cry. The woman led her inside and made her sit down. Lily looked up at her with horror in her eyes.

'They've got my boy. They've got my Michael. I don't know what to do!'

Chapter 6

PC Edgar Pring, the village policeman, had just cycled over from Threshfield where he'd been investigating a barn fire. His police-issue bicycle weighed a ton and he wasn't as fit as he might have been. His exertions didn't put him in a good mood.

'Right, Maureen. What's all this about a missing lad? I've had ter break off an important investigation ter trail across here.'

He sat down in a chair opposite Lily, breathing heavily, still with his cycle clips on his trousers and sweat running down his heavy jowls. He removed his helmet and wiped his face with a large, grimy handkerchief.

'Any beer in t' pantry, Maureen? I could murder a light ale.'

'There's a couple o' bottles, but yer'll have to make it up to Vernon in t' Bell tonight — will yer be going in?'

'Can a duck swim, Maureen? I need to be there to keep law and order.'

'Edgar, the only time law and order needs keeping in that place is when you've had a few.'

Lily listened to this meaningless banter with tears in her eyes. It was as if her problem didn't exist. She felt like screaming at them to shut up and find out where her Michael was.

'My four-year-old son's missing, in case anyone's interested. He's been taken by some people called Oldroyd who were living at number seventy-four not four weeks ago. I know this because we stayed with them overnight. We came on a coach trip and we met them in a tea shop in Grassington. They seemed very nice people. I just don't understand what's happened.' The words tumbled out, closely followed by tears.

PC Pring wasn't best pleased at having his conversation interrupted. 'Who's we?' he asked, gruffly.

'Me and my son, Michael,' sobbed Lily. She lifted her tearful eyes and looked directly at him. 'My husband was killed in France two weeks ago and now these people have taken my boy. Could you find him for me, please?'

'I'll make us all a cup of tea,' decided Maureen, going into the kitchen. Another dimension had been added to this poor woman's troubles and it seemed to her that beer was an unsuitable drink for such an occasion. The policeman took a notebook from his breast pocket and a pencil from behind his ear.

'Right,' he said. 'I'd best take some details.'

Lily's waters broke before Maureen came back with the tea. The policeman heaved out a great sigh, which might have been exasperation or relief. He went off to the phone box to ring for an ambulance with barely a page of notes in his book. Six hours later Lily gave birth to another boy, by which time PC Pring was drinking his second pint in the Bell. His notebook, with its incomplete statement, was in his uniform pocket, hanging on a hook behind his kitchen door.

Monday 30th April

Baby Robinson, who was born in the early hours, was being kept in a side ward, with him being jaundiced and slightly underweight at five pounds three ounces. Lily had been assured that this was a perfectly normal procedure and whenever the baby needed feeding he'd be brought to her. In the meantime she needed rest.

'Do you have a name for him yet?' the matron had asked her. 'We do like to give them names as soon as possible.

'What? No.'

Lily's mind was in a turmoil. The labour of the previous evening had been long and excruciating, leaving her in need of a substantial blood transfusion. The only name running through her mind was that of her lost son, Michael. It had been there throughout all the pain and trauma of the birth. It was the name she constantly screamed as she pushed her baby out into this bloody awful world that took away husbands and children. She hated this world and everything in it. She hated the nurses and doctors and the police who kept asking questions about Michael, instead of being out there looking for the people who had taken him. She told them all she knew, but throughout the day different policemen kept coming back with more questions. This time it was a detective from Leeds, DS John Bannister.

'I'm sorry to trouble you at a time like this but the first twenty-four hours is usually the most important in the case of a missing child and we seem to have lost a couple of days already.'

'I didn't realise he was missing until . . .' Her voice trailed off. She'd momentarily lost track of time. Bannister nodded understandingly.

'These Oldroyd people,' he said, 'the ones who are supposed to have taken your son – could you tell us what you know about them?'

'What do you mean *supposed* to have taken him? There's no *supposed* about it. They came to my house in Leeds and took my boy away to a house in Grassington.'

'What were they doing in your house, Mrs Robinson?'

'They read about my husband being killed and came to offer their condolences – and their help. They offered to take Michael off for the weekend to give me a break.'

'And how well did you say you knew these people?'

Lily was frowning with disapproval of her own stupidity. This was all her fault. Larry had often said she acted without thinking, but he also said it was one of the things he loved about her. He wouldn't love her for this.

'I only met them the once – a few weeks ago. They put me and Michael up overnight in their house. We'd gone on a coach trip out to Grassington and met them in a tea shop.'

'I see – and this house would be Lark House, would it?'

'Yes.'

Lily began to cry. She turned to an attending nurse and asked, 'Could you bring me my baby please. I want to hold him.'

'Would you leave that a few minutes, Nurse?' said the

detective. 'I've just got a few more questions to ask Mrs Robinson.'

'Mrs Robinson's very weak and very distressed,' said the nurse, quite sharply. 'I'll give you five minutes but I'll be staying here to keep an eye on her.'

'Thank you, Nurse, that'll be fine.' He returned his attention to Lily, who was still weeping.

'You say you gave these Oldroyd people permission to take Michael. In fact you actually asked him and his wife to look after the boy for a couple of days?'

'It wasn't quite like that. They offered, I accepted – after they told me about the bombing.'

'What bombing's that?'

'Oh, they told me the Germans were going to attack the Leeds munitions factories. The last time they did that they hit our streets.'

'And you believed that?'

'At the time, I suppose I did. I don't any more. I talked to one of my neighbours who more or less told me it was rubbish so I rang the Oldroyds to tell them I wanted Michael to come home. I missed him so much.'

'So you actually rang them?'

'I tried but the number they gave me wasn't a proper number, which is why I came out on the bus.'

'And this house is number seventy-four High Bank Lane in Grassington – Lark House?'

'Yes, but the lady living up the road from there said she's never heard of them and that it's been empty for four years. That can't be right. I mean, we stayed there. How can that be ri . . . ?' Her voice tailed off and her eyes flooded with tears once again.

'I think that's enough for now,' said the nurse.

'I understand, Nurse, but I do need to ask her more questions as soon as possible. A small child is missing and Mrs Robinson is our only source of information. Time is of the essence.'

'So is Mrs Robinson's health.'

The detective rang his boss, Inspector Foster, at Millgarth Police Station in Leeds. 'To be honest I'm not at all sure what's happened, sir. The story she tells sounds strange. It appears she allowed a couple she hardly knew to take the boy away and look after him for two days.'

'I understand she claims that she and her son stayed at the house in Grassington with the man and his wife earlier this month? But the house has been empty for four years, and no one in the area has heard of these Oldroyds.'

'That's right, sir. It's beginning to sound most odd.'

'I'm not sure "odd" is the word I'd use, Sergeant.'

'She seems a perfectly decent woman.'

'Her husband was killed in France a couple of weeks ago, Sergeant. People react in different ways to bereavement – and if we throw her pregnancy into the mix . . . who knows?'

'Indeed, sir. Have her neighbours in Leeds managed to throw any light on things?'

'Not really. She told some of her neighbours that her son had gone off to stay with an uncle and aunt for a few days. None of them saw this uncle or the aunt – Mr and Mrs Oldroyd or whoever it was, come and take the boy away. Nor had she ever mentioned them.'

'Did anyone see a car come to her house, sir? I'd say visiting cars are a rarity in that street.'

'No, Sergeant, they did not – although it was pouring down around that time. You wouldn't expect too many people to be out in the street, or looking through the windows in such weather.'

'Perhaps not, sir.'

'I've also spoken to a bobby up in Grassington,' said the inspector. 'He sounds a real bloody plod. I think you might need to go over there and take a look around yourself.'

'In the meantime, do you want me to continue questioning her, sir? She's very distressed, as you might imagine.'

'Distressed or not I think we need to get as much information as we can out of her, Sergeant. Also, you might want to try and trick her into contradicting herself. Let's find out if she's telling us the truth, or what she thinks is the truth.'

'Sir.'

'In the meantime I'll check her background to see if she's had any form of mental health problems in the past and apply for a warrant to give her house a search from top to bottom, including the cellar. I'm beginning to get a very nasty feeling about this, John.'

Lily looked into the eyes of her baby. 'I'm sorry I've got no smiles for you, little boy . . . some nasty people took them all away. But the police'll catch them and bring your big brother back to us.'

She longed for Michael, she longed for her husband and, from time to time, she longed for her miserable life to end. But she knew that was selfish. The child in her arms needed her. It also needed a name. On the opposite wall was a crucifix. She looked down at her son.

'I wonder if they'd let me call you Jesus? Jesus Christ Robinson. Couldn't go wrong with a name like that eh? Or I could just call you Christ Robinson – Chris Robinson for short. Christopher Robinson: almost like the boy in the Winnie the Pooh books.'

A nurse came to her bedside, Lily looked up at her. 'Nurse, I'd like you to meet Christopher Robinson.'

The nurse's smile broadened. She reached behind her neck, unclasped a silver necklace and handed it to Lily. 'Here,' she said. 'It's a St Christopher – the patron saint of travellers. I'd be honoured if Christopher would have it as his first gift.'

Tears once again from Lily, who took the necklace and gripped it in her hand so tightly that blood flowed from between her fingers, much to the consternation of the nurse.

'Lily, open your hand, you'll get me into terrible trouble.'

Lily looked down at her hand and slowly opened it, not knowing what she'd done, only now feeling the pain. The necklace was covered in blood. Her eyes widened as if she'd suddenly realised the awful truth of her situation. She dropped the necklace on the bed and screamed, 'I want Michael! Please, I want my boy back!' Then she broke down into a fit of desperate sobbing.

The nurse took the baby from her. A second nurse arrived and tended to her injured hand. Lily gradually stopped crying and was squeezing her eyes together. Shutting out the horror of it all.

'I'm so sorry,' she murmured. 'I just don't know what I'm doing. I just don't kno—'

'Mrs Robinson, I wonder if I might have another word,' said the detective, who had arrived at the other side of the bed in time to see and hear all this.

Half an hour later the detective sergeant was on the phone to his inspector. 'I've had another chat with Mrs Robinson, sir.'

Inspector Foster listened intently as Bannister related Lily's story. 'Did you find any contradictions in her version of events?'

'None, sir. It all sounds plausible until you realise that the house didn't belong to the Oldroyds – if that's their real name.'

'Or even if the Oldroyds exist?'

'Quite, sir.'

'Did you ask her why she went out to Grassington to get her boy back just two days later?'

'I did, sir. It seems the Oldroyds had told her that the Germans intended bombing Leeds any time now and that the boy would be safer out in the country. The next day she heard that no such bombing was going to happen so she rang the number Oldroyd had given her and was told by the operator that no such number existed so she went out there on the bus.'

'She's certainly got a good story going, Sergeant – too good, you might think.'

'On the face of it she sounds very plausible, sir, but one odd thing did happen in the hospital. A nurse gave her a St Christopher medal, with her calling her baby

Christopher. Mrs Robinson took the medal and squeezed it so tightly that her hand bled. She didn't know she was doing it, sir. The wound looked very painful and required dressing.'

'And she didn't know she was doing it? Would you say that was unbalanced behaviour, Sergeant?'

'Possibly, sir.'

'Yes. Well, I think we need to tread very carefully here, Sergeant. Firstly we need to take a good look around her house. I'll arrange it.'

'How do we enter, sir? The old-fashioned way, or do we politely ask her for her key?'

'I think the less she knows the better at this stage, John. I suggest we engage the services of a locksmith.'

'Are we allowed to do that, sir?'

'Yes, if we have grounds for suspicion of a crime having been committed. I do not want a repeat of what happened last year.'

'No, sir.'

Bannister put the phone down and thought about the event to which his boss had been referring. The parallels to this case were too much to ignore. They'd been called to a house in Harehills in Leeds at two o'clock in the morning. A young woman had staggered out into the street shouting for help. She was holding her five-month-old baby girl and screaming that she'd been attacked in her home and her baby was dead, strangled by the attacker.

It was a most odd case, seemingly motiveless. The woman hadn't been sexually assaulted and nothing had been stolen. In fact she lived in a poor area where the pickings for any robber would be very slim indeed. Apparently the killer had come in through an unlocked door, gone up the stairs, strangled the baby and thrown the woman down the stairs. She was taken to hospital with several broken ribs. There were no clues whatsoever as to who had done this. Foster had been a chief inspector back then. The detective inspector in charge of the case had decided the woman, who'd had a recent history of depression due to her husband being killed in France, was the main suspect and had ordered for her to be taken into custody once she'd been discharged from hospital. He accused her of strangling the child herself then throwing herself down the stairs. The woman vehemently denied this.

Chief Inspector Foster looked at the evidence, all of it circumstantial. He also took into consideration the implications if the woman had been wrongly charged, which he thought was quite probable. The police were already getting atrocious publicity for locking up this poor woman. Her friends and neighbours had begun a protest, keeping a vigil outside the police station, shouting slogans, waving placards. He backed down and ordered her release. Within forty-eight hours she had killed her only other child, a three-year-old boy.

Chapter 7

A black Wolseley police car pulled up outside number 13. A van marked Woodhouse Locksmiths Ltd pulled up behind. The curtain twitched at number 14 across the street as Hilda Muscroft peered out.

'Hey up, Arnold, there's a police car outside Lily's.'

For the next five minutes she gave her uninterested husband a running commentary on how a man from the van seemed to be trying to unlock the door.

'There, he's done it. I wonder if Lily knows what's happening. Bet she doesn't. Makes yer wonder, dunt it, Arnold? I 'ope the lass is all right. I haven't seen her nor young Micky fer a couple o' days. By the 'eck Arnold! I hope she hasn't done nowt daft!'

Four uniformed police entered the house under the watchful gaze of Mrs Muscroft. After ten minutes one of them came out, knocked on the door of an adjacent house and stood there for several minutes talking to the occupant. This frustrated Mrs Muscroft, who was more than willing to impart any information they required in exchange for any information she could glean from them. Hilda Muscroft was an expert at gleaning information. She went to her door and stood there with arms folded, looking eager to help. The constable was making his way to the next house when she called out to him.

'Can I help yer, love?'

He turned and looked at her and decided her nosiness might be worth exploiting. As he got closer he became aware of her body odour, a problem no one dared mention to her. He took a step back.

'I'm making enquiries about Mrs Robinson who lives at number thirteen, and in particular her son, Michael.'

'What is it yer want ter know?'

'Well, the boy's missing and we need to know when he was seen last.'

'Missin? Lily reckons she sent him off ter stay with an uncle and auntie fer a while. Yer know she lost her husband in Germany, don't yer?'

'Yes, we know that. It's just that we can't trace this uncle and aunt nor the boy. If you know anything at all that might help we'd be most grateful.'

'I'm not sure I can help. Last time I saw young Micky were a few days ago. Friday, I think – no, I tell a lie, it were last Thursday. I know that cos it peed it down on Friday. What's that? Five days ago. He were out playin' in t' street wi' some other kids.'

'And you haven't seen him since?'

'No.'

'What about Mrs Robinson? Have you spoken to her recently?'

'Well, me and me husband went over on Thursday ter give us commiserations about her Larry.'

'And how did she seem?'

'She were bleedin' heartbroken. How else would she

seem? We didn't go inside or nowt. Just went to 'er door'

'Yes. I understand that, but did she seem as though she might not be able to cope?'

'What? As though she might do summat daft – like top herself, yer mean?' Mrs Muscroft had never been one to mince words.

'Not exactly, but she apparently sent her son off to an uncle and aunt who don't appear to exist. I wonder if you could throw any light on the matter.'

'Bloody hell! Aw no! What's she gone and done?'

'As far as we know she hasn't done anything. We're just trying to track the boy down.'

'Well, it sounds ter me like she's bloody done summat. I know nowt of no uncle or auntie.' She turned and shouted into the house. 'Arnold! Do you know owt about an uncle an' auntie what Lily sent her lad off ter live with?'

'Just shurrup. I'm listenin' ter t' wireless. They're sayin' Hitler's dead.'

Mrs Muscroft turned to the policeman. 'D'yer want ter come in an' listen?'

The policeman nodded and followed her inside to listen to the news bulletin that was saying Adolf Hitler had committed suicide in his bunker in Berlin.

Arnold stood got to his feet and gave his wife a hug. She responded in a manner that indicated she wasn't used to such treatment.

'Give over, yer barmy beggar!'

Arnold shook the policeman by the hand and went to the pantry to get a bottle of beer.

'Will yer have one with me?' he asked the constable,

whose nose had had as much as it could take of Hilda's pungent aroma, to which Arnold seemed immune.

'No, thanks. I'm on duty.'

He jotted a few notes down in his book and thanked them before walking across the street to find a more likely, and fragrant, source of information. Mrs Muscroft followed him to the door then went back into the house to discuss things with her husband.

'Did you hear all that, Arnold?'

'All what?'

'All what that bobby were sayin'?'

Her husband, who was now halfway through his bottle of beer, and still listening to the wireless, shook his head.

'God, yer bleedin' useless, you are,' she grumbled. 'We've only got a bleedin' murderer livin' opposite us. Done her lad in, like as not.'

'They reckon he committed suicide,' said Arnold, 'did yer hear that?'

'Let's face it,' Mrs Muscroft said. 'A bobby's not jus' gonna come right out with it and tell me she's done her lad in.'

'What?'

'Aren't yer bloody listenin'? That copper reckons the lad's gone missing an' she's lyin' about him goin' to some uncle an' auntie what dunt even bleedin' exist. Yer dunt need ter be a genius ter know what gone on. Bloody hell! Poor little bugger. That's what they've been doin' over at her house – searchin' fer his body.'

'I think I might bob round ter t' pub,' said Arnold,

finishing off his beer. 'I reckon there'll be a few in celebratin'. Bloody suicide, eh? Fancy that.'

He got to his feet and took his coat off the peg behind
the door, then reached into his waistcoat pocket for his
teeth, which he jammed into his mouth.

'Where d'yer think you're goin'?'

'Down ter t' boozer. I've a bit o' celebratin' ter do.'

'You come back drunk, Arnold Muscroft, an' yer'll
find t' bloody door locked and yer tea on t' back o' the
bloody fire!'

Arnold grinned 'Ee, yer a rough-tongued woman,
Hilda Muscroft.'

He danced out of the door and marched down the
street, swinging his arms and holding an imaginary rifle
– a rifle which had been real when he'd learned to march
back in 1914. He sang to the tune of Colonel Bogey:

> Hitler has only got one ball,
> Göring has two but very small,
> Himmler is very similar,
> But poor old Goebbels has no balls at all.

His wife followed him to the door and stood there with
folded arms watching and waiting for the police to bring
out a small body from number 13. After an hour the
police left empty-handed. Mrs Muscroft was disappointed but still hopeful that her interpretation of events
was correct.

Chapter 8

Lily was sitting in a chair beside her hospital bed, breast-feeding Christopher. Her mind was by no means on the job. The mysterious loss of her son had left her almost mute with despair, barely able to believe her own version of events. Had she imagined the Oldroyds? Had she imagined the stay in Grassington? How could she when she saw the actual house they'd stayed in? She remembered the interior layout of the house; the bedroom she and Michael had slept in; the view from the bedroom window. She remembered all that as clear as day. She felt a desperate urge to go inside the house and check that she was right. Check she hadn't imagined it all. Check she wasn't going mad. *Check she wasn't responsible for Michael's disappearance.*

The police, who had been to see her every day in the four days she'd been there, seemed to be growing less and less sympathetic; their questioning harsher. Maybe this was because she didn't answer them properly, causing them to get annoyed. Her brain was so clogged up with grief she couldn't think straight.

One had just arrived and was waiting at the other side of the curtain which had been drawn to give her privacy.

He was no doubt to here ask the same questions she'd failed to answer the day before, and the day before that. A nurse poked her head round the curtain just as Lily was finishing. She gave a smile and came in to take Christopher from her.

'I'll put him down for a sleep while you talk to the policeman. I'll leave the curtains closed.'

'Thank you.'

The nurse was placing the baby in the cot at the other side of the bed as the policeman came through. He waited until she'd finished before speaking to Lily. He was DS Bannister, the one she'd seen a couple of times just after she'd had Christopher.

'Hello, Lily. How are you today?'

She shrugged as if to say she'd never be all right until she got her boy back.

'He's a fine-looking boy is young Christopher.'

'Yes he is.'

Her voice was faint but it was a response if nothing else. She seemed to be trying, for a change.

'Are you OK to answer a few questions to help us find Michael? There are all sorts of things that don't add up and I'm hoping you'll be able to help.'

Lily thought for a while, then came out with her longest speech for four days. 'My whole story doesn't add up. I bet you find it hard to believe Mr and Mrs Oldroyd exist. I bet you think I never stayed in that house in Grassington with it being empty for years.' She waited for a response but none was forthcoming. This exasperated her. She demanded an answer.

'Well?'

'What we know, Mrs Robinson,' said the detective, 'is that the house has been empty since the owner died over four years ago. No one in the area has ever heard of a Mr and Mrs Oldroyd, including the nearest neighbour. None of your neighbours in Leeds saw this Oldroyd couple but they say you told them that you'd sent Michael off to stay with an aunt and uncle for the week-end. On top of which you lost your husband very recently, which must be hard to cope with.'

Lily stared at him, realising how totally unbelievable her story sounded. If only she could inject an element of proof into it. Enough to make them give her story a chance.

'Have you been in the house?' she asked him.

'No, I haven't.'

'Has anyone from the police?'

'Er, no. We haven't had cause to.'

'Really . . . well I'm going to give you cause to. I'd like you to write this down.'

John Bannister sat on the edge of her bed, took out his notebook and looked up at her expectantly. Her words came out in a rush.

'You go through the front door and there's a big hall-way. To the right is a door to a . . . a sort of study, to the left is the main living room. Under the stairs is a small toilet with a washbasin. The door doesn't shut properly so we didn't use it.' She furrowed her brow as she tried to picture the house's interior. 'Beyond the stairs are two doors, one to a very big kitchen, the other to a dining room. Am I going too fast for you?'

The policeman scribbled for a few seconds, then

looked up and repeated her last words. 'Beyond the stairs two doors to a big kitchen and dining room. Go on, this may well be helpful.'

She slowed down and became more fluent. 'Upstairs there are five bedrooms and two bathrooms, one attached to the main bedroom. I know that because Mrs Oldroyd showed me round the whole house. The other bathroom is the one we used. It's got a shower as well as a really deep bath and a big brass bolt on the door. The bedroom we stayed in was the first room on the left along the landing. It's got wooden beams across the ceiling and an old, cast-iron fireplace.' She stopped and looked at him. 'I couldn't know all this just by looking through the windows, now, could I?'

He finished writing and looked up at her. 'No, Lily, I don't suppose you could – providing this checks out.'

'Well, if it doesn't you might as well take me away and lock me in a loony bin.'

'I'll check it out myself tomorrow.'

'Thank you. Then I'd like you to come back to me and tell me I'm not going mad. You see, when reasonable people stop believing in you there comes a time when you've got to question your own sanity. I really need to know this house is as I described it. If it isn't, I've got to assume I've imagined everything I've told you – although I doubt if anyone's imagination has ever been as strong as that.'

It occurred to the detective sergeant that if this woman was sane enough to question her own sanity then surely she couldn't be insane. He had several questions to ask her but decided to leave them for another time. He was as curious as she was to see if this part of her story was true. If it was, the case would take on a whole new, very weird dimension.

Chapter 9

DS Bannister got out of the police car and introduced himself to PC Pring who was standing outside Lark House, still wearing his cycle clips. The constable looked exactly like he'd sounded on the phone.

'Do you have the keys, Constable?' Bannister asked him.

'Well, I'd hardly come all this way without them,' grunted Pring, taking a bunch of keys from his pocket. He wasn't happy with a sergeant from Leeds taking over a case within his jurisdiction. But his bosses in Skipton didn't have the manpower to get involved in time-consuming mysteries, so they were happy to let Leeds get on with it.

Pring handed the keys over to Bannister, saying, 'I picked them up from Weetman and Penn's estate agency in Grassington. Told them you'd drop them off on your way back to Leeds.'

'Well done,' said Bannister. 'I like a man who can think on his feet.'

PC Pring didn't pick up on the sergeant's sarcasm and followed Bannister up the gravel drive to the house. He unlocked the front door and entered the hall, checking the layout with the notes he'd taken of Lily's description. It had since occurred to both him and his inspector that Lily might have acquired her detailed knowledge of the house's interior some other way. The hall was devoid of all furniture.

'Constable, I wonder if you could check all the doors and windows – in fact every possible entry and exit on the ground floor, to see if it might be possible for someone to come and get in here without a key.'

The constable, happy to have been given a job of some responsibility, took off his helmet and looked around for somewhere to put it, before placing it carefully on the floor. He then headed for the kitchen as DS Bannister checked the ground floor layout against his notes. Everything was as described by Lily, as were the upstairs rooms and the view from the bedroom window, below which PC Pring was standing, surveying the house from the back lawn. Bannister unfastened the sliding sash window, pushed it open and called down.

'Anything?'

'Nothing that I can see.'

Pring took out his notebook and read out loud enough for Bannister to hear. 'Three doors soundly locked. Six sliding sash windows all locked from the inside. No windows broken, no obvious tampering to any door or window, no obvious recent repairs and no cellar. Anything up there?'

Bannister was mildly surprised that Pring seemed to have made such a thorough job but, there again, it was a job within the constable's everyday sphere of competence, so perhaps he shouldn't be.

'Nothing,' he said, closing the window. He reminded himself to ask the estate agents if there had been any signs of a break-in recent months but he felt confident that Pring's assessment was accurate.

As he descended the stairs it struck him that no one had asked about the furniture. Where had it gone? Was it in storage? Had it been in storage during the time Lily claimed to have spent time there? He asked the question of PC Pring, whose answer didn't surprise him.

'No idea. I should ask Weetman and Penn.'

'Thank you, I will – and thanks for your help.'

The estate agents were situated in a stone building on the main road which wound through a village of similar buildings. The detective parked his unmarked police car, went inside and identified himself. There were times when he wished he was still in uniform and not obliged to offer identification, with him looking most unlike a police detective. Given the willpower he'd take up exercise and lose a few stones. He was five feet eight inches tall and had what he referred to as a 'low centre of gravity', a man difficult to knock down when it came to the rough stuff. His face had been battered during his days as an amateur rugby league player which had left him with a broken nose and a cauliflower ear but, that said, his face was quite genial, more the face of a club comic. And there were many times when not looking like a copper had decided advantages. Miles Penn stared down at the policeman's identification, then up at the man the photo was supposed to match. 'This is you, is it?'

'It's definitely me.'

He put the keys on the counter. 'Keys to Lark House as promised by PC Pring. Would you be Mr Weetman or Mr Penn?'

'I'm Miles Penn.'

'I wonder if I might ask you a couple of questions about the house?'

Bannister was hoping this man who had deliberately fussed over his identification might also be uncooperative about answering questions, whereupon Bannister would exert his police authority in no uncertain terms; the sergeant was an expert in exerting authority over civilians. Perhaps the determined expression on his face convinced Penn to become friendly.

'Certainly. Perhaps you'd care to come through to my office.'

Bannister followed the man through and sat down. He took out his notebook to remind him of the questions he needed to ask.

'Firstly, could you tell me the recent history of Lark House since the last owner died which, I believe, was about four years ago?'

Penn took a file out of a cabinet and sat down at his desk opposite the detective. He opened it and nodded. 'Mrs Ethel Ramsden, the owner, died in January 1941. The house was placed for sale with us in October 1941 but withdrawn from sale in January 1942.'

'What was the reason for this?'

'I believe the new owner received his call-up papers and decided not to go ahead with the sale until after the war. He thought that prices might shoot up.' Penn sat back in his chair, still holding the file and added, 'Not sure if he's right about that.'

'Could you give me details of the owner?'

'I can give you what we have – and I can also tell you that he's currently in the army, probably in France or Germany or somewhere. Went over on D-Day. His name's George Ramsden – Ethel Ramsden's son. He lives here in Grassington but he hasn't been home for several months. The last time I saw him was back in . . .' He paused to consult the file. 'Back in March this year. He wanted us to arrange a contents sale for Lark House, which we did.'

This took care of one of Bannister's questions. 'Really? When did this sale take place?'

'Let's see.' Penn flicked over a couple of pages. 'I did the auction myself. Saturday, April the seventh.'

'And where did it take place?'

'Well, we find that house content sales are always best done in the actual house – as was this.'

'So, the people who came to the house would be able to walk all around the house to view the furniture and stuff?'

'More or less. We do ensure that we have several of our own people on the premises for security reasons.'

Bannister looked down at his notes. He had no more questions written down, just one in his head. 'Do you have a list and description of the items you sold? And who you sold them to?'

Once again Penn flicked through the file. 'I have a list of all the lots up for sale, plus the amounts they sold for and the names and addresses of some of the buyers – the ones who required delivery. Anyone who paid cash for a lot which they could take away themselves were given a cash receipt and not required to give any details. The descriptions we have here were all for our own benefit simply so that we could identify them. They aren't detailed unless the lot was particularly expensive. There weren't too many valuable antiques in Lark House, I'm afraid.'

Bannister tried to picture Lily's house. Just one thing stood out in his mind. 'Was there one of those clocks that hangs on a wall? A fairly old one.'

Penn ran his forefinger down the list. 'Yes, antique wall clock. Sold for seventeen pounds ten shillings – cash. No name or address I'm afraid.'

'Do you have a description of the clock?'

'Sorry. It was the only one for sale so we didn't need to describe it precisely.'

'Can *you* remember what it looked like? I mean, if I brought you a photograph?'

Penn gave his question some thought then shook his head. 'Sorry. I'm not sure I can. There were so many lots in this sale that I probably didn't look at it for more than a couple of seconds – I doubt if I'd be able to iden- tify it if you stuck it in front of me. I do a lot of house content sales. For me to remember an individual lot it would have to be fairly special.'

'But you did sell an antique wall clock in Lark House?'

'Yes, we did.'

Bannister thanked Penn for his trouble and went out to his car planning on asking Lily where her wall clock came from. It was unlikely that she'd have paid seventeen pounds ten shillings for it. Money such as that seemed beyond Lily Robinson's means, but he had nothing else to go on.

Chapter 10

It was ten thirty in the morning, nine days after Lily had given birth to Christopher. An ambulance delivered the two of them back to 13, Perseverance Street in Leeds. There was still bunting hanging across the street from the VE Day party the previous Sunday. Before the driver got the back doors open a small crowd had emerged from neighbouring doors. Mainly women who would normally be sympathetic to Lily's plight, and dying to take a look at the new-born child. Not this lot. Hilda Muscroft had done an expert job in spreading her poison. She was the first to call out as Lily stepped from the ambulance.

'Where's your Mickey, then?'

Lily looked at her, wondering at such a question. Surely they all knew that Michael was missing. The disgust on their faces took her aback. In that instant she knew she'd be getting no sympathy from any of this lot. Quite the opposite by the look of it. She turned her back on them and walked to her door with Christopher in her arms. Hilda called out again.

'Nowt ter say to us, then?'

She turned back to face the women and shook her

head. 'What do you want me to say?' Her voice was still weak from her ordeal.

'I asked where yer boy was. What have yer done with him?'

Lily's voice gathered strength. 'What?'

'You heard.'

'Michael's missing.'

Her reply provoked a dissatisfied rumbling from the women, who moved towards her as she fumbled for her keys. The ambulance driver took them from her and opened her door, ushering her inside and taking her bag in for her.

She thanked him and wondered if she ought to apologise for the rudeness of her neighbours; neighbours with whom she'd been on good terms until all this; neighbours who had rallied round and supported her when Larry died. The driver asked if she'd be all right now. She said she would so he left her to it.

Lily glanced through the window to see that the crowd had largely dispersed, leaving only Hilda Muscroft talking, animatedly, to a couple of women, occasionally pointing at Lily's house. Albert Pilkington approached and paused by the gossiping women who tried to engage him in their conversation. Albert pulled a face, shook his head at them, and walked on. A possible ally, thought Lily; although maybe a short-lived ally. She'd noticed Mrs Pilkington in the crowd.

She sat down, still holding Christopher, and never in her life had she felt so alone. Her own mother had died when she was a baby, her father had been unknown and she'd been brought up in various children's homes.

Larry's middle-class parents had totally disapproved of him marrying her; convinced that she'd trapped him into marriage by getting herself pregnant.

In truth her pregnancy had been the result of two very good friends having too good a time in the Crown and Mitre one evening and ending up in bed at her lodgings in Leeds. Her friends considered that her becoming pregnant had worked more in Larry's favour than hers as there was no way she'd have married him otherwise. Larry had always fancied her like mad and proposed the evening she told him she was pregnant. She wasn't at all sure it was what she wanted.

'I didn't tell you for that,' she had said. 'I told you because . . . well because I thought you should know.'

'So, what are you going to do?'

'I don't know.'

'So, marry me. You and I get on OK, don't we?'

'We get on great, Larry. Always have, but . . .'

'But what?'

'Well, apart from anything else you live in a nice house in Roundhay and I live in lodgings in Meanwood. You work at a bank and will probably end up a manager. I work in Marks and Sparks selling underwear. Me getting pregnant is no foundation for marriage.'

They were in Roundhay Park, standing by a lake. Ducks were heading their way hoping for breadcrumbs. Larry was staring at them, hoping for inspiration. All he could come up with was:

'If it's any help I actually love you, Lily.'

Lily probably knew that already. What she didn't

know was the strength of her feelings for him. Were they strong enough to endure a lifetime of marriage?

'And I'd make a good dad.'

Lily also knew that to be true.

'And if I married you I'd hardly need go chasing after other women like some husbands do.'

Lily smiled. Larry was a great friend but not a womaniser. She and he had got together because she felt more comfortable with him than with any other human being. He made her laugh and he had a strong shoulder to cry on. He put his arm round her. It wasn't an arm she would ever shrug off.

'I know you don't love me like I love you – that would be impossible. But I know you love me a bit.'

'Do you now?'

'Yep. I can tell by the way you're letting me hold you. Come on, right now, who would you rather marry than me?'

'I don't know. Maybe I haven't met him yet.'

'Hmm.' He tried another tack and murmured into her ear. 'This er, this baby of ours. Did you enjoy making it?'

'I believe I did. Having said that I've never done it before so I've got nothing to compare it with.'

'Oh, take my word for it. It doesn't get any better.'

'Oh, really? There speaks a man of the world. How many girls have you done it with?'

'Including you?'

'Yes.'

His lips moved silently for several seconds as if adding up a long list. 'You mean properly, like we did?'

'Yes.'

'Altogether . . . one – including you.'

She laughed with relief that they'd broken their ducks together, as it were. Why would she be relieved? Why did she want to be his first? They sat down on a lakeside bench and stared at the water silently for several minutes. Afternoon sun glinted on the water. It took her another week to say yes to him. But by that time she was as sure as she could be of any man. Not that she'd known many men. He wasn't Errol Flynn but he had too much going for him for her to say no.

The memory of that had brought a smile to her face. It was still there when a shattering of glass brought her back to reality. A brick had come through the window, missing her and the baby by inches. Still holding him she ran to the door to see a neighbour's boy running away. Hilda Muscroft was standing in her doorway with arms folded, laughing. Lily stepped into the street and shouted at her, angrily.

'That brick nearly hit the baby! What's so funny, you brainless woman?'

Hilda just went on laughing. Albert Pilkington appeared and walked towards Lily. 'Now then, love. What's up?'

Lily turned and looked at him. 'Would you hold my baby, Albert?' she said.

Albert took the infant. Lily marched across the street to the still-cackling Hilda. 'You think harming babies is funny, do you?'

'You should bleedin' know. You did fer your lad! That's what the coppers think, anyroad, an' there's no smoke without fire, that what I say!'

'What?'

'Come off it. Everyone round here knows yer went loopy after Larry died. No need ter do your lad in, though.'

Lily, in a rage, pushed Hilda and had the bigger woman staggering sideways and tripping over the kerb. She banged her head against a street lamp and slid to the ground, dazed and bleeding.

'Oh, bugger,' muttered Albert, giving Christopher back to Lily. 'There'll be 'ell ter pay fer this.'

'She deserved it,' said Lily, taking her baby back into the house.

Back inside Lily sat down in a daze. She was aware that her story sounded unbelievable but this was the first time anyone had accused her of *killing Michael*. How could anyone think that? What had she said? *Yer went loopy after your Larry died. No need ter do your lad in, though.* Is this what the police think?

She looked around the room and saw certain things out of place; not where she usually kept them. Someone had been in her home without her permission. She gave it some thought and came to the most likely conclusion. Probably the police. Suspicious of everything she'd told them, just like her neighbours. The wind blew small shards of glass into the room and she wondered what to do, how to fix it. Christopher began to cry. He needed feeding. She glanced through the broken window and saw no sign of Hilda. Good. Maybe the stupid woman would know not to make such vile remarks next time.

In her busy days after hearing of Larry's death she'd prepared her baby's cot and all the stuff needed for a mother to bring up a baby. He'd be sleeping in her room for the time being, then sharing with Michael. The thought brought tears flooding.

'Oh, Michael. Where are you, my darling boy?'

After feeding Christopher she put him into his pram and eased it down the front step on to the pavement. Lily had a desperate need to get out of her house which seemed in more danger from her neighbours that it ever had from the Luftwaffe. She had one eye on the house opposite to see if Hilda might make another appearance, but the Muscroft door remained firmly shut. In fact the Muscroft house looked empty, which suited Lily. It could stay empty for good as far as she was concerned.

It was a bright enough day to be out walking her baby. From the corner of her eye she saw curtains twitching and faces at windows. No one came to their door to ask how she was, and has Michael been found yet? Hilda Muscroft's venomous tongue, it seemed, had been hard at work. The rumour didn't trouble Lily too much. She had barely enough room inside her head to cope with her Michael being missing without worrying about the lies going up and down this street. Since she moved in there had always been a hint of jealousy from her neighbours, with her and Larry being the only ones in the street to actually own their own house. All the others were rented.

She walked past Quarry Mount school where Michael should be going next September. Children were playing in the school yard; hopscotch, whip 'n' top, rounders, marbles, leapfrog and many other games she remembered, even from her own fractured childhood. She stopped to watch them and envisaged her boy playing there, running round, chasing his school friends, shouting and laughing. He laughed a lot, did Michael. He was a happy kid, never any trouble; never moaned if he couldn't have his way; accepted her decisions with equanimity and a cheeky smile that sometimes made her give in to him. Tears were streaming down her face as she stood by the school gates. A teacher on playground duty came across to her.

'Are you all right, madam?'

Lily blinked away her tears and forced a smile. 'Yes, I'm fine, thank you. Just got something in my eye, that's all.' It was an obvious lie but better than having to explain the truth to a complete stranger.

She pushed the pram down on to Meanwood Road, up Buslingthorpe Lane then the long drag up Scott Hall Road towards the fields where she'd often taken Michael to play with his football. Exhausted, she sat down on a bench and took in the panoramic view of Leeds city centre which, as usual, had a cloud of smog hanging over it from the myriad tall chimneys belching out smoke. Barrage balloons floated in the air, some reflecting the sunlight and looking quite decorative. At this end of the war, decoration was all they were good for.

Leeds was known as the Holy City due to this protective cloud of muck obscuring the city centre and the Hunslet engineering works from the Luftwaffe. It was a long way north and a long way inland, leaving the Luftwaffe at the limit of their range with not enough fuel to hang around searching for their target. Most of the bombers simply guessed where Leeds was and jettisoned their load. Woodhouse and Headingley had taken several hits, the city museum had been badly damaged but few, if any, bombs landed on or near their intended targets.

She could see the white Parkinson Tower of Leeds University, built just before the war, where her Michael would have gone when he was eighteen, after he'd completed his secondary education at Leeds Grammar School – that's if Larry's salary would run to it. But Larry was gone now, so he'd have to pass his scholarship and go to one of the state-run high schools. She favoured Roundhay High, with it being in such a good area. Her eyes misted over again and she headed for home, keeping her head down to avoid curious glances from passers-by who might wonder why she was crying.

Chapter 11

DS Bannister was standing near the front desk of Millgarth police station when he heard the name, Mrs Lily Robinson, repeated over the phone by the desk sergeant.

'What was that about, Alf?'

'Disturbance on Perseverance Street. Some woman's just flattened a neighbour. Lily Robinson? Isn't she the one whose boy's gone missing?'

'Yeah – she's just had a baby. Is she all right?'

'As far as I know. She's the one who did the flattening. The victim's a Mrs Hilda Muscroft. She made a complaint from the LGI where she's having her head stitched up. Sounds like we need to bring the Robinson woman in.'

'I'm on her case, Alf. I'll need a WPC to come along with me. Someone with maternal instincts.'

'I'll see if Eileen Morley's available. The others are more likely to eat a baby than look after it.'

'Thanks. Tell the LGI to hang on to Mrs Muscroft. I want to speak to her first.'

John Bannister and WPC Eileen Morley made their way up Union Street, past the council swimming baths, to where the detective's car was parked. From there they headed for the Leeds General Infirmary to interview Mrs Muscroft, whose version of events would prove most damning.

'So, what do you think, Eileen?' asked Bannister as they drove towards Lily's house.

'I think Mrs Muscroft's a woman I wouldn't like to get on the wrong side of,' commented the WPC. 'I dread to think what Mrs Robinson's like if she won the fight.'

'According to Mrs Muscroft it wasn't a fight, it was an unprovoked attack,' said Bannister. 'The action of an unbalanced woman.'

'Is that what Mrs Robinson is?'

'Mrs Robinson is an enigma,' said Bannister, thinking back to when Lily cut her own hand with a St Christopher medal. 'She's very plausible but we mustn't be taken in by her. If she can harm both herself and a woman like Mrs Muscroft we can't discount the possibility of her harming her own son.'

'So, you don't believe the story she tells of her son being taken by this man Oldroyd?'

DS Bannister had filled her in on the case on the way to the hospital. 'I've no idea what to believe. She gave me an accurate description of the interior of Lark House which she would only be able to do if she'd been inside the place.'

'Which supports her story.'

'Only if there was no other way she could have taken a look round.'

'And is there?'

75

'In my experience, Constable Morley, which is considerable, there's usually another way. For example there was a house contents sale at the house in April. Who's to say she and her son didn't take a trip out to Grassington that day and call in to see that? Maybe even buy something.'

'Such as?'

'Well, inside her house is an antique wall clock that looks out of place there, and a wall clock was sold at the contents sale.'

'That sounds a bit a bit tenuous if you don't mind me saying, Sarge.'

'Everything about this case is tenuous, but out there is a small boy and we don't know if he's alive or dead.'

'I notice we haven't given the story to the papers. Wouldn't they be able to help?'

'That's been held in abeyance. If this man Oldroyd has got the boy we don't want to spook him into doing something drastic. He may well think he's got away with it and drop his guard at some point. We're going to give it another couple of days and then release the story.'

'Sounds a risky strategy.'

'Ours not to reason why, Constable. This is the brain-child of our chief superintendent.'

She looked at him questioningly. He explained: 'A few months ago a two-year-old girl went missing in Wakefield.'

'I remember that, but that was all over the papers from the beginning. She was found within a week, wasn't she?'

'Ten days,' said Bannister. 'And during that ten days

76

the woman who took her didn't read a paper, nor did she listen to the radio, with her not having one. She thought she'd got away with it and took the girl out for a walk. She was spotted within half an hour.'

Eileen followed his reasoning. 'But we're assuming that Oldroyd will be reading the papers and listening to the radio so we're giving him nothing to read about or hear about.'

'Precisely. We're calling it the No News is Good News theory. In a couple of days we'll have the lad's photo in every paper in the country. If he's out there and Oldroyd's dropped his guard, we'll have him.'

'Right,' said Eileen, unconvinced.

'That's if Oldroyd exists,' added Bannister.

Chapter 12

Home now, and with Christopher safely tucked up in his cot, Lily had set to work doing a makeshift job on the broken window. She had flattened a large cardboard box she'd found in the bin yard on her way home and had cut it into the shape of the frame, then she put on a pair of Larry's gloves and eased out all the remaining glass. She was tacking the cardboard into place when Bannister's car arrived. Because the window was completely blocked by the cardboard she didn't see the two officers getting out of the car, although she'd heard a car arrive.

She still had the hammer in her hand when she went to the door in response to Bannister's knock.

'Have you found Michael?'

'I'm afraid not.'

Her grip on the hammer tightened instinctively. She half raised it.

Bannister looked at it. 'I don't think you'll be needing that, Mrs Robinson.'

Her mood was such that she went immediately on the attack. 'Really? So what do you suggest I use to fix my broken window? A brick came through it not two minutes after I got home with my baby. It missed him by inches. Would such a crime interest you, Sergeant Bannister, or have you come to ask what I've done with my missing son?'

'May we come in?'

She didn't reply but simply stood back and allowed them through before following them and laying the hammer down on the table, to the WPC's relief.

'We're here about the altercation between you and Mrs Hilda Muscroft?'

'Did you ask her about my broken window?'

'Are you saying she did this?'

'I'm saying she was out in the street, laughing about it when I went to the door.'

'Mrs Muscroft told us about that. Apparently it was a local boy who did it.'

'I saw a boy running away – and I know who it was. Mrs Muscroft will have known. Did she tell you who it was?'

'She said she didn't know.'

'Of course she knows. He only lives at number twenty-four. His name's Harry Bridges. If that brick had been a few inches to one side you'd have been arresting him for murder. That'd have given Hilda Muscroft something to laugh at.'

Tears were streaming down Lily's face as she spoke. Upstairs Christopher began to cry. Without bothering to excuse herself Lily left the room and went upstairs to attend to him. Bannister and the WPC looked at one another.

'Bit awkward, all this, Sarge.'

'Hmm, I could have done without this Mrs Muscroft complication. If she doesn't withdraw I'll have to think about charging Mrs Robinson with assault. I wonder if there was a witness?'

Bannister looked at the door through which Lily had recently left them to attend to her baby. 'I think you should go up. Check she's OK.'

'She's probably feeding him.'

'Probably – that's one of the reasons I brought you along. Have a chat, woman to woman. See what you make of her. I'm blessed if I know.'

As the WPC went upstairs Bannister took a close look at the wall clock. It was a highly decorative piece set in a walnut case, with a large brass pendulum. His wife wouldn't object to having such a clock on their wall at home. It was completely out of place in this room but it wouldn't have been out of place in the Lark House drawing room. Lily Robinson would need to tell him where it had come from. Her answer might even have a bearing on her future.

It was ten minutes before the WPC came down, followed by a red-eyed Lily holding her baby. Bannister asked her to sit down, which she did. He sat down opposite, not wishing to appear overbearing.

'Lily, the reason we're here is because Mrs Muscroft has made a very serious allegation that you assaulted her, causing her to receive hospital treatment.'

'So Eileen told me,' said Lily, looking at the WPC. 'It's about par for the course for me. I get a broken window, my baby nearly gets a smashed skull and who gets the blame?'

'We're not blaming anyone,' said Bannister. 'Mrs Muscroft said you assaulted her, we'd like to hear your side of the story.'

Lily took a while to gather herself together. 'For some reason,' she said eventually, 'the people round here seem to think I killed my son Michael. I've got no idea why.' She looked, accusingly at Bannister and added, 'Except that I know you don't believe my story of how he went missing. I also know someone's been in this house while I've been away and I can only assume it was the police. Was it?'

Bannister struggled not to look guilty. 'It was a routine investigation,' he said. 'No reflection on you.'

'Rubbish! Why didn't you tell me about it, then? How did you get in?'

'We used a locksmith. Your lock wasn't damaged.'

'Really? I had my keys with me in hospital. Why didn't you ask to borrow them?'

Bannister gave up his pretence. 'OK,' he said. 'Your story just doesn't add up. We had to check you out. No one in Leeds or Grassington has ever seen or heard of this Mr Oldroyd.'

'I described the interior of the house to you. Have you been to check?'

'Yes, I have, and you described it accurately.' He paused, then added, 'But that doesn't prove that you stayed there with your family. It simply proves that you've been in the house at some time.'

'When? Are you saying I got the bus out to Grassington and broke into the house just to give myself a good story to tell?'

'No, I'm not saying that. I'm saying . . . for example there was a house contents sale in April. It was pretty much an open house as far as I can tell.'

'April? It was April when we went there.'

'Really. When in April?'

'April the fifth. It was the day after my birthday. It was a Thursday. We met the Oldroyds in a teashop on the lunchtime, went back to their house and ended up missing the coach back and staying over. Mr Oldroyd ran me into Skipton the following day with there being no through buses from Grassington to Leeds.'

'I see.' Bannister was staring at the wall clock. 'Do you mind telling me where you got that clock?'

His eyes turned sharply on hers as he asked the question. So did Eileen's. Lily frowned and looked up at the clock.

'Why do you want to know that?'

It slightly troubled her because the clock had been a present from Auntie Dee and, knowing Auntie Dee, it was quite possible the clock wasn't kosher. But no way could Bannister know that. Surely. He spotted the flash of guilt on her face.

'Just answer the question.'

'It was a wedding present.'

'Oh. So you've had it how long?'

'Well, we were married nearly four years, so I'll let you work it out, Sergeant. Do you have any other daft questions?'

He glanced at Eileen who gave a slight shake of her head, advising him not to pursue it. He could check it out later so he changed the subject.

'Tell me what happened between you and Mrs Muscroft.'

Lily gave a sigh that said she'd had enough of this for one day. 'The stupid woman accused me of killing Michael. I reacted normally.'

'How did you react?'

'I lost my temper and pushed her. She tripped over the kerb or something and banged her head on the lamp-post.'

Bannister nodded. He really wanted this charge to go away. It was getting in the way of the real investigation. Mrs Muscroft had told them that Lily had attacked her with her fists. If this statement proved untrue he'd make sure the charge would be dropped. He took out his notebook and wrote something down, then asked:

'Did anyone see this?'

'Yes. Albert Pilkington. He lives down at number twenty-five – or is it twenty-seven? It's got a green door.'

Bannister got to his feet and looked at the patched-up window. 'That's not safe. Would you like me to send a glazier round? I know a man who's quite reasonable with his prices. I'll see if I can get him to come this afternoon. I'll also have a word with young Harry Bridges. Tell his parents to cough up the cost.'

'I wouldn't bother. There's only his mother at home and she hasn't two ha'pennies to rub together. She'll give you a right mouthful and tell you what an angel her little boy is.'

'I'll still have a word. Mark the lad's card. It'll stop him bothering you again.'

'Thank you. Is that it, then?'

'Possibly — if Mr Pilkington verifies your story. If not, we'll have to take you down to the station to make a formal statement.'

Chapter 13

Two days later Albert was walking down the street, heading for the lavatory block. Lily had been sitting by the window all afternoon, waiting for him. Albert was a creature of regular habits. She was consumed with what was, perhaps, a disproportionate sense of betrayal. He was the only one whom she thought had been on her side and therefore the only one in a position to betray her. She laid Christopher in his pram and eased it down the two steps to the pavement. Then she called out to him.

'Albert!'

He turned and a look of guilt spread over his face like thick margarine. He looked undecided as to whether to retreat to the sanctuary of the lavvies or face up to her. The lavvies seemed the best bet to him.

'Don't you walk away from me, Albert Pilkington. I'll wait for you if I have to.'

He stood there like an errant schoolboy being caught playing truant, his *Yorkshire Evening Post* clasped in his hand, as Lily pushed the pram towards him.

'I just thought you'd like to know that my husband was mentioned in dispatches. I got a letter this morning. I'm ever so proud of him.'

'I'm very pleased for him.'

'I'm guessing you told lies about me because you're afraid of your Vera. I notice she was one of the crones cackling at me when I came home with Christopher. Pity you're not brave like my Larry or the courts wouldn't have found me guilty of attacking Mrs Muscroft with my fists. All you had to do was come forward and tell the truth but you lied to the police and told them you didn't see what happened.'

Albert muttered something which she couldn't make out, then she saw a look of concern on his face as he looked over her shoulder. His wife and Hilda Muscroft were approaching. Lily turned to face them.

'I was just telling Albert about my husband being mentioned in dispatches – this means he was a brave and outstanding man, unlike poor old Albert who's scared stiff of you two lying old crones.'

Hilda's face turned into a mask of hate. 'The court found yer guilty, which means yer've gorra criminal record for violence.'

'They only found me guilty because of your lies and his cowardice!'

Lily jabbed a thumb towards Albert, who wished he was anywhere but here. She returned her attention to the two glowering women.

'Do you know why my Michael's still missing? He's missing because no one's bothered to help look for him. Not even the bloody police. It's easier for them to think I've murdered him and hidden him somewhere. One of these days I'll bring Michael home alive and well, but I don't expect either of you to apologise for being nasty to me. Only decent people apologise.'

Vera went to Albert and dragged him away. He yanked himself free and walked off to the lavatory yard, humiliated.

Lily watched him go, then turned to Vera. 'You might be able to order your husband around, but his bowels have a mind of their own.'

Vera shook her fist. 'One o' these days yer'll swing fer what yer did ter your lad! Bloody murderer!'

Lily flushed with anger, let go of the pram and took a couple of quick strides towards Vera who foolishly stood her ground. Being told she'd killed her beloved son was like being stabbed in the heart. Lily clenched her fists and punched out at Vera with all her strength. She wasn't a big woman but the adrenalin now surging through her veins made up for that. In a flurry of punches she caught Vera flush on her nose and then in the eye, knocking her to the ground. People appeared at doors and windows. Hilda retreated; she had no intention of helping out her stricken friend. Albert, alerted by the commotion, came out of the lavatory block and looked on as his wife was being beaten up by the smaller woman. Then he went back inside, not wishing to be seen witnessing this and not helping.

Leaving Vera lying on the ground with her face covered in blood, Lily went back to the pram, spun it on its wheels and headed home. Her belligerent demeanour began to collapse as she approached her house. The confrontation had taken a lot out of the steel out of her and she didn't have much left in her to begin with. The previous day she'd had to endure a supercilious woman magistrate castigating her for an act of unbridled violence for which she'd been fined seven pounds ten shillings. What the hell was going to happen to her now?

By the time she got back inside she broke down into uncontrollable tears. She'd had just about all she could take and was still crying and rocking Christopher in her arms when the police arrived half an hour later. They knocked, tried the door and walked in. Eileen Morley and a male constable. Lily looked up at them through tear-stained, defiant eyes.

'I'm not like this. You people made me like this. You people told them I killed Michael. The woman out there called me a murderer for killing my son. What do you expect me to do? Every minute he's missing is tearing my heart out and I've got to put up with people like that.'

'We didn't tell them anything of the sort,' said Eileen gently.

'Your lot obviously hinted at it.' Lily got to her feet and walked to the window. 'That's enough for the idiots out there.' She turned to face the WPC. 'Let's face it. Mr Bannister doesn't believe my story about Oldroyd. And if he doesn't believe that, what does he believe?'

The constable with Eileen grew impatient at all this chatter. He placed a hand on Lily's shoulder. 'Lily Robinson, I'm arresting you for common assault on Mrs Vera Pilkington. You do not have to say anything but anything you do say may be taken down and used in evidence against you.'

Lily stood there in silence, still rocking Christopher, as the constable stood back to await her reaction.

'I'll take care of the baby,' said Eileen.

'No, you will not!' said Lily sharply. 'He stays with me. I've already lost one child by handing him over to someone else.'

Eileen held up placating palms. 'All right, all right. You can bring him to the station but while you're being interviewed you'll have to let me take care of him. I'll hand him back to you, I promise.'

Lily looked at her long and hard, then hung her head and breathed a long, mournful sigh. 'How did it come to this? Why are we all turning against one another? I've never hit anyone in my life before all this.'

'I don't think the war has helped,' said Eileen. 'Do you need a coat?'

Lily knew that to put on her coat she'd have to give up Christopher, even if only momentarily. 'No,' she said, 'it's warm enough without.'

Eileen glanced at the wall clock before they left and wondered if it would do any harm, while they were in the area, to ask the neighbours if they'd seen it on her wall before last April. But she decided against it. That wasn't her job. It might, in a Chinese whisper sort of way, add to the rumours going around about Lily. She wasn't a detective. Let DS Bannister sort his own problems out. She was guessing that Lily would get a custodial sentence for this attack, which would keep her out of harm's way long enough for the DS to ask all the questions he liked.

Chapter 14

The courts in Leeds Town Hall were designed by the Victorians to be dark and intimidating. The only concessions to comfort were the cushions on the seats of the magistrates, and the only concession to coloured decoration was the Leeds Coat of Arms on the wall at the back of the magistrate's bench, featuring three miserable-looking owls and a dead sheep. What owls and sheep had to do with Leeds, an engineering city, was anyone's guess. Lily was taken to the dock by the court usher. She gripped the sides as she gave her name and address and pleaded guilty to the charge of assault. Her thoughts were on Christopher whom she'd handed over to Eileen Morley just minutes before.

'What if they lock me up? What will happen to him? I'm breastfeeding him. How can I do that in prison?'

'Look, Lily, just plead guilty. Tell them the story you told me about these women accusing you of killing Michael. Mention your husband getting killed in action. Give them a sob story and you'll most likely get off with another fine – it'll probably be a lot more than seven pounds ten, though. Just be polite and don't forget to call them your worship. I'll be waiting with Christopher outside the door.'

There were three magistrates, all men. In the middle sat Mr Iredale, the chairman, from whom she needed sympathy. He looked to be a well-fed man in his early forties: too old for this war, too young for the last. He wore a tweed coat, a tie of regimental design, a badge in his lapel and epaulettes, possibly to give him a military appearance. But his weak-jawed, flabby face let him down. Lily's heart sank as she looked at the three of them. Not too much sympathy on show here. One of the other magistrates spoke first.

'Could you give the court your name and full address?'

'Mrs Lilian Marie Robinson. Thirteen, Perseverance Street, Leeds.'

'Mrs Robinson, you have been charged with assaulting Mrs Vera Pickersgill of number twenty-seven, Perseverance Street. How do you plead?'

'Guilty, Your Worship.'

'And do you have anything to say in mitigation of your actions?'

Lily nodded, still wondering how Christopher was faring. She heard nothing from outside in the corridor. The bench was waiting for her to reply. The magistrate repeated his question, impatiently.

'Oh, I'm sorry,' said Lily. 'Yes, I'd like to say that I haven't been myself in recent weeks since I got news that my husband was killed in the war.'

Mr Iredale spoke for the first time. 'You have our sympathy, Mrs Robinson, but you're not the only war widow in this country. If every war widow behaved as you did this country would descend into anarchy.'

'I also lost my son, Michael.'

'We know about this, Mrs Robinson, and we're not here to question why you handed him over to a man you hardly knew unless you're claiming that your mind is unbalanced?'

The police had given the story to the newspapers and for three days it had received dwindling exposure at a time when the main news was the progress of the Allied armies in Europe. Michael remained missing and it increased the police's suspicions that Lily wasn't telling them everything she knew about his disappearance. A hint had also been passed on to Iredale that it would suit the police to have Mrs Robinson held in custody for a while. Being sent to prison turns a citizen into a non-person: a person without rights. Becoming a non-person has the effect of reducing a prisoner's resolve to maintain secrecy under interrogation, especially a prisoner who's never been locked up before. The police reckoned that a few weeks in prison would soften her up enough to tell them what she'd done with Michael.

'No, I'm not unbalanced, Your Worship. I was just confused, sad at losing my husband – a brave man who was mentioned in dispatches. I had no one to turn to. I have no family, you see. I was brought up in children's homes and my late husband's family wanted nothing to do with me, nor my children.'

'And why was this?'

'They thought I wasn't good enough for him.' She wasn't about to mention that Michael was conceived out of wedlock.

'Hmm.' Mr Iredale looked at his notes. 'I see you were married in the August and your son was born just five months later. Would this have any bearing on their antagonism towards you?'

Lily was taken aback by the question that seemed to have no bearing on her case.

'I don't know, Your Worship.'

'Really? Tell me what you *do* know, Mrs Robinson.'

Lily took a deep breath. This wasn't going her way at all. This man had come out gunning for her. 'I'm really sorry I hurt Mrs Pickersgill. I'm not like that, honest. She was so nasty to me that she made me lose my temper. She accused me of murdering Michael. It's bad enough having your son abducted without people who don't know what they're talking about accusing you of murder. My Michael's still out there and nasty people saying things like that won't help to bring him back.'

She knew Vera Pickersgill and Hilda Muscroft were in the public seats but she chose not to look their way and acknowledge their presence.

'This isn't the first time recently that you've attacked one of your neighbours, is it?' said Iredale.

'I didn't attack Mrs Muscroft. I just pushed her because she accused me of murdering Michael as well. If she'd told the truth in court I wouldn't have been found guilty.'

'Liar!' screamed Hilda. 'I had to have six stitches in me bloody head!'

'That's because she tripped and banged her head on a lamp-post,' said Lily. She spoke, nervously, without looking Hilda's way. Iredale banged a gavel and asked for silence in the public seats, then addressed himself to Lily.

93

'Nonetheless, Mrs Robinson, you've been found guilty of two counts of assault in the space of a few days. Do you have anything further to say which might persuade us not to give a custodial sentence?'

Lily remembered Eileen Morley's words of advice. *Be polite*. 'Yes, Your Worship. I'm sorry for what I did but I have a new-born baby boy who's still being breastfed. To take me away from him at this time would be very harmful.'

Mr Iredale glared at her. 'Mrs Robinson. I'm not entirely sure you're a fit person to be a mother. My colleagues and I will retire to consider our verdict.'

It took them twenty minutes, during which time Lily remained in the dock while the court officials chatted with each other and prepared the rest of the day's cases. A policewoman was standing just behind Lily's shoulder. Lily turned to her.

'What do you think they'll do?'

'I don't know love, but you picked the short straw getting Iredale. He's what we call a confirmed bachelor – doesn't much like women.'

'Oh,' said Lily, wishing she hadn't asked.

The magistrates returned in solemn procession and sat down. Iredale put on a pair of spectacles and read from a piece of paper he was carrying.

'Mrs Robinson. We have taken into account the fact that your recent unfortunate experiences appear to have adversely affected your mental state. It's with this in mind that the judgement of this court is that you be sent to a secure establishment for psychiatric treatment until such time as it is deemed that you're a fit person to be safely returned to the community. During this time your child will be taken care of by the authorities.'

The verdict numbed Lily. 'What?' she said. 'For how long? How long are you sending me away for?'

'For as long as it takes, Mrs Robinson.'

Lily's self-control exploded. 'This isn't fair! None of this was my fault.' She pointed to Hilda and Vera. 'It was the two sniggering witches over there! I had my son stolen from me and the police are too damned lazy to do anything about it and then I have to put up with you three bloody stooges who can't see right from wrong!'

She darted from the dock and made for the unguarded door which she pushed open. Outside was Eileen holding Christopher. Lily snatched him away from her and ran down the corridor. It had all happened so quickly that it was several seconds before a court usher followed Lily out of the door.

'Where did she go?' he asked Eileen.

Eileen pointed down the corridor that led to double doors, then followed the usher through them. A policeman and other court officials followed them.

Through the doors was a staircase, from the top of which Lily could see two policemen on the floor below. She headed upstairs and was out of sight when the usher and Eileen came bursting through the door. The usher carried straight on and the policewoman flew down the stairs. Lily ran along a corridor, trying doors as she went. One was open. She took a cautious glance inside. It was a dark room containing a wooden table and six chairs. Still clutching Christopher she hid beneath the table, out of sight of anyone who chose to open the door and give the room no more than a cursory glance. After five minutes she heard voices in the corridor, one of them saying that she couldn't have left the building otherwise she'd have been seen.

'Check all the unlocked doors.'

She held on to Christopher tightly, knowing it was just a question of time. If they knew she was definitely in the Town Hall they wouldn't bother extending their search to the streets, and even if they did, how long before she was captured or had to give herself up? What she did know was that they were going to take her baby off her and put her in a loony bin.

Tears streamed down her cheeks. She tried to suppress her sobbing. The door to the room opened then, after no more than five seconds, closed. The searcher had given the room just a quick glance and had seen nothing. She clung to Christopher as the searching feet faded away in the distance. Lily's hopes rose. Ten minutes went by during which time she'd just heard the odd hurried footsteps approaching – giving her a heart-stopping moment – but not slowing down and then passing. A door at the end of the corridor would bang and then nothing. This happened three times. She began to plan what she would do once outside the building. First she would go to the bank and draw out all her money. She had her bank book in her pocket. She always took it with her in case of emergencies and today had looked like being an emergency day. There was enough to keep her going for a while. Then she could track down Auntie Dee who lived in Shipley. She'd never been to her house and she hadn't seen her since she and Larry got married.

Auntie Dee, who wasn't one for keeping her opinions to herself, had *had words* with Larry's parents at the wedding reception. Dee had apologised to the newlyweds and subsequently thought it best she stay away and not make further trouble for them. She wasn't a proper auntie, but she was the nearest Lily had to a relative. Auntie Dee worked on the markets, that's how she'd find her. Auntie Dee would get this mess sorted out. Her plans were making progress when more feet arrived. A man's voice shouted, 'Have these rooms been checked?' He sounded like a policeman. Lily's heart began to pound.

'I don't know,' came a distant voice.

'Does anyone know?' The man sounded exasperated, his voice boomed along the corridor. 'Is anyone keeping a check on what rooms have been searched and what haven't? We could be here all day at this rate. Let's start acting as if we know what we're doing. I'll do this side, you do that. WPC Morley, you stay in the corridor to catch her if she tries to escape – that's if you can manage it after letting her go once already.'

'I didn't let her go, Sarge,' protested Eileen. 'I didn't know she'd been given a custodial.'

'Well you know now!'

Lily now hated this policeman who was dashing her hopes of freedom. Freedom for her and Christopher who was to be taken away from her by an efficient copper, whose face she'd never seen. She kissed Christopher on the forehead.

'They're going to take you away from me, my darling. But it won't be for ever. We'll be back together before you know it. What they're doing isn't right. Your mummy hasn't done anything wrong. The world is full of bad people, like the Germans who took your daddy away. Now it's our own people, who are just as bad.'

The door opened again. This time it didn't shut straight away. She saw boots come into the room. The big black shiny boots of a policeman. She held her breath but containing her sobbing was incredibly difficult. The boots walked all around the room, clumping against the worn parquet floor. They stopped in front of a window. She heard him sliding it open, then she heard him strike a match. She smelled tobacco smoke. He was sitting on the window ledge now, one foot on the floor, one foot dangling, enjoying his cigarette. Finding Lily was obviously the last thing on his mind. Maybe he'd been in court and had sympathy for her. Maybe luck was on her side. The world wasn't entirely full of evil people like Hilda Muscroft and that horrible magistrate.

She kept absolutely quiet for the three minutes it took him to smoke his cigarette. Christopher had mercifully fallen asleep in her arms. In the outside corridors the sound of the searchers dwindled. They probably thought she'd made it out to the street. The boots were both back on the floor now and the window was sliding shut. She held her breath. Another few seconds and he'd be gone. The boots headed for the door and stopped. She could almost sense the brain, six feet above the boots, ticking away. Her own thoughts were trying to push him on his way.

Just go. Please go.

She saw his legs bend. One knee rested on the floor,

then a hand, then his face came into view. It was a young face. A face disappointed at finding her.

'Oh, please,' she said, 'don't tell on us.'

He stared at her for a full five seconds, then got to his feet. He went outside the door. For a second she thought he'd heeded her plea. His shout was loud.

'She's in here, Sarge – Room thirty-seven.'

Voices echoed along the corridor. 'We've got her. She's in Room thirty-seven!'

There was an approaching rush of feet through the door. Faces appeared all around her but no one was making a move. One of the faces was Iredale's, the magistrate who'd just condemned her to a psychiatric hospital. They stared at each other in silence until the hatred and defiance in Lily's eyes forced him back to his feet. She looked down at Christopher, trying to memorise every tiny bit of his face. He woke up and smiled at her, or perhaps it was wind.

'Mummy will come back to you, my darling,' she whispered. 'I promise.'

Legs and feet were all around her now. A strategy was being discussed about how to get her out from under the table without doing any harm to them or to her baby. No mention of not doing *her* any harm.

'She's a woman with a propensity for violence,' she heard Iredale say.

'No, I'm not,' she sobbed. 'You're just too stupid to be able to see the truth.'

More people came into the room. The odd face bobbed down to take a look at her then quickly withdrew without speaking to her.

She screamed hysterically, 'What am I? Some monkey in a zoo that you've all come to gawp at? My husband's been killed and my son stolen but I haven't done anything. Why are you trying to hurt me?'

Her outburst brought them to silence. One voice that she recognised spoke. The owner of the voice bent down and spoke to her.

'I think you'd better give Christopher to me. This can't be doing him any good.'

'What the hell are you doing here?' sobbed Lily.

'I happen to be a magistrate.'

'A pal of the three stooges, no doubt. Was it you who put him up to having me sent away?'

Just for a brief second, before Godfrey Robinson, her late husband's father, got to his feet, she saw guilt on his face. She'd hit the nail on the head.

'I'm right, aren't I?' she screamed. 'You persuaded them to lock me up so that you can have my son!'

Above the table there was an awkward silence. Several people had heard Lily's accusation. She hadn't finished.

'I wish the Germans had won the war. They can't have been any worse that you! And to think your son died for the likes of you!'

She heard Godfrey say, 'Perhaps it's best if I stay out of this for now. I'll be outside.' Lily watched his feet leave the room. Eileen bent down and smiled at her.

'Lily, we're not going to drag you and Christopher out of there, but it'll be better all round if you come out of your own accord. It's not good for Christopher isn't all this.'

'What's going to happen to him?'

'Nothing bad. He'll be placed in good care until you're feeling well again, I promise you.'

'Until I'm well? There's nothing wrong with me that giving me my Michael back won't cure. Why is everyone trying to hurt me? All I want is my boy back. Is that so unnatural?'

'No, Lily, it's not unnatural, but unfortunately you've broken the law.'

'So, I'll pay a fine. I don't care how much.'

It was obvious that the policewoman was feeling sympathetic to Lily's cause. She got to her feet. Lily heard her ask, 'What exactly was her punishment? Why is she acting like this?'

A voice Lily didn't recognise said, 'She's been given an indefinite sentence in a psychiatric unit.'

'Which means her baby's to be taken away from her,' said Eileen. 'All this on top of losing her other son. And you lot are wondering why she's acting strange.'

'It's not for you to be giving opinions,' said Iredale testily. 'I'll thank you to do your job and retrieve the woman and child from under this table.'

Eileen sighed and squatted down again. 'Come on, Lily,' she said gently. 'You can't win this one. Give Christopher to me.'

Lily stared at her for a long moment, realising the utter futility of her predicament. Sobbing loudly, she kissed Christopher on his forehead and handed him over to the WPC. Then she heard Iredale's voice as he spoke to the male constables in the room.

'Right, get that damned woman out from under that table and handcuff her, using whatever force is necessary.'

Lily felt a hand behind her grab her leg and yank her out, roughly. Her hands were forced behind her back and handcuffs snapped on to her wrists. She heard Eileen's voice call out.

'There's no need for all that!'

Iredale shouted at her. 'Quiet, Constable, and hand the child over to its grandfather! He's outside.'

'No!' Lily screamed. 'Don't give my Christopher to that bloody man! He doesn't love him.'

'Get her out of here,' barked Iredale, 'and send for a Black Maria.'

Chapter 15

Lily's new home was Room 36, Ecclestone House Hospital, out on the Yorkshire Moors, seven miles northwest of Haworth. It was a secure hospital funded by the government but it had a poor record for curing the inmates who were mostly a mixture of alcoholics, depressives, and people with learning difficulties who had found themselves on the wrong side of the law. A few of them had been there for years. The suicide rate was high and never publicised. Working at Ecclestone House was not the most sought-after occupation – reflected in the quality of employees the job attracted. Some of them were little better than the inmates they were caring for; particularly Dr Freeman who ran the hospital.

From the minute Lily came through the door, handcuffed to a police constable, Dr Freeman had his designs on her. Beneath all the angst etched into her face he saw a beautiful young woman. Her body was a bit plump around the belly but he knew this was because she'd recently had a baby. This was OK. He never took advantage during the first month. A woman needed to be gently subdued by drugs and what, in his opinion, was his charming bedside manner, before he joined them in their bed.

It was all part of the therapy, he told them. He'd been doing it for years and no one had ever complained. Few could actually remember the incidents clearly enough to make a complaint and his position would be so difficult to refill that no one would take the word of a criminal woman above his. The lucky women, the ones who spent the least time there, were the plain ones.

Lily was shivering with acute distress as she was taken up to her room. Freeman walked behind and sent a nurse to bring a strong sedative. 'This one needs to sleep,' he told the police officer. 'It's my suspicion that she's a manic depressive but I'll know more tomorrow when she wakes up after a good night's sleep.

What he didn't say was that Lily wasn't due to wake up completely for some time to come. She lay on her bed and watched as Freeman emptied a syringe into her arm as he murmured soothing words into her ear.

'You'll be all right, my dear. This will ease the pain you're suffering.'

She didn't like this man. Not too long ago he wouldn't have got away with injecting her without giving her a detailed explanation of what it was and why it was necessary. Not today. Her defences were shattered. They'd taken away everything that was dear to her and now they were sending her to sleep. She was hoping it would be a good long sleep, preferably an endless one.

She was drugged into a haze of semi-oblivion which would dry her tears and dull the memory of her two sons, her dead husband, Hilda Muscroft, Vera Pickersgill and the Oldroyds. She would wake up each morning not quite knowing where she was, what time it was, what day it was, where she had come from and why she was here.

She quickly became compliant, quiet and didn't eat much. In many ways she was Dr Freeman's ideal patient. A patient out of favour with the police, with no close friends, no living relatives that anyone knew of, and very pretty.

Lily had been there a week when Freeman began making his late-night visits to her. She was vaguely aware of someone being there but she'd been pumped too full of psychoactive drugs to know who or even worry about it. On occasions she might have sensed her bedclothes being pulled back and her nightdress being lifted over her thighs. She was wearing nothing underneath and normally she'd have kicked and screamed at such a vile intruder but she didn't. She just lay there, out of it, as his hands wandered all over her body, into parts hitherto known only to herself and her late husband. Dr Freeman felt she wasn't ready to be penetrated, but that time would come. For this he needed her to be more awake, more responsive. In the meantime he made do with straddling her and relieving his lust all over her naked stomach. He was always careful to wipe all evidence of his ejaculation from her before any nurse saw it. Lily was never really aware of what he was doing. There'd be a time when she'd become aware of it but she'd be so compliant as to not complain to him or anyone. Freeman knew this.

After two weeks he eased off on the drugs; she had enough in her system to have lowered her resistance to his advances. He added what he thought to be personal charm to the prescription, smiling at her, talking sweetly to her, stroking her hair and allowing his hands to brush against her breasts pushing against the thin cotton of her nightdress. On some days he would ask her to lie back on her bed and to lift up her nightdress as he needed to examine her breasts for lumps. She did as he asked. He was a doctor; why wouldn't she? She was wearing no undergarments but she was too weary to give the matter much thought. She was too weary to notice his erection as he ran his hands over her breasts, stroking each nipple in turn, then running his hand over her stomach down to her pubis. His eyes fixed on hers, but hers were blank. Unfeeling and unaware what he was doing to her.

Chapter 16

A month went by. To Lily it could have been a week, a day or just a few minutes; she had so little concept of time. In all this time she hadn't left her room other than to go to the bathroom just down the corridor. Her level of consciousness allowed her to walk and to talk in short sentences, to eat and take her drugs. She was losing weight simply because the drugs had taken away her appetite, her willpower and most of her common sense. She was totally reliant on Dr Freeman, a man she instinctively disliked.

He still hadn't penetrated her. He was worried about a forthcoming inspection ordered by the board of trustees which would involve him explaining the treatment of each patient. Up until now he'd always been able to wing it, with one of the trustees calling in from time to time to enjoy the same perverted persuasions as Freeman. But now a government department had taken an interest and he'd been warned that the inspections would be much more meticulous than before. His decidedly unethical treatment of Lily for manic depression would be a major problem, unless . . .

She was lying on her bed, in her nightmare

dreamworld, when he came into her room and sat beside her.

'Lily,' he said, 'we're putting you on a new treatment.'

He knew she wouldn't respond, in fact he doubted if she was listening.

'It's a minor operation to relieve the pressure on your brain. Afterwards you won't need all these drugs that make you sleepy. You'll feel like a new woman and no doubt we'll be able to release you within a week or two. What do you think about that?'

Lily said nothing. She just stared at him with nothing but emptiness behind her eyes. Freeman went on.

'It's called a prefrontal lobotomy. It's cured thousands of manic depressives like you.'

He chose not to tell her that it involved drilling through her skull to cut through the frontal lobes of her brain. He also chose not to tell her that it was an unproven operation which the visiting surgeon, Mr Goodchild, had only performed four times before in the Ecclestone House Hospital, with mixed results. The symptoms of two of his patients had been relieved temporarily, another had shown marked deterioration and the third had been transferred to Keighley Hospital and was currently little more than a cabbage. The inspection was due in two days so it would help Freeman's cause if the inspectors found Lily in recovery, with her head bandaged and still drowsy from the previous day's strong anaesthetic.

'We'll be operating tomorrow morning,' he told her. Lily gave a faint nod and went back to sleep. Freeman left her, satisfied that he'd done his duty in keeping his patient informed of all forthcoming treatment. He'd mention that to the inspectors, including the part where she was most grateful to be having the operation.

The following morning Lily was awakened by a male nurse who told her she was being taken down to pre-op. Lily didn't know what that was but she eased herself out of bed and into a waiting wheelchair. She'd totally forgotten what Freeman had said to her the previous day. She was now being taken through a part of the hospital she'd never been to before.

'Where am I going?'

'For your operation, Lily.'

She was suddenly scared, the first emotion of any kind that she'd felt since arriving there and being injected with her first drugs.

'What operation? I don't want an operation.'

'It's for your own good, Lily. It's a very clever operation that'll make you better. You ought to be grateful.'

She was wheeled into the anaesthetic room where she was asked to climb on to another bed. The nurse went over to a table, filled a syringe and turned towards her.

'What's that?' she asked.

'It's what you need to make you feel relaxed, Lily. There's nothing to worry about, I promise.'

'Do you?'

'Yes, of course . . . just a little scratch.' He injected her in her arm.

'What sort of operation?' she asked again.

'A necessary one, Lily. Shortly we'll be putting you

to sleep and when you wake up you'll feel so much better.'

Michael and Christopher moved, fleetingly, across her mind and she felt immensely sad, but she couldn't remember why. It would be good to feel better.

Chapter 17

The rider of the motorcycle combination stopped at a crossroads to check a map against a road sign. The helmeted head shook in confusion. The leather-clad biker got off and reached into the sidecar to take out a bottle of whisky. After a couple of deep swigs the bottle was replaced and the map re-examined as if the drink had helped sharpen the mind. Then the goggles were reset over the eyes, the rider remounted and, with a throaty roar, set off again up the narrow, winding, uphill road. A heavy mist was shrouding the Pennine tops. It was mid-morning in late June. In an hour the sun would be warm enough to burn it off, but right now there was a real pea-souper up ahead.

The mist swept down like a dirty grey cloak and the rider switched on the headlight, more to alert oncoming vehicles than to improve vision. The beam just bounced back off the fog. Suddenly, to the right, about two hundred yards away, the swirling mist cleared and revealed a large stone building which might well be the rider's destination; hard to tell in this mist, even though the biker had spent time there. If it wasn't it might provide sanctuary for a while until the weather improved.

The motorcyclist slowed down to a walking pace; eyes glued to the right-hand side of the road, looking for the dirt road that would lead to the house. There it was, an eight-foot-wide track that would take most motor vehicles going one way. Rarely did two vehicles meet each other coming the other way out here.

There was a wooden sign saying *Hospital No Through Traffic*. The biker gave a smile as bleak as the weather and took the machine up the track. After a less than a minute the hospital came into view. It was a substantial stone building which had begun life as a country house before a descendant of the original owner decided it was no fun living out here on the cold, cheerless moors and sold it to a company which converted it to a thirty-bed hospital. The government took it over during the First World War and used it for treating wounded soldiers, before turning it into a psychiatric hospital, with Dr Freeman in charge.

The noise of the motorcycle combination brought a young man in a white coat to the front door just as the rider was dismounting.

'Can I help you?' asked the white coat, peering at the face behind the goggles.

The rider lifted the goggles and returned his smile. 'I do hope so. I'm told that Dr Freeman still works here. Is this true? I'm an old friend of his.' The voice was low and gruff – a smoker's voice. The rider hitched the goggles up to the front of the helmet. Scarf round the neck, tucked into the leather windcheater. Face still barely visible.

'Yes, he's still here. Can I tell him who you are?'

'Still here, eh? Hidden out here for all these years – twenty to my knowledge. Is his wife still around?'

'No, I believe Mrs Freeman left before I came to work here. Who did you say you were?'

'Did a bunk eh? Can't say I blame her. We had some high old times, Benny Freeman and me. High old times. Tell you what. Why don't I surprise him? He'll like that. Great man for a practical joke, old Benny. Where is he?'

'He's in his office.'

'Good, no need to show me. I know the way. The rider pushed past the young man, entered a large vestibule, went up a curving staircase to the first floor. Along a corridor to the right was a door bearing a sign saying: *Dr Freeman. Do not enter without knocking and waiting.* The rider entered without knocking and waiting. Behind a large desk sat a man in his sixties who was in the act of quickly withdrawing his hand from the young woman at the side of him. By the way she smoothed her dress and hitched up her underwear it was obvious where his hand had been. The young woman was wearing no uniform and had the drawn look of a psychiatric patient. Other than that she was quite pretty.

'Good morning, Benny Boy. Still up to your old tricks with the patients eh? Still lying your socks off? Still abusing the inmates? I thought you'd have grown out of it by now, you seedy old creep.'

Freeman's face turned puce. 'Who the hell are you?'

The rider took off the helmet and scarf. Freeman's puce face blanched within the space of two seconds. Delilah Maguire smiled down at him, showing an array of gleaming white teeth that could only have been false.

She was a tall, strongly built, hard-looking woman in her mid-fifties and she looked to have lived every year of it to the full. Her eyes were bright blue and full of life. Her nose was on the long side but it gave her face character and strength. As she removed the helmet her hair sprang out as if desperate to be released. It was long and wild and wiry and sprinkled with grey. She stuck her left hand behind her head in an automatic movement, twisting her hair into a ponytail which she tied into place with an elastic band that had somehow appeared in her right hand.

'I suggest you postpone this consultation until another time, Benny Boy. I have serious business to discuss with you.'

Freeman's white face reddened as he sent the young woman from the office. Delilah plonked her helmet and goggles down on the doctor's desk, sat in the chair opposite and rested her booted feet on his desk. 'You have my niece, Lily Robinson, staying here.'

'What? How the hell did you know that?'

Delilah grinned triumphantly, swung her feet off the desk and leaned forward. 'Actually, I didn't, you rapacious old goat – until you just told me. I knew the bastards had sent her to a nuthouse but they wouldn't tell me where. Jesus! This is the first place I should have looked.'

'If you're a bona fide relative you have a right to know where she is,' said Freeman, nervously. 'If you're not, you've no right to be here.'

Delilah laughed out loud. 'Bona fide? When was I ever bona fide anything? I wasn't even a bona fide nutter when they sent me here. It never occurred to me that young Lily would follow in my footsteps. When I read about her in the paper I checked every hospital in West Yorkshire to try and find her – and here she is, under the care of the great Dr Freeman, pervert of this parish.'

'Get out before I call the police!'

Delilah's face turned ugly; she pulled out a long-bladed knife from inside her jacket and leaned across the desk, holding the knife at Freeman's throat.

'If you've been screwing young Lily I'll swing for you, Benny Boy. You know I'll do it.'

Freeman pushed himself back in his chair but the knife followed him, drawing a speck of blood.

'Jesus! You mad bloody woman! She's only been here a month. What the hell do you think I am?'

'I know what you are, Benny Boy.' She took the knife away from his throat, but still held it at the ready. 'Take me to my niece. I'll ask her myself.'

'I thought you said she wasn't your niece.'

'She's the daughter of my best friend who died a year after Lily was born. I swore on her mother's deathbed that I'd look out for her and I would have if the bastards hadn't kept locking me up. Better late than never, eh?'

The knife was once again hovering not far from Freeman's throat. He knew this woman of old and what she was capable of. She'd once done time for seri-ously stabbing a vicious gangster in a knife fight. He got to his feet.

'OK, but when you see her you'll realise what a mistake you're making. Lily is in need of treatment.'

'Just take me to her.'

Freeman made for the door. Delilah put the knife away and picked up her helmet and goggles. She followed him, whispering in his ear.

'Just remember, I know what I know. If I open my mouth and give the police names they'll bang you up for a ten stretch at least. So far I've kept it to myself because it was of no use to me, but now it is. I do that, you see. I keep stuff in reserve. I'd practically forgotten about you. Just goes to show, eh? My old mother used to say, "Delilah girl, never throw anything away if you think it might come in handy one day." '

Freeman led her back downstairs and along a corridor to a room marked *Pre-op*.

'Pre what op?' asked Delilah sharply, stopping outside the door

'She's scheduled to have a very necessary operation.'

'What sort of operation?'

'You wouldn't understand.'

'Try me. You'd be amazed.'

'It's called a prefrontal lobotomy.'

Delilah froze for a moment, then said, 'And you think I don't know what one of those is? Do you think I don't read? Do you think I don't know that most of the people who have that operation are never right in the head again?'

She pushed past Freeman into the room. Lily lay on a bed, on her side, face away from the door, wearing a surgical patient's gown which revealed her naked buttocks.

'Has she been anaesthetised?' snapped Delilah, adjusting the gown to protect Lily's modesty.

'Not yet. She'd had a pre-med but the surgeon hasn't arrived yet. I imagine it's due to the fog.'

'Where's the anaesthetist?'

'I'm qualified in that field.'

'You? Do me a favour. You're not even a qualified human being.'

Delilah went over to the bed and touched Lily on the shoulder. Her voice changed. It was softer, friendlier. The voice of an affectionate auntie.

'Lily, it's Auntie Dee.'

Lily had heard them come in but she was so subdued with narcotics that she took little notice. Dee leaned right over her, so her face was inches away from Lily's ear.

'Lily. It's me, Auntie Dee. I've come to take you home.'

The sound of a friendly and familiar voice penetrated the drug-induced fog. She turned over. Dee was shocked at what she saw.

The radiant young woman she'd last seen, on Lily and Larry's wedding day, had aged twenty years. Her face was drawn and pale, dark rings encircled her eyes, her hair was lifeless, her lips colourless, and she'd lost too much weight for a woman who'd been slender to start with. She looked up at Dee and tried to speak, but nothing came out. Dee took a couple of steps towards Freeman and held the knife at his throat.

'Pre-med my arse! She's drugged up to the eyeballs and you're going to anaesthetise her and drill a hole though her skull. You're a bloody monster. Bloody hell! Hitler should have had you working for him, you vile bastard! When she comes round I'm going to ask her if you've been screwing her. If you have I'm going to kill you and you must know I don't make idle threats!'

'Apart from necessary examinations I haven't touched her.'

'Which means you've been feeling her up. What else, you low-life lizard?'

'Nothing. I haven't done anything . . . illegal to her.'

'The operation's cancelled. I'm taking her away with me.'

'You can't just take her away.'

Freeman's voice was weak with fear. This woman was more than capable sticking her knife in him.

'Why not?'

'Because she has to be discharged and she's not in a fit state to be discharged. When the drugs wear off she'll become very depressed.'

'I should think she will be depressed after what's been done to her. Husband sent to his death, and two sons stolen from her, and what you've done to her. Do you know who's got her baby?'

'I don't know. They don't tell me these things.'

'Well I'll tell you, shall I? Her stuck-up bloody in-laws, that's who. They had no time for the family when their son was alive, now they've decided they want her baby.'

It was something Dee had found out during her search for Lily. Lily had rolled over again. Dee tugged her shoulder.

'Lily, I'm taking you with me.'

'You can't do this,' Freeman protested.

'Oh yes I can, you bastard!'

Dee looked down at Lily and then out of the window at the moor outside. Was the mist lifting or was it just wishful thinking? She looked up at the watery sun that seemed to have a lot of work still to do to if the mist was to clear any time soon. Then she turned her attention to Freeman, glaring at him with gimlet eyes.

'I've got a list of women you abused over the years. Got it from your darling wife just before I left here. I promised I'd do something about it to bring you to justice – another promise I failed to keep, with them banging me up in jail. God, she loathed you, did that wife of yours. It wouldn't take much for the police to track these women down. Put all their evidence together and make your wife happy at last. Is she still alive?'

Freeman said nothing. Dee pressed the point of the knife into his groin. His mouth opened wide in shock.

'I asked you a question.'

'I've no idea,' Freeman bleated, bending his body away from the knife. 'I haven't seen or heard of her since she left with all the money from the safe.'

Dee laughed out loud. 'Robbed you, did she? Good for her. Didn't know she had it in her.'

Lily was now sitting up and watching proceedings with some bemusement. All the anger left Dee as she sat beside her and put an arm round her. 'You're coming home with me, Lily. Then me and you are going to get your boys back. Do you understand what I'm saying?'

She felt Lily squeeze her in return, which brought a rare tear to Dee's eye.

'Can you stand up?'

Lily pushed herself off the bed and stood quite still, as if waiting for further instructions.

'She can walk well enough,' muttered Freeman. 'She walked here.'

'I wasn't talking to you, you creep! Where are her clothes?'

Freeman pointed to a pile of clothes on a chair in the corner of the room. Dee picked up the clothes, examined them and threw them to the floor.

'Does she have any clothes other than these bloody rags? I don't imagine she arrived dressed like this. Smart girl, our Lily.'

Freeman said nothing. Dee took him by his collar and dragged him to the door. 'Right. You and me are going to take Lily down to your office. On the way there you'll act as if all is in order, nothing for anyone to worry about. If you don't, the person who'll have the most to worry about is you. When we get there I want Lily to be brought the smartest change of clothes you have in this dump – her own, preferably. Plus a good, warm coat if she didn't come in one.'

'You can't just take her off her medication like that, she'll get massive withdrawal symptoms.'

'You'd better hope she's OK then . . . *Doctor.*' Dee spat out the last word, 'Because you'll be fully responsible for her, having discharged her. What symptoms are we talking about?'

'She may get a fever, and hallucinations. I don't know. Everyone reacts differently to medication. Just give her aspirin to control her temperature and make her drink plenty of water to stop her dehydrating.'

'How long will this take?'

'Two or three days, maybe longer, but she's young and fit. She should come out of it OK.'

'She *was* young and fit until you got hold of her, you evil bastard.' She held her knife to his throat. 'Jesus, I could slit your gizzard here and now . . . but I need you to sign a document that says she's fit to be released back into the community. That's what the court requires, and that's what you're going to do.'

'Very well! I'll sign the discharge. Then what?' He held his hands up in complete surrender, trying to ease his neck away from the knife.

Dee held him in her contemptuous gaze for several uncomfortable seconds before deciding.

'Then I will leave you to your perversions because part of this deal is that you inform the relevant authorities that Lily has been quite properly released.'

'And what about this list that my wife gave you?'

Dee took a piece of paper from her pocket and held it up for Freeman to see. He recognised his wife's handwriting – a list of maybe twenty names. Some he knew, most he'd forgotten.

'You give me Lily's discharge, I give you this and we leave you alone – providing you're telling the truth about not screwing her.'

'It's the truth.'

Dee chose to believe him because the alternative was too vile to contemplate.

There were many faces at the windows as Dee led Lily out to her motorbike. The sidecar was open to the elements so Dee put her crash helmet on her charge, more for warmth that safety. One of the nurses has brought her a choice of coats, one an army greatcoat which would have gone round Lily twice, but Dee selected it.

She helped Lily into the sidecar through the small door in the side and checked that she was sitting comfortably and safely. The army coat swallowed her to the extent that just a couple of inches of pale skin were to be seen beneath the crash helmet. Dee wrapped her scarf round her face and kicked the bike into action. Then she checked her pocket to ensure the discharge was there, gave a sweeping V sign to the watchers at the windows and took off into the mist, away from this place of danger to which the courts had sent Lily.

Chapter 18

By the time they'd reached Dee's home in Shipley, near Bradford, the mist of the Pennine moors had given way to summer sunshine. This, coupled with a fever that Lily was developing, had her sweating profusely, despite sitting in an open sidecar with the wind blowing in her face. The crash helmet protected only her head. Goggles would have helped but Dee needed the one pair she had. Dee drew the machine to a halt in the short driveway of a pleasant-looking, three-bedroomed semi-detached in a smart, residential area and wasted no time in helping Lily out. She'd sacrificed safety for expediency on the way back and had driven flat out knowing that it was important to get Lily into bed. After that, all Dee could do was her best. She had no idea what drugs Lily had been on and even if she had it wouldn't have helped.

What she did know was that it was important to keep Lily's existence at her house a secret until she was sure the police weren't looking for her. She'd give it a few days then ring that creep Freeman. Scare him into telling her exactly what the score was. If there was one thing Dee was good at, it was scaring the likes of Freeman.

Over the next forty-eight hours it was Dee who was

scared. On a couple of occasions she almost rang for an ambulance, once when Lily was hallucinating and once when she got violent shivers. Luckily both of these withdrawal symptoms went away before Dee took drastic action.

She gave Lily regular aspirin, the only drugs she had in the house, and made her drink plenty of water. She hadn't needed Freeman to tell her that aspirin kept the temperature down, nor that drinking water warded off dehydration. However, she was reassured that Freeman had told her the truth in that respect, so maybe he'd told the truth in *another* respect.

Lily drank her water and took her tablets because she'd been indoctrinated into taking whatever tablets she was given. Over the first two days her body temperature dropped from 103 degrees down to ninety-nine. On day three her head began to clear and she ate a bowl of breakfast cereal. On day four she managed eggs and bacon; she also managed to talk a little and, gradually, Dee pieced together the story of how Lily had ended up in Ecclestone House Hospital – a place she didn't remember much about, fortunately.

'Hilda Musgrave and Vera something or other eh? I must have a quiet word with them.'

Lily wasn't too good at remembering names as yet. She'd just had her breakfast and was sitting in an armchair having a cup of tea.

'No, no, no you mustn't.'

'Why not?'

Lily gave it some thought. 'Because they're my neighbours.'

'Not any more they're not. You can't go back there. Not after what's been in the papers about you. They've all but called you a child-killer.'

Lily remembered being called such a name by Vera and she burst into tears. 'Auntie Dee, I want my baby. Where is he? Where's Christopher?'

Dee hesitated before telling her. 'He's OK, love. He's being looked after by his grandparents.'

'What?' It took Lily a few seconds to unravel the significance of this. 'You mean Larry's parents? But . . . they hate me, don't they? They wanted nothing to do with us. How can they look after Christopher? They can't possibly love him.'

'We'll get him back, Lily. You mark my words. But our first priority is to find Michael. Christopher's safe enough where he is.'

'Will I be able to go and see him?'

'First things first. I need to be sure the police aren't looking for you.'

'Oh. Did I escape or something? How did I get here? Where am I by the way?'

'You're in my house in Shipley.'

'*Your* house? It's a nice house. Do you actually own it?'

'Actually I do. No mortgage, nothing.'

'Must have cost a bomb.'

'Well, it was kind of a gift from a man called Johnnie Eccles. Both the house and the jewellery stalls. Although when Johnnie had them they were just tat stalls he used to launder money.'

'Launder money?'

'Yeah, it's the crook's way of justifying his ill-gotten gains to the law. He pretends his stalls are making the money that comes from his other business.'

'What other business?'

'He was a fence – dealt in stolen goods. He even organised some of the blags and let the mugs do the thieving while he made most of the money. Never got his hands dirty, our Johnnie. He had me working for him for a while in another business.'

'What as?'

'That doesn't matter.'

She didn't want to tell Lily she'd been acting as a madam in a brothel. She took the job for the money but also to look after the girls, who would otherwise have been put under the care of a pimp.

'It only lasted a year, but I made it my business to learn everything about his dodgy dealings. I took a good look at his crooked books and I knew exactly where he kept them. I knew most of his thieving associates and details of the jobs they'd pulled. Times, dates, places, everything. I figured at some stage he'd try and do the dirty on me and I had to be ready for him. The business he had me running was raided one day and he fitted me up to take the blame. Told the law it was nothing to do with him, it was all me. He'd set it up like that. For me it was the difference between a twenty-pound fine and three years inside.'

Lily was curious to know what sort of business this might have been, but chose not to press the matter. Dee continued:

'I kept schtum about his dodgy businesses and was given bail. Then I rang him up and told him I had enough on him to put him away for a ten stretch. He knew I could as well. I told him I wanted a grand to keep quiet. Promised to do my time like a good girl and keep him out of it. Silly sod fell for it. Absolutely scared to death of having to do bird.'

'Bird?'

'Jail time. Some people just aren't cut out for it and Johnnie Eccles was one of them. He said he didn't have a grand but he'd sign his house and his jewellery business over to me. What I didn't tell him was that I'd done a deal with the law, who'd been after him for years.'

'As soon as I got the deeds to his house and ownership of his jewellery business I shopped him to the police. I got his house and business. He got nine years.'

'Weren't you worried he'd come after you when he got out?'

'He actually sent one knuckle dragger after me but I got word he was coming and I was ready for him. I hired a couple of heavies of my own to take care of him. Then I went to visit Johnnie in Wakefield nick and told him I'd put some money inside the prison to sort him out if he tried it again.'

'And would you have done that?'

Dee shrugged. 'I wouldn't know how, but I knew it could be done and I knew he wouldn't put it past me. That's all I needed. Anyway, not long after that he had a heart attack and died. Lucky me eh?'

'How long ago was this?'

'Thirteen years ago, during which time I learned the imitation jewellery business and established proper contacts to buy high quality merchandise.'

Lily sat up in her chair and took a sip of her tea, realising she didn't really know Auntie Dee. She was a formidable lady, right enough, and thank heavens for that.

'So, is that how you got me out of that hospital place – blackmail?'

'You were legally discharged but I had to lean on the doctor who discharged you. I just need to know your discharge is kosher. We don't want the police arresting you the minute you turn up on the in-laws' doorstep.'

'How do we do that?'

'By ringing Dr Freeman.'

'Who's he?'

'He's the creep I had to lean on. The man in charge of the hospital where you've spent the last month. A worse man than Johnnie Eccles ever was.'

'Freeman? Was that his name? I remember someone. He had a white coat. Didn't like him. Was I there a month?'

Yes, and you'd have been there a damned sight longer if Freeman had had his way, Dee thought.

'I need to know the name of the copper in Leeds who's leading the hunt for Michael.'

Lily had to think long and hard about this one. It was a name emblazoned on her memory just over a month ago. 'It's something to do with stairs . . . Balustrade, I think.'

'Funny name. Are you sure?'

'No.' Lily screwed up her face in thought, then her face cleared, as did her mind.

'Bannister. His name's Bannister.'

'I assume he's a detective.'

'Yes. He doesn't wear a uniform. He's a sergeant I think. Yes, Detective Sergeant Bannister.' Lily smiled at her own achievement.

Dee was one of the few people in her street who had a telephone. She also had the number of Ecclestone House Hospital, along with the numbers of every other psychiatric establishment in West Yorkshire. Freeman answered on the second ring. He was obviously in his office.

'Benny Boy. This is your good friend Dee Maguire. I'm ringing to confirm that you've sent the discharge notice to the Leeds Magistrates' Courts and Leeds Police.'

There was a long hesitation before Freeman said, 'I have – that's what I agreed isn't it?'

'Yes, but you're a weasel and I don't trust you. I'm going to ring a certain Detective Sergeant Bannister of the Leeds Police right now and ask if Lily's been officially released. If anyone knows, it's him. What will he tell me?'

'He'll tell you what you want to hear.'

'Good because if he doesn't I'll give him the list your wife compiled in her own fair hand.'

'And how are you going to do that? I burned it.'

Dee laughed. 'Oh, how gullible you weasels are. Do you think I didn't make a copy of all the names? I have it here. Ruth Ingham, Dolly Marshal—'

'All right, all right, so you have a copy. I kept my side of the bargain. I expect you to keep yours. The courts and the police have been informed, in writing, of her discharge. I've also confirmed it by telephone. She's a free woman. How is she, by the way?'

'She's OK, no thanks to you.'

There was a long pause before he said, without conviction, 'Then you'll know I didn't screw her.' He was hoping Lily wouldn't remember what he *did* do to her.

'Do I?' said Dee mischievously. 'I'll see what Sergeant Bannister has to say about her discharge being official. If it isn't, you're in deep trouble.'

'It's official.'

Dee put the phone down and smiled at Lily, who was standing beside her. 'You're in the clear, Lily. Free as a bird.'

'This Dr Freeman, do you think he might have molested me?'

'I don't know, Lily. What do you remember?'

'Not much, but I have images of . . .' She shuddered. 'I don't know what.'

'Try and forget the images, Lily. He had you drugged. All sorts of weird images come to you when you're drugged. He most probably didn't do anything.'

Dee doubted that very much, but it was better that she think otherwise. Lily had enough on her plate right now without her being the victim of a perverted doctor who would get his comeuppance anyway.

But Lily wasn't fooled.

'Auntie Dee, suppose he's made me pregnant?'

Dee sighed. 'Lily, if he did *that* to you it wouldn't be just images. You'd know for certain. He likes his victims with a bit of life in them, otherwise it'd be like doing it to a corpse. I remember him of old. I know his sick ways. On top of which he always uses protection.' Then she added hastily, 'But he won't have raped you. Never think that.'

'Are you going to be ringing Sergeant Bannister now?'

There was apprehension in Lily's eyes. At the back of her mind she knew that Bannister had never been a bringer of good news.

'I could do, but he might start asking awkward questions, such as who am I and where are you?' She gave it some thought then decided, 'No, there'll be no need for that. Freeman wouldn't dare bluff me with so much at stake for him.'

'What list were you talking about?'

'Oh, just a list of Dr Freeman's patients. Women he wouldn't want the police to be visiting and asking awkward questions.'

'Women he molested?'

'Women who actually remember being raped by him, which is why I'm sure he didn't rape you.'

'And will the police be visiting them?'

Dee let out a roar of laughter. 'You bet your life they will, Lily! Now that we know you're in the clear I'll make damn sure Freeman gets what's coming to him. I should have shopped him years ago. He'll get ten years for what he's done. My God! Why on earth do these idiot men trust me to keep my mouth shut?'

Chapter 19

Godfrey and Jane Robinson lived in a four-bedroomed detached house on a leafy street in the more opulent part of Roundhay in Leeds. Godfrey was a butcher with four shops and he'd been doing very nicely out of the war due to a black market scam he was running. He had land out near Wetherby where he raised pigs for pork and bacon. It wasn't difficult to kill two pigs and hide one from the food inspector. Larry had known about this and had told Lily on condition she didn't mention it to the authorities. She hadn't given the matter a second thought as she never had any time for Larry's snobby parents. Luckily for Godfrey, Lily, still recovering from the damage caused by her stay with Freeman, had pushed such trivialities into a dark recess of her memory.

Dee's motorbike combination pulled to a noisy halt outside the Robinsons' house and both women sat for a few moments taking a look at it. Lily had only been there once, to meet Larry's parents. It hadn't been a memorable meeting, especially as Larry had omitted to mention to Lily that her parents always called him Laurence. Her calling him Larry met with instant disapproval. They were devout Christians and members of the Lord's Day Observance Society. Lily thought she might catch them at their best on the Sabbath.

The house was an old stone property set well back from the road, with large, beautiful gardens that Lily knew were tended by a gardener. Godfrey wasn't a man for any kind of manual labour. He didn't even chop his own meat.

'Comfy-looking gaff,' observed Dee, dismounting from the bike and taking off her helmet and goggles. She turned to Lily. 'Are you sure they'll be in?'

'Yes. On a Sunday they go to church in the morning and then stay in – observing the Lord's Day.'

'How are we going to play this? I mean, Christopher is your son. As far as I know they have no legal right to keep him. You could just thank them kindly for looking after him and tell them you'll be taking him to live with you, where he belongs.'

Lily was shaking with nerves. 'I know – but what if they kick up a fuss?'

'Then we'll threaten them with the law.'

'Larry's dad's a magistrate. He'll know the law better than we do.'

'That doesn't mean he can break it. Look, leave the talking to me. I can be really diplomatic when I try. Trust me.'

They approached the front door together and rang the bell. Mrs Robinson came to the door and stared first at Dee, then at Lily, whom she didn't appear to recognise at first. She was a starch-faced women in her late forties who had apparently come from a background as humble as Lily's.

'Oh, it's you,' she said, feigning delayed recognition.

'Yes, it's your daughter-in-law, Mrs Robinson,' said Dee, brightly, holding her crash helmet under her arm in the manner of a policeman with his helmet 'She's been through a lot recently, as you no doubt know, and she's come to collect Christopher, but not without thanking you and your husband for looking after him.'

'Collect Christopher? How do you mean?'

'Well, he is my son,' said Lily politely. 'He belongs with me.'

Mrs Robinson turned and shouted back into the house. 'Godfrey! I think you'd better come and listen to this.'

Godfrey Robinson appeared in the doorway. He was a large man with heavy jowls, a completely bald head and a face that had set itself into a permanent grimace many years ago. His stomach protruded well over the waistband of his trousers that were held up by both belt and braces.

'Go on. Tell him what you just told me,' his wife said to Lily.

Dee spoke first, not intimidated by this man. Her voice now took on a steely edge. 'Your daughter-in-law's come to collect her son. Where is he?'

'Daughter-in-law? We no longer have a son. How can we have a daughter-in-law?'

'I don't care about that,' said Lily. 'I've come to collect my son.'

Robinson's face went puce. He took out a handkerchief to wipe off the beads of sweat that were forming on his brow as he glared at Lily. 'Who the hell do you think you are? I think you'd better go away and find the other son you've lost before you come back here claiming our grandson. Cheeky young madam!'

'You've no legal right to keep him,' said Dee firmly. 'She's his mother.'

Robinson let out a loud, unpleasant laugh. 'Mother? Mother you call her? She's lost one son – strongly suspected of killing him, she's been sent to a lunatic asylum for attacking innocent women and you want us to hand our grandchild over to her. What sort of grandparents do you think we are who'd place him in such danger?'

'We could always call the police,' said Dee. 'I know you're a magistrate but you can't just make up your own laws.'

'Call Winston Churchill if you like! We happen to be the legal guardians of the child – or didn't you know that? If this lunatic wants him back she'll have to fight us through the courts.'

Lily was now in tears. 'Can't I just see him?'

'No, you can't damn well see him! Now get off my doorstep before *I* call the police.'

He slammed the door in their faces. Dee kicked at it, then tried the handle but it had locked itself. She opened the letter box and shouted through it.

'We'll have you locked up for this you bloody child-snatchers!'

Lily was already walking away, desolate. Barring a miracle, she had no chance of getting Christopher back off these mean and powerful people, not with her reputation. If only she hadn't let Michael go with Oldroyd.

That man was the key to all this. They must find him. He must be somewhere.

She was living with three gaping holes in her heart, one left by Larry, one by Michael and one by Christopher. The one left by Larry would heal with time, but time would never heal the holes left by her boys.

Chapter 20

'I'm beginning to think they did the right thing sending me to a psychiatric hospital.'

They were in a café in Bradford. It was the day after the confrontation with the Robinsons. Dee had taken Lily to see a solicitor to find out how she could get Christopher back and how quickly. The news wasn't good. Despite being discharged from the hospital Lily had a criminal record and the authorities had a responsibility to make sure Christopher didn't come to any harm at her hands. Right now he was in the legal care of two respectable citizens who happened to be the boy's grandparents and who also happened to be wealthy enough to put up a good fight in court. Morosely, Lily sipped at her tea. Since Larry's death her demeanour had ranged from sadness to heart-rending depression.

'Honestly, Auntie Dee, I just feel empty. Useless. I brought all this on myself by letting Michael go off with people I hardly knew.'

'Lily, you were eight months' pregnant, you'd just lost your husband and these people had been kind to you. I think they've stolen Michael for themselves. People do this, you know.'

'Auntie Dee, you never mentioned this before. I thought . . . well, I don't know what I thought. The worst usually. For themselves? But they're old.'

'Old? I thought you said they were in their forties.'

'Well, that's what I told the police. I don't know how old they are. A lot older than me, I know that much.'

'Well I didn't want to mention it to you but it's odds-on that's what's happened. Childless people sometimes get into their forties and get really broody for children before it's too late. Then, when they find they can't have any, they take someone else's.'

'Really? Do you think that's what happened? So, you think Michael's being well cared for?'

'I'm sure of it, love. I think both of your boys are being well cared for but it mustn't stop you getting them back.'

Lily let out a deep sigh. 'The answer to all this is me getting Michael back. If I do they'll have no good reason to keep Christopher. The problem is, where do I start?'

Dee corrected her. 'The problem is,' she said, 'where do *we* start?' She passed a cigarette over to Lily, who'd started smoking again. 'And I think you should get a job where you have a very sympathetic employer who'll give you as much time off as you need to search for your son and who will even help you find him.'

'What about applying to the courts to get Christopher back?'

Dee gave this some thought. 'Godfrey and the Gorgon have got money, respectability, and they've given Christopher a good home, away from his mother who was locked up for being mentally unbalanced. This is

138

how the courts will see it, Lily. I think you should bide your time.'

'I miss him, Auntie Dee. He's my baby and he's growing up without a mother. Maybe if I applied for some sort of access?'

'Possibly, but with their money they could make it a very slow and expensive business, getting their lawyer to ask for adjournments and the like.'

'I need to give it a try,' said Lily. She lit her cigarette and allowed a plume of smoke to leak from the side of her mouth. 'You want me to come and work for you on your market stalls?'

'Correct. It's not easy running a stall on your own. You need eyes in the back of your head to stop people thieving, especially the stuff I sell.'

'Auntie Dee, you sell fake jewellery.'

'Hey! *Imitation* jewellery – and not all of it's imitation. With me you pays your money you takes your chance. My customers know this. Some of it's the good stuff: mebbe one piece in fifty. It's up to them to work out which is which. I just act dumb and say I buy the stuff in job lots, so I don't know for sure. The trick is to buy in the real stuff that looks rubbish and imitation stuff that looks great. When someone buys a piece of the good stuff I have a quiet word in their ear. I says to them, "I don't do this for everyone, love, but you take it to a jeweller's to get it valued and if it's worth less than you paid I'll give you the difference." '

'Why do you do that?'

'Why? Take brooches for example. Generally speakin' old brooches allus look crap. I had a genuine diamond and ruby brooch on my stall for three months marked up at four pound seven an' six. It looked so manky no one'll touch it. Then a couple o' weeks ago this feller came up wanting a present for his missis. He asked me if it was real. I said I'd got no idea but if it is I'm doing meself out of thirty odd quid. Anyway he haggled me down to three pounds ten and bought it. I had a word in his ear about having it valued.'

For the first time in weeks Lily was vaguely interested in something other than her personal problems.

'And did he?' she asked.

Dee grinned. 'Oh yes. I knew he would. He were a gloater, y'see. I can spot a gloater a mile off. He came back the next market day to tell me it were worth forty quid.

I said, "Oh, bugger me, mister! I wish I'd known that." He's standing there, waving this valuation certificate under me nose, and there's poor old me looking embarrassed with a crowd gathering round me – plus I made sure I had a load o' brooches on me stall that day. Sold the lot for a fiver each. I didn't pay more than ten bob for any of 'em.'

Lily smiled for the first time in weeks.

'I've been doin' it fer years,' Dee told her. 'Word gets round that there's a barmy old bird selling real jewellery at knock-down prices. I call 'em loss leaders. People turn up specially to come to my stall. Mostly they're paying well over the odds for old tat but the trick is to send the odd one away with a bargain.'

'Is it illegal, what you do?'

'No, not a bit of it. Look, they buy what they see. I never tell anyone it's the real stuff. For every twenty quid loss I make on a real gem I reckon I make four times that on the crap stuff – which is high-class crap, I might add. There's women going round wearin' fake diamonds an' pearls, what they're not gonna risk havin' properly valued, who thinks they're the Queen of bleedin' Sheba. I never tell 'em no different. What they don't know don't hurt no one.'

'Do you ever get real jewellers coming round? People who can tell the good from the fake?'

'Not so much nowadays. I could smell a real jeweller a mile off – specially when they bring their eye glasses out. I tells 'em to piss off. "This isn't a bleedin' trade stall!" I tells 'em. "This is for ordinary folk who like to pick up a bargain now and again." They seem to have got the message.'

Lily finished the tea and put the cup back in the saucer with a decisive flourish. 'How much do I get paid?'

Dee grinned broadly. 'That's the ticket, girl. Welcome back to the world. You start Thursday. I'll get your pockets jingling and together we'll get your boys back.'

Chapter 21

Charlie Cleghorn looked at the gleaming machine on display in the window of Morgan's Bikes.

> BSA M24 Gold Star 500 1938. Good as new. Low mileage. Unused since 1939. POW owner killed in Burma.

It was his dream bike and for sale at £38 15s 0d – less than half the original 1938 price of £82 10s. He had £39 16s 9d left from his demob money, most of which had gone to repay certain gambling debts he'd incurred during the war. When a man spends the war gambling with his life he doesn't worry too much about gambling for money. If he bought the bike he wouldn't have anything left to buy Beryl the engagement ring she was expecting. She would also expect him to be saving for their marriage and he wasn't sure if he was ready for that. What he needed was time to think things over, but what if the bike got sold while he was doing his thinking? He went inside the shop and took a closer look. A salesman appeared by his side. He was middle-aged and wore a regimental badge from the First World War.

'Climb aboard, soldier,' he said. 'Get a feel for her.'

Charlie was wearing his army khakis. He felt the uniform might give him a bit of an edge when negotiating the price. He threw a leg over the bike and sat on it. Leaning forward and gripping the handlebars, he knew he must have it.

'Would you go down to thirty quid?'

The salesman shook his head. 'We'll get the asking price, no problem.'

'Really? I'm told it's been for sale for a month.'

'I'll have a word with the boss, see if he'll go down to thirty-five.'

'It'll have to be thirty. I haven't got thirty-five, but I can pay cash.'

'We're in business to make a profit.'

'You'll still make a profit, just a smaller one.'

The salesman smiled. 'What mob are you in?'

Charlie hesitated. He wasn't in any mob. Not any more. But he desperately wanted this bike.

'Special Forces.'

'What, commandos?'

'No.'

'I see.'

Charlie's reluctance to tell the man his regiment meant that he was in one of the elite groups: SAS, SBS or Long Range Desert Group. His uniform gave nothing away, no regimental insignia. The only things on display were two strips of medal ribbons. The salesman recognised one of them as the Military Medal, as Charlie was hoping he might. It was a properly won medal, but perhaps using it to negotiate a decent price for a motorbike might be frowned upon by the military.

'I could stretch it to thirty-two pound ten,' said Charlie.

'Tell you what. Leave me a fiver deposit and if we haven't sold it in a month I'll get in touch. If it's sold, or you don't want it, you get your money back.'

Charlie gave this a few moments thought them stuck out a hand. 'Deal,' he said.

The man nodded at his medal ribbons.

'Where'd you get the MM?'

'Italy,' said Charlie.

'I've seen this wedding dress in Marshall and Snelgrove's,' said Beryl. 'It's absolutely beautiful.'

'Marshall and Snelgrove's? Aren't they a bit snooty?' said Charlie, still thinking about the Gold Star.

'Charlie, you have to pay for quality. I don't want to be seen walking down the aisle in any old tat.'

They were in the Town Hall Tavern in Leeds. Charlie was drinking a pint of Tetley's bitter. Beryl was sipping a port and lemon, which she considered to be a sophisticated drink.

'You don't want me walking down the aisle in any old tat, do you, Charlie?'

'What? Oh, no.'

'You can hire your morning suit from Moss Bros. They do lovely morning suits. I can't wait to see all the men in top hat and tails.'

Charlie was now picturing his demolition contractor dad in top hat and tails. It was a difficult image to conjure up.

'Top hat and tails? I thought I might just buy a nice

suit from John Collier or somewhere. At least I'd get to keep it.'

He thought she was jumping the gun a bit, considering they weren't even engaged yet. She seemed to have taken a lot for granted since he got back from the war.

'Oh, and we need to get formally engaged, and put it in the *Yorkshire Evening Post* – not the *News*. Only common people use the *Evening News* for formal announcements.'

'Right.'

'I thought a spring wedding next year. I've always wanted to be a spring bride. April would be nice.'

'April?' said Charlie. 'Doesn't it rain a lot in April?'

'Well, May then, if that's what you want. I don't want you to feel as though I'm making all the decisions. If you want a May wedding that's what we'll have.'

Charlie, who hadn't realised he wanted a May wedding, looked at her over the top of his pint glass. Beryl Townsend was a looker and she knew it. He'd admired her from afar before his call-up and they'd got together on one of his leaves. She'd been more than generous with her affections. That had helped cement their relationship. If only she wasn't so pushy.

'Has your demob money come through yet?'

'No, it's still a bit tied up,' lied Charlie.

'Marlene's brother got his money the day he was demobbed.'

'I know, most blokes do, but with me being in Italy there's a lot of red tape and stuff.'

It was a lie he'd told before and he hoped she wouldn't ask for details.

'Anyway,' she said cheerfully. 'If you haven't got it

yet you can't be tempted to spend it. I always look on the bright side of things. Haven't you noticed that about me?'

'Er, yes, I have.'

'When you've finished that beer why don't you get us a glass of wine each. You should know all about wine with the time you spent in Italy.'

She was right there. Charlie had spent many a night carousing with the Legione SS Italiana – the Italian SS. A brigade of ultra-fascists which he'd infiltrated, using the identity of a dead Italian soldier. He played a convincing drunk, having perfected a trick of swapping his full glass with someone else's almost empty one. Getting drunk was never an option in his work. And all the time he was drinking the enemy's wine he'd been dreaming of Yorkshire beer.

'Beryl. I've had enough Eyetie wine to last me a lifetime.'

'You must wear your medals on your morning suit. Oh, I'm going to be so proud of you. Will you be proud of me, Charlie?'

'Prettiest girl in Yorkshire, why wouldn't I be proud of you?'

'Stop it, Charlie. You're making me blush.' She smiled, coquettishly, then added, 'Tell me what you see when you look at me.'

Charlie looked at her and all he could see was his Gold Star disappearing into the distance at ninety miles an hour.

Chapter 22

Dee worked three days a week – Skipton market on Tuesday and Wednesday, and Leeds market on a Thursday. On the other two weekdays she visited a Dutch wholesaler of imitation jewellery and toured auctions and antique shops, where she bought the good stuff which she would mark down by as much as eighty-five per cent from the cost price. She loaded her wares into the sidecar of her 1936 BSA Blue Star. It was Thursday and Lily had ridden pillion to Leeds where they had their stall set up and open by nine a.m.

Kirkgate Market in Leeds was a covered market that had been selling an endless variety of goods since its opening in 1904. Adjacent to it was a lively open market that had been selling goods for much longer. In this market, in 1884, Michael Marks opened his first Penny Bazaar which led to the founding of Marks and Spencer in 1890. Here Dee worked her Thursday stall, opposite one selling crockery. She'd chosen her stall because the crockery salesman, Danny Muldoon, had been selling crockery for over twenty years and had offered as much entertainment as the Leeds City Varieties theatre just ten minutes' walk away. Danny was a comedian, a salesman, a juggler and a shrewd businessman. During his spiel Danny's assistant would throw him a complete, twenty-four piece dinner service, piece by piece, until Danny held them between his outstretched arms as his assistant placed a soup tureen on his head like a German helmet. His hilarious routine drew the biggest crowd in the market which suited Dee down to the ground as the crowd would disperse past her stall which had a reputation as good as Danny's, but for different reasons.

Lily helped with the layout. There were rings, bracelets, necklaces, jewelled hairslides, hair bands, cocktail rings, earrings and even a couple of tiaras. When the set-up was complete Lily cast her eye over the whole display, nodding her head in approval.

'OK,' she murmured, 'I give in. Which is the good stuff?'

'You can't tell? That's good. That's how it should be.'

'Well, I've never had much experience of the good stuff – only this,' Lily said, looking down at her engagement ring. It was a half-carat diamond solitaire and had cost Larry a month's wages.

Dee took her hand and assessed the ring. 'Well, it's definitely the real thing. He probably paid thirty-five quid for it – more 'n' a month's wages for most.'

'Thirty-two,' said Lily. 'I went to choose it with him.'

Dee looked around to make sure she wasn't being overheard. 'Those earrings in the second row down are real pearls. I paid twenty-five quid for them. A valuer would put them at thirty-five, minimum.'

Lily looked at the earrings, which didn't look in any

way superior to half a dozen other pairs of earrings on display. They were marked at three pounds fifteen shillings.

'And that diamond solitaire – it's a genuine, point eight carat diamond set in nine carat gold. It set me back thirty-five quid.'

The ring was for sale at four pounds seven and six but it was the least impressive of the rings on display.

'Anything else?' Lily asked. There were over a hundred items on the stall.

'No,' said Dee. 'Two's enough. If we sell one of these today and word gets out that it's the genuine article it's enough to keep my reputation as a crazy old bird intact.'

It was late in the afternoon. Danny Muldoon had just finished one of his half-hourly routines and those among the crowd who weren't waiting to buy his amazing bargains were dispersing past Dee's stall, many of them still laughing at his cheeky jokes. A young man stopped to examine a tray of Dee's rings with obvious purpose but little expertise.

'Can I help you?' Lily asked.

'Er, yeah – I'm looking for a ring that looks real enough to fool my girlfriend long enough until I can buy her a real one.'

'I see.'

He grinned at her. 'I spent all me demob money on a motorbike and she's expecting me to propose to her tonight. She's a real beauty. Goes like the clappers.'

'Does she really? What's she called?'

'BSA Gold Star, 1938.'

Lily found herself smiling. 'What? Oh, right. And

what does your girlfriend think about you buying a motorbike?'

'She doesn't actually know yet. I haven't found the right moment to tell her.'

'So you've been in the forces?'

'Yeah, army – got an early demob due to the job I was doing. So, what do you think? I've got a fiver between me and the workhouse and I want to take Beryl out tonight for a slap-up meal with the full works, so it'll have to be no more than four quid.'

He had china-blue eyes that looked older than the rest of him and Lily wondered just what horrors those eyes had witnessed. Had they seen the same sort of things as her bank clerk husband?

'What were you before the army?'

'Me? I was a demolition man. Still am when I go back to it – work for my dad's firm, actually.'

Without hesitation and without sparing a glance at Dee, Lily pointed to the real diamond solitaire.

'Yeah,' he said. 'I think that might fool Beryl for quite a while.' Then he frowned. 'Four pounds seven and six. Doesn't leave me much to take her out. You need ten bob nowadays for a decent night out.'

Lily slid it on her ring finger beside her own engagement ring. 'My ring's a real diamond,' she said. 'Can you tell the difference?'

'Blimey! None at all, except this one's a bigger diamond.'

Dee moved in. Lily was expecting her to put the young man off this ring and recommend something else.

'Are you local?' Dee asked.

'When I'm back in Blighty I'm local. Up to getting demobbed I haven't been around Leeds for nigh on two years – and then only on leave.'

'He was in the army,' Lily explained.

The young man grinned at Dee. 'I remember you. You've been working this market since I was at school.'

'Thirteen years,' said Dee. 'Tell you what, seeing as how you're a soldier of the King I'll let you have it for four quid.'

'*Used* to be a soldier of the King. Four quid eh?' The young man took the ring off Lily and examined it. 'Blimey! It looks real enough to me.'

'I buy job lots,' Dee explained. 'For all I know, it might well be the real thing but my eyes aren't what they used to be. But if that's imitation it's top quality and worth four quid of anyone's money. Get it valued. You never know.'

'Right. I might just do that. Hey! If it's a real diamond I'm not giving it back.'

'I don't expect you to.'

Lily and Dee watched him walk away, happy with his purchase. 'Are you mad at me?' Lily asked, still with her eyes on the soldier.

'Not this time – just don't do it again, that's all. If he gets it valued, which I suspect he will, he'll tell all his mates in the pub. Word'll get round.'

'If word gets round to his girlfriend he'll be in trouble.'

Dee shook her head. 'If he's got any sense he'll tell her he knew it was a real diamond when he bought it. It'll keep my reputation intact.'

By the time they packed up at four-thirty they'd sold twenty-eight pieces of jewellery. Total cost to Dee, including the diamond solitaire, seventy-three pounds. Total takings, ninety-eight pounds.

'If we'd sold the genuine pearl earrings I'd have still broken even on the day,' Dee said, licking the end of a pencil with which she was working out the day's profit. 'As it is we've made twenty-five, less the cost of the stall for a day . . . one pound ten . . . less a gallon of petrol and wear and tear on the bike . . . six bob. Net profit before tax, twenty-three pounds four shillings. Of which you get a fiver clear. Not bad money for a day's fun, is it?'

'It's more than I used to earn in a week. What do I do about tax?'

'We'll worry about that as and when we have to. At the moment the government owes you for one husband and one month's freedom.'

Lily nodded and took her fiver. The fact that she was earning somehow empowered her. Not only that but she was in a higher income bracket than the coppers who were looking down their noses at her. Her mind was clearer. Her chances of getting her boys back didn't seem quite so hopeless. She kissed Dee on the cheek.

'Blimey, girl. What was that for?'

'Oh, for all sorts of stuff, Auntie Dee. You've been like a mother to me.'

'I promised your mam I'd look after you – a promise I severely neglected, I'm afraid.'

'Well, you're certainly making up for it now.' Lily paused and asked, 'What was she like? I mean, I've heard you talk about her but never even seen a photo of her.'

Dee stared at her for several seconds, as if coming to a decision. Then she opened her handbag and brought out a man's wallet inside which were several photographs. Dee selected one and handed it to Lily.

'Sorry love. I didn't realise you'd never seen her photo. That's me being thoughtless. This is your mam – I took it on a day out to Scarborough.'

The photograph was of a vivacious young woman sitting on the railings in front of a deckchair-strewn beach with the sea in the background. Standing beside her, with an arm round her, was a young man in slacks, braces and a white shirt with the sleeves rolled up. They looked an obvious couple. Also in the photograph, down at ground level, was a cheeky young boy who was standing on the beach and poking his head under the railings and pulling a face at the camera. Lily stared at the woman, who looked younger than she was now. But she could see her own face there.

She looked up at Dee. 'Is this my mother?'

'That's her, Margaret Mary Windsor – everybody called her Peggy.'

'Auntie Dee, she was beautiful.' Lily clasped her hand to her mouth to choke back a sob, but it didn't stop the tears arriving. 'And this young man. He looks nice. Who's he? Is he someone you met in Scarborough?'

Dee took the photograph from her and studied it, shaking her head slowly. 'No, he came with us. We went as a foursome.'

'So, he was my mam's boyfriend? Do you remember his name?'

'I do. His name was Frank Nuttall. Lovely feller. Fancied him myself, but I had to settle for his brother, Ernest.' She smiled. 'Frank and Ernest. We always thought their parents must have had a sense of humour.'

'What happened to him, this Frank?'

'He died, love – Spanish flu. Went all through the first war without a scratch then died of flu.'

'How well did she know him?'

'They were very close, love – too close some might say. When I say *some*, I don't mean me.'

'Auntie Dee. What do you mean?'

Dee hesitated for a while then said, 'Frank was your father, love. He fully intended marrying your mother but . . .'

'But he died.'

Lily almost snatched the photo back and studied it with intense interest. 'So, this is my mam and my dad?'

'Yes, love.'

'He was very good-looking. Was he a nice man?'

'Lovely feller. Put it this way. If he hadn't set his cap at yer mother I'd have made a play for him.'

'Who's the boy in the background?'

'No idea – some cheeky young beggar who thought he'd get in on our photo.'

'Can I keep it, please?'

'Of course you can.'

'But it says father unknown on my birth certificate. Why didn't anyone tell me all this before?'

Dee hadn't told her this before because she'd only just made the story up. It was a much better memory to live with than Lily knowing that her mother had been a

154

prostitute and her father a client. The person in the photograph was a young man they'd met that day in Scarborough and had never seen since. Dee couldn't even remember his name. Frank Nuttall was the name of an old boyfriend, killed at the Battle of the Somme along with tens of thousands of others four years before Lily was born. She smiled at the look on Lily's face.

'There was only me knew, love – and I never really got a proper chance to tell you. Sorry.'

Lily sat on the empty stall for a full fifteen minutes as Dee loaded her wares into the sidecar hoping her lie sounded plausible. Lily's eyes remained glued to the photograph, placing it to her lips, occasionally, and kissing it; making Dee feel guilty. But the lie was told, the seed had been sown and she'd now have to run with it, making up additions as time went on. Suddenly Lily looked up at her.

'Auntie Dee, this has given me the first useful idea I've had for weeks.'

'What sort of idea?'

'Oh, one that might come to nothing, but I need to call in at Perseverance Street on the way home.'

'OK, but if there's any fighting to be done, I'll do it.'

Someone had written MERDERER on her front door in white paint, the letters growing smaller as space ran out. Lily stepped out of the sidecar and glanced at it, shocked.

'Take no notice,' said Dee. She looked over Lily's shoulder and murmured, 'Fat woman living opposite, who's that?'

'Hilda Muscroft. It'll be her who wrote it, probably.'

'You go in. I'll be with you in a minute.'

'Auntie Dee—'

Dee winked at her and waved her protest away. Hilda was at her door, arms folded having been alerted by the sound of the motorbike. Dee sauntered across to her with a smile on her face. 'Are you Mrs Hilda Muscroft?'

'What's it ter you?'

'Nothing . . . except I've been hearing horrible stuff about you, from your neighbours.' She pointed at Lily's door. 'You spelled it wrong, by the way – did you not go to school?' Then she stopped in her tracks, two yards away, and wafted her hand in front of her face. 'Woooaagh! It's true what they all say about you! Good God, woman! Have you never heard of soap and water? Has your husband never told you that you stink like a pig?'

Hilda was too taken aback to respond.

Dee backed away holding her nose. She turned to follow Lily into the house, happy that she'd delivered a grade-A insult.

Hilda stormed back into her house to report this outrage to her husband. Arnold, who had long since become inured to his wife's pungency, comforted her with the words, 'Nay, lass, yer smell a bit, but yer all right.'

Lily was already coming out of her house by the time Dee got to the door. She was carrying a small bundle of letters and an unimpressive-looking box camera.

'Does that actually work?' Dee asked, nodding at the camera.

'Of course it does. It might not look much, but it takes good snaps in the right hands.'

'How many does it take?'

'Eight, but we only took about four. I took two of Michael then Mr Oldroyd took a couple of us both.'

'And you think the Oldroyds might be on the ones you took of Michael?'

'I'm not sure but I do know their table was behind where Michael was sitting. I'll drop the film off at the chemist's in the morning. I should get them back in three or four days.'

'You will not. I know someone who'll have it developed tonight.'

'Is it right about your Mickey?'

The question was asked by Tony Lafferty who had approached down the pavement and was standing just a few feet away with hands on hips and his wishbone legs wide apart. Lily looked down at him and asked, 'Is what true?'

Tony frowned and shifted his feet nervously. 'Is it true that yer killed your Michael?'

Lily looked down at him. He'd asked as innocently as such a question could be asked.

'No it's not true. Michael's missing. We're looking for him.'

The frown left Tony's face. 'That's what me mam said. She said yer wouldn't do a thing like that. D'yer want me to help yer find him? I'm good at looking for stuff.'

Lily broke into a smile. 'That'd be a real help, Tony. How is your mam?'

She scarcely knew Mrs Lafferty but it seemed impolite not ask about the only neighbour she knew about who didn't think she'd murdered her son.

'She's a bit brassed off.'

'Oh dear. Why's that, I wonder?'

'It's me dad. He's not comin' home from t' war.'

Lily was shocked. 'Oh dear, Tony. I'm sorry. How's your mam. Is she OK?'

'No, she's as mad as 'ell. She says he's gone off wi' a French tart.' He squinted up at Lily. 'What's a French tart, Mrs Robinson? Do they taste nice?'

Lily looked at Dee, then back down at Tony, not knowing what to say.

'He's not sendin' us no money and we're skint. I'm supposed to have some new boots but we can't afford 'em. Grown outta me old boots.'

Lily, who knew all about boys growing out of boots, looked at his feet. Two big toes poked out of the cut-off ends of his plimsolls. He looked scruffier than usual and somewhat emaciated. She guessed he existed entirely on free school dinners. But he had a mother who believed in her. Strange world.

'Wait there, Tony.'

She went back into the house leaving Dee and the boy standing looking at each other. Tony wiped a sleeve across his perpetually runny nose. Dee tapped a foot on the pavement wondering what Lily was doing. Lily was back out within a couple of minutes with an envelope in her hand which she gave to Tony.

'This is a note for your mam, and here's a shilling for you if you deliver it to her without losing it.'

She pressed a coin into the boy's other hand. He looked at it in wonder. This was the most money he'd ever had.

'Straight to your mam. No messing about.'

'No, missis.'

'How much was in the envelope?' asked Dee as they both watched the boy gallop off, slapping his backside and whooping with delight at his new-found riches.

'A tenner,' said Lily. 'It's all I have at the moment. I need to borrow a couple of quid from you, of course.'

'I'll go halves,' said Dee, after some deliberation. 'Should pay for a new pair of boots and keep 'em both well fed for a few weeks. Poor little sod.'

'At least he's got his mam at home,' said Lily, her eyes still on the galloping boy. 'And she loves him enough to cut the toe out of his pumps so his feet don't hurt. And I'll bet he has a new pair of boots tomorrow. He's better off than some.'

Four hours later Lily was sitting at Dee's kitchen table, looking at a photograph of Michael grinning at the camera. Just behind his left shoulder was a large man talking to a woman who was sitting half out of shot to Michael's right; both of them were oblivious to the fact that they were being photographed.

'That's Oldroyd,' Lily had confirmed. She found herself suddenly in tears, caused by the black and white evidence that she hadn't been imagining all this. In the second shot of Michael, the Oldroyds had moved their heads so that they were both looking away from the camera.

'They must have seen you taking that one,' Dee guessed, 'but I'm guessing they don't know about the first one. Lily, girl, we have a photo of Michael's abductor.'

The following day Dee went back to her photographer friend who isolated Oldroyd's head and printed off half a dozen seven- by five-inch copies plus another half-dozen of the original photograph.

DS Bannister showed the photographs to Inspector Foster, explaining who they were purported to show.

'And she wants us to print this in the papers, does she?'

'She does, sir.'

'And if we do – even saying it's a man we only want to question *in connection* with the Michael Robinson abduction and he turns out to be a completely innocent man who's had the bad luck to be in the background of a photograph, just how much damage do you think it'll do to him, Sergeant?'

'I don't imagine it'll do him much good, sir – people always believe there's no smoke without fire.'

'He could sue the force, Sergeant. It's happened before. Us barking up the wrong tree and causing an innocent man damage. Could cost us hundreds, maybe even thousands, depending who he is.'

'Sir, with respect, this is all about what happened last year, isn't it?'

'Of course it bloody is, John! I'm responsible for the death of a three-year-old boy. Do you blame me for treading carefully?'

'But can we allow what happened last year to influence how we handle this case? Last year we had protesters defending a mad woman. Mrs Robinson's neighbours are dead against her and she doesn't appear to be the least bit mad to me. According to WPC Morley what happened in court was a travesty of justice.'

Foster sighed, heavily, and shook his head. 'Look, John, this is my decision, not yours. The answer is no, we don't print the photos. Libelling a man on the word of a woman who's recently been sentenced to serve time in a psychiatric hospital. I doubt if I'd survive something like that.'

'Sir.'

'I was quite surprised to hear she'd been released so soon.'

'Discharged, sir – declared sane.'

'Hmm . . . I've never been declared sane, have you, Sergeant?'

'No, sir.'

'To be declared sane you have to have been insane at some stage.'

'You know that aunt of hers, Delilah Maguire, gave us the names of several women who she said had been sexually assaulted by a Dr Freeman who ran the hospital Robinson was sent to. I sent the information through to Keighley.'

'So I understand. Have we heard from them?'

'This morning, sir. They're investigating and it seems there's some truth in what the Maguire woman says. They picked Freeman up for questioning.'

'And do you think there's a link between this and

Freeman giving the Robinson woman a clean bill of health? Maybe a bit of blackmail – only Maguire and Robinson didn't keep their side of the bargain.'

'Could be, sir, although I doubt there's much anyone can do. Evidently, when Mrs Robinson was captured in the Town Hall she accused her father-in-law of using his influence as a magistrate to have her put away in a loony bin. According to WPC Morley it could explain why she was sentenced so severely. The in-laws have now got custody of her baby.'

'Have they now? Well, I think the magistrates might want to let sleeping dogs lie on that one.'

'It seems there's more to this Mrs Robinson woman than meets the eye, sir.'

'I'm not all sure about her – never have been.'

'I understand that, sir. So how do we play it – bearing in mind that she could be telling the truth?'

The inspector sat back in his chair and ran his fingers through his hair. 'Bloody hell, I could do without this. Right now we've got a manpower problem that's not going to be resolved any time soon. I personally think this woman's trying to distract us from the truth.'

'The truth, sir?'

'Another version of the truth, John. The truth that she knows perfectly well where her son is. To have got herself out of that nuthouse in double-quick time by whatever means, she has to be a devious woman who could waste us a lot of time – time we don't have.'

'So, what do we do, sir? We can't ignore a missing child.'

'No, but we *can* ignore its devious mother. We'll

continue to conduct our enquiries along our own lines. In the meantime I think we send these photos to the Grassington plod.'

'I don't think he's the enquiring type, sir.'

'Luckily that's not our problem, Sergeant.'

Chapter 23

They were walking down the street towards Dee's motor-bike. Lily didn't know whether to be angry or distressed. Angry was better, she knew that, but she also knew that the police thought she was a murderer. They hadn't spoken since Bannister had come to the front desk to tell them of Foster's decision not to publish the photographs.

'I think I'll buy a van,' Dee mused. 'This motorbike and sidecar's OK for a single girl but it's highly unsociable when you've got company. You and me can talk in a van – discuss tactics and stuff.'

'They think I murdered my boy,' said Lily. 'They think I'm a murderer. There's no point even bothering with the police if that's what they believe.'

'I think you've got that right, girl. You and me can handle this on our own.'

'We'll have to handle it on our own,' Lily said, 'the police aren't going to be any help to us now. Trouble is, what do we do next?'

'We go to Grassington,' said Dee. 'We find the café where you took the photographs and we ask around – see if anyone recognises Oldroyd and his wife, or whoever he really is.'

An hour and a half later they were in the Dales Café in Grassington showing the photographs to the proprietor, who was shaking his head.

'Passing trade most probably,' he said. 'Like ninety per cent of our trade. Very few locals coming here to buy a cup of tea, they've all got their own kettles and teapots at home. I'll show it to the wife, see if she recognises either of them, but I doubt it.'

He took the photographs through a door behind the counter and came back a minute later still shaking his head. 'No, sorry, like I said, they must have been passing trade. Were they anybody special? Long-lost relatives or summat?'

'Not relatives as such,' said Dee. 'But they're people near and dear to us who we'd like to get in touch with.'

'There might be a reward, say two pounds or something,' said Lily. 'If someone knew where they are.' She looked at a board in the window displaying many local advertisements. 'Would it be OK if we stuck the photos in the window for a few weeks?'

'For a tanner a week you can have them both in for as long as you want.'

Dee took out her purse and handed a two-shilling coin over to the man. 'There you go, we'll have it in for a month. Do you have a piece of paper we can stick them on and write a little reward notice with a telephone number?'

Five minutes later they were both standing outside the café looking at the notice they'd just placed in the window. It read: *Do you know the identity and whereabouts of either of the people in these photographs? If so please ring Bradford 36214. £2 reward.*

Lily nodded at it approvingly, then wondered, 'Do you think we should have gone over the top and made it five pounds?'

Dee shook her head. 'No, if we offer too much money we might get too many chancers ringing us up. As it is, I think we might get quite a few time-wasters.' She clapped her hands together decisively. 'Right, seeing as we're in the district I think I'd like to take a look at this mystery house. Is it far?'

'It is if you're walking, with a full-term baby in your belly,' said Lily. 'But it's about five minutes by motorbike.'

Five minutes later they were walking up the pathway that led from the road to Lark House. Lily stood back as Dee looked through all the windows and walked all around the house. When she'd finished her inspection Dee returned to Lily who was sitting on a garden seat on the overgrown front lawn.

'Seen enough?' asked Lily.

'Yeah, I just wanted to get the full picture. To see what you saw that day. To try and get an idea of how you must have felt. I imagine coming back here must bring back bad memories.'

'Good and bad, actually,' said Lily. 'Good when I came here with Michael, and bad, really bad, when I came here the last time. I expected Michael to be here, probably in the back garden, or leaning over the fence feeding the horses, or maybe playing in the stream. What I found was what you see now: an old, empty house, with no one in it. No people, no furniture, no Michael . . . nothing.'

'And you nearly nine months' pregnant,' said Dee. 'Doesn't bear thinking about.'

'The trouble is I *do* think about it. I have to think about everything, and to try and make some sense of it. Somewhere there's a clue as to where Michael is.'

Dee turned to look back at the house, 'Oh, if only you could talk, big old house. If only you could give us that clue.'

'Maybe we could get some flyers printed,' Lily suggested. 'Stick them all around the Dales.'

Dee suddenly turned back to Lily and slapped the palm of her hand against the side of her head in exasperation.

'You idiot, Maguire! Why didn't you think of this before?'

'Think of what?' Lily asked.

'The *Craven Herald*.'

'What about it?'

'It's the Dales newspaper, in Skipton. I know a reporter there who might help us, in exchange for a good story.'

'Do you think they'll run the photographs?'

'I imagine so. It covers a decent area – a lot wider than a café in Grassington.'

Lily got up and took a last look at the house she hoped she'd never see again; the house which had been the cause of all this misery. She followed Dee to the motorbike.

The *Craven Herald and Pioneer* was one of very first newspapers to publish photographs; the first example was a society wedding in 1905. Forty years later Lily and Dee were hoping they'd publish a photograph of Michael's abductors. Dee's reporter friend had already been working on the *West Yorkshire Pioneer* for fifteen years when it was taken over by the *Craven Herald* in 1934. Henry Smithson was a fifty-year-old graduate of what he called the school of hard knocks. He was married to a woman whom he called Frosty Freda and he supplemented his inadequate conjugal rights with a weekly liaison with Madge from the typing pool. There had been a time when he'd set his cap at Dee but Dee told him straight, she was many things but not a marriage breaker. They were, however, good friends, with Dee having a more understanding ear than Madge. Between them, according to Henry, she and Madge made a far better wife than Frosty Freda. He studied the photographs at his desk in the corner of the newsroom which wasn't quite as busy as Lily imagined a newsroom would be.

She told him her story in full including her time at the psychiatric hospital. It shocked him. He lit his pipe which, Lily found, had a pleasant aroma. The pipe matched the man, as did his sports jacket complete with leather elbow patches. He wore a red and white spotted bow tie, three pens clipped into his breast pocket and a regimental badge pinned to his left lapel.

'I can see why the police were reluctant to have these photographs published in connection with your son's abduction. It'd be difficult to write an article along with these photographs and that article not be libellous.'

'Henry, are you not going to take my word that this man abducted Lily's son?'

Henry looked at Lily through narrowed eyes as if assessing her character. She returned his gaze with a similar one of her own, which made him smile. He leaned back in his chair with the pipe jammed into the corner of his mouth, linked his hands behind his head and closed his eyes.

'He's thinking,' said Dee. 'He does a lot of that.'

After a long minute Henry opened his eyes again, withdrew the pipe from his mouth, said, 'Blast!' and proceeded to light it once again.

'Let me get this straight,' he said. 'All you want to do is to locate these people? You're not planning on making a citizen's arrest or anything daft like that?'

'For now, that's all I want,' said Lily. 'I just want to know where they are and preferably who they are.'

'We can take it from there,' said Dee.

'And God help them,' said Henry. 'What I can do is print these photographs as though they're missing people, with concerned relatives trying to locate them. We mention nothing about the boy's abduction, nothing that can be construed as being in any way libellous.'

With his pipe relit he resumed his recumbent position, smoke billowing while he puffed vigorously. He looked from one woman to the other.

'So, how does that sound?'

'It sounds good,' said Lily.

'And I get the exclusive rights to the story?'

'You do,' said Dee, 'providing you give us any help you can along the way.'

'Sounds like we've got a deal,' said Henry, happy

now that his pipe was behaving itself. He leaned forward and thrust a hand towards Lily. She took it happily, knowing that this man was also on their side. Now there were three of them. Henry shook hands with Dee and got to his feet. 'Right, ladies. It'll be in next Thursday's edition, hopefully on page two.'

'No chance of the front page then?' said Lily.

'No chance at all,' said Henry. 'The front page is reserved for advertisements, better known at this newspaper as our bread and butter.'

Chapter 24

'You knew it was a real diamond didn't you?'

It was Thursday – Leeds market day. Lily looked up from the stall at the soldier from last week. The previous day she'd been to see a solicitor about the prospects of either regaining custody of Christopher or at least having some sort of access. It appeared that Auntie Dee was right about the problems her ex-in-laws could create.

'A real diamond? Really?'

'Really. I had it valued. It's worth fifty pounds. But you already knew that, didn't you? What I don't understand is why you sold it to me for four quid.'

Lily looked at him, genuinely puzzled. 'What I don't understand is why you'd grumble – and why on earth would we do a thing like that? We're in business to make money.'

He was quite tall, probably over six feet. His hair was dark brown and quite luxuriant. He'd either been out of the army for some time or they'd relaxed their rules about short haircuts. His build was athletic, probably due to army training. His nose was perhaps larger than average, his ears stuck out a little but, all in all, it was a pleasant face, bordering on handsome but not quite there. His best feature, his blue eyes, were right now boring into her accusingly. Dee was standing nearby, taking it all in. She left the stall, ostensibly to talk to Danny Muldoon. In reality she'd decided to leave this one to Lily.

'So, did the Beryl like the ring?' Lily said to him. 'I assume congratulations are in order.'

'She didn't get to see it. I found out, just in time, that she'd been seeing other blokes while I was away. I tackled her about it and she seemed to think she had every right to play the field as she thought I'd been killed.'

'Why would she think that?'

'Because I'd been reported as missing in action. I'd actually got a transfer to a special forces unit.'

'Special forces, you?'

Under any other circumstances this might have sounded like a made-up fantasy concocted by a young man out to impress. But this young man wasn't out to impress anybody, least of all Lily. She stared at him for a while.

'Good heavens! You're telling me the truth, aren't you?'

He frowned, slightly taken aback. 'Why would I lie about something like that?'

'I don't know. Sorry. But I can maybe understand why Beryl thought you were dead.'

'There's a big difference between being missing and being dead. It's the difference between loving someone and not loving them. That's the way I see it. Anyway, she'd apparently been putting it about before my Missing in Action came through. On top of which I realised that

I didn't love her, and I couldn't spend the rest of my life with her. I'd known her since before I got my call-up. I didn't know any better back then. I was just a boy.'

'And now you're a man.'

'Well, I have grown up a bit in the last two years or so, enough to know when people aren't being straight with me. Not quite so green, you might say.'

'Are you accusing me of not being straight with you?'

'Yes.'

'So, you're accusing me of charging you four pounds for a fifty-pound ring. Have I got that right?'

'I've been around long enough to know when people are lying to me. It's a knack I acquired in the forces. It's saved my life more than once.'

'Well, I don't think this knack has saved your life this time. If you want to give me the ring back, I'll gladly refund your money.'

'Oh no, I'm not falling for that. There's something fishy going on here and I want to know what it is.'

Lily was becoming irritated with the young man who didn't know when he was well off. 'Look,' she said. 'If you think we're dishonest, report us to the police. If not, clear off and stop wasting my time before I report *you* to the police!'

He stared at her for long moment, as if undecided what to do for the best. Then he gave a slight shake of his head and walked away. Lily was still watching him when Dee reappeared by her side.

'What was all that about?'

'I'm not sure. It was all very confusing. He's split up with his girlfriend. One minute he's opening his heart to me, the next minute he's having a go at me for selling him a fifty-quid ring for four quid.'

'Fifty quid? Hmm, I paid thirty-five. Was he drunk?'

'Don't think so. He thinks he's rumbled something, only he doesn't know what. Could be he thinks we've got him involved in something dishonest. Beggars belief if you ask me.'

'Oh, take no notice. All sorts of people think they've rumbled us, but they still come back to try their luck. They think they've got nothing to lose and a lot to gain, and maybe they're right.'

Lily glanced in the direction the young man had gone, perhaps hoping he might still be in sight. But he was a damned nuisance and she had other things to think about.

'Do you think we'll get any phone calls tonight?'

It was the day the photograph went in the *Craven Herald*. 'Both photos are on page two. Large as life and twice as ugly,' Henry had confirmed. 'I'll stick you a copy in the post tonight.'

'Henry said that if anyone's going to ring at all they'll ring by tomorrow night,' Dee said. 'After twenty-four hours it's fish-and-chip paper.'

'Twenty-four hours?' said Lily. 'That means one of us should be waiting by the telephone.' She looked at her watch: three-fifteen. 'Maybe one of us should be there right now.'

'Damn! That's a good point,' Dee said. 'We'll close up now and get back.'

Chapter 25

It was three minutes after five when they got in the house. The phone rang at five past.

'Hello,' said a woman's voice. 'I'm ringing about them photos in t' paper. D'yer still not know who they are?'

'As a matter of fact you're the first to ring about it,' said Dee. 'Who am I speaking to?'

'Me name's Mrs Rachel Clegg, I live in Ilkley. I think I know who t' feller is, only when I knew him, which is a year ago, he didn't have a 'tash, but I'm sure it's t' same bloke.'

Dee stuck a thumb up as Lily looked on. 'Do you know his name and where he lives?'

'He told me it were Arthur Williams, but I'm pretty certain that's not his real name. What I do know about him is that he used ter work as a caretaker in a school in Bradford.'

'Do you know which school?'

'Yeah, it were Jubilee Street primary. Phyllis, she's a neighbour of mine, used to live in Bradford and went to that school. She saw him coming out of our house and she remembered him working there when she were a

175

girl, only she couldn't remember his name. Anyroad I've just shown her this photo from t' paper and told her the tale – she reckons it's definitely him.'

'When you say you're pretty certain that Arthur Williams is not his real name why would he give you a false one?'

'Because he's a bloody wrong 'un, that's why. I told Phyllis at the time and that's when she told me she knew him. It's my guess that he's done you out of some money and yer trying to track him down. Am I right or am I wrong?'

'You're spot on, Rachel. Only it's not money, it's something far more valuable. The police won't help us, so we're having to be as devious as him.'

'Yer'll have your work cut out there, love. He's a real tricky customer, is Arthur. He got thirty quid from me for a washing machine what I never got delivered. Like I said, it's about a year ago now. He just knocked on our door one day and asked me if I wanted ter buy a really cheap Bendix washer. He had one in t' back of his van. He showed me it and told me it were worth seventy quid and if I didn't believe him I could check up on t' shop prices. I asked him how much he wanted for it and he said that particular one were sold but if I wanted one he could let me have one for thirty quid cash in advance. He said he needed t' cash ter give to t' wholesaler. It all sounded dead right to me, he's a very convincing bloke.'

'So I understand,' said Dee. 'I gather you gave him the thirty quid and never saw him again.'

'Well, it were a couple of weeks later. I did check on t' shop price and they were selling the same model in

Brooke's in Keighley fer sixty-six pounds fifteen and six pence. I had ter borrow a twenty-five off t' tally man. At twelve and six a week over twelve months I worked out it'd cost me an extra tenner, which still made t' washer a bargain at thirty quid – that's if I'd got t' bloody thing, which I didn't. He were supposed ter come back t' day after I paid him but I never saw hide nor bloody hair of him. I've only just finished payin' off t' tally man. I had ter take on an extra job ter do it. I tell yer, missis. I've had a bloody bad year because o' that thievin' sod.'

'Did you tell the police?'

'I did, but they didn't seem all that interested. They just took a few notes and buggered off. Me husband'd go mad if he ever found out – which he won't. He's in t' army and I reckon he's had enough ter worry about over t' past year. He's still over in Belgium or somewhere, sortin' out displaced persons. God knows when his demob'll come through.'

'And you're sure it's the man in the photograph?'

'Well, I drew a tash on t' photo and it were him all right. If yer find him, I'd like ter know his whereabouts meself. I'll fettle that thievin' bugger.'

'So,' said Dee, summing it all up. 'What you know about him is that he worked as a caretaker at Jubilee Street School in Bradford – how long ago will that have been?'

'Oh . . .' said Rachel to herself. 'How old's Phyllis now? Coming up ter thirty I reckon. She were only ten years old when she left there, so it'll be goin' on twenty years since she knew him.'

'And do you know anything else about him? His build, the way he talks, any peculiar mannerisms? I just want to be absolutely certain it's him. Look, I'll put you on to my friend. I never actually met him. She's the one he stole from.'

Lily took the phone and heard Rachel describe Oldroyd: his height, his age, his build, his Yorkshire accent, the cigarettes he smoked, his plausibility. They were both talking about the same man, no question. Lily felt a faint thrill of hope run through her for the first time since Michael's abduction.

'D'yer want ter take me details so that if yer do track him down yer can let me know?' said Rachel.

'Of course,' Lily said. 'In fact we'll let you know before we let the police know. You've been a damn sight more help than them.'

'D'yer mind if I ask what he stole from yer?'

Lily paused for a long time before saying, 'My son.'

'Bloody hell!' said Rachel.

Lily thanked her, said her goodbye, then looked at Dee. 'It's definitely him. We need to go to this Jubilee Street primary school tomorrow.'

'That's my girl. You know, there's a bit of colour coming back to your cheeks and a bit of a spring to your step. Don't tell me the old Lily Robinson's on her way back.'

'I'll not be back 'til my boys are.'

Chapter 26

The following morning they rode the full half-mile length of Jubilee Street without seeing a school. It was now the middle of July and the weather was warm, even in Bradford. On one side of the road was a plot of waste ground covering an area of maybe two acres. If there had ever been a school on Jubilee Street it had to have been there. Dee pulled into the kerb beside a newsagent's shop and dismounted. Lily was still sitting on the pillion seat with a look of disappointment on her face.

'You wait there,' said Dee, taking off her crash helmet. 'And don't look so miserable. No one said it was going to be easy.'

Lily dismounted but didn't follow Dee into the shop. Her mood swings were frequent and erratic and her current mood was low. She leaned against the shop window smoking a Capstan and gazing vacantly upwards at the bus cables above. A trolley bus approached, pale blue with a white strip down the middle, advertising Swan Vestas and going to Clayton, its only sound a low hum and the rush of tyres on tarmac. It was full of people, most of whom would not have her troubles. She looked at them with envy. How many of you lot have lost a husband and two sons recently? In the other direction a horse-drawn bin wagon clopped over the cobbles; together it and the tram illustrated the old and the new. Horses had been vanishing from the roads all her life, to be replaced by buses and trams and cars. Too many things were vanishing from her life.

An ice-cream cart attached to the back of a bicycle headed her way. The pedalling vendor called out to her. 'Want an ice cream, love? Do yer more good than that fag.'

His cheerful words forced out a smile. Her mood took an upward lurch. She dropped her cigarette on the ground and stamped on it. He pulled to a halt and opened the back of his cart.

'I'll have a tuppenny cornet please.'

'Tuppenny cornet coming up. Want a strawberry squirt on it?'

'Please.'

He gave it a squirt of red juice and handed it over. Other customers were arriving to form a queue. 'See,' he said, 'yer've brought me luck. Pretty girls always do that.'

Lily smiled at his innocent compliment and retreated back to the shop window. Inside the shop Dee was also in a queue. When it was her turn she asked for a quarter-pound of Mint Imperials.

'Didn't there used to be a school on this road – Jubilee Street school?' she enquired conversationally, as the woman behind the counter weighed out her order on the scales.

'Bombed in 1941,' said the woman. 'That'll be sixpence, love.'

Dee handed over a sixpenny piece. 'I hope it happened at night when the kids weren't there.'

'It actually happened on a Saturday night. No one was hurt. I think they only dropped half a dozen bombs on Bradford all through t' war and that were one of 'em.'

A man behind her in the queue commented, 'The Nazzies reckoned bombin' Bradford'd only improve it, so they didn't bother.' He chuckled at his joke.

'Actually,' said Dee, 'I knew someone who worked there and I'm trying to track him down, must be twenty years ago now. You don't know where they all went, do you?'

'No idea, love, sorry.'

A woman standing in the queue had been listening to the conversation and chipped in: 'The headmistress took early retirement and took over t' post office on Canal Street.'

'Really? Do you remember her name?'

Chapter 27

Lily and Dee entered the Canal Street post office and were relieved to find that it was almost empty. There was just one old man at the counter buying a dozen penny stamps. The woman behind the counter looked to be in late middle age and could well be a retired headmistress. Lily, whose turn it was to make enquiries, stepped up to the counter as the old man shuffled off.

'Excuse me, but are you Mrs Harrison who used to be the headmistress at Jubilee Road School?'

'Yes, I am.'

She looked at Lily through narrowed eyes as if trying to identify her. 'Do I know you? Were you one of our pupils?'

Lily smiled and shook her head. 'No, nothing like that. I'm trying to track down a man who used to work there. I don't know his name, but I do know that he was a caretaker there about twenty years ago. I was wondering if you were there around that time?'

'Twenty years ago? Yes, I was teaching there then, and the name of the caretaker was Armitage, Bernard

Armitage. What was it you wanted to know about him?'

There was a suspicious look on her face, as if she knew something about this Bernard Armitage and wondered if Lily did as well.

Dee spotted this look. 'What was he like?' she asked.

'In what way?'

'I mean, was he a trustworthy person?'

Mrs Harrison hesitated for a while before answering this. 'No, I'm afraid he wasn't. As a matter of fact he was sent to jail for stealing money from the school. That will have been about, let me see, ten or eleven years ago. I know he was sentenced to a year and I haven't heard anything about him since then – due to lack of interest, mainly.' She looked at Dee, quizzically. 'Might I ask why you're looking for him?'

'I've had something very valuable stolen from me,' said Lily 'and I have reason to believe that he is the person responsible.'

'Ah, I see. Well, I've pretty much told you all I know about him, which isn't that much I'm afraid.'

Lily took the photograph of Oldroyd and his wife out of her handbag and showed it to Mrs Harrison. 'This is a recent photograph of the man I'm looking for. Would you say this is Bernard Armitage?'

Mrs Harrison scrutinised the photograph. 'It certainly looks like him, only he didn't have a moustache back then and obviously he was a lot younger.'

'Do you know anyone who might be able to tell us where he is now?' Lily asked.

Mrs Harrison shook her head. Another customer

came in and was standing obediently behind Lily and Dee.

'Do you mind if I serve this customer?' said Mrs Harrison.

'No, not at all,' said Lily, 'you've been a great help.'

Dee was tugging on Lily's coat sleeve as they left the post office. 'Hey!' she said in a loud whisper. 'We can't leave it like that. We need to know more about this Armitage bloke. We need to know what he was like. The things he got up to when he was working at the school.'

'Auntie Dee,' said Lily, as they stepped into the street, 'Mrs Harrison told us everything we need to know about this man. Bernard Armitage is obviously his real name – not Bernard Oldroyd or Arthur Williams – and he was sent to jail ten years ago for stealing money from Jubilee Street school in Bradford. All we have to do is pass this information on to Mr Bannister and let the police track him down.'

Dee gave a sigh and scratched her head. 'Yeah, I suppose you're right, girl. It's just that over the years I've learned to have not too much faith in the coppers, which is probably my own fault as I've not given them good reason to have much faith in me.'

'There's no reason why we can't continue to look for him,' said Lily. 'It's just that the police should be able to find him a lot quicker than we can, and they've also got the authority to arrest him.'

Dee held up a finger as if an idea had just struck her. 'Give me a minute,' she said and went back in the post office.

In less than a minute she returned. Lily raised questioning eyebrows.

'Just gave her one of me cards,' said Dee, 'in case she remembered anything. You never know.'

Chapter 28

Millgarth police station was a stone's throw away from Leeds open market and just around the corner from Union Street Baths where Lily had spent a lot of her childhood. It was Saturday morning. They'd called in to see DS Bannister but he wasn't due in until the afternoon. Dee had gone for a scout around the antique shops. Lily had bought herself a swimming costume from the market and had gone for a swim, which was something she'd done quite regularly to get herself back to a reasonable level of fitness after her ordeal in Ecclestone House Hospital. She was changing into her costume in one of the poolside cubicles which afforded modesty from shoulder to ankle, when she spotted him diving in from a platform at the deep end. He surfaced and went into a fast crawl, taking no time at all to cover the twenty-five-yard length of the pool; possibly even faster than Lily, who had represented Leeds schools before the war.

She emerged from her cubicle and walked to the shallow end, waiting for him to arrive at the end of his third length. She allowed him to touch and turn before she dived in and surfaced alongside him, taking up her stroke on equal terms with him. She had on a swimming cap, also bought from the market, so he didn't recognise her, but he did recognise a challenge when one presented itself. He picked up his pace, which was matched by Lily, stroke for stroke. People by the poolside stopped to watch. Some swimmers got out and went up into the balcony for a clearer view. Rarely had Union Street baths seen swimmers with such obvious ability racing each other. The onlookers began to take sides, mainly cheering on Lily who was the obvious underdog and trailing by a yard or so after five lengths of racing. The fact that she was also an attractive-looking young woman helped encourage her supporters.

Lily was going flat out, hoping that the extra three lengths he had already swum might tire him out and allow her to catch him up and pass him. But, after another two lengths, it was obvious that this wasn't going to happen. He now had a lead of three yards. Halfway down the pool he turned over on to his back to take a good look at this person with whom he'd been competing and he smiled when he saw it was a woman. He stopped swimming and allowed her to pass him at speed. She arrived at the bar, turned and noticed he'd stopped. He swam lazily towards her, still not realising who she was.

'OK, you win,' he said, drawing in deep breaths. I'm more of a hundred-yards man myself. You had me doing double that. Hang on. Don't I know you?'

'You've met me, but you don't know me,' panted Lily. Her swimming cap disguised her long dark hair and he'd certainly never seen her in a swimming costume before. 'You bought a ring for Beryl,' she said, 'only it turned out she wasn't worth giving it to.'

His face broke into a broad grin. 'Ah, the ring lady. You're obviously better at swimming than you are at selling rings at a profit.'

'I think I might have given you a better race a few years ago,' Lily said.

'You gave me a pretty good race just now. I couldn't have kept up the pace much longer.'

'Nor me,' she admitted.

They both heaved themselves out of the pool, still attracting glances of admiration from the onlookers who were disappointed that the race hadn't reached a proper conclusion. This time the admiration was not for their swimming prowess but for their good looks, which was unusual down at Union Street baths.

The young soldier's body was hard and lean and tanned. He had a tattoo of a red rose on his right shoulder. In contrast, Lily's body was pale and slim but with curves in the right places. Since leaving the psychiatric hospital she'd put quite a few pounds back on and regained some of the bloom to her cheeks. Together they made an attractive couple.

'I suppose I'd better introduce myself,' said the soldier. 'My name's Charlie, and you are . . . ?'

'Lily'

'Well, Lily, I think I owe you an apology for being so ungracious about the ring.'

'Apology accepted – and yes, you were a bit ungracious. Do I take it that you've managed to work out why we do it?'

Charlie nodded. 'I'm guessing that you're appealing to the gambling instinct in people who know that there are odd items of genuine jewellery on your stall, which you don't know about – only you do know about them, don't you?'

Lily just smiled.

'Only that doesn't quite explain why you pointed the ring out to me.'

She pointed at his red rose tattoo. 'Does this mean you're a Lancashire lad?'

'Born and bred in London,' grinned Charlie. 'We moved to Leeds when I was ten years old.' He twisted his head towards his tattoo. 'This is my freedom tattoo – Beryl hated 'em. I had it done the day we split up.'

'Good job she hated them, eh? Otherwise you might have been stuck with her name on your shoulder for the rest of your life.'

Charlie laughed. 'Hey! That's true. Never thought of that.'

'And how's the Gold Star running?'

'Ah, you remember. Oh, she's a beauty. You'll have to come for a spin one day – if you don't mind riding pillion.'

Lily, who had been riding pillion less than an hour ago, made no comment. She knew this couldn't have been anything other than a chance meeting, but it still seemed as if their paths crossing three times in just over a week was more than a coincidence. He was an attractive young man; a young man she could get on with, but she felt uncomfortable even contemplating this so soon after Larry, the father of her lost boys, had died. Charlie sensed he'd said the wrong thing and glanced down at her wedding ring.

'Oh, sorry. I should have remembered – you're married. Look, I wasn't trying it on or anything. I just—'

'That's OK. No offence taken.'

She smiled and dived in. He stood at the edge; watching her plough through the water; wondering whether to follow her, then he decided against it and went back to his cubicle. She was married. No future in that. Shame, though. She put Beryl Townsend into the shade, no doubt about that.

An hour later, Lily and Dee were standing at the desk in Millgarth police station, waiting to see Detective Sergeant John Bannister. He appeared behind them and invited them into a musty interview room, lit only by a high window that needed a good clean. They sat round a table. Lily took the photographs from her bag and placed them in front of him.

'His name's not Oldroyd, it's Bernard Armitage,' she said. 'Ten years ago he was sent to prison for stealing money from Jubilee Street school in Bradford.'

Bannister picked up one of the photographs. 'And where did you get this information from?'

'From a Mrs Harrison who used to be the headmistress of the school before it was bombed in 1941. She works at the Canal Street post office in Bradford now. He was also recognised by an Ilkley woman called Rachel Clegg. He swindled her out of a lot of money last year. She knew him as Arthur Williams.'

'I'd think with that sort of information dropping into your lap you should be able to find him quite easily,' said Dee, without disguising the disdain in her voice. Lily threw her a glance of caution.

'I'm aware that you think I'm responsible for my

son's disappearance,' she said to Bannister, 'which is why your investigation is going nowhere.'

'And why we're having to do your bloody job for you!' added Dee. 'Lily's applying for custody of baby Christopher, but while the responsibility for Michael's disappearance is still hanging over her head like the sword of bloody Damocles it's gonna make things difficult.'

Bannister knew that there was a lot of truth in what they said about the investigation, although he wasn't about to admit it. He put the photograph back down on the desk and picked up a pen.

'OK, I'll run with what you've told me. First I'd like details of these women who appear to know him, and I'd like to know how you brought the photos to their attention.'

'We had them published in a paper, like we wanted you to,' said Dee pointedly.

Bannister ignored her dig at him. 'Which paper was that?'

'*Craven Herald*, last Thursday. Mrs Clegg rang us on Thursday evening. Recognised him straight off – as did Mrs Harrison when we showed her the photos. He didn't have the moustache when they saw him but they're sure it's him. Amazing what you can do if you put your mind to it. You should try it some time.'

They were back at Dee's house in Shipley when the phone rang. Dee answered.

'Hello, Dee Maguire.'

'It's Mrs Harrison from the post office. You came in yesterday enquiring about Bernard Armitage?'

'I did, yes. Do you have anything for me?'

'Well, I don't know if it's of any use but I have the address where he was living when he worked at Jubilee Street school in 1935. With me being the head mistress I had a ledger with the names and addresses of all the staff and co-workers. I rescued it from the rubble after the school was bombed.'

'That'd be most helpful,' said Dee, sticking a thumb up to Lily who was wondering who it was. Dee picked up a pen and opened a notepad on the telephone table, repeating the woman's words as she wrote. '"Bernard Armitage: Twenty-three Farrar Mount, Bradford four." Thank you, Mrs Harrison, you've been most helpful.'

Chapter 29

Twenty-three Farrar Mount was a substantial terraced house built of millstone grit, quarried from the moors to the west of Bradford, consisting of three storeys and a cellar. Dee drew the motorbike to a halt in a cloud of blue exhaust smoke and raised a staying hand to Lily who was getting out of the sidecar. There were times when Lily preferred the relative comfort it afforded compared to a pillion ride.

'You wait there,' Dee said 'I know what him and his woman look like. If they see you, God knows what they'll do. If one of them answers the door I'll tell them I'm selling bargain jewellery which I've got in my vehicle – there's some cheap stuff under your seat.'

'What if someone else answers?'

'Then I'll just ask for Bernard, Bernard Armitage – as if I know him.'

'And what if he comes to the door? What will you say to him, having asked for him by name?'

'Bloody hell, girl! Let's not get ahead of ourselves. If he comes to the door I'll play it by ear.' She gave it some thought. 'I'll tell him I'm Rachel Clegg's auntie and I've come for her washing machine or her money back or we go to the police. Come to think of it, that's not a bad idea at all. He's hardly going to want the police knocking on his door.'

Lily looked up at the rainy sky and settled back into the sidecar, satisfied with Dee's plan but not entirely sure she'd stick to it.

Dee walked up to the door and knocked loudly. It was a substantial door which seemed to require a decent knock. In fact it required several. Dee was about to give up when she heard a man shouting inside.

'All right, all right . . . I'm comin' as fast as I damned well can!'

Dee arranged her face into a winning smile to disarm the annoyed man coming to the door. It wasn't Oldroyd. It was a man well into his seventies who looked as if he'd struggle to make it into another decade. He glared at this unwanted visitor, wheezing at the effort he'd been forced to make to come to the door. His words were punctuated by further wheezes.

'What d'yer want? I don't have visitors, me . . . At my time o' life I make it a point not ter bother wi' visitors . . . An' if yer tryin' ter sell me owt, yer can just bugger off. I've got no brass ter throw about on stuff I don't need.'

Dee maintained her smile. 'I'm not trying to sell you anything. I'm wondering if Bernard Armitage still lives here. I know he used to.'

'Is that what yer know? Well, yer know more than me. Bernard Armitage? Who is he, when he's at home?'

'He was a caretaker at Jubilee Street school. This is the last address I've got for him.'

'Is it now? Well, we used ter take in lodgers years ago but I can't remember names . . . I can scarce remember me own name at times.' He gave a frightening laugh at his own joke. Dee showed her appreciation of his humour by laughing as well.

'If I tell you he was sent to jail for stealing from the school, would that help you remember?'

'Sent ter . . . ? Bugger me, I do remember him. What did yer say his name were?'

'Bernard Armitage.'

'That's him. I remember him. Left owin' me rent money. Next thing I knew he were in jail. Never saw him again. There were summat about him that I never liked. My missis never liked him, neither. She's dead now, poor owd cow. Died two years ago.' His rheumy eyes misted over at the thought of his wife.

'I'm sorry about that,' Dee said. 'I imagine you loved her very much.'

'What? Aye. Happen I did. Never really told her. One day she were there, makin' me dinner, next thing she were dead. Stroke or summat, so they said.'

'So, Bernard Armitage. You've no idea how I could find him?'

The old man scratched his mop of white hair, and somehow swivelled his false teeth within his mouth, ruminatively.

'I know when he lived here he spent a lot o' time in t' Conservative Club up Lumley Road. He reckoned he were better than us with him bein' a Conservative.' He gave another wheezy laugh. 'Hey, I bet they kicked the bugger out when he went ter jail. They don't like

195

jailbirds, don't them Conservatives. Mind you, if it were up ter me, I'd lock a few o' the buggers up. Bloody Conservatives! What's all that about? No interest in the working man.'

'So maybe someone there knows him.'

'Aye, happen they do. If yer find him he owes me twenty-seven shillings fer week's rent an' board.'

'Thank you, you've been a great help, and I'm sure your wife knew you loved her without being told.'

'D'yer think so? Aye, happen yer right. I allus tret her right, yer know. Never raised me hand to her once.'

'I'm sure you were a fine husband.'

'D'yer think so?' He gave his teeth another swivel. 'Aye, happen yer right.'

He closed the door on her without further comment, leaving her smiling to herself.

Chapter 30

There was a strong element of incongruity about the Lumley Conservative Club insofar as it was situated in an unmistakable working-class area. It was early evening when Lily and Dee walked in. They found themselves in a small vestibule with three doors leading off, marked, Bar, Lounge and Games Room.

For reasons Lily didn't understand Dee led the way into the Games Room. Inside were two snooker tables, both occupied, with other players waiting. Eyes briefly turned to the two women, the only women in the room. Dee walked up to the bar, being tended by a middle-aged man who seemed surprised by their presence but not put out.

'What will yer have, ladies?'

'Do we have to sign in or anything?' Dee asked him. 'We're not members.'

'Eventually. Yer can have a drink first if yer like.'

She scanned the beer pumps. 'Right, well, I'll have a pint of Tetley's Mild. What about you, Lily?'

'I'll have a brandy please.'

The barman took a clean glass from a shelf above their heads and proceeded to pull Dee's pint.

'We've actually come to enquire about a man who was a member here many years ago.'

'Well, I were here many years ago,' smiled the barman. 'Been pulling pints here for twenty-six years. What's his name, this feller?'

'Bernard Armitage.'

The man's hand froze on the beer pump. He looked up at them. 'D'yer mind if I ask what it is yer want ter know about him?'

'We just wanted to know if he's still around these parts.'

'Was he a friend of yours or something?'

'Not really,' said Dee. 'I assume you know him?'

He finished pulling the pint and turned to pick up a brandy glass.

'Well, I knew him.' He nodded at the other men in the room. 'We all knew Bernard, but . . .'

Lily sensed what the barman was going to say next and she didn't want to hear it.

'You say you *knew* him?'

'That's right, love,' said the barman, turning his attention to her. 'I'm afraid Bernard's not with us any more. He was killed in a road accident about a month ago; walked out in front of a trolley bus. There are some who think it was suicide.'

Lily felt all hope drain away from her in that instant. The only connection she had with her missing son was dead. She felt herself going faint. Dee spotted this and helped her to a chair. Then she fetched the brandy and told Lily to drink it, but Lily was shaking so much she couldn't hold the glass.

'It's all right, girl. Just another setback.'

'Is she OK?' the barman was asking. 'I thought yer said he wasn't a friend.'

'He wasn't,' said Dee. 'Her son's gone missing and we think this Armitage man might be able to help us find him. Was he married, do you know?'

The barman shook his head. 'Not any more. Got divorced years ago. His wife got fed up with him playin' around. He always had a woman in tow.'

Dee surveyed the room where most of the men turned their attention from snooker to the two women who were so upset at Bernard Armitage dying.

'Did any of you see him with a small boy about four years old?'

The men looked at each other, shaking their heads. 'He wasn't our most popular member,' said the barman. 'There was something about him we didn't trust, but we couldn't put our fingers on it.' He looked over at the men on the nearest table. 'That's right, isn't it fellers?'

'I don't like ter speak ill of the dead,' said one, 'but he were a bit of a pillock. He's done time, yer know.'

'Yes, I know that,' said Dee. She took out her purse to pay for the drinks.

'Two and eightpence,' said the barman.

She gave him three shillings and told him to keep the change, then asked, 'Do you know where he lived?'

'Well, he moved about a bit, but t' last I heard he were livin' off Lumb Lane. We'll have his address some-where, but yer'll have to ask a committee member. It'll be in t' office.'

'Are there any committee members in here?'

199

The barman called out to one of the men sitting waiting for his turn to play.

'Barry, while yer doin' nowt could yer dig out the late Bernard Armitage's last known address for this lady.'

As Barry went off to get the address, Dee sat down next to Lily who was now sipping her brandy; her mind racing as to what to do next.

'There's more than one way ter skin a cat, girl,' Dee said. 'I think we should mebbe take what we've just found out to Bannister. If nothin' else at least he might realise you're trying a lot harder than he is to find Michael.'

'I want to go to his house first,' said Lily, swilling down her brandy and getting to her feet. 'For all we know Michael might still be there – with that bloody woman.'

'Now yer thinking, girl.'

That bloody woman was nowhere to be found at Bernard Armitage's last known address, which was a small rented terrace house just off Manningham Lane. There was a To Let sign in the window with the address and phone number of the letting agent. Within five minutes Lily and Dee were standing at the agent's counter.

'We've come to make an enquiry about the house you have to let on Bertha Terrace.'

The agent was a tall, thin young man with a pale face, thick lens spectacles and a row of pens sticking from his top pocket. Lily suspected he'd been deemed unfit for duty in the armed forces.

'I'm afraid we let it last week, madam. The people

who do our signs obviously haven't taken it down yet. We have another similar hou—'

'We're actually enquiring about the previous tenant of the Bertha Street house,' interjected Dee, 'the late Mr Bernard Armitage.'

'Oh yes, oh dear. Poor Mr Armitage. He was one of our tenants for just over two years. What was it you wanted to know?'

'Well,' Dee went on, 'I understand he lived with a woman, perhaps his wife. I wonder if you know what happened to her.'

The young man frowned and shook his head. 'His wife? As far as I know he lived there on his own, but just let me have a look in our ledger. We keep a full record of all our tenants.'

From a drawer beneath the desk he took out a large, leather-bound ledger and opened it at page one where the As were to be found. He ran a bony finger down to the bottom and turned the page over.

'Here we are . . . Mr Bernard Armitage, single tenancy.' His eyes were magnified through his lenses as he looked at them. 'Yes, he lived on his own. In fact I do remember seeing the obituary notice in the *Telegraph and Argus*. There was only the one, from friends and members of the Lumley Road Conservative Club. It stuck in my memory because he didn't look much like a Conservative to me.'

'You're sure he couldn't have had a woman living with him without telling you?' Dee pressed.

'I don't see why he'd want to keep her a secret. The rent would be the same no matter how many were living there – unless he was sub-letting. We don't allow that.'

'Sub-letting?' said Lily, now clutching at straws. 'Is this something he might have done? We know he was a very dishonest man who's been to jail.'

The young man shrugged. 'I don't know too much about him. He did fall behind with his rent on occasions, in fact I had to go there a couple of times to collect his arrears. But I didn't see any signs of a woman. In fact, after he died I went round with a solicitor to remove his belongings and I have to say there were no women's things about the house. He apparently died intestate with no known relatives.' He paused and added a devious thought of his own. 'But perhaps she removed them when she heard he'd died. Maybe if you ask some of the neighbours.'

'Thank you,' said Dee, 'We'll do that.'

Chapter 31

Asking the neighbours drew a blank as Lily suspected it might. Bernard Armitage hadn't been a very neighbourly neighbour. The people living on either side of him knew him to nod to but they didn't even know his name, despite him living there for over two years. They knew he'd been killed by a trolley bus because it had been in the *Argus* along with his photograph and street address. None of them had seen a woman going in and out of his house. Him dying intestate with no known relatives was of no help either.

Dee reported their findings about Armitage's death to Bannister, who commented, 'Sounds to me as if he's not much of a loss to the world.'

'He's a loss to us. He was the only connection we had to Lily's son. Tell you what. You concentrate on what you're good at – arresting innocent people. Me and Lily'll find her boy without your bloody help!'

Having nothing to lead her to her beloved son, Lily descended into a deep despondency which Dee couldn't shake her from. Dee's neighbours asked her about her niece, whom she referred to as Our Lily from Leeds who didn't enjoy the best of health. It was a plausible explanation, disguising Lily's true identity as the infamous Lilian Robinson, the woman who was suspected of killing her own son. Luckily, during all her trials and tribulations no newspaper had run a photograph of her. In fact she was now very old news and no paper had even bothered to report her release from psychiatric custody. Anyone who remembered Lilian Robinson's story would no doubt assume she was still locked up. Lily had heard from her solicitor regarding her custody application and was told that Christopher's grandparents were going to fight the application vigorously.

Dee had tried to comfort her. 'At least we know he's OK, Lily.'

'But I miss him, Auntie Dee. If I had him with me I'd be able to cope better.'

'I know that, love, but we have to play the cards we've been dealt. We've got truth and right on our side. Hold on to that.'

In rare moments of mental clarity Lily's mind locked on to Michael and ways of tracking him down. So far, running the story in the newspapers was the only thing she could come up with. She mentioned this to Dee who pointed out the pitfalls.

'You'd need to run it in the nationals, love. Which would mean a reporter asking questions about you which you wouldn't want to answer.'

'What sort of questions?'

'Well, they'd want to know where you live, for a

start. When a paper runs any sort of story they need a hook to hang it on and *your* story is the hook, not Michael's. They'd dig a lot deeper than you'd want them to, believe me.'

Chapter 32

Ogden Beakersfield had been staring into the window for several minutes, screwing his eyes up most of the time because his eyes weren't what they used to be and he'd left his glasses on the kitchen table. Eventually he walked away, muttering to himself and called in the pub for a beer. It was market day and they'd been open since ten a.m. – an hour ago. He was still muttering to himself as he sank his pint.

'Stop yer chunterin', Oggie, lad,' scolded the landlady. 'Yer mekkin' everyone's beer go flat.'

'I'm minding me own buggering business,' muttered Ogden. 'An' two pound's a lorra brass for a man on a low pension.'

'What the heck is he talkin' about?' asked the landlady of no one particular.

'I'll tell yer warram talkin' about if yer lend us yer glasses for two minutes.' Ogden pointed at the landlady's spectacles. She stared at him for a brief moment, sighed, then took them off and handed them to him. He stuck them in his top pocket and shuffled out of the door, much to her consternation.

'Hey! I never said yer could walk outside with 'em.

Bloody hell! Where's he gone wi' me glasses? Daft owd beggar!'

The daft owd beggar had gone over the road to the café, where he donned the spectacles and stared at the photograph on display in the window. His wrinkled face creased into a toothless beam as he confirmed what he'd previously seen. He took a crumpled piece of paper from his pocket and wrote down a phone number, using one of the many bookie's pencils he'd accumulated. He then stuck the glasses back into his pocket and returned the pub for a celebratory pint. As he paid for it he asked the landlady, 'How do I mek a telephone call ter Shipley? Is it long distance? Will it cost much? I'm not used to all this new-fangled telephone business.'

'New-fangled? Oggie, telephones have been around for years.'

'Not round my bloody 'ouse, they haven't. What do I do?'

'Yer go ter that big red box up t' road and yer pick up a black thing what yer stick to yer ear'ole, then yer dial 0 and ask t' operator ter put yer through to whatever number yer want. She'll tell yer 'ow much ter put in.'

'What, they mek yer pay afore yer use it do they?'

'Aye, just like I mek yer pay fer yer pint afore yer drink it.'

Ogden screwed his face up. 'I 'ope it's not much. I've not got money ter flash around, yer know.'

'Aye, I think we've all noticed that, Oggie.'

'I've mos' prob'ly missed me chance, anyroad. Prob'ly someone's beat me to it. Story of my life – bein' beaten to it.'

207

He finished his pint and shuffled outside, up the road to the telephone box where he dialled 0 and asked the operator for the Shipley number he'd seen in the café window.

'Put tuppence in the box, caller, and press Button A when your call is answered.'

'What if I don't get no answer?'

'You press Button B for your money back.'

'Right.'

Ogden carefully placed two pennies in the slot, dialled the number with a shaky index finger and pressed the telephone to his good ear.

Chapter 33

'Well, damn me! Aren't you supposed ter be in jail?'

Lily looked up at the woman confronting her at Dee's stall in Leeds market. It was late morning and Dee had gone to buy them a couple of sandwiches for lunch. Since finding out that Bernard Armitage had died, her world had almost died with him. He'd taken with him the precious secret of her son's whereabouts. Dee had virtually bullied her out of the house and back to work, afraid of what she might do if left alone.

'What?' said Lily dully.

Hilda Muscroft was standing there with a carrier bag full of vegetables. Her voice grew louder, wanting people to hear.

'Yer got locked up in a nut'ouse, didn't yer? How come they let yer out? Yer still look doo-lally ter me. Bloody 'ell! We're not safe in us beds wi' nutters like you around. Killed any more of yer kids lately?'

Lily, who had been sitting down, got to her feet but didn't have the mental ammunition to retaliate. She went paler than usual and began to shiver. Hilda was laughing out loud at her triumph over this woman who, along with her blowzy friend, had humiliated her. She turned and addressed the small crowd which had gathered, sensing something going on.

'Hey, d'yer know who this is? It's Lily Robinson – her what killed her son and got sent to a nuthouse for attacking me in t' street.'

Lily wanted to run away but this meant deserting Dee's stall, so she stood her ground, drip-white and shocked to the bone. People who remembered her story were looking at her with contempt. Hilda's vicious diatribe grew in venom and volume when she realised that she was in no danger of retaliation from Lily, who looked totally harmless and on the verge of a breakdown. Angry comments came from the crowd, eagerly encouraged by Hilda. One woman stepped forward and spat on a tray of rings. Hilda sniggered out loud.

'That's right love. Step forward and spit on the child killer! Lily bloody Robinson. What's she doin' workin' among decent folk?'

Another voice, much louder than Hilda's, joined in. 'That horrible smell isn't coming from the fruit and veg stall, ladies and gentlemen – it's coming from this stinking woman!'

Dee took Hilda by the scruff of her neck and twisted her coat so tight that she had her choking. She then hurled her to the ground. The carrier bag burst, scattering her vegetables. Then she confronted the woman who had spat on her stall.

'You, wipe your filthy spit off my stall before I throttle you!'

She took the woman by the hair and thrust her face into the spit she'd just deposited. Effortlessly, she held the woman's face down as she spoke to the crowd.

'My friend hasn't killed anyone, which is why she's a free woman. She's a victim of brainless idiots like this old bag and old smelly knickers down there.'

Dee let go of the old bag and took a kick at a large cabbage that Hilda was reaching for. It flew into the crowd like a football, bringing broad grins from some of the watching men. Then she gave the kneeling Hilda a kick up the backside, sending her sprawling and rousing the men into cheers. When she turned back to the stall Lily had gone.

She was just leaving the crowded market and heading towards the West Yorkshire bus station when she heard a voice behind her.

'Are you OK, Lily?'

She stopped but didn't turn round, having recognised the voice. Charlie. He came alongside her. 'I saw it all kick off back there – including the mayhem caused when your friend turned up. She seems a very formidable lady.'

Lily couldn't think of anything to say. She felt his hand on her shoulder and it felt unbelievably welcome, strong and comforting and undemanding. Now she turned to him. He was dressed for work, in a dark blue boiler suit, a pencil stuck behind his left ear.

'What are you doing here?' she asked him. This fourth meeting must be more than a coincidence.

'Well, maybe I thought I might bump into you.'

'Oh,' she said, then added, 'Did you believe what you heard?'

211

'No.'

His answer came almost before she finished asking the question. Brief and unequivocal.

'What do you believe, then?'

'I believe the story you're going to tell me when we go for a drink in this pub.'

The Yorkshire Hussar, which stood at the bottom of Eastgate, was just opening its doors. Charlie escorted her into the taproom.

'I'd take you into the lounge but I'm not exactly dressed for it,' he said apologetically.

'I don't mind.'

He selected a table for two in a corner where they wouldn't be disturbed, sat her down like a head waiter might, removed the pencil from behind his ear and stuck it in his pocket. The bar was practically empty, but would soon fill up with early lunchtime drinkers; beer was twopence per pint cheaper than in the lounge. He bought her a brandy while he settled for a small lemonade.

'How do you know I like brandy?'

'I don't. Seems to me as if you need one.'

'Good guess.' She eyed his drink. 'Not a drinking man yourself, then?'

He grinned. 'Oh, I can drink with the best of them but not during the working day and not while I'm driving. The army instills all sorts of strange disciplines into you.'

'Driving? Do you have a car as well as your motorbike?'

'Firm's van. The old man gave it to me as a sweetener to persuade me to go back into the family firm.'

'*Were* you going to work somewhere else?'

'It crossed my mind to *do* something else. I'm afraid the army messed up my mind for Civvy Street. Anyway, I'm back to knocking things down for a living – for the time being at least.'

'You sound as if you had a hard time of it in the army.'

He went quiet for a brief moment, then said, 'We're here to talk about your problems.'

She gave a wan smile and swilled her drink around in the glass. 'Oh, I don't think you want to know about my problems.'

'Actually, I do – and the first thing I want to know . . .' He glanced at her ring finger. 'Tell me to mind my own business if you like – but I assume you're married?'

'If you assume I'm married why have you come looking for me?'

'I've learned that not everything is as it seems. Or is it?'

Lily looked down at the two rings on the third finger of her left hand and, without looking up, said: 'My husband was killed in France on April the eleventh this year. He was mentioned dispatches.'

She added the last bit to emphasise that her Larry had died the death of a brave soldier. People who asked about him should know that.

Charlie felt guilty at the fact that his feelings were mixed at this answer. 'I'm truly sorry to hear that.' He took a sip of his drink. 'Got a Mentioned, did he? Sounds a good man. Just weeks before the end. That was hard luck.'

She gave a slight nod and felt a desperate need to unburden herself on this young man whom she hardly knew. Over the next thirty minutes the whole story tumbled out. He sat there, quietly, interjecting nothing but an occasional question to clarify something. At the end of it he went to the bar and came back with two brandies. She looked at them and then up at him.

'I thought you didn't drink during a working day.'

'This stopped being a working day about ten minutes into your story. I'll ring the old man up and give him some lame excuse about me needing to take the afternoon off, then I'll run you home.'

He looked at his watch. 'In my experience,' he said, 'there's always a way out of a problem. Blimey, I've wriggled out of a few tight spots in my time.'

'This isn't the army, Charlie.'

'Same principle. Just needs thinking about. As Mr Micawber once said, "Something will turn up." '

'*David Copperfield*.' Lily smiled, unaccountably relieved that she had Charlie on her side. Dee was a tower of strength, but a loose cannon. Charlie was different. He seemed resourceful and dependable. Somehow she had faith in Charlie, a man she hardly knew.

'What's your surname?' she asked him.

He winced slightly. 'Cleghorn. Beryl hated it. Hated the idea of one day becoming Beryl Cleghorn. Still, she doesn't have that to worry about any more.'

'She must be mad to lose you.'

Charlie grinned. 'She going out with a bloke called Arthur Sirrell now. Hey, if she marries him she'll be a mouthful.'

Beryl Sirrell made Lily smile once again. He did that, did Charlie.

'Do you want to come in for a cup of tea?' Lily asked him as he drew the van up outside Dee's house.

'Don't mind if I do.'

They'd just settled down to drink their tea when the phone rang. 'It'll be Dee, worrying about me like a mother hen,' said Lily, going into the hall.

'Hello, Shipley four–eight–six–two.'

'Is that two quid still up fer grabs?'

'Pardon?'

'Oh, bugger! Can yer hear me all right?'

'Yes, I can hear you. Two pounds? Which two pounds is that?'

'That photo what yer put in t' caff winder. I know who it is, if that two quid reward's still up fer grabs.'

Realisation set in. 'Oh, right. Look, I'm sorry, we've actually identified the man.'

'Oh bugger! Story of my life. So, I'm not gonna get no two quid, then?'

'I'm really sorry, but—'

'Buggeration!'

He banged the phone down. Lily shouted over the dial tone. 'Don't ring off! Oh blast!'

She put down the phone and went back into the living room as Ogden trudged back to the pub disconsolately, muttering to himself. Charlie looked up from his tea.

'Was it Dee?'

'No, it was someone claiming a reward we were

offering to anyone who could identify photo of the man who took Michael.'

'And this person said he knew who he was?'

Lily paused before saying, 'Yes he did.'

'So, did you ask him any questions about Oldroyd or Armitage?'

'Didn't get the chance. He caught me a bit unawares. I told him we'd identified the man. He swore because he wasn't going to get the two quid then he put the phone down before I could ask him anything. Good God, Charlie! My mind's all over the place. Do you think the telephone people will know who rang?'

'Dunno. I imagine the police might be able to have the call tracked somehow. Did it sound like a private number or did you hear any coins drop as you answered?'

Lily cast her mind back. 'I heard coins drop – it was a telephone box.'

'I see. Where will he have seen this photo?'

'He mentioned a caff. It'll be the one in Grassington. We put a photo in the window.'

'Then we should go to Grassington and ask around.'

'What – now?'

'No time like the present. It may well be a wild goose chase but it has to be done.'

Chapter 34

'Was there anything distinctive in his voice that might set him apart from other men?' Charlie asked her as he drove the Morris van along the A650 towards Skipton.

Lily thought for a moment, running the telephone conversation through her head. 'Well, his voice was a bit raspy as though he was quite old . . . and he used the word bugger three times. Actually, there were two buggers and one buggeration in a thirty-second conversation.'

'Good. His vocabulary might well single him out.'

'There is one problem,' she said. 'I haven't got two quid on me. He sounds like the sort of person who'll want money in advance to talk to me.'

'Oh,' he said. 'Well I've got about thirty bob on me but I'll need to stop for petrol which is getting a bit low. If I put three gallons in, that'll take about six bob, leaving me twenty-four. You haven't got sixteen bob have you?'

Lily checked her purse. 'Fourteen and tenpence ha'penny,' she said, after counting it. 'That leaves us, what? One and three ha'pence short.'

'I'll just put two gallons in. That should do us.'

'I'll pay you back for all this.'

Charlie grinned. 'One way or another I'll make sure you do.'

'What's that supposed to mean?'

'Dunno,' he said, still grinning. It was a pleasant grin, one she didn't mind at all. She looked out at the passing grey buildings of Keighley and felt that a small part of the weight on her heart had been lifted.

Chapter 35

It was market day in Grassington, which meant the pubs were open all day. By two-thirty p.m. when Lily and Charlie arrived, Ogden Beakersfield was in the Black Horse, well in his cups.

Charlie parked the van and the two of them walked into the centre of the village, heading for the Dales Café which was doing good business. The photograph was still in the window, due to be taken out within a couple of days, Lily reckoned. They went inside and Lily asked the proprietress if a man had been showing interest in the photograph that day. They were trying to track him down.

'I'm sorry, love. We've been run off us feet all day. I haven't had a minute to notice anything.'

Charlie leaned forward and said in a low voice, so as not to offend the delicate ears of the customers, 'He er, he uses the word, "bugger" a lot and we think he might be quite old.'

The woman pulled a face and said. 'Now that sounds like Oggie.'

'Oggie?'

'Ogden Beakersfield – I know, but it's his name not mine.'

'And where would we find this Oggie?'

'Most prob'ly in a pub, drunk as a skunk, grumbling about somethin' or other. Never known a man who could find so much ter grumble about.'

'I don't suppose you could describe him, could you? Lily asked. 'You see, he knows the man in the photo we put in your window and he rang me up this morning only we got cut off.'

'I'm surprised he didn't ring yer back. There's a reward, isn't there?'

'Yes, two pounds.'

'Well, he's a little feller, in his seventies, miserable as sin and bald as a coot, only he'll be wearing a black bowler that's seen better days. Rarely takes it off, even inside. Oh, he wears his Boer War medals on his coat. I reckon the only fighting he saw were in the army canteen.'

'Do you know where he lives?'

'Out Threshfield way, I think. I should just have a look round the pubs. He'll be in one of 'em.'

Ogden was in the third pub they tried. He was sitting at a table in the corner of the bar, fast asleep, snoring, head lolling back, his bowler tipped forward, half covering his face and revealing most of his completely bald head. The clincher was the row of four medals on his tattered coat. Charlie went to the bar and ordered two small shandies. He inclined his head towards the sleeping old man.

'Is that Oggie?' he asked the barman.

'Aye, and I wish he'd clear off and annoy someone else. Whether he's awake or asleep he's an annoying old

220

sod. Yer can have these on the house if yer'll tek him off me hands.'

Charlie laughed and paid the man the last of their spare cash. Then he and Lily walked over to Oggie's table. Charlie shook him by the shoulder quite vigorously. Oggie woke up with a start.

'What the buggerin' 'ell?'

'Afternoon, Oggie,' said Charlie cheerfully.

Oggie sat up, adjusted his bowler and looked from one to the other. 'Who are you?'

'I'm the woman you were speaking to on the phone earlier today,' said Lily. 'It was about the photograph in the café window.'

'Wha . . . ?'

Charlie was trying to assess if the old man was sober enough to talk any sense. 'Do you remember?' he asked.

Oggie frowned, searching his memory. 'Course I remember. Two quid reward wasn't there? Only it's gone.'

'It might not have gone,' said Lily. 'Depends what you can tell us about the man in the photo.'

Oggie's frown deepened, trying to work out what was happening. He held out a bony hand. 'Money first,' he said.

Charlie took out a ten-shilling note and placed it in Oggie's hand. 'When you've given us ten bob's worth there might be another ten bob,' he said, 'and so on.'

Oggie's hand closed over the note like a claw, and said, 'I know his name.'

Lily was about to say, *So do we*, but Charlie stayed her with an upraised hand.

221

'All right, what is it?' Charlie said, with a slight challenge in his voice, as if he was testing the veracity of Oggie's story.

'I know his rank as well, and I know where he's stationed.'

Lily and Charlie said nothing. Oggie was talking about a different man, probably the wrong man, but it would do no harm to let him ramble on. No way would they get their ten bob back.

'He's a sergeant.' Oggie screwed up his eyes trying to think of the man's name. 'Aw, bugger me! I 'ad his name when I rang yer. Same as that comic from Lancashire. Vulgar little bugger. George summat or other, no, Fred . . . Frank . . . Frank Randle. God! He meks me laugh, does that feller.'

'So, this man's name's Frank Randle?'

'No, this bloke's a sergeant. Sergeant Randle. In fact I know his first name. I remember that because it's my middle name. Ogden Bernard Beakersfield.'

'His name's Bernard?' said Charlie, looking at Lily. This sparked her interest. Yet another Bernard. Was the last one just a coincidence, or was Oggie's man the one she was looking for?'

'Where did you meet him?' she asked.

'Met him in Skipton.'

'When?'

'About a year ago – it were in some pub or other. He were havin' trouble with 'is motor. I fixed it fer him so he gave me a lift home, and he gave me a pair o' nylons fer me missis. I sold 'em fer ten bob. I don't have a missis. She buggered off years ago.'

Lily stopped herself saying she wasn't surprised. Instead she said, 'Is Randle married?'

'He is. He were with her that day.'

'What's her name?'

Oggie's face screwed up once more. 'Buggered if I can remember.'

'Could it have been Edith?'

'Hmm, not sure.'

'This car of his. What model was it?'

Oggie's face brightened. 'Austin Seven, love, 1937. Good little motors, them. I used ter be a mechanic, see.'

Lily looked at Charlie. 'Oldroyd's car was an Austin Seven. I know this because Larry mentioned us getting one some day.'

Charlie was nodding. 'The other people who saw the photo hadn't seen him for donkey's years, before he grew his tash. This man's seen him quite recently.' To Oggie, he said, 'You say he's in the army? Seems a bit old to me. What mob is he in?'

'No idea. He's stationed at a place called . . . oh buggeration! I knew that as well this mornin'. It's where they keep all them Eyeties locked up.'

'What? Eden camp?' said Charlie.

'That's it. He were told old fer combat with him havin' been in t' first lot but he's looking after Eyeties. It's near Malton.'

'It is,' said Charlie. 'I went there myself once or twice before I got sent overseas.'

'What for?' Lily asked.

'As a translator. I'd learned Italian as part of what I had to do, so they decided to make use of me before

223

they kicked me over to Italy. There used to be Italian POWs and Italian nationals over there. I think they moved the Italians out last year. Mainly Germans now, as far as I know.' He smiled at Lily. 'I think the women who thought the man in the photo was Armitage were just plain wrong.'

'I agree. This man sounds a much more likely prospect,' Lily said. 'He was in the first war, as Oldroyd told me he was, and he's got an Austin Seven, although I am wondering why he would use a false surname but his own first name?'

'To avoid slip-ups in general conversation,' said Charlie. 'If his wife started calling him Fred you'd wonder if he was genuine.'

'Oh, it's the same feller all right,' Oggie assured them. 'Do I get the rest of me brass, now?'

Charlie looked at Lily. 'There's another reason he's a more likely prospect,' he said.

'What's that?'

'He's alive.'

Charlie took out another ten shilling note and gave it to Oggie, who looked at it with mixed feelings.

'I thought yer said two quid.'

'We don't know for certain it's him yet,' said Charlie. 'If it turns out to be him we'll send you the other quid. I can't say fairer than that. I'll need your address, though.'

Oggie wrote his address down on a beermat, which Charlie stuck in his pocket. They were outside the pub, heading for the van, when Lily asked, 'Why didn't you give him the full two pounds?'

'Because we need more petrol if we're going to Eden

Camp today, and I haven't eaten since breakfast. I reckon our spare quid should be enough for another two gallons plus a decent fry-up, don't you?'

'We're going today are we?'

'Unless you'd like to leave it until tomorrow, or maybe let the police know what we've found out.'

'No, I want to go right now. Why would we leave it? It's my son we're talking about.'

'Look, we're heading into the unknown a bit here. We could be there a while. Perhaps we should have left some sort of message for your friend. She'll be worried about you.'

Lily looked at her watch: two forty-five p.m. 'She'll be on the market until half past four, home at half five. I'll ring her then.' She smiled at him. 'You do have a tendency to think ahead, don't you?'

'It's something I've had drilled into me. Life's like a game of chess. Always stay two moves ahead. It's kept me alive more than once.'

She said nothing. If he wanted to talk about the war he would, when he was good and ready.

Chapter 36

Eden Camp was situated near Malton in the East Riding of Yorkshire. It was built in 1942 and originally housed around 250 Italian prisoners of war and civilians. In 1944, the year after the Italians surrendered to the Allies, they were replaced by German prisoners, many of whom were destined to be held in this country until 1948. The camp comprised forty-five prefabricated huts and a brick office block within a barbed-wire enclosure. Most of the prisoners had been put to work on nearby farms. Few attempted to escape. In 1944 there was nowhere for them to go. Germany was overrun by the Allies.

It was quarter past four when Lily and Charlie arrived at the camp. Charlie had a pal whom he thought might still be stationed there.

'We'd both been on the same language course in Scarborough only Jimmy didn't get into the Regiment so they kept him on here.'

'The Regiment?'

'Yeah. Jimmy broke his leg during parachute training. He's still got a bit of a limp.'

It was common knowledge that most of the men who were returning from the war didn't talk about it much, especially those heavily involved in combat, so Lily didn't enquire further.

There were two gates, one to the prisoner compound and one to the adjacent guard compound, both were wide open with the black and yellow barriers up and men wandering in and out, seemingly at will, many with the letter P painted on the trouser leg of their dark uniforms. The soldier on duty at the guard compound gate was smoking a Woodbine when Charlie and Lily arrived in a van marked *Cleghorn Demolition*. The guard rested his rifle butt on the ground, swivelled his cigarette round in his hand so it was hidden by his palm and leaned in through the van window.

'Name and business, sir?'

'Charlie Cleghorn and I was stationed here for a few weeks in '43. I'm trying to track down an old pal of mine – Jimmy Dunkersley. Is he still here?'

'Jimmy? Yeah.'

'Where would I find him?'

'He's in charge of the pay office.'

The guard stepped back and took a surreptitious drag of his Woodbine as Charlie drove through.

'Security seems a bit lax,' said Lily. 'He didn't ask for any form of identification or anything.'

'Security's slackened off a lot since the war ended.'

Lily looked across at the prisoners wandering around their compound, mostly in small groups with the odd British guard standing around, not displaying too much concern or alacrity. In the guard compound were two machine-gun posts and four gun batteries, all unmanned.

'The murdering sods seem well fed,' she commented

grimly. She felt a surge of hatred towards these men who belonged to the same army that had killed her Larry.

'The Germans in here are better fed than most of the civilian population of this country,' said Charlie. 'They're also taking up jobs on the farms that belong to men coming back from the war. Cheap labour. There's a lot of bad feeling about that.'

'Unbelievable,' said Lily. 'Makes you wonder who won this war.'

'There's going to be a lot of disquiet in the coming years,' said Charlie. He pulled up in front of a long wooden hut marked Camp Office. 'I sometimes think I'm lucky I didn't have a wife and family to come back to, with the wife turned all independent and kids all strangers to me.'

'How d'you mean?'

'Well, mebbe the wife's had a job of her own for the past few years. Mebbe she's found another feller. It's beginning to happen. I've seen it among my mates.'

'It happened to you, didn't it – with Beryl?'

'Fortunately, yes.'

He nodded at a group of prisoners playing football. 'Some of those guys will have British girlfriends, and not all of these girlfriends will be single women. The quicker they get repatriated the better. Trouble is there's millions of 'em all over Europe. It's gonna take years. I'm lucky I got an early demob otherwise I'd still be over in France or Belgium or somewhere, taking care of displaced persons. Not a job I'd relish.'

'Did you relish the job you did over there?'

Charlie froze for a second, with his hand on the door

handle. 'Well . . . it helped move the war along,' he said, before getting out.

They entered a reception area occupied by a pretty, but bored-looking ATS corporal who looked up with interest at these strangers who weren't British soldiers or German prisoners. Charlie gave her a smile which she returned with interest, provoking in Lily a spasm of jealousy.

'I wonder if you could point me in the direction of Jimmy Dunkersley. He was a private when I was here last.'

The ATS girl's smile remained as she held Charlie in her gaze. 'Charlie bloomin' Cleghorn, as I live and breathe. Word was that you'd be out of your depth when you qualified, but here you are.'

Charlie stared at her for a few seconds. 'Ah, you've changed your hair . . . and you're looking a lot slimmer . . . Not that you were ever er, not slim.' He was struggling to remember her name, although he'd once taken her to the cinema in Malton.

'I'm also a corporal now.' She flung her arms out. 'Mistress of all I survey.' Charlie did a quick survey of the office and saw two typist's desks, both unoccupied.

'What, all of this? You must be drunk with power.'

'One's gone to the bog, the other's off sick – probably a hangover but I've put it down as a migraine because I'm an understanding boss. Oh, and my name's Brenda – just in case you forgot.'

'Of course I knew it was Brenda,' lied Charlie. 'It was your surname I was struggling with.'

Brenda gave a giggle. 'I don't remember you ever

229

calling me by my surname. It's Witherspoon – Corporal Witherspoon B – senior clerk/typist.'

Lily was beginning to take a dislike to this Brenda Witherspoon woman who had so far ignored her existence.

'Is it possible for you to tell Jimmy that Charlie's here to see him?' she said curtly.

Brenda turned her attention to Lily. 'Of course I can, madam. I'll get him myself if you'll give me a minute.'

She got to her feet and went through one of the three doors leading out of reception.

'Did you have a fling with her?' Lily wasn't sure why she'd asked.

'Took her out once as I recall.'

'Did Beryl know?'

Charlie turned to her and smiled. 'What's it to you?'

Lily didn't answer. It was nothing to do with her. Within a few seconds the door opened and a young man came bursting through. He had a pronounced limp as he approached Charlie and shook his hand vigorously. He was wearing just uniform trousers and a khaki shirt and tie. No rank insignia.

'Never thought you'd make it back from that mad mob you were in, Charlie boy. What was it like?'

'Not sure I'm allowed to tell you.'

'What rank did you end up with? I got three stripes up . . . when I wear 'em.'

'Yeah, me too, but it was only to give me some sort of authority over the local civvies we were working with. Still, I got sergeant's pay.'

'Wish I'd been there with you. I hear you got a decent gong – MM wasn't it?'

'Hey, where d'you hear that? We were supposed to be a hush-hush outfit.'

'I'm in the Royal Army Pay Corps. We get to know stuff.'

The army small talk went on for a while with Lily becoming increasingly impatient. She sat down on a chair on the opposite side of Brenda's desk and took out her cigarettes. Out of politeness rather than friendship she offered Brenda one.

'No thanks. I find it tends to make your breath smell.'

Lily's dislike of her mounted at this veiled insult. 'Depends how often you clean your teeth,' she commented, lighting up.

Brenda smiled, showing off an array of gleaming white teeth. 'After every meal,' she said. 'And *always* before a date.'

Lily gave her a display of equally white teeth and found herself countering Brenda's barbed comment. 'I wouldn't know too much about courting – my husband was killed in France just a few weeks before the war ended.'

Brenda looked up at Charlie, then back at Lily, trying to work out the relationship. Lily enlightened her.

'Just acquaintances. I have a problem he's helping me with.'

'Oh, right. I'm sorry about your husband.'

She sounded genuine and Lily relaxed a bit. She gave Charlie a dig with her elbow. 'Charlie, why don't you introduce me to Jimmy?'

'Oh, sorry, Lily,' said Charlie. 'I've forgotten my manners. Jimmy, this is Lily. Lily, Jimmy Dunkersley – who's very clumsy when he jumps out of aeroplanes.'

Lily got to her feet and shook Jimmy's hand. 'Pleased to meet you, Jimmy. We're looking for a Sergeant Bernard Randle. Is he still on this camp?'

'What? Old Randy Randle?' said Brenda. 'Yeah, he still hangs around here, like a bad smell.'

'So, you don't like him either, then?' said Lily, now warming to Brenda.

'What's to like? He's a two-faced old sod. I don't know how his wife puts up with him.'

'You mean Edith?'

'Yeah.'

Brenda gave a casual nod, out of all proportion to the boost it had just given to Lily's hopes of getting her son back. The name Edith sealed it. This man was most definitely the one she was looking for; the one who had taken her son, *and he was here, on this camp*.

'Mind you,' said Brenda, 'Edith's got a right mouth on her. I think they deserve each other, those two. Saves making two other people miserable.'

'He's a bit of a Jekyll and Hyde,' Jimmy explained. 'What do you want him for?'

'Is there somewhere where we can talk?' Charlie said, 'preferably somewhere where Randle isn't. I just want to know what you know about him.'

'We have a canteen,' Jimmy said. 'We can talk there. It'll be OK. Randle never goes in.'

'He never goes anywhere where he has to spend money,' commented Brenda.

Charlie turned to Lily. 'You won't have tasted army canteen tea, will you?'

'Not that I remember.'

'It's like NAAFI tea only not quite as tasty.'

'You'll need an asbestos stomach,' said Brenda. 'Hey, I do hope this means trouble for Old Randy,' she called out as they left. Lily paused on her way out and said, 'I hope so, too.'

Brenda flashed her teeth again; so did Lily, this time without malice.

Chapter 37

No one brought up the subject of Sergeant Randle until they'd finished drinking their tea. This was because an adjacent table was occupied by men with stripes on their sleeves who might well have taken an interest in a conversation about one of their colleagues.

'Right,' said Jimmy, in a low voice, when the men had left. 'What's Randle been up to?'

Lily and Charlie looked at each other, wondering who should answer. Lily spoke first.

'He's got my son,' she said. 'He pretended to be a man called Bernard Oldroyd who lived in Grassington and him and his wife took my four-year-old son. I thought they were taking him for a couple of days in the country. My husband had just been killed, you see, and I wasn't thinking straight.'

'Right,' said Jimmy, trying to take in the enormity of what she'd just told him. Charlie went on to explain the problem in more detail. Jimmy's face grew more and more sombre.

'Jesus, Lily. It's a wonder you're still sane!'

'I'm not sure I am sane, Jimmy. What I need to know

is have you seen Randle with my son? Has anyone seen him with a four-year-old boy?'

Jimmy shook his head. 'Randle's an unpleasant character who can put on a good-guy act when it suits him, but I haven't seen him with a kiddie.' He looked at Lily. 'He fiddles everything else and gets away with it, with him being a throwback from the first war, but I've never heard anything about him liking kiddies.'

'So,' said Charlie, 'Did you get on OK with him?'

Jimmy gave a wry smile, 'For most of my time here he outranked me and gave me a hard time just for the fun of it. He used to accuse me of faking my limp just to get out of active service. When I got my third stripe he tried it on again, only this time I gave him a real good hiding. One he won't forget.'

'Did you get into any bother?' said Charlie.

'No. He was drunk. I claimed I'd struck him in self-defence and they believed me.'

'No witnesses, then?'

'Oh yes, plenty of witnesses – mostly my mates and none of them came forward. No action was taken. Just two men of equal rank letting off steam.'

Lily took out her photograph and showed it to Jimmy. 'Just so there's no mistake, is this him?'

Jimmy only needed a glance to confirm that it was Randle. 'And he abducted your son? Bloody hell! Why on earth would he do that?'

'I've got no idea, Jimmy,' Lily said, then she turned to Charlie. 'But it's got me frightened has this, Charlie.'

'Do you think we should bring the police in at this stage?' Charlie asked her.

'Probably,' said Lily, 'but I'd prefer to confront him face to face myself, with you at the side of me, and see what he has to say for himself. I want to know where Michael is, and I want to know now.'

'Well, he'll probably be at home,' said Jimmy. 'He hasn't been around all day so I suspect he'll be on duty tonight. He looked at his watch,

'It's half past four. I'm off at half five, if he's not back on camp by six I'll take you round to his house.'

'I'd like to go round right now,' said Lily.

Jimmy looked at Charlie, who shrugged.

'OK.' Jimmy pointed to four blocks of terraced brick houses standing just outside the compound. 'Block on the right, red door. I think it's number six.'

She looked at Charlie and held out her hands as if to say, *Well, what are we waiting for?*

Chapter 38

Lily recognised the car instantly. Small, square, black. Too small for a big man like Randle. She looked at the red door, behind which was the man who had stolen her son from her. The venom within her began to build; as did the fear of what she might discover when she confronted Randle. What had he done with Michael? Her heart was pounding as she and Charlie walked up the concrete footpath leading directly to the door. He sensed her emotions and put his arm round her shoulders. He knocked on the door, firmly. Randle opened it. Lily stepped in front of Charlie. She wanted to be the first one he saw, to see the expression on his face.

His face was expressionless. For twenty seconds they faced each other in silence, then Randle spoke.

'It's er, it's Lily, isn't it? What are you doing here, Lily?'

'I think you know very well what I'm doing here – Mr Oldroyd whose real name is Randle. Where's Michael? Where's my son?'

Randle looked beyond Lily at Charlie. 'Oldroyd? What is this? Who are you?'

'I'm a friend who's helping her find the son you took from her,' said Charlie, marginally surprised at the man's coolness.

'Ah, you're still at it are you? Accusing us of taking your son. I thought you might have seen sense by now. Why would you think I've got him? What would I do with him? This is just plain ridiculous!'

Lily's voice became shrill with frustration. 'Because you came to my house and took him away to Grassington where you said you lived.'

'We've never lived in Grassington, you ridiculous woman. We met you in Grassington but we never lived there. Whatever gave you that idea?'

A woman came to the door. 'Lily,' she said. 'What's this about?'

Lily stood her ground. She was on the verge of hysteria. 'Is Michael in there? If he is, I want him back, NOW!'

'Now Lily,' said Edith. 'Why would we have Michael?'

'Because you took him from me, that's why?' Lily was in tears now. She suddenly pushed past the Randles and charged into the house where she ran from room to room shouting her son's name. She flung open cupboard doors, wardrobe doors, the back door which led out on to a tiny garden with a small shed at the end of it. She ran to the shed and tried the door, which was locked. She started kicking at it, screaming Michael's name.

'Oh, for God's sake get the key to the shed before she wrecks it!' said Edith sharply.

Randle took a key off a hook and ran down the

garden where he opened the shed door. It was full of garden tools. No Michael. Lily sank to the ground, sobbing.

'Satisfied?' said Edith. 'I know you've had problems but it's no excuse for making such an accusation. If you carry on like this we'll sue you for slander. Strikes me you need some sort of treatment.' To Charlie, she said. 'Is she having any treatment?'

'Oh, she's had plenty of that, if you're talking about ill-treatment.' He knelt beside Lily to console her. Then he looked from Randle to his wife and back. 'How do you know Lily?' he asked, helping Lily to her feet.

Randle's words tumbled out. 'We met her and Michael in a café in Grassington.' He looked at his wife for confirmation. 'Is that not so, Edith?'

Edith nodded. Randle continued: 'She was taking a photo of her boy and I offered to take one of the two of them. I took Edith over to Grassington so she could get a house ready for a house contents auction. We got friendly with Lily and Michael and we all went over to the house together so that young Michael could play in the back garden. He had a lovely time, feeding horses in the back field and playing in the stream.'

'Really? You befriended them, did you? How long after you met Lily and Michael did you decide to take them off on this little jaunt?'

'I don't know – an hour, maybe.'

'Why would your wife go right over to Grassington to get a house ready? It must be forty miles away.'

Edith answered. 'I used to live near Grassington. I worked as housekeeper for the lady who lived there.

The estate agents trusted me with all the contents, some of which were quite valuable.'

'You just said you never lived in Grassington,' said Charlie.

'What I meant was *I* never lived in Grassington,' blustered Randle.

'When did you last see Lily?'

'Just after we heard about the tragic death of her husband,' Randle said. 'We went over to her house in Leeds to offer our condolences. I wish we hadn't bloody well bothered now!'

'Have you seen her since?'

'No.'

'So, when did she first accuse you of taking her son?'

'What?' said Randle, confused.

'A few minutes ago you said she'd previously accused you of taking her son. How could she do that if this is the first time you've seen her since you went to her house to offer your condolences?'

Charlie looked from one to the other.

'When?' he repeated. 'When did she accuse you of taking her son? Simple question.'

No answer.

'The truth is that she hasn't seen you to be able to accuse you of anything.'

No answer.

'So, you've given yourselves away, haven't you? So, where's the boy?

'We don't know what you're talking about!' snarled Randle. 'Now clear off!'

Charlie shook his head and held them both in his

contemptuous gaze as he said, 'I think we'd better let the police deal with this scum, Lily.'

'I agree,' said Randle harshly. 'I'll be damned well contacting them myself just as soon as you've gone! Stupid bloody woman!'

Charlie walked her back to his van. Before getting in she turned to him and said, 'He's a liar, Charlie. You know that, don't you?'

'Of course I know. I knew that before he said a single word.'

They were both in the van as Charlie explained. 'When he came to the door he pretended not to recognise you at first. How could he not instantly recognise a beautiful woman like you? He admitted to spending half a day with you in Grassington, then he came to visit you in Leeds and yet it still took him ages to speak when he came to the door.'

He started the vehicle and drove off towards the main road.

'I didn't speak either,' said Lily. 'I didn't know what to say to him.'

'I know, and that didn't help him. He and his wife will have anticipated such a moment and they'll have rehearsed it until they've almost convinced themselves they are telling the truth. With you turning up so unexpected like that he needed time to remember his lines. Obviously he slipped up when he said you'd previously accused him of taking your son. When was that supposed to have happened?

'His wife got straight into the act with her having had a bit more time to think. On top of which they

241

answered all my questions as though I was a copper, not just an ordinary bloke who'd no business asking such questions. They were going through a rehearsed routine. Trust me. They'd practised answering these questions before. And there's something else that gave them away . . .'

'What's that?'

'Well, the way they spoke to you just now tells me that they're an intrinsically unfriendly couple. I doubt if they've got many close friends.'

'None, according to Jimmy and Brenda,' said Lily.

'And yet, on their own admission, they befriended you and Michael to the extent that they took you off in their car within an hour of meeting you. Jimmy said Randle was a Jekyll and Hyde character which means he's obviously a man who can turn on the good guy act when it suits him and it suited him and his wife that day back in April.'

'Charlie, how do you know all this stuff?'

'I've been well trained in the art of being someone else – and I've spent a long time actually *being* someone else.'

'So, you believe Randle took Michael.'

'Absolutely. There are only two stories here: yours and theirs. You're the genuine article. No question of that. What I don't know is what they've done with him.'

'Or why they took him.'

'That's the real baffler. One of our problems is that we've now put them on their guard for when the police start asking them questions. I doubt if they'll slip up quite so easily again.'

'Are you saying we should have left it to the police, instead of barging in like that?'

Charlie shrugged. 'I don't know. Anyway, it's a bit late worrying about that now. However, they've given themselves away to me, so they'll know there are at least two people who know what they've done – not just you. They won't like that.'

He turned on to the A64 and headed west. 'If it comes to it,' he said, 'I could probably get the truth out of Randle, but it would have to be a last resort. People like Randle are basically men of straw. He'd crack fairly quickly if he thought the alternative was death.'

'Can you really do that?'

'I'm afraid so.'

'It wouldn't bother me what you did to him. Jesus! Charlie, what's happening to me? I'm not a cruel person.'

'You're a step closer to your son, that's what's happening to you.'

'So, what next? Are you going to go round there at four in the morning to torture him?'

'No. I think you should go to the police and tell them everything you know. You've got a match for the photograph. See what they can dig up about him.'

'But the Randles will just give the police the story they gave us, without the slip ups.'

'Oh, they'll no doubt give the coppers a much more convincing version – the full rehearsed script. But they'll be panicky, which is what I want them to be. To be found guilty of child abduction puts them in jail for a long time, they're bound to worried sick right now. After all this time they'll have thought they got away with it.'

'Which police? The ones in Malton?'

'Do no harm. The Randles are in their jurisdiction. The Malton boys will no doubt get in touch with the Leeds coppers.'

Chapter 39

'Mr and Mrs Randle, a very serious allegation has been made against you both and I'm duty bound to question you about them.'

'By "duty bound" I assume you mean you don't believe these allegations because they're being made by a poor young woman who's not right in her head?' said Edith.

DS Bannister was in the Randles' house along with a detective constable from Leeds and a uniformed sergeant from Malton. There was no doubt that the man in the photograph, whom Lily claimed had taken her son, was the man sitting across the table in front of him. The other person in the photograph, half out of shot, was his wife, Edith. They'd both admitted this. But being in a photograph isn't a crime unless the photograph is incriminating in some way, which it wasn't.

'Mrs Robinson says you went to her house on the afternoon of Friday the twenty-seventh of April this year and you left taking her son, Michael, with you – ostensibly to give her a break during her bereavement and to give Michael a weekend in the country, namely Grassington in the Yorkshire Dales.'

'Sergeant,' said Randle, 'we went to see her to offer

our condolences but we left alone. Why would we lie about this? There was never any mention of us taking him. We don't live in Grassington, we live here. On the day we met Lily and Michael we took them to a house in Grassington but it wasn't our house, it was a house where Edith needed to do a bit of work before a house contents auction. If you don't believe us, ask the estate agent.'

'The man dealing with it is Mr Penn,' added Edith.

'Yes, I've already spoken to Mr Penn,' said Bannister, looking at them to see if this raised any sign of worry in their faces. It didn't.

'Mrs Robinson says that she and Michael stayed the night at a Lark House, which she assumed was your house.'

'I'm sorry but Lily knew full well it wasn't our house, Sergeant,' said Edith. 'We talked about how we'd like to live in a grand place like that. I only went there to do a bit of dusting and tidying before the auction. Lily left late that same afternoon. She'd missed her coach back so we dropped her off in Skipton to catch the bus. What time was it when you ran her into Skipton, Bernard?'

'Well, I know her coach was leaving at five and she didn't realise what time it was until it was half an hour too late. We took her in soon after that – I reckon about six because we had to get home. I was on duty that night. I think she got a bus direct through to Leeds.'

'Early the following morning the auctioneers were due to go in to set up,' said Edith. 'It'd look well for them to turn up and find us in one of the beds and Lily and her son in another room.'

246

DS Bannister made a note that Randle should have been on camp the night Lily said he was in Grassington. If there was any record of that, her story would crumble. Also he needed to check with the estate agent that their auctioneer had gone round early the following morning and found the house empty; and that Mrs Randle had once been a housekeeper there; and that she'd been employed to do some dusting and tidying before the auction.

He also needed to check with Lily the time she said she'd left the house that morning. On the face of it, he should be able to disprove her allegation within twenty-four hours. Check with the camp records, check with the estate agent, talk to Lily again. Ask her why she's lying.

Ask her what she did with her son.

Chapter 40

'How did you know where I was?' Lily asked Bannister.

They were in Dee's house. It was the following after-noon. Dee and Charlie were there. Charlie had taken a week off work, much to his dad's annoyance. But it seemed to Charlie that Lily was at a crucial point in tracking down her son and she needed all the help she could get.

'I'm a detective, Mrs Robinson. It's my job to detect people.'

It wasn't much of an answer but it was obviously the only one she was going to get so she didn't pursue the matter.

'I've done some checking on Bernard Randle,' he went on, 'and it seems he was on night duty at Eden camp the night you say he was at Lark House.'

'What?'

'The army keep duty records. I checked them this morning. He was on duty from ten p.m. until six in the morning.'

'He has a reputation as a fiddler,' said Charlie. 'Who's to say he hasn't fiddled the duty records?'

Bannister gave this some thought and sighed. 'On the

night you say you were at Lark House what time did you go to bed?'

'Not late,' said Lily. 'I'd say about ten o'clock.'

'And Randle was there when you went to bed?'

'Yes, he was.'

'You see my problem? Army records have him at Eden camp at ten o'clock.'

'Army records are wrong then,' said Lily adamantly.

'You'll find that's not so unusual,' said Charlie. Bannister wished he'd shut up.

'The following morning,' Bannister went on. 'What time did you leave?'

'Oh, fairly early. I was up at seven, so I reckon it was about eight o'clock. Randle and his wife took us to a transport café for breakfast, then dropped us off in Malton.'

'I see.'

This put paid to a challenge he had in mind. The auctioneers had arrived at the house at nine o'clock. Charlie interrupted again.

'A transport café? You mean they couldn't manage to rustle up some breakfast in their own house?'

Lily tried to cast her mind back. 'They had no milk for tea or cereal or anything. I remember this because Randle was just coming in the house as I got downstairs. He said he'd been to the village to get some milk but nowhere was open.'

'I'm not surprised,' said Charlie. 'What sort of village shop opens before seven o'clock to sell milk? I reckon he'd just got in from camp, Sergeant.'

'I'd appreciate it if you wouldn't interrupt, Mr—'

'Cleghorn,' said Charlie. 'Do you mind if I ask Lily a question of my own?'

Bannister sighed and said, 'If you must.'

'Lily,' said Charlie. 'You say that the Randles took you for breakfast to a transport café?'

'They did, yes. In fact they took us to the same café the previous evening for a meal.'

'Did they now?' said Charlie, looking at Bannister. 'Tell me, all the time you were at the house did they provide any sort food or drink – maybe just a cup of tea and a biscuit?'

Lily thought back and shook her head slowly. 'No . . . I don't think they did.'

'Of course they didn't,' said Charlie. 'It wasn't their house. There'd be no food there. Did you not think it odd that they only fed you in that café?'

'At the time, no. They just went on about how good it was and what good value it was. They said they often dined there.'

'And was it good?'

'It was passable, but I wouldn't make a habit of it.'

'Mr Bannister,' said Charlie, 'might I suggest you ask some questions at the café? See if anyone remembers seeing the Randles with Lily and her son having breakfast on Friday April the sixth. Maybe they'll also have some duty roster they can refer to.'

'That's a very long shot,' said Bannister. 'People come in and out of cafés all the time. Who's going to remember a face from four months ago?'

'Do no harm to try,' said Charlie. 'Lily could go with you. She has a memorable face, you have to admit.' He turned to Lily. 'Is there anyone at the café you remember? Maybe someone spoke to Michael – or had a joke with you if you'd been there twice in the space of what, fourteen, fifteen hours?'

'It was the same person both times – I remember that,' said Lily. 'A man. I think he ran it with his wife and daughter. His wife did the cooking. There was hardly anyone in at breakfast time. The previous evening it had been packed.'

'What do they call it?' Bannister asked, taking out his notebook.

Lily shook her head. 'I don't remember. Yes I do – it's the Wharfedale Café. It's on the main road from Grassington to Skipton, probably halfway to Skipton.'

Bannister scribbled something in his book and got to his feet. Dee followed him with her eyes and spoke for the first time. 'You thought you'd got Lily bang to rights, didn't you, Sergeant? I bet there's a constable sitting in your car outside to assist with her arrest.'

'The Randles took Michael, Sergeant,' Charlie said. 'Didn't you notice how plausible they both were? A ready answer to every question you could throw at them. Aren't you trained to take such people with a very large pinch of salt?'

Bannister looked at Charlie and said, 'We're trained to collect evidence, Mr Cleghorn, and there's no evidence against the Randles except Mrs Robinson's word and, so far, she hasn't behaved in a manner to encourage me to take her word as gospel. I'm aware she went into hysterics in Randle's house yesterday – I have the evidence of their next-door neighbour to that effect.'

251

He walked to the door, then paused with his hand on the handle. 'We're also trained,' he said, 'to take with a very large pinch of salt the word of unstable people. I'm very sorry about your husband, Mrs Robinson, but I have to play it as I see it. I'll be back.'

'Hold on a minute, Sergeant,' said Dee, going to a drawer and taking out a packet of photographs. She gave Bannister the one of Lily and Michael that Randle had taken. 'If you're going to that café you'll need to show the man this.'

As Bannister drove back to Leeds, along with the constable he'd brought along, he didn't know what to think. Mrs Randle's story checked out with the estate agent who confirmed that she'd once been the house-keeper at Lark House and that they'd employed her to help prepare the house for the auction.

First thing tomorrow morning he'd be at that transport café between Grassington and Skipton with photos of Randle, Lily and Michael. He was secretly hoping that the man would recognise them and confirm Lily's version of events, but he wasn't holding his breath.

Chapter 41

Bannister stood in front of the Wharfedale Café with his hands on his hips and a look of resignation on his face. It was eight a.m. and the place was closed and up for sale. He walked round the back to see if there were any living quarters but all he found was a garage, kitchen, toilets and some sort of storeroom. On the way it had occurred to him that he ought to call in to Malton police station purely as a matter of courtesy to inform them of what he was doing on their patch and to ask what they knew about the owners, but it seemed a waste of time. Not any more. He needed to find out where the owners had gone.

The estate agents were Weetman and Penn, the same as the ones selling Lark House and he wondered if this was a coincidence. Probably not. Estate agents weren't exactly thick on the ground in Grassington, but it might be more fruitful to ask them where the café owners were.

Ten minutes later he was outside the offices of Weetman and Penn, mildly cursing at a sign that said they didn't open until nine. He was peckish, having had no breakfast, so he drove around Grassington looking for a café that might be open or a shop that might sell him a bar of chocolate. But the entire village, it seemed, didn't open until at least nine o'clock. He remembered Lily saying that Randle had been down to the village to get milk but couldn't get any. If her story were true, that part of it would make sense.

The problem with her story was that the overall picture didn't make sense. If Randle had abducted the child for sexual purposes – and Bannister couldn't think of any other reason – a man of his age would have some sort of history in that field, especially if his wife was in it with him. But Randle had no criminal record of any kind and his military record was unblemished, albeit unheroic. The Randles had no children of their own and had never been seen with any, particularly around the time Michael had been abducted. Nor had Randle ever shown any unhealthy interest in children. Bannister's enquiries at Eden Camp had been discreet but thorough. He knew how to do his job. He thought about Charlie's interruptions the previous day and muttered to himself. *Don't try to tell me how to do my job, Mister!*

Penn arrived at five minutes to nine and parked at the back of the offices. Bannister was standing in front of the door as Penn opened it for business.

'Ah, it's er . . . ?'

'Detective Sergeant Bannister of the Leeds City police.'

'Of course. How can I help you, Detective Sergeant? I assume it's to do with the events at Lark House, last April.'

'It's in connection with that – but what I need to know is the whereabouts of the owners of the Wharfedale

Café which you appear to be selling on their behalf. They may be able to help us with our enquiries.'

'Oh, I see. Well, I can only give you the whereabouts of one of the joint owners, that is the wife – Olga Fairclough. You see, they split up in May. Apparently he ran off with one of the part-time waitresses. A young woman half his age. No idea where he is, but his wife might know. She lives here in Grassington but I'm not sure how obliging she'll be. She's taken this whole thing very badly.'

'Right, well, could you give me her address and directions, please. I believe they have a daughter who worked there.'

'Yes, she lives with her mother. You might get more sense out of her.'

Olga Fairclough and her eighteen-year-old daughter, Peggy, had both taken a good look at the photographs Bannister had showed them and neither recognised Lily, Michael or Randle.

'It will have been about a month before, er . . .'

'Before me husband ran off with that bloody woman!' said Olga. Her daughter put a hand on her mother's arm.

'Mum and I both worked mostly in the kitchen. We didn't get to see many of the customers.'

'But your father will have seen them.'

'Oh yes,' said Olga bitterly. She stabbed a finger at Lily's photo. 'He'll have clocked her all right, pretty woman like that – and he'll probably remember her.'

Peggy was nodding her agreement. It seemed as though her father had made enemies of both of them.

'But you don't know where he is?'

'No idea,' snapped Olga, 'but he'll crawl out from under his stone when the café gets sold, tryin' ter claim his half of the money. I tell yer, he's got a shock comin' to him. He'll get bugger-all if I have owt ter do with it. This house is in joint names as well – bought and paid for, but I'm stayin' put. He's not sellin' this from under my feet. Yer can tell him that when yer see him.'

Bannister scratched his head. 'That's the problem. I can't see him if I don't know where he is.'

'If we hear anything we'll let you know,' said Peggy.

'Thank you. I'll see myself out.'

He got into his car wondering if he should call in at Malton police station. He should by rights have called in as soon as he came on to their patch, so he might have to apologise for that to start with. He knew he'd have to grit his teeth and call in because they just might have a clue as to the whereabouts of the errant café owner.

They didn't.

Chapter 42

Time moved on for Lily at an excruciatingly slow pace. She was missing Christopher, she was missing Michael and she was missing Larry. She knew who the man was who'd taken Michael but she couldn't do anything about it. The police couldn't, or wouldn't. Dee would if she only could. Her only hope seemed to be to take up Charlie on his offer to beat the truth out of Randle.

Dee was wondering whether or not to offer her motorbike combination in part exchange for a van she'd seen in the paper. She'd mentioned it to Lily, who had other things on her mind.

'Charlie thinks he could get the truth out of him,' she said.

Despite her own propensity for violence, Dee was dead against it. 'If anything happens to Randle, Charlie will be number one suspect. I don't know too much about what he did in the army but he sounds as if he was trained to do some very dodgy stuff. You know Charlie's potty about you, don't you?'

'We're just friends, that's all.'

'Well, I should have a word with that friend of yours and tell him you don't want him charging in. Using force could ruin things for all of us, especially for Michael.'

'I know, but it's been a month since we found out about Randle and we're no nearer getting the truth out of him. I sometimes feel like going over there and beating it out of them myself.'

'You and me both, girl.'

'They must be laughing at me right now.'

'If they are,' Dee said, 'I might have an idea to make them laugh on the other side of their faces.'

'What's that?'

'Well, from what I gather, Randle isn't the most popular kid on camp.'

'Pretty much the opposite according to Jimmy and Brenda.'

'Who's Brenda?'

'She's in the ATS. Works at Eden camp as some sort of receptionist.'

'And she's not a fan of Randle?'

'You could say that. She's got a right mouth on her. Didn't take to her at first, but when I realised how much she disliked Randle I sort of warmed to her.'

Dee smiled. 'She sounds about right. We need everyone on that camp to know what the Randles have done. We need to find someone who'll spread the story.'

'Ah . . . and you think Brenda's the one? She might enjoy it.'

'What about asking that pal of Charlie's as well?'

'Jimmy? Yeah, he might help.' Lily thought for a few moments. A rumour about child abduction would turn everyone on camp against the Randles. 'If such a rumour takes off it could be really poisonous for the Randles,' she murmured.

'Oh dear,' said Dee. 'That would never do.'

Within the hour Lily was talking to Brenda on the phone, telling her the full story. Brenda was instantly on Lily's side.

'Oh my God, Lily! I knew there was something he'd done to you but I didn't think it was as bad as that. I asked Jimmy but he wouldn't tell me. Said he didn't know, but I didn't believe him.'

'Jimmy knows all about it, so does Charlie. They can tell who they like. So can you.'

'Lily, are you and Charlie, er . . . ?'

'Charlie and I are friends.' Lily found it a hard answer to give.

'Right. I quite fancied him myself at one time but I've got a feller of my own now. RAF officer based at Church Fenton.'

'Brylcreem Boy eh?'

'Oh, he's lovely. Flight Lieutenant James Durkin-Smyth. Met him at a dance.' She paused for a few seconds, then said, 'Lily, I hardly know you. Why have you told me all this?'

'Because I think people should know what the Randles have done to me. Even the police think he's guilty but they can't break him.'

She'd made up that bit, but it added credibility to her story.

'So, you actually *want* me to start spreading the word about that creep, is that it?'

'Something like that. I'll be speaking to Jimmy as

well. See if I can persuade him into backing you up, saying he's heard the same story.'

Brenda gave a short laugh. 'With the two of us at it, it'll be round the camp in a day, and all over Malton by the day after that.' Lily detected a note of glee in her voice. 'In fact,' added Brenda, 'I reckon I can have it all over Church Fenton RAF camp by the weekend.'

'So, you'll do it?'

'Do it? Try and stop me! I don't hear stories like this every day about a pillock like Randle. Believe me, Lily, in a couple of days he won't dare come out from under his stone.'

'Thanks, Brenda.'

Lily put the phone down and looked at Dee with raised eyebrows, happy with herself to have taken some action against Randle.

'I take it she's agreed to do it?'

'With knobs on,' said Lily. 'Randle's in trouble. Do you think we should mention this to your pal on the *Craven Herald*?'

'Do no harm to tell him,' said Dee. 'He might be able to make something of it if he doesn't mention any names.'

Henry Smithson of the *Craven Herald* decided against running such a destructive unsubstantiated rumour in his newspaper but wished Dee the best of luck with it.

'If the rumour becomes public knowledge I might be able to do something with it, but right now it's just inviting an indefensible libel action. I'd be obliged if you keep me up to date with how things are going with all this.'

Ten days later Squadron Leader Hector Manders,

DSO, DFC, of RAF Church Fenton, put a call through to the officer in command of Eden camp. His voice oozed authority.

'Am I speaking to the officer in command?'

'You are. This is Major Bykers. To whom am I speaking?'

Bykers knew exactly who he was speaking to. Manders was a well-known war hero. Bykers' telephonist had told him who it was, but he didn't like this man's tone of voice.

'Squadron Leader Manders, Church Fenton.'

'How can I help you, Squadron Leader?'

'Well, there's a particularly nasty rumour going around this camp regarding some of your men abducting children for disgusting purposes. Children who subsequently and mysteriously disappear.'

'And you actually believe this nonsense, do you, Squadron Leader?'

'It matters little what I believe. Such a vile rumour will do His Majesty's forces no end of harm. There's just one actual name being bandied about – that of a Sergeant Randle. I take it you've heard this rumour.'

'I've heard the original version of it. It's obviously become much more lurid as it spread. It's completely untrue of course.'

'Do you have a Sergeant Randle?'

Bykers chose not to prolong this conversation. This man's attitude was annoying him. He was of equivalent rank and he didn't have to kow-tow to Manders. 'Thank you for letting me know, Squadron Leader. I now have urgent matters to attend to.'

He put down the phone. His face was red with anger that this bloody silly nonsense should have spread as far as Church Fenton. One of his officers had already had a word in his ear about the rumour which, at that time, was indeed confined to one man – Sergeant Randle. He also knew the police had been questioning Randle about a missing boy, but the police had taken no action so he'd chosen to leave well alone lest he give this appalling rumour credence. Things had apparently gone too far. He went to his office door and spoke to a corporal sitting at a desk.

'Corporal, bring Sergeant Randle to my office at the bloody double.'

Chapter 43

Had DS Bannister known the outcome he might not have let slip the name Dee McGuire when he was interviewing Randle. In general conversation, after he'd become convinced that the Randles had nothing to do with Michael's abduction, he had mentioned that Lily was living with a woman of that name in Shipley. It took Randle just a few minutes to track down her address in a Bradford phone book. It was entered under D. McGuire but it was the only D. McGuire in the book.

Randle had watched the house for five hours, from seven a.m. until noon. He'd seen Dee leave on her motorbike at eight and watched as Lily came out to put some rubbish in the bin at quarter past ten. All during that morning no one else came in or out. He wanted to make sure that no one else was in the house, particularly the young man who'd brought Lily and Dee out to camp. The man's van wasn't there. There was no van of any description outside the house. He had to be sure she was in on her own. At five past twelve he walked past the house. He was wearing a flat cap pulled down over his face, and workman's overalls; had she looked up from her book she would have seen him but wouldn't have recognised him. He saw her, alone in the front room, reading.

He walked up the drive, whistling loudly, and knocked on the door. It was the standard cheery knock that usually represented a friend, a neighbour or a sneaky salesman. Lily put down her book and went to the door. Randle was standing with his back to her, checking that no one in the street could witness what he did next. As soon as he heard the door open he spun round, pushed her back into the hallway, strode inside after her and slammed the door behind him.

'Now then you bitch! What have you been saying about me? What lies have you been telling?'

Lily was frozen with shock. The only dealings she'd ever had with Randle had been amicable, albeit false on his part. This was a different man, totally unbalanced. His teeth were bared and he was snarling like a mad dog. She said nothing. She knew that anything she might say would only make him worse, if that were possible. He put a hand round her throat and squeezed until she couldn't breathe.

'Give me a reason why I should let you live, bitch! Have you any idea how much damage your lies have done?'

He let go of her throat just as she was about to pass out. She sank to the floor, coughing and spluttering. He knelt down beside her, with his mouth an inch from her face, spraying spit as he spoke. 'Your brat of a boy is dead. He wouldn't behave, so he's dead, just like you'll be dead very shortly. No one spreads filthy lies about me and lives. Do you hear me, bitch? I'm going to kill you for what you've done!'

Him saying that Michael was dead filled her with a mixture of despair and rage. She hit out at him with her fists and began screaming. 'Murderer! You murdered my little boy, you filthy murderer!'

He put his hand over her mouth to stifle her screams and began to laugh at her, enjoying her despair.

'Like mother like son. He screamed just like you did when I told him he was going to die. Cried his snivelling little eyes out he did. Cried for his mummy. I want my mummy! Snivelling little brat! It was a pleasure choking him to death just to shut him up.'

Lily collapsed to the floor in floods of tears. Her Michael was dead. She didn't care what this vile man did to her. He could kill her if he wanted to. He put his hands on her throat and began to squeeze, still laughing. She closed her eyes. All she could think of was Michael. There was a roaring sound in her ears. Was this it? Was this the sound of death? The roaring grew louder.

She could breathe again. The pressure on her throat had gone. Her breath was coming in short gasps. She opened her eyes and looked up at the ceiling. He was gone. The roaring had stopped. Someone else was there: Auntie Dee. Leaning over her; looking down at her; asking what had happened. Lily couldn't form any words yet. All she could do was cough. Dee could now see red marks on her neck.

'Lily, who did this? What the hell's happened?'

It took a full minute before Lily could get out the name, 'Randle.'

'Randle? Where?'

'Here. He was here.'

Lily exploded in a fit of coughing

'Take it easy, girl. I'll get you some water.'

Dee went into the kitchen and saw the back door was open. Randle had gone, but there was time to deal with him. She knew where he lived, so did the police. She took a glass of water to Lily, who had stopped coughing now but was weeping profusely.

'Lily, it's OK. He's gone. We can have him arrested now. We can get Michael back.'

Lily looked up at her with intense despair in her eyes. 'Auntie Dee, Michael's dead. He killed him.'

Chapter 44

Tom Cleghorn arrived on site in a firm's lorry and walked over to where Charlie was using a pneumatic drill to cut a series of holes in the base of a brick railway bridge in preparation for packing them with demolition charges.

'A woman's been on the phone back at the yard asking for you. She said it's urgent.'

He didn't seem too pleased to be delivering such a message – a message that might take his son away from an important job. Charlie put down the drill.

'Who was it?'

'A woman. Calls herself Dee or something. She sounded a bit harassed. She says you know her number.'

'It's Lily's friend. Give me a minute.'

Charlie went up the road to a nearby phone box and dialled Dee's number. She answered first ring.

'Dee, it's Charlie. Is there a problem?'

'You could say that! Randle's been round to the house and tried to kill Lily. If I hadn't come home when I did she'd have been a goner.'

'You saw him, did you?'

'No, I think the noise of my motorbike scared him

off. The exhaust's blowing – saved Lily's life more than likely – and to think I nearly swapped it for a van last week. He tried to strangle her.'

'Have you told the police?'

'I rang DS Bannister in Leeds. He's been and gone five minutes ago.'

'To arrest Randle, presumably.'

'I bloody well hope so.' She paused before continuing. 'Charlie, Randle told Lily he'd killed Michael. She's in a right state. I can't console her. I think you should come over.'

'I'm on my way.'

He went back onto the site. His dad knew Lily's story.

'Randle's attacked Lily, tried to kill her. I need to go over there.'

His dad looked less than pleased. 'It's a police matter, son. You start interfering, you'll get your fingers burned.'

'She's a friend, Dad. Would you mind finishing off here? I've practically done all the prep.'

His dad didn't look at all pleased.

'Dad, I wouldn't ask if it wasn't important.'

'Yeah, this job's important as well.'

'I need to see her, Dad.'

Tom Cleghorn sighed. He was immensely proud of his son, who done well in the army and was also a highly qualified explosives expert. Much of his training he'd got under his dad's tuition before he was called up, but the army had put some fine finishing touches to his expertise. Charlie knew more about explosives than his dad ever would.

'Look, son, I'm going to have to get another licensed

268

explosives man in to replace you. We can't go on like this.'

'What? You're sacking me?'

'No, I'm just not relying on you until you've sorted your life out. We've got plenty of work on, so you can come in, as and when you like, and you'll get paid for the hours you work.'

'Fair enough,' said Charlie, stripping off his boiler suit. 'I take it I still get use of the van?'

'For the time being,' his dad said. 'But it is a firm's van. The firm takes precedence over your private life. Better that you use that bike of yours.'

When Charlie arrived Lily was sitting on the settee in the front room, drip-white, arms round her knees, rocking to and fro. He sat down beside her.

'He's lying,' said Charlie. 'That's what he does. That's what he's good at.'

Lily said nothing for a while, then she asked, in a tiny voice, 'About M . . . Michael, you mean?'

'About everything, Lily. It's all he's done since you first clapped eyes on him. Michael's alive.' He gave Lily a squeeze. 'He'll be lying to the police right now.' He looked up at Dee. 'Did anyone other than Lily see him?'

Dee shrugged. 'Not that I know of.'

'If they did,' said Lily, 'they probably wouldn't recognise him as Randle. I didn't myself for a few seconds. He was wearing overalls and a flat cap.'

'He'll have an alibi,' surmised Charlie. 'No doubt his wife. Once again it'll be Lily's word against theirs.'

'Well, Lily didn't attack herself,' said Dee heatedly. 'Who the hell will the police think did it?'

'Bannister might well think it was Randle, but without independent witnesses he won't be able to prove it,' said Charlie. He gave Lily another reassuring squeeze. 'Right now him and his wife'll be lying their socks off. They'll have prepared his alibi very carefully just as they prepared the story about them not taking Michael.'

'Why did he take Michael, do you think?' Lily asked.

There was an obvious answer which neither Charlie not Dee wanted to contemplate. They both wondered if the same thought was on Lily's mind.

'I don't know,' said Charlie, 'but he didn't take him just to kill him, where's the sense in that? And he's got no record of being a man who ... likes children. Michael's alive, Lily. Don't let him get to you.'

'I was terrified,' said Lily. 'He was like some evil madman.'

'Jimmy said he was a Jekyll and Hyde character,' Charlie remembered.

'Charlie, he's a monster,' Lily said. 'He would have killed me if Auntie Dee hadn't turned up.' She turned to look at him. 'Do you honestly think my boy's alive?'

There was too much desperation in her voice for him to say anything other than, 'I most definitely do, Lily, and I know you don't want me to, but if he gets away with this, as I suspect he will, I'll get the truth out of him my way.' He looked from one to the other. 'Any objections?'

Lily and Dee looked at each other then shook their heads. 'That's it, then,' said Charlie. 'I'm glad you agree, ladies, because you're my alibis.'

Later that evening, when Lily was in the bathroom, Dee asked Charlie the truth.

'Do you honestly think Michael's alive?'

'I honestly think Randle's an inveterate liar whose word can't be trusted so I don't see why we should take his word about anything. More than likely he was just saying it to add to Lily's misery before he killed her. He probably enjoyed saying it. There are people like that around, you know.'

'I know, but how certain are you that Michael's still alive?'

Charlie looked at the doorway into the hall to make sure Lily wasn't listening. 'About sixty per cent sure,' he said quietly. 'No more.'

'Me too,' said Dee.

Chapter 45

Charlie had learned from Jimmy that Randle would be leaving camp at two a.m. having come off duty. He'd be walking back to his quarters. It was three days after the attack on Lily and, as Charlie predicted, Edith had given Randle an alibi and Randle had told the police that he wouldn't be surprised if all the harm done to Lily was self-inflicted just to frame him.

DI Foster called the sergeant into his office when the complaint was made via the Bradford police.

'Bradford are trying to pass this one over to us with it being part of an ongoing case. The thing is, do we want to waste time investigating such a matter on their patch?'

'Apparently, she does bear the marks of an attack, sir.'

'Didn't she harm herself when she was in hospital having her baby?'

'Yes, sir.'

'Is there any reason to suppose she couldn't have done it again simply to get Randle arrested. If he hadn't got an alibi he'd be in custody by now.'

'Well, I'm not sure how she could strangle herself, sir. That would take a very determined nutcase, and she doesn't strike me as being such a person.'

'With women like that anything's possible, John. She could certainly inflict strangulation wounds on herself if she was sufficiently disturbed mentally. Randle claimed he didn't even know where Robinson lived. I mean, where would he get her address from? She was living in hiding with that Maguire woman.'

Bannister felt a twinge of guilt but said nothing.

'I'm going to bounce it back to Bradford, John, along with our view on the matter. Is this OK with you?'

'Yes, sir.'

'Good. If Bradford are daft enough to follow it up it's their problem.'

Brenda had been called into Major Bykers' office. She'd already started a rumour about there being paedophiles among the ranks and had been tracked down as one of the instigators of the story. Under serious questioning by the major she'd admitted that Lily had asked her to start the rumour.

'But only because I think she's right, sir,' she'd added in mitigation. 'I never said anything about anyone else doing anything, just him, sir.'

'Really? Perhaps you should have had the common sense to foresee the repercussions of your foolishness. Corporal Witherspoon, for bringing this camp into disrepute you are now reduced in rank to Private Witherspoon. That is all.'

'Sir.'

It was now one a.m. Charlie was ten miles from Eden camp and about to go into action for the first time since his last mission in the Lombard province of Northern Italy, which had still been occupied by the Germans in June 1944. He'd spent six months in Allied-occupied Sicily, brushing up his Italian, in particular the Lombard accent. His job was to go up to Porto Valtravaglia on Lake Maggiore and infiltrate the Legione SS Italiana.

His new identity had been provided for him by Carlo Graziano, a dead fascist from Varese, a young man who wouldn't be missed. He was the of same age, appearance and build as Charlie and had been killed and buried without trace. Killed to order, purely because of this resemblance. Charlie took Graziano's identity papers, now altered with Charlie's photo replacing the dead man's, and including Graziano's Republican Fascist Party membership card which was virtually a passport throughout German-occupied Northern Italy.

Charlie's infiltration into the Italian SS was eased by an Italian SS officer who was working undercover for the partisans. Charlie's job was to supervise the destruction of two ammunition dumps: one in Porto Valtravaglia and one in neighbouring Laveno-Mombello. His expertise with explosives was well up to the job required, as was his combat training as a soldier of the elite SAS where he'd served first in North Africa and now Italy. It was this expertise plus his language skills which had got him this job. Charlie was one of life's natural linguists. He'd won a scholarship to a grammar school where he'd struggled with maths and science but excelled at French and Latin with a special gift for accents. Italian came later, as did German.

His fake, but accurate, Lombard accent was never

suspected when he joined the Italian SS. He lived, worked, ate and slept with the enemy for four months before he put his skills to good use. It had been the best and worst four months of his life. The worst because of the constant threat of being found out and handed over to the Gestapo; the best because he'd got through it and carried out the job successfully.

For an Englishman to impersonate an Italian takes more than just language skills. He needed to think like an Italian, act like an Italian and have Italian mannerisms, all of which were alien to his English background. Charlie had proved to be uniquely talented in this field, but the danger to his life was real and constant.

He'd once stepped in when two SS soldiers decided to rape a local woman during a routine three-man patrol. At first, Charlie had pretended to go along with the rape then, at an opportune moment, had moved behind them and knocked them both unconscious with the butt of his rifle before sending the terrified woman off to make contact with the local partisans who took the soldiers away to a fate Charlie didn't want to think about. His only demand was that the men never be seen again, alive or dead.

He'd returned to camp and reported them to his captain as deserters. 'I last saw them heading for the Swiss border, Capitano, not five miles away. They tried to persuade me to go with them but I refused.'

'You should have shot them.'

Charlie had thrown out his arms, expressively. 'That very thought did occur to me, Capitano, but how would I have explained it to you? I could never have proved they were deserting.'

Desertion was not uncommon during this time. Many soldiers, especially Italians, could see an inevitability about the war's outcome and they didn't want to end up on the wrong side. Charlie's story was accepted and he was accorded the dubious privilege of wearing a red, Waffen–SS collar tab.

A month later, under his close supervision, two groups of Italian partisans blew up the Porto Valtravaglia ammunition dump at midnight and the dump at Laveno-Mombello at four a.m. The massive explosions lit up the night sky for several minutes on each occasion and could be seen fifty miles away in Milan.

It was a major blow to the Italian SS; to the fanatical Brigates Nere (Black Brigade) and to the MVSN (Milizia Volontaria per la Sicurezza Nazionale), who were all active in the area and supposedly on top of the partisan problem. The local populace braced themselves for the usual murderous reprisals but Charlie had arranged for enough subtle evidence to be left at both scenes to indicate that the attack had been carried out by British commandos and not local partisans, who wouldn't have had the expertise to carry out such a brilliant raid.

When word got back to Hitler he took his reprisals out on the senior officers. Many of them, both German and Italian, were sent to the Russian Front where Germany was suffering badly against the Russian counter-offensive.

At five a.m. Charlie and the undercover officer were over the border in Switzerland. The action earned Charlie a Military Medal and an early demob.

The action he was about to embark tonight on might earn him a substantial prison sentence, if not worse.

Then he thought about Lily and smiled. She was most definitely worth the risk.

Sergeant Bernard Randle kept his head down as he left the compound and made his way to his quarters. The vile rumour was still rife. He'd first been told about it by another sergeant; the one who usually never spoke to him; the one who had once given him a good hiding. Not that that would have happened in his younger days. In his younger days he'd have given Dunkersley a sound beating. He'd been given a severe roasting by the CO, despite his protestations of innocence, and now he was being stared at by everyone, even by the German prisoners. Someone who could speak German had passed the rumour on to them and, apart from the prisoners themselves, he only knew of one man on camp who could speak fluent German. Sergeant Jimmy bloody Dunkersley.

He knew it was time to call his army career a day. Joined up at eighteen, two years before the First World War and had spent the full four years of that war fighting in France. He could apply for a discharge any time he wanted and he wanted out now. Along with his army pension they had enough money to see him into a comfortable retirement; enough to buy a nice bungalow somewhere down south. Bournemouth maybe. He'd never been to Bournemouth but he liked the sound of it. So did Edith. Respectable place full of respectable people. Respect was what he craved right now. The bitch Robinson had taken all that away. She deserved to die and no mistake. Pity he'd been disturbed.

He'd killed a few in his time, over in France, and he'd grown to like it. He'd killed one or two of his own by mistake but no one knew. In the fury of battle it was bound to happen. He could fire off the ten rounds from his Lee-Enfield 303 almost as fast as a machine-gun. He'd devised a method of pretending to fall back in the trench after the order was given to go over the top. He would do this a couple of times before managing to climb out, thus creating a shield of protective men between him the murderous machine-gun fire coming his way. He would kneel beside the first dead Tommy he came across, acting as if the man was still alive and he was trying to help him. Then he'd take cover behind the body of the dead man as the German guns mowed down the men in front of him by the hundred, occasionally looking out from over the body to fire off a few rounds in the general direction of the Hun. It was inevitable that he'd shoot a couple of his comrades in the back from such a position but, in the heat and the smoke and the noise and the mud, no one actually knew what he'd done and there were no close friends among them – he knew that because he had no close friends – so what the hell? They most probably would have been killed by the Hun anyway.

At one point his ruse had been rumbled by a sergeant who cursed him for being a coward and threatened to shoot him if he didn't move forward. A shell had exploded nearby, knocking the sergeant off his feet. Randle looked around to see if anyone was watching, then shot the sergeant through the heart and, for the first and last time, followed his comrades towards the

German lines, knowing the sergeant was dead, but not quite sure if it had been the exploding shell or his bullet that killed him.

Killing the Robinson bitch would have given him more satisfaction than all of the Hun he'd killed put together. Too late now. He'd missed his chance. To go back and try again was just asking for trouble. The police were not *that* stupid. He smiled to himself at the way he'd pulled the wool over DS Bannister's eyes. Told him lie after blatant lie and the silly bugger believed him. No wonder crime was so rife in this country.

He was so engrossed in thought that he didn't hear the quiet footsteps behind him. He stopped for a couple of seconds to take the house keys from his pocket. In that couple of seconds the man behind him took up a stance at a ninety-degree angle to Randle's back.

The classic, reverse karate chop to the carotid artery behind Randle's left ear was delivered with such skill and precision that he knew nothing about it. The next thing he did know was when he regained consciousness in the back of a van, blindfolded, his hands and feet bound, and a gag over his mouth.

Lily was unaware of what Charlie was doing. She knew she'd given him carte-blanche to extract information from Randle in any way he could and that didn't bother her as much as it might have done in recent weeks. She had to know for certain if her son was alive. Charlie's assertion that he *was* alive made sense, but she also knew that Charlie was saying that to save her from complete despair. What she did know was that Randle was perfectly capable of murder. But why would he kidnap her son just to kill him? Not for the first time she cast the obvious answer out of her mind as too awful to contemplate.

But somehow Charlie's assurance that Michael was alive had buoyed her spirits. Charlie's very presence in her life buoyed her spirits just at a time when she needed that. She went to bed that night thinking about him as well as about Michael and Christopher. Larry was in there somewhere, but was gradually receding from her heart. For this she felt guilty. But first things first.

First she had to find her boy. His prolonged absence from her life was gnawing away at her very soul. If she could only get definite confirmation that he was still alive it would ease this constant pain and give her renewed hope. Bringing Michael home alive and well was the answer to everything.

Randle felt the van leave the hard road and go onto an uneven surface, some sort of cart track. His hands were tied behind his back and the bindings attached to his feet were tied in such a manner as to allow him to just about stand up and walk, as and when required. He was guessing this requirement wasn't too far off. There was a familiar, not unpleasant smell in the van. The smell of cordite. It reminded him of his time in the war. Cordite was a propellant for guns. What he didn't know was that a certain ex-army man, now in the demolition business, had found a use for it in his work.

The van stopped. The driver's door opened and closed. Randle's heart was racing. He thought this might be something to do with the Robinson woman but he couldn't be sure. Over the years he'd made quite a few enemies, done his share of back-stabbing, got a few soldiers into unnecessary trouble, but nothing that would merit this.

The back door opened and he was grabbed by the feet and pulled out of the van until his head banged against soft ground. He could hear a soft rushing sound, the sound of water. Then a man's voice. Irish.

'On yer feet, scum!'

Jesus, he hadn't made an enemy of any Irishmen to the best of his knowledge. He struggled, first to his knees and to his feet. An owl hooted, wind rustled through nearby trees, a dog barked in the distance and the water rushed on. It was obviously a river; either that or a very busy stream. Probably a river, most likely the Derwent.

'Walk.'

From behind he felt a hand on each shoulder, pushing him forward. His heart was racing with fear. He couldn't talk to this man because of the gag. He couldn't scream out or have any conversation. Couldn't ask what this was all about. Maybe it was a case of mistaken identity. If he could speak he could clear that up in a second. He was stumbling down what was probably a river bank. He felt his feet enter cold water. He stopped and was pushed further forward until the water was almost up to his knees. Hands behind his head undid the gag.

'Don't speak until yer spoken to.'

The voice was harsh. Northern Irish he reckoned. Randle didn't speak. What the hell was all this about? The voice clarified the matter.

'I'm a friend of Mrs Lilian Robinson's husband. Does this explain ter ye just how much trouble yer in – scum? Does this tell ye just how much longer ye have left ter live?'

Oh Jesus! Randle said nothing. He was now quaking with fear. The man suddenly reached underwater and took Randle by the ankles, pulling them back and up, forcing Randle to fall forward, until his head was beneath a good foot of water.

Instinctively, Randle managed to take half an inward breath before he went under. His head was now on the muddy bed of the river, his legs held in the air and his arms tied around his back. He was underwater and totally helpless; totally at the mercy of this unknown man who might just hold him there until he drowned. After half a minute he was certain he was going to drown and the ensuing adrenalin surge sent a massive shiver of terror throughout his whole body, to the extent that Charlie could feel it. He held him there for another few seconds then let go of Randle's legs, allowing the man to struggle to his knees, coughing and spewing out river water. Charlie allowed him time to stop coughing, then grabbed him by the scruff of the neck and yanked him back to his feet.

'I'm going to ask ye this only once and if I don't get a satisfactory answer I'll assume I didn't keep ye under for long enough, and ye go under again – and ye'll keep going under until you've told me the truth or yer drowned like the sewer rat y' are. So, where's the boy, Michael Robinson, who ye took from his home last April?'

There was a moment's hesitation then Randle, who wasn't thinking straight, blurted, 'I don't know!'

Charlie said nothing. He just took hold of Randle's ankles once again and held him underwater, for exactly the same length of time as before, only he knew it would seem an age longer to Randle, who was on the verge of collapse when Charlie let go of his legs for a second time.

Randle flailed about in the water, gasping and choking, trying to push himself up but having little strength to do so and getting no help from Charlie. Eventually he struggled back to his feet and Charlie placed him in position once more, leaving no doubt what the future held for Randle if he didn't cooperate.

'Right, scum, ye know the question, give me the answer or ye'll keep going under fer a whole lot longer. It strikes me yer a feller who likes the water. So, where is the boy?'

'I . . . I . . . sold him,' gasped Randle.

Charlie felt himself smiling. Randle had just told him that the boy was alive. Even that snippet of news had made this enterprise worthwhile, but he required more, much more. He now wanted the boy back.

'Sold him? Who'd yer sell him to – a gang o' filthy paedophiles, was it?'

'What? No, nothing like that. He's OK. He's g . . . gone to a wealthy family.'

'Yer lying ter me, yer bastard!' screamed Charlie. He hit Randle across the side of his head, knocking him into the water.

The bad guy act didn't come naturally, but the

memory of what Randle had done to Lily drove him on. Randle was sobbing with fear as he struggled to his feet.

'Please, I swear to you I'm not lying.' Charlie put him in position again and stood behind him. His voice went into deranged mode.

'Wealthy family ye say? Which wealthy family?'

Randle hesitated, still gasping for breath. Charlie had reached into the water and had him by the ankles again, ready to pull him back under. Randle knew he was in no condition to survive another ducking. The next time he went under would be the last.

'No, no. Please, I'll tell you. Just give me a—'

Charlie's voice was now laced with a spine-chilling calm. 'Mister, if I think fer one minute yer telling me a lie I can assure ye, you'll regret it for the rest of yer life. However, the good news is that ye won't be regretting it for long – just the sixty seconds or so that it takes ye to die. I'm told that the quickest way out of this life is to take in a great gobful of water the minute yer head goes under. Ye might like ter try that.'

'Please, let me think. I'm trying to remember his . . . his name. He wanted a son to take home to his wife.'

Charlie's grip grew tighter around Randle's knees. 'Don't!' screamed Randle. 'Please, please . . . I'm trying to think of his name!'

'Think well,' said Charlie, still in his venomous Irish accent, 'because after ye've told me what yer know, yer staying wid me until I find the lad, and if I don't find him alive yer a dead man, so y'are.'

'OK, OK. I promise he's not dead. Look, I sold him to one of the Italians . . . oh, Jesus, what's his name?'

Charlie knew he'd scared Randle witless and that it was probably his fault that the man's memory was failing him. But he also knew from experience that Randle had so far told him the truth. He tried another method of interrogation. Break the questions down into easy-to-remember answers.

'Ye mean an Italian soldier?'

'Yeah . . . real fascist bastard when you got to know him.'

'How much did you sell him for?'

Hesitation, then. 'Two thousand pounds. Jesus, man! You can't expect me to turn my nose up at that sort of money. It'll buy me a decent house.'

'OK. What rank was he? Was he an officer?'

'Hello?'

The shout came from Charlie's right. He looked through the trees and saw a group of dark figures fifty yards away, advancing on them. Charlie cursed under his breath. Another shout came.

'Are you OK over there?'

Whoever it was had no doubt heard Randle's screams. Charlie thought he'd selected an area where they wouldn't be disturbed late at night, but he hadn't allowed for night fishermen.

Randle screamed, 'Help me!' His voice was hoarse but loud enough to carry to the approaching men.

Charlie stepped away from him, cursing under his breath. The men were now running towards him. He ran off down the river bank, his intention to lead them away from his van. He looked back. If they found it and stayed with it he was lost. They'd reached Randle and it seemed that a couple of them had stayed with the distressed sergeant, but there were at least four in hot pursuit, two of them way out in the lead. Sprinting had never been Charlie's strong point, but he was agile. His motto in extreme situations was: Do what you do best. A few yards to his right was a big sycamore, shielded at ground level by a bush. He darted behind the bush and leaped up to grab one of the lower branches, pulled himself up with ease and shot up the tree like a monkey. The chasing men were all shouting, masking any sound he made. By the time they'd rounded the bush he was halfway up the tree, still as stone, trying to control his breathing. Beneath him two men arrived, one of them shouting.

'Which way did he go?'

'It's got to be that way.'

They set off, heading further downriver. Two more arrived and headed after them. Charlie waited for a few seconds before climbing down, dropping silently to the ground and heading for his van, hoping that Randle hadn't had the presence of mind to mention the incriminating vehicle to the men with him. When he got to the van there was no one about. He could hear Randle's whining voice from down by the river, maybe fifty yards away.

He opened and closed the van door as quietly as he could and hoped the engine would fire first time. Sod's law, it didn't. He cursed and tried again. The starter motor was snarling into the silent night air giving him away to anyone within a quarter of a mile, and still the engine didn't start. He could hear loud voices and the sound of approaching men. If the engine didn't fire this time he'd abandon the van and scarper. It was a very bad idea but the only one on offer. He pressed the starter again. The engine turned over, slowly. He kept the starter button depressed. Out of the corner of his eyes he saw two men emerge from nearby trees, running towards him. The engine was spluttering into life just as they reached the van. He was nursing the accelerator as they banged on the side. He knew if he pressed it too quickly the engine would die. He shielded the side of his face with his left hand as someone tried to open the passenger door. But he'd had the presence of mind to lock it. He encouraged the engine with a low curse.

'Come on you bloody thing!'

The engine came to life. He depressed the clutch and used his right hand to put the van into first gear, his left hand still shielding his face. Someone was kicking at the side panel. He'd covered up the firm's lettering with brown paper and sticky tape to hide it from inquisitive eyes and he was hoping they wouldn't think to tear it off, but they were only interested in getting at him; this beast who'd been trying to drown a poor man in the river. The wheels spun on the grass and the van moved away, very slowly, churning up mud. One of the men stood in front of it but jumped to one side when it became obvious that this murderous driver wasn't going to stop for him. Men were running alongside him. He moved up into second gear as the wheels took a firmer grip. The men dropped behind. With his lights turned off, so they wouldn't illuminate the number plate, Charlie drove back along the cart track by the light of a half-moon, but he'd operated under worse conditions. He turned on to the road and switched his lights on. As he drove off, an adrenalin-driven grin creased his face. It'd been a while since he'd put himself in such a tricky position. No immediate threat to his life but a very real threat to his immediate future – many years of it, probably.

Who the hell were these men? Probably night fishermen, he concluded. Had they managed to read his number plate? No, not in that light. It was pretty grimy to start with, almost unreadable by daylight never mind in the dark. Tomorrow morning he'd give the van a good wash. Clean all the mud off the tyres. Make it look as if it hadn't been off-road for quite some time. Throw his boots away, so they couldn't match his footprints to the ones he must have left. In fact get rid of every stitch of clothing he'd been wearing. It had been a close call, but had it been worth it?

He still didn't know where Michael was but he was fairly certain Randle was telling the truth due to the extreme pressure he'd been under. The man had thought he was going to die if he didn't tell the truth and he wasn't a man trained to withstand torture to the point of death; nor had he any good reason to do so. Some brave men might have gone to their deaths under such pressure; men willing to sacrifice their lives so that loved ones might live, but Randle was a cheap crook who'd committed the most heinous of crimes for personal reward. His own life was the most precious thing he had. Under such pressure he'd have given away military secrets that might have seen any number of his comrades die rather than sacrifice his own life.

He'd been telling the truth all right. Michael was alive and had been sold to a wealthy Italian soldier who wanted a son to take home to his wife. Yet the Italians had left Eden camp a year before Michael's abduction. But he was sure that Randle had had the truth scared out of him.

Charlie's heart was still pounding as he headed towards Shipley. All that violent play-acting and the near-miss at the end had taken it out of him. He gathered and arranged his thoughts and worries as he'd done so often in the past. One thing you must do, he said to himself, is to send Ogden Bernard Beakersfield the outstanding pound note. He thought of the drunken old reprobate who had led them in the right direction and the thought made him smile to himself and lifted his spirits. To keep in good spirits was essential for survival.

He arrived at four in the morning after alerting Lily and Dee of his imminent arrival by phoning them from a call box. He parked the van around the corner from Dee's and walked quickly to her back door which was already open. The two women were waiting for him. Charlie sat down to tell them what he'd found out.

'First of all he told me Michael's alive – and I believe this.'

Lily felt a flood of uncontrollable tears rush down her cheeks.

'So, what happened exactly?' Dee asked him.

'I put the absolute fear of death in him,' said Charlie, 'and I'm sure what he told me was the truth. The problem was that just as we were getting to the lowdown we were disturbed by a group of fellers and I had to scarper.'

'What did he tell you?' asked Lily through her tears.

'Well, he admitted taking the boy and he told me why. He did it for money – two thousand quid to be precise. He sold him to some wealthy Italian soldier. Trouble is I didn't get the Eyetie's name. He couldn't remember it, which might have been my fault. I put him in a state of very severe shock, which didn't help the memory one bit.'

Lily wondered how Charlie had managed to do that but decided not to ask.

'Another few minutes and I'd have had the feller's name,' Charlie went on. 'I think they must have been fishermen. Why can't they do their fishing during the day like civilised human beings?'

'Maybe they were poachers,' suggested Dee.

Charlie shook his head. 'I doubt if poachers would have been so keen to make themselves known.'

'So,' said Lily, who wasn't interested in the fishermen. 'You're saying Randle stole my son from me to sell to an Italian prisoner?'

'Something like that,' said Charlie. 'The trouble is that all the Italians left the camp a year before Michael was taken.'

'What does that mean?' asked Dee.

'It means we have another mystery on our hands, but at least we know the boy is definitely alive and possibly living in comfort somewhere. What's more I think he might well be still be in this country. The Italians are being repatriated but I don't think he'd take the risk of taking Michael with him so soon after the war's over. I think he might want to let the dust settle a bit, then sneak him over to Italy.'

'If that's the case he'd have to be living in some sort of closed Italian community,' said Dee. 'An English boy living with an Italian man'd stick out like a sore thumb.'

'More likely he's already in Italy,' said Lily.

'Perhaps,' said Charlie, 'but he's still alive, Lily, and in no danger. Hold on to that thought. He's just with the wrong people.'

'Like Christopher,' said Lily.

'At least we know where Christopher is,' said Charlie.

'I need to see Christopher, Charlie. I need to hold him.'

'I understand that, Lily.'

Charlie had a strength about him that Lily found uncommon in such a young man. From it she gained strength of her own. She gave his hand a grateful squeeze.

Chapter 46

DS Bannister tracked Charlie down to his mother's house in Wetherby, a few miles north of Leeds. It was the evening of the morning Randle had been attacked. Charlie's mother, with whom he lived, was out when Bannister asked the inevitable question.

'Where were you between the hours of two o'clock and three o'clock this morning?'

'Why would you want to know that?' Charlie asked, innocently.

'Because a serious crime was committed at that time and I need to eliminate you from our enquiries.'

'You mean I'm a suspect in some crime or other? What sort of crime?'

As an ostensibly innocent man Charlie knew his rights.

'It's just a matter of procedure, Mr Cleghorn. Sergeant Bernard Randle of Eden camp was assaulted in the early hours of this morning. I'm aware that you had a grievance with him and I just want to eliminate you.'

'Assaulted? Any life-threatening injuries – or is that too much to hope?'

'Just tell me where you were?'

'You know when Lily accused him of assaulting her? Where did he say he was at the time?'

'He was at home with his wife. Mrs Randle verified this.'

'Well, with me it's a very similar story. At two o'clock this morning I was with Lily Robinson and Delilah Maguire and they'll verify that, Sergeant. Oh, don't get me wrong. Lily and Dee live in a three-bedroom house. We had a bedroom each. We'd been up until at least two o'clock wondering how to persuade you police people that Randle is the man who abducted Lily's son. Is there any other reason why you suspect me?'

'Is that your van outside?'

'Technically it's a firm's van but I have the use of it.'

Charlie's van was pristine clean. Not a speck of mud on it.

'Do you always keep it that clean?'

'I have a dirty job, Sergeant. If I don't wash the van regularly you'd hardly be able to see it for dirt. My dad's a stickler for clean vehicles. A dirty vehicle gives the firm a bad name. Why do you ask?'

'Randle says he was thrown into a van that smelt of cordite, which I understand is a propellant for guns. Do you have a use for cordite in your business, Mr Cleghorn?'

'Yes, I find it has its uses.'

'But not to your normal demolition contractor – more to someone who's learned his skills in the army.'

'I did all my explosives certification training before I went into the army, Sergeant Bannister. My dad taught me everything I know.'

293

'Not quite everything, I suspect. If I inspected your van would I detect the smell of cordite?'

Charlie laughed. 'I think you'd detect all sorts of smells, Sergeant. What I smell right now is the smell of Randle trying to frame me.'

'Really? I'm not sure that Randle ever knew you were in the demolition business. I certainly didn't tell him that you were. Why would he make that connection?'

'Perhaps us turning up at his house in a van marked *Cleghorn Demolition* might have given him a clue.'

Bannister winced at this sharp answer to what he thought would be a tricky question. Neither of the two witnesses who had chased the van remembered seeing any lettering on it.

'Is he in hospital or anything?' Charlie asked.

'He's in Scarborough hospital for observation.'

'Pity the *police* didn't keep him under closer observation, Sergeant. It could have saved Lily a lot of trouble.'

Bannister knew in his bones that Charlie was lying, despite the fact that Randle had said the man who assaulted him was Irish. He'd checked on Charlie's military background, as far as he was allowed, and had learned that, among many other attributes, Charlie was an expert linguist; and linguists are usually able to master different accents.

'Did Randle give any reason for this assault, Sergeant?' Charlie asked innocently. 'Does he think it could have been anything to do with him attacking Lily?'

'Mrs Robinson's missing son was the apparent reason for the assault, which is why I'm here.'

'I can well imagine her dead husband's army pals not being too happy at having her son stolen by a fellow soldier. Are you investigating that line of enquiry?'

Bannister was annoyed at being told his job by this man who was the most obvious culprit, although the assailant had told Randle that he was a friend of Lily's dead husband.

'I could investigate many lines of enquiry, Mr Cleghorn, but I always find it better to eliminate the most obvious suspects first.'

'I'm pleased to hear that I'm being eliminated. Tell me, Sergeant, have you heard the latest rumour about Randle?'

'What rumour's that?'

'The one about him selling young Michael Robinson to an Italian soldier who may or may not have already smuggled the boy over to Italy. Just a rumour, Sergeant, no idea where it came from, but it's probably worth-while you following it up.'

Bannister stared at Charlie, knowing full well where he'd got this information from, and how it had been obtained. He knew that Charlie had been in special forces and he knew he'd been awarded a Military Medal. Someone like that would have little trouble in scaring information out of Randle. From what Randle told him, if they hadn't been disturbed by fishermen, the Malton police would have had a murder case on their hands. Charlie Cleghorn didn't look a dangerous man but his military record said otherwise.

He got to his feet and said, 'I'm not an idiot, Mr Cleghorn. I know exactly what's been going on and if I find one scrap of evidence to implicate you in the assault on Randle I'll have you inside so fast your feet won't touch the floor!'

Charlie ignored Bannister's threat and sat back in his chair, with arms folded, as he looked up at the policeman. 'Tell me, Sergeant. Do the Randles strike you as a couple who make friends easily?'

They both knew the answer to that. 'It's not a crime to be unfriendly, Mr Cleghorn – but it's a serious crime to torture people.'

'So, you do agree that the Randles aren't the types to make friends easily?'

The question was rhetorical. Bannister said nothing. He left the house to see if Lily and Dee would corroborate Charlie's story. He knew they would and he also knew they'd be lying, but he had to go through the motions. It was a matter of procedure.

As he drove over to Shipley he ran through Charlie's story about Michael being sold to an Italian and wondered if it was worth following up. It was a very strange story and he knew what his boss would say if he put the matter to him. *Forget it, John. We've enough bloody crimes to solve without chasing wild rumours.*

Then he thought about the two words *ulterior motive* and he couldn't help but agree with Charlie. The Randles had been pleasant enough with him, but he'd sensed it wasn't genuine. Plenty of people put on an act when talking to the police, so it hadn't bothered him at the time.

But maybe, with the Randles, it should have bothered him.

Chapter 47

Jane Robinson wheeled the pram along Street Lane until she came to the newsagent's. It stood on its own a couple of hundred yards away from the main shopping parade and on the other side of the road, the same side as she and Godfrey lived. She depressed the brake pedal with her foot and went inside, as she did every morning. She called it her morning constitutional. Every morning she'd make the ten-minute walk from her home to the shop to get her *Yorkshire Post*, and the ten-minute walk back, pushing her grandson in his pram. Every morning she left him outside rather than suffer the effort of taking the huge pram into the shop and it getting in everyone's way.

It had never occurred to her that there was any danger in leaving an unattended child in a pram. This was a respectable area with no undesirables hanging around. The man walking towards the pram looked eminently respectable. He wore a trilby and had a neat moustache. His suit was grey pinstripe, possibly a demob suit, but there was no shame in that. Many men who could afford better wore their demob suits as a badge of honour. He was carrying a large shopping bag; no shame in that either. Men doing the shopping for their wives were to be applauded, according to most women.

Other than him that part of the footpath was deserted. He reached into his bag as he reached the pram and took out a large doll, probably the same size as a six-month-old child. He paused for no more than the few seconds it took him to swap young Christopher for the doll and move on. No one saw this happen. By the time Jane Robinson emerged from the shop the man had turned a corner and was out of sight with the sleeping boy in his shopping bag.

She released the footbrake and headed for home, scarcely glancing in the pram at what she assumed was a sleeping baby. It wasn't until she arrived home that she let out the scream which told the world that Christopher was gone.

When Lily and Dee got back from Skipton market that evening, Bannister and a constable were in his car outside the house. As Dee's motorcycle combination roared up the drive Bannister got out and followed them. Lily saw him first as she swung off the pillion.

'Sergeant,' she said apprehensively. 'What are you doing here?'

He looked at her, trying to assess her demeanour before he said, 'I'm afraid I have some bad news, Mrs Robinson.'

His eyes held hers, watching for any flicker of guilt. But her eyes showed only fear of what was to come. 'Bad news? What bad news, Sergeant?'

'At ten o'clock this morning your son was taken from a pram outside a shop in Leeds.'

'You mean he's missing?'

Bannister nodded, still not taking his eyes off Lily's face, which showed nothing but shock.

'Did anyone see who took him?' Dee asked, taking off her helmet.

Bannister looked at her and shook his head. 'Apparently not. Mrs Jane Robinson didn't notice the infant was missing until she arrived home.'

'What? She pushed an empty pram home and didn't notice there was no baby inside?'

'The baby had been replaced by a doll of similar proportions.'

'And this bloody woman can't tell the difference between a doll and a real baby?'

Bannister returned his gaze to Lily, who was now crying. 'Maybe we should go inside,' he said. 'I need to ask you both a few questions.'

'And to search the house,' said Dee sarcastically, 'in case Christopher's in there.'

'I haven't got a warrant to search your house but it would help if I could do that with your permission. You do appreciate that we need to eliminate you from our enquiries.'

'We haven't got him,' sobbed Lily. 'Why did she leave my baby on his own outside a shop? Why has a woman like that got custody of him? Will you be able to find him, Mr Bannister?'

'We've got thirty men on the case right now. You would have been contacted earlier, but we didn't know where you were.'

'Working,' said Dee. 'In Skipton market since nine

299

o'clock this morning. You can ask any of the other stall-holders. What time was the baby taken?'

'Around ten o'clock.'

Bannister signalled for the constable to get out of the car and the four of them went into the house, which was searched thoroughly by the two policemen. No sign of Christopher. Bannister didn't expect to find him. This new twist to the case was baffling him.

'We wouldn't do anything as stupid as this, Mr Bannister,' sobbed Lily. 'For God's sake, I'm applying for custody of him.'

'It wouldn't surprise me if Randle's taken him,' seethed Dee. 'I wouldn't anything past that lying creep!'

'The Malton police have already investigated that end of things,' Bannister told them. 'Bernard Randle has a rock-solid alibi. He was in his CO's office at ten o'clock this morning.'

'What about his wife?' Dee asked.

'His wife claims she was at home alone all morning.'

'So, she doesn't have a solid alibi.'

'Not as such, but—'

'Then arrest her.'

'We can't go round arresting people just because they can't prove where they were at a particular time.'

Lily was sitting in a chair with her face in her hands, her shoulders heaving with great sobs. She eventually looked up at Bannister. Imploring him.

'Mr Bannister. If you find Christopher, will you bring him to me, please? I'm his mum. I haven't seen him since he was a month old. Why were those awful people allowed to take him off me?'

'Mr and Mrs Robinson are perfectly respectable people. Your son is being well taken care of.'

'Is he really?' A vague memory came to her mind. 'The man's a crook.'

'Lily,' said Bannister reprovingly, 'I know you're upset but there's no cause to start making false accusations.'

'I'm not,' said Lily. 'He sells meat on the black market. My Larry told me. He doesn't declare all his pigs to the food inspector . . . or something.'

'Really? And how come you didn't mention this when your son was put into their care? Or have you just made it up?'

'I know what you're thinking, Sergeant,' said Dee, 'but Lily's not that devious. Nor does she know enough about the butcher's trade to have made up a story like that.'

'I thought about telling someone when they took Christopher,' Lily said, 'but I promised my Larry I wouldn't say anything to anyone, which was daft of me because Larry would probably shop them himself for what they've done to me.'

'Well, if that's true we'll have it looked into.'

'It is true. My Larry wouldn't tell such a lie about his own father.'

'We'll do whatever we can,' said Bannister. He looked from Lily to Dee. 'Maybe you should get a doctor to see her.'

'She's had enough of doctors, Sergeant. I'll look after her. There is one thing, though.'

'Yes?'

'Lily's been driven out of her home in Leeds by her neighbours. The people round here don't know who she is. As far as they're concerned she's just our Lily from Leeds who's come to stay with me for a bit. If word gets out who she is, well, she'll have to move on.'

'They won't hear anything from the police,' said Bannister, looking at the constable who nodded his assurance. Bannister drove back to Leeds convinced that Lily and Dee had had nothing to do with this. He was also becoming more and more convinced of her overall innocence of everything that had been thrown at her. What he didn't know was what he could do about it. Her two boys had vanished into thin air and the only possible suspect, Randle, had a rock-solid alibi.

Chapter 48

Charlie arrived just a few minutes after Bannister and the constable had left. Dee opened the door to him. Charlie followed her inside.

'Charlie, have you heard?' she said, over her shoulder. 'Christopher's been taken.'

'Yeah, I know that. I've been waiting for Bannister to leave.'

She half turned. 'What? Why?'

'I needed him to interview you first, and for you to be completely convincing.'

Dee turned to face him. 'Charlie, what are you talking about?'

Charlie held opened the handles of the shopping bag he was carrying and showed the contents to her. 'So far he's been fed twice and had his nappy changed twice, although I think he's done another one. He's a great kid. No trouble.'

Dee's mouth hung open with shock as she looked down on Christopher. 'Charlie, what the hell have you done?'

'I've brought Christopher to see his mum.'

He looked up just as Lily came to the living-room door. 'Hiya, Lily. Hey, look who I found.'

Lily darted forward and looked in the bag. She held her hands to the sides of her face as she gazed down on this boy she hadn't seen for five months of his six-month life. He'd altered so much she didn't immediately recognise him. She looked up at Charlie.

'Is this really Christopher?'

'I do hope so,' said Charlie, 'otherwise I'm in deeper trouble than I thought.'

He was more than twice the size he'd been when she last saw him, under that table in Leeds Town Hall, surrounded by unfriendly feet, when she'd kissed him goodbye, not knowing if she'd ever see him again.

With tears streaming down her pale cheeks she lifted him from the shopping bag and took him in her arms. Within seconds she knew he was her Christopher, the son she'd given birth to all those awful months ago. Dee and Charlie stood back, smiling, as she kissed him all over his head. Then Dee took Charlie's arm and led him into the kitchen.

'Good God, Charlie! What the hell are you playing at? You can't do things like this. As soon as the police find out that Lily's got him they'll take him off her and she'll have no chance of custody. On top of which we could all end up in the slammer!'

Charlie placed a hand on each of her shoulders. In the background they could hear Lily singing to her son. 'Dee, I know what I'm doing. Lily needs this time with her son, no matter how brief that time is.'

'Brief? How do you mean?'

'I mean, she can't keep him for more than a couple of days, then he goes back. In two days' time Christopher is found and his grandparents are totally discredited as unfit guardians when the custody hearing comes up.'

Dee sat down and lit a cigarette. 'Might work, especially with the police investigating Godfrey about his black-marketeering.'

'Black-marketeering eh? Didn't know about that.'

'Neither did I. Lily reckons he didn't declare all his pigs or something. That's what she told Bannister.'

'If Lily said it, I believe it.'

Dee smiled. 'How are we going to prise Christopher away from Lily in two days' time?'

'Ah, well, I thought that's something best left to you. You must tell her the situation right now so she knows the score. We need her fully aware of the situation for her own benefit. Has Bannister searched the house?'

'Yes, thoroughly. I gave him permission.'

'That's good. So Christopher can stay here, then. Hey, he's a great kid, doesn't cry much at all. I've got all sorts of baby stuff in the van. Baby milk, clothes, nappies, dummies. I figured you could make a bed up in a drawer, he's still only tiny.'

'You've been planning this for some time, haven't you?'

'About a week. I had to do a recce on his grandma's movements. Fortunately she's a creature of habit – one of them a particularly bad habit.'

'What? Leaving the kid outside the shop?'

Charlie nodded. 'Every morning, outside on his own. Sometimes for as much as ten minutes as she chatted to the shopkeeper. It's lucky *I* took him and not someone more sinister.'

'Yeah, he's such a lucky boy,' said Dee, drawing on her cigarette, shaking her head but beginning to see the method in Charlie's madness. 'You know, Charlie, I thought I was a lunatic, but compared to you . . . God! I'm the sanest person alive.' Dee looked up at Charlie and began to laugh. 'Jesus, Charlie you're a real, genuine, twenty-four carat madman.'

Charlie shrugged at this dubious compliment. 'Look, I'm going. I want to be at home when Bannister comes calling on me. I have an alibi for ten o'clock this morning when Christopher was taken.'

'Who's that?'

'My mum. She's been helping me look after Christopher all day.'

'Your mum! I don't believe this. Does your dad know?'

'No, Dad's a bit of a worrier. Mum's been great – always had faith in me. She and my dad divorced when I was a boy. I live with Mum but she can be a bit unpredictable. Dad couldn't do with it. She drove him mad at times and I can understand why. Now they're divorced they get on a lot better.

'Look, give Lily a happy hour before you tell her what's happening.'

Dee nodded. 'I'll definitely do that. If anyone deserves a happy hour it's Lily. Then I'll tell her what the deal is and see if she goes for it but, to be honest, I don't think you've thought this through clearly.'

Chapter 49

It was the following evening. Bannister had been and gone. Charlie's mother had provided her son with an excellent alibi, to the extent that Bannister totally believed her. Not only that but he seemed quite taken by her, to Charlie's irritation. She'd asked Bannister if he was married and his answer was a most reluctant yes.

'Mum, you're a blatant flirt,' Charlie said, after Bannister had left. 'He's a copper. You don't go round flirting with coppers.'

'Bit of fun, Charlie, boy. Anyway he's my age, why shouldn't I flirt with him?'

Charlie shook his head. The phone rang. It was Dee, who was understandably cautious.

'Can you talk?'

'Yes. Bannister's been and gone. We're all in the clear – for now.'

'For now's right, Charlie. She won't part with him. I've been trying to make her see sense since last night.'

'She's got to give him back, Dee.'

'Try telling Lily. Ever since I told her we'd have to give him back she won't even let me hold him. She even takes him into the bathroom with her. It's weird, Charlie.'

'I'll come over.'

He put the phone down and looked at his mother who had already figured out the problem. 'She doesn't want to send him back?'

'No,' said Charlie.

'I could have told you that.'

'Why didn't you?'

'Because you've never taken too much notice of anything I ever said. There's a lot of your father in you in that respect.'

'It'll blow the whole deal if she tries to keep him.'

'That depends on how quickly you get Michael back. He's the key to all this. You get Michael back and all the people giving Lily problems will crawl back under their stones.'

'He could be in Italy. Or he could be still in this country, or anywhere in the world for that matter.'

'You need to track down this mysterious Italian who bought him.'

'Short of grabbing Randle again and asking him, I'm not sure how to do it.'

'Ask your pals at Eden camp. Maybe they know something.'

Lily was sitting at the dining-room table with Christopher on her knee when Charlie arrived. He sat down opposite her.

'Sorry for all the trouble I've caused', he said. 'I should have kept my big nose out of it. I should have known you wouldn't let Christopher go. The trouble is, keeping him is just about the worst thing you could do, under the circumstances. You'd never get proper custody if the court found out what you'd done. In fact he'd probably end up in some children's home or other.'

Lily smiled at him. 'I know what you're doing, Charlie. I doubt if you can be any more persuasive than Auntie Dee's been, but I can't let him go. It'd be like you wanting me to have a leg chopped off – worse even. Maybe if you had a son of your own you'd understand.'

Dee was standing in the doorway. 'Charlie, can I have a word?'

Charlie got to his feet and followed Dee into the front room. 'I actually know how she feels,' she said. 'If I'd known what you had planned I'd have told you that she wouldn't be able to part with him. You'll have to think of an alternative plan.'

'I see.'

'Not sure you do.' Dee sat down and lit a cigarette, composing a story as Charlie waited for her to speak. 'My full title,' she said at length, 'is *Mrs* Delilah Maguire.'

'You're married?'

'Was married for a whole year, to Ernie Maguire. He died in 1919 of flu.'

'I'm sorry to hear that. I didn't know. The big epidemic, eh? I was only a toddler when that broke out.

'My son died as well.' She was lost in thought for a few seconds. 'James – he was eight months old. He died three weeks after my husband. I'd handled Ernie's death OK, but losing my boy was like having my heart ripped out. What's happened to Lily's sons since would have destroyed many women. She's been immensely strong to cope as she has.'

Charlie nodded and left a respectful pause before asking, 'How did you cope?'

'Well, I was left with no money, no child, no job, no qualifications and no skills so I used what assets I had to make money. I'm not proud of how I lived after that but I got by.'

Charlie thought it wise to change the subject. 'Do you think Lily's getting over losing Larry?'

Dee drew on her cigarette and smiled at him, allowing the smoke to drift from her mouth. 'Now, why would you ask such a question?'

'Just wondered, that's all.'

'Her marriage to Larry was much like my marriage to Ernie Maguire – a marriage of necessity – better than having a child out of wedlock. Don't get me wrong, I was very fond of Ernie and Lily was very fond of Larry, but neither of these were great love stories.' She held him in her gaze. 'It might be too late for me to find that sort of love, Charlie, but not for Lily.'

'I don't know how Lily will go on if she doesn't get Michael back,' he said.

'But you understand about Christopher?'

'About her not giving him up?' said Charlie. 'I suppose I do, but I don't know how we're going to manage. He can't stay inside this house indefinitely. Kids have a tendency to grow up.'

'That's why we need to find Michael before Christopher gets much older.'

'Right, best tell her, then.'

They both went back into the kitchen. Charlie held up his hands in mock surrender. 'OK, Lily, we give up.

You keep him, but we all have to tread very carefully. Act as you would if Christopher had really been stolen.'

'Like Michael, you mean?'

'Yeah, no one knows better than you how to do that, but I suggest you ring Bannister every other day and ask if there's been any news of Christopher. If he's out leave messages for him to ring you if there's any news. You'll get on his nerves to the extent that he'll want to keep his distance from you, which suits us down to the ground. Trouble is, there's about thirty coppers out there looking for him. How do you feel about that?'

'You mean do I feel guilty? Not really. It's about thirty more coppers than bothered looking for Michael so I'm struggling to have any sympathy for the police. Do you have a plan to get him back?'

Charlie looked at Dee. 'Dee and I, we're working on one.'

'So,' said Dee, 'you can leave him with me from time to time. No need to take him to the bathroom with you.'

Lily looked from one to the other as if assessing the truth of the situation.

'Lily, don't look at us like that. You can trust us,' said Dee. 'Here, let me take him.'

Lily breathed a sigh of relief, then got to her feet and handed Christopher over. She then looked at Charlie. 'What's the plan?'

Charlie winced slightly. 'First I need to find out who this Italian is who bought Michael.'

'Are you sure he was telling the truth?'

'Lily, if you'd been there you'd know he was telling the truth. The information's solid, believe me.'

She now wondered what excruciating torture he'd put Randle through to get this solid information. Bannister hadn't been very forthcoming about the nature of the assault.

'What did you do to him?' she asked. Her eyes forced a truthful answer from him.

'I kind of tricked him into believing that he was definitely going to drown if he didn't come up with truthful answers. When the choice is death or the truth, truth wins out. It's a tried and tested tactic.'

'And was he in any danger of drowning?'

'Well, there's always that danger if you don't know what you're doing, which makes it such an effective method of interrogation. Acting comes into it a lot. You need to convince the subject that you're slightly mad and well capable of carrying out your threat – but I haven't lost one yet.'

'So, you're an expert on this, are you?'

Charlie didn't answer this. 'I thought I might ask Jimmy if he knows anything,' he said.

'Or Brenda?' suggested Lily.

Charlie shook his head. 'Brenda got demoted for spreading that rumour. Not sure how helpful she'll be.'

'Oh dear, that'd be my fault.'

'Probably, but it was in a good cause, so I shouldn't worry too much. Major Bykers is a fair man. Brenda should get her stripes back when we nail Randle.'

Charlie sat down to examine his thoughts, thinking back to what Randle had said about the Italian. 'You know, Randle said this Italian was *a real fascist bastard, when you got to know him* – those were his exact words, and he paid two thousand pounds for the boy.'

'So, he must also have been a fascist bastard with access to cash money,' said Dee. 'Which begs the next question. Where would an Italian POW get that much cash from?'

'It would have to be someone on the outside,' said Charlie. 'British fascists who weren't locked up as security risks – some of Mosley's lot, maybe.'

'How would he have made contact with them? Lily asked.

'A few months after Italy surrendered in September 1943,' Charlie told her, 'the Italian prisoners were given the option of becoming cooperators. Most took up the option and were put to work outside the camps. A man could have had money passed to him on the outside.'

'Money to buy a child?' said Dee. 'Why would a fascist sympathiser do that?'

'It could have been his own money being passed on to him,' said Charlie. 'Money being sent from Italy, possibly via a Swiss bank.'

'Can they do that?' Dee asked him.

'Actually, I dunno,' admitted Charlie. 'This is all kind of educated guesswork.'

'So,' said Lily, 'your educated guesswork tells us we're looking for a wealthy Italian soldier who's got friends among the British fascists.'

'Or we could be barking up the wrong tree altogether,' said Dee.

'True, but until we find out otherwise, it's the only

tree we've got,' said Charlie, looking at Lily, who was smiling at him.

'I like this tree,' she said. 'Thanks, Charlie.'

The look she gave him made him glad he'd stolen Christopher back for her. It was a look that held a lot of promise – but only if she got Michael back.

'One of our main problems,' he said, 'is that we can't involve the police. I've been operating on the wrong side of the law and if we let them too near us they're going to sniff me out.'

'I think they might sniff Christopher out before they get to you,' said Lily, wrinkling her nose. 'I think he needs changing. It's OK, I'll do it upstairs.'

As Lily left the room, Charlie ran his fingers through his hair then scratched his head. 'My mother's volunteered to help us,' he said. 'In fact she practically insisted. What do you think?'

'I don't know your mother. Is it a good thing or a bad thing?'

'Could be either. She's got her own car. 'And she speaks five languages.'

'She sounds just what we need. A mobile linguist.'

'She's also very charming when she puts her mind to it. She had Bannister eating out of her hand.'

'Charming could be handy.'

'Well, I can't see Lily wanting to hang around here while you and I are off tracking Michael down. Mum could look after Christopher at her house.'

'Well, I suppose another recruit will do no harm.'

314

Chapter 50

'It was you who tried to drown Randle, wasn't it?'

Charlie and Jimmy Dunkersley were in the Green Man in Malton. Charlie had asked to meet him, only not on camp.

'Jimmy, if I'd tried to drown Randle he'd be dead now.'

'You know what I mean.'

'What makes you think that?'

'Motive, method and the fact that you asked me what time Randle would be off duty that night.'

'All circumstantial, Jimmy.'

'What did he tell you?'

Charlie leaned forward. The pub was quite full and noisy enough to drown confidential conversation.

'He told me he'd sold Michael to an Italian soldier.'

'But there weren't any Eyeties on camp when the boy was taken. They'd been sent all over the country last year when we took in the Germans.'

'I know that,' said Charlie, 'but this could have been provisionally arranged before the Italians left, and the boy to be delivered as soon as the war was over.'

'What? You mean an order placed for one small boy

to be delivered as soon as Hitler topped himself? Come on, this is ridiculous!'

'Ridiculous, but true. Obviously I don't know any details but Randle definitely took the boy.'

Jimmy looked at him. 'I was questioned by a copper called Bannister. He asked me if I knew you, and had you been asking me about Randle's movements. I told him, no.'

'Thanks.'

'Jesus Christ, Charlie! If Randle took the boy, this is very serious stuff!'

'Oh, he took him all right. The trouble is that me and Lily are the only ones who know that for certain. I got Randle thinking I was some mad Irish friend of Lily's husband. I got him into such a state that he wouldn't have dared lie to me, but I can hardly tell the police that. I told them about a new rumour that Randle had sold Michael to an Italian but I didn't know where the rumour came from. He can't prove it, but Bannister knows I'm the one who half drowned Randle so he knows full well where I got it from. I also think he's coming round to thinking Lily's been telling the truth all along.'

'So, do you think Bannister might go for Randle?'

'Doubt it. Bannister's just one copper, and only a sergeant at that. The police obviously don't think this case merits a senior officer. Jimmy, you speak Italian, what I want to know is did you ever hear any of the Italians talking about children?'

'And saying what, exactly?'

'That's just it. I don't know why an Italian would want to buy a British child.'

'Are we talking . . . perverts here?' said Jimmy, shocked. 'I've heard about such stuff, but surely not to a little lad like that.'

'We must hope not, Jimmy. I know one thing, the army wouldn't want anything like that to get out. One of their own sergeants abducting a child for whatever purpose. It'd be worse than treason in the eyes of the public.'

'Bloody hell! Too true. That'd be hushed up and no mistake.'

'The police don't seem too keen on investigating it either,' said Charlie. 'They'd sooner believe Lily killed her boy and buried his body somewhere.'

'Did Randle say anything else?'

'He said the Italian was a real fascist bastard.'

'That might narrow it down a bit. We had over two hundred of them. A few were dyed-in-the-wool fascists, but not too many. Most of 'em hated the war – and Mussolini.'

'I know,' said Charlie. 'I actually worked with that group of partisans who captured old Musso back in April and executed him and his mistress. They were merciless buggers, I tell you. I once handed them a couple of Eyetie SS lads who were trying to rape an Italian woman; dread to think what happened to them. Their top commander was an Italian count called Pedro Bellini, but I mainly dealt with a local bloke called Leonardo. I used to call him Loony Lennie – lucky for me he didn't speak a word of English.'

Charlie went quiet for a while as his mind drifted back to his time with the Italian partisans, then he came back to the present.

317

'Anyway, this bloke also had a lot of money – or access to it. I'm thinking he spotted that Randle was as bent as a nine-bob note and made an approach to him. I'm guessing he was an officer; wealthy Italians tend to be officers.'

Jimmy shook his head. 'I can't think of anyone. I didn't have much to do with them, actually.'

'Could you ask around? Randle said he was a real fascist *when you got to know him*. This tells me that he hid his fascism.'

'The known fascists weren't allowed the same privileges as the cooperators,' said Jimmy. 'My guess is that this bloke was a cooperator because it suited him. If he was an officer he wouldn't have been made to do any work like the non-coms.'

'So, you're looking for a secret fascist who's probably an officer and rich enough to pay two grand for a small child.'

'Two grand?' Jimmy whistled. 'That's quite a few years' pay for Randle. I can see why he'd be persuaded to do something like that.'

'Would two grand tempt you to steal a child from its mother?'

'I bloody hope not!'

'No, me neither, nor any half decent bloke, but we're talking about Randle who also tried to murder Lily, by the way.'

'I know that, Bannister mentioned it.' Jimmy looked at Charlie and said, 'She's a bit of a looker, this Lily. Are you and her . . . ?' He gave a meaningful nod, with eyebrows raised.

'I like her a lot.'

'Which is why you're going to all this trouble, putting your neck on the line for her. Does she like you a lot?'

'We get on OK, but she's got too much on her plate to bother with romance.'

'There's something else I meant to ask you,' said Jimmy pointedly. 'I was reading in the paper about that baby boy who was taken from his pram in Leeds. Apparently he was in the care of his grandparents – Jane and Godfrey Robinson. I remember when Lily was telling us about her in-laws looking after Michael she mentioned her father-in-law's name. And there can't be too many Godfrey Robinsons looking after their six-month-old grandsons in Leeds. So I assume it was him.'

'So?'

'So – you haven't mentioned a word about Lily's other son being abducted, which you would if it worried you.'

'You think I took him?'

'Did you?'

Charlie's shrug told its own story.

'You need to be on your guard, mate,' warned Jimmy. 'They could throw the key away on you after what you've done for Lily.' He finished off his pint and plonked the glass down on the table. 'Anyway, I'll ask around and do what I can, but a lot of the blokes on guard duty now weren't here when the Eyeties were. Quite a few went over with the D-Day lot.'

'I know you'll do your best, Jimmy.'

Chapter 51

Bernard Randle had a half smile on his face as he walked into his house. It wasn't an expression Edith had seen too much of recently. It was a week after Charlie had met Jimmy in the Malton pub.

'You look like the cat that got the cream.'

Randle's grin broadened. 'I'm the cat who's just been discharged from the army. Too psychologically damaged by that psycho pal of Robinson to serve another day.'

'What? Discharged on mental health grounds?' said Edith, getting up from her chair to look at the contents of an envelope he'd just taken from his pocket.

'Medical grounds,' said Randle. 'Honourable discharge on full pension, plus ninety pounds demob money and a new suit,' he said, handing it to her. 'Pack your bags Edith, we're away from here in the morning.'

'Leaving? Where to?'

'Bournemouth.'

'Bournemouth? At this time of year?'

'It's an overcoat warmer down there, Edith, even in November. We'll find some digs then set about finding ourselves a house. We could have a nice new home by Christmas.'

'What about all our furniture and stuff?'

'Most of it's too old to be worth anything. Leave it for the next mug who comes to stay here. We'll just take the odds and ends that are worth taking.'

'I've been thinking we could buy a boarding house with the money we've got put away,' Edith said.

'I don't care what we do. I just want to get away from this place and away from that bloody Robinson woman and her vicious bloody cronies. She's getting too much of a nuisance, Edith. I don't want that lunatic pal of hers coming after me again. We need to make a clean break.'

He hadn't mentioned to her that he'd told his attacker about an Italian who'd bought Michael for £2,000. Better she didn't know this. No one would ever know who this Italian was, much less track him down. He'd arranged to have his army pension paid into his bank as he had no forwarding address as yet.

'Do we have to tell the army where we've moved to?'

'Edith, right now thousands of men are leaving the army every month. Most have got homes to go to, many haven't. The army's got better things to do than to keep track of all its old soldiers.'

'What about the police? Won't they want to know where you are?'

'Why should they? I've done nothing wrong.'

'What about the boy? Supposing he gets found?'

'And how's that going to happen? He's a thousand miles away, and the police have no way of tracking him down. By now he'll have a different name, a different identity and he'll be learning a different language. What's

321

more he's probably forgotten who his real mother is. Kids of that age don't have much of a memory. The lad'll have a far better life ahead of him than he would living with that Robinson cow.'

Chapter 52

Tuesday 27th November 1945.

Christopher had been officially missing for a month and Michael for seven months. Bannister was getting fed up with Lily's constant phoning. Her distress was genuine, fuelled by the lack of progress in finding Michael, about whom she also asked. She found the detective a good outlet for her frustration at the police's reluctance to spend too much time looking for her older boy.

'Has any progress been made in the search for my boys?'

His reply was always the same: 'Nothing yet, I'm afraid, but we'll be in touch the minute something breaks.'

'Do you still believe I killed Michael, because while you do you're not going to put your heart and soul into looking for him?'

'We have no evidence to support that, Mrs Robinson.'

'What about the rumour that Randle sold him to an Italian soldier?'

'The only person I've heard that rumour from is Mr Cleghorn.'

'It was in the papers, Mr Bannister.'

Dee had eventually persuaded Henry Smithson to publish the story of the rumour in the *Craven Herald*. No mention of Randle, just that a British army soldier was rumoured to have abducted a missing Leeds boy and sold him to an Italian POW. A couple of nationals had picked it up but, with nothing to substantiate it, the story occupied just a couple of column inches in one edition before being dropped.

'I'm sorry, Mrs Robinson. We can't allocate police resources to a lead based on a rumour.'

Charlie's mother, Mary Cleghorn, had proved an invaluable help in looking after Christopher. On the days when Lily went to work the market with Dee they'd worked out a routine whereby Mary would reverse her car to the end of Dee's drive and the baby was transferred from house to car without being seen by curious eyes. Lily had gone back to work in Leeds market, despite her altercation with Hilda Muscroft. Dee had suggested this as a further ruse to throw the police off the scent as to Christopher's whereabouts.

'They know I work Leeds market,' she'd said. 'I've been told they've been asking around about me – and you for that matter. Stands to reason they'll keep an eye on my stall from time to time. If they see you and me there, and no Christopher, it'll reinforce our story and keep them off our backs.'

The police did keep off their backs, as did Hilda Muscroft, who still visited the market but gave Dee's stall a wide berth. The fact that Lily still had the cheek to work there, after all the trouble she gone through to shame her, frustrated her no end.

Jimmy's investigations around camp about this wealthy Italian fascist POW who might have shown an interest in children had come to a swift halt. He'd been foolish enough to mention Randle's name in connection with his enquiries and word had very quickly got back to Major Bykers. Jimmy ended up being hauled in front of the officer and given a dressing down.

'As you no doubt know, Sergeant Dunkersley, one person has already been reduced to ranks for starting this unseemly rumour, do you wish to follow in her footsteps?'

'No, sir.'

'Then not another word about it, Sergeant.'

'Sir.'

Lily and Dee had just got back from Skipton market when she sat down and mentioned that her son had been missing for seven months to the day.

'Seven months is a long time in the life of a four year old, Auntie Dee. I know kids of that age forget things very quickly. Do you think he'll have forgotten me by now?'

Dee had put an arm round her. 'His memory might fade, Lily girl, but not his love for his real mum. If you walked in on him right now he'd know you instantly. Wherever he is, no matter how well he's being looked after, he won't be getting a proper mother's love. Kids forget many things but not that.'

'Do you really believe that, Auntie Dee?'

'Oh, I know it, love.'

Half an hour later the phone rang. Dee answered.

'Could I speak to Lily Robinson please?'

'Who's speaking?'

'My name's Brenda – Brenda Witherspoon from Eden camp. Lily knows who I am.'

'Lily,' called out Dee, 'it's Brenda Witherspoon.'

Lily came to the phone, murmuring, 'Oh dear. I got her demoted . . . Hello, Brenda. Look, I'm sorry about what happened.'

'What? Oh, never mind that. I'm leaving the army at Christmas. Just got engaged. I'll be an RAF officer's wife on Valentine's Day.'

'Oh, congratulations.'

'Thanks. Look I should have been ringing you a month ago but Jimmy never told me, you see. He only mentioned it today when I found out he'd had a roasting back then from the CO.'

'Mentioned what?'

'About Major Mancini, the Italian who was asking about kids. Well, I say asking, it just came up in general conversation. He was a nice bloke and we got talking—'

'What?' exclaimed Lily. 'You know an Italian who was asking about children?'

'Well, yeah. He kind of confided in me that he and his wife couldn't have children of their own. Men do that, you know. Confide in me. I'm a good listener.'

'I see.'

Lily tried to contain her excitement. This phone call could lead her to her son.

'I used to take the post across to the prisoners' compound,' said Brenda. 'Obviously, this was before the Italians left and after they'd surrendered, so the security levels were relaxed a bit. Prior to that we weren't allowed to fraternise with the enemy, so there were a few months before they left when I got quite friendly with one or two of them.'

'And this Major Mancini – you got friendly with him?'

Brenda giggled. 'Only to talk to. He's a bit too old for me – anyway he's married.'

'And rich, I'm betting.'

'I got that impression. And Jimmy mentioned this bloke he'd been looking for might be one of them fascists.'

'And is Mancini a fascist?'

'Well, I never heard him grumbling about Hitler or Mussolini like some of the others. I think he only signed up as a cooperator so he could enjoy the privileges without being made to do manual work – with him being an officer. He told me he didn't need the money.'

'Do you mean he had money inside the camp?'

'He was never short of a bob or two when he needed it.'

'Where did he get it from? Through the post?'

'No, all post was checked, even after the surrender.'

'So someone on the outside must have been handing it to him.'

'I imagine so. It wouldn't have been too difficult. They were all allowed out of camp under curfew. He

327

might well have had pals on the outside who gave him money.'

'They sound more like sympathisers than pals,' said Lily. 'Fascist sympathisers. I mean, where's an Italian going to find pals like that in Yorkshire? The people round here have barely enough money to feed themselves. It had to be British fascists who were acting as some sort of go-betweens from Italy to here.'

'I suppose you could be right. By the way, there was a rumour that he'd put a Malton girl in the family way. So, if there was a problem having kids, it wasn't his problem.'

'Nice man,' said Lily.

There was a pause in the conversation as Lily framed her next question. The all-important one. 'Brenda, when he confided in you about him and his wife not being able to have children, did he say anything else on that subject?'

'That's why I'm ringing you,' said Brenda. I went over one afternoon and he'd been drinking. Some of our guards weren't above taking a back-hander from the Eyeties. I reckon Randle was one of them.'

'Go on,' said Lily, eager to hear this part of her story.

'Well, I took the post over. He was in charge of distribution and he had his own little office. He was sitting there behind a bottle of whisky when I got there. Well in his cups. He asked me how he might go about buying an orphan child from one of our children's homes.'

'Why would he want to do that?'

'Well, he was rambling a bit but I got the impression

328

that he wanted to take one home with him after the war. He confided in me that he wanted to surprise his wife by taking a ready-made child home with him. I told him I didn't think our orphan children could be bought like that.'

'And what did he say to that?'

'Say? He just picked up the bottle and finished it off. Then looked at me as if I was an imbecile. He said anything can be bought if the price was right and he had the money to buy anything or anyone he wanted. Then he started spouting a load of Italian which I don't speak, so I left him to it. Can't do with drunks, me. Never thought any more about it until Jimmy told me about his roasting from Major Bykers.'

'So, do you think it's possible that he paid Randle to get him a child?'

Without hesitation, Brenda said, 'Absolutely! That sleazy old sod'd sell his wife if the price was right – not that he'd get much of a price for her.'

'Do you know when Mancini left Eden camp and which camp he was sent to?'

'I think the Italians left around May last year and I think they were sent to all sorts of different places, not just prison camps. They're being held in football grounds, racecourses, parks, tents, country houses. As far as I know no German or Italian prisoners ever managed to escape back overseas so the odds are that Mancini's still in this country, but I've got no idea where he ended up. I know some were sent to York racecourse. He could be there. Jimmy might know. He's got access to records.'

'I bet Randle knows,' muttered Lily.

'Randle's gone,' said Brenda. 'Didn't you know?'

'Gone? Gone where?'

'He got himself a medical discharge about three weeks ago. He and his wife vacated their quarters and went off leaving no forwarding address, just a house full of furniture, apparently. Didn't Jimmy tell you?'

'No – we're not in regular touch with Jimmy. Charlie last spoke to him just after Jimmy got his roasting. He was doing us a favour.'

'Hey. I know all about doing you favours.'

'Sorry about that.'

'Like I said, it doesn't matter. I quite enjoyed it at the time.' Brenda paused for thought then added, 'Look, Lily, your story makes sense to me after what I know from this end, so I want to help. Would you like me to have a word with Jimmy about where Mancini ended up?'

'Would you? Brenda, that would be so helpful.'

The pips went on the line, indicating that it was time to put more money in or be cut off. Brenda said, hurriedly, 'Either me or Jimmy'll get back to you.'

'Thanks Bre—'

The disengaged tone came on and Lily put the phone down and looked at Dee who been intently listening to her end of the conversation.

'I think we might have the name of the Italian who's got Michael,' Lily said. 'It's a man called Major Mancini and Brenda's trying to find out where he was sent to from Eden.'

'Lily, that's excellent news!'

'Mixed news, really. The Randles have done a bunk so we won't be getting any more information out of them. I think I should ring Charlie and see what he thinks.'

Chapter 53

Brenda watched in some consternation as Jimmy limped across the guard compound towards the CO's hut. It was a miserable late November day, cold, windy and raining.

It was she who'd set these wheels in motion by telling Jimmy about Major Mancini, and if Jimmy got busted for what he was about to do she'd feel it was all her fault, despite the idea being his. She liked Jimmy and would have said yes if he'd ever asked her out. But he was a man with principles and she was a girl who always had a current boyfriend, sometimes more than one. Still, she had the man of her dreams now. Her RAF officer.

Jimmy, the man with principles, felt it was all wrong that this information about Randle and Mancini shouldn't be made official. He gritted his teeth as he tapped on Major Bykers' door.

'Come!'

Jimmy entered and clicked his heels to attention in front of the major's desk. The officer wasn't wearing a hat so a salute wasn't necessary. Jimmy's uniform was soaked from his short walk from the camp office and he was wishing he'd put his topcoat on. Bykers didn't look up from the papers in front of him. He didn't seem to be in the best of moods. On the wall behind him was a large-scale plan of the camp and a photo of a very pretty woman in WAF uniform. Jimmy knew this was Bykers' wife and wondered why she'd chosen him. A woman like that could have had the pick of the crop. Bykers was many things, but handsome wasn't one of them.

'Yes?' said Bykers, still with his attention focused on his papers.

'I've er, I've been doing a routine check through the camp records and diaries, sir, and the records of one of the prisoners is missing. I just thought I'd better report it . . . sir.'

There was a leak in the roof and a bucket was in place, catching the constant drips. Jimmy was wondering if he might have picked a better day. Bykers, recognising the voice, looked up. 'Sergeant Dunkersley. Are you on an efficiency drive to make up for your recent misdemeanour? Why bring this direct to me and not to Lieutenant Danvers?'

'I couldn't find him, sir,' lied Jimmy. 'I think he must be off camp. I was checking the prisoner lists against their personal files and records, sir, and I couldn't find any records for an Italian prisoner – Major Mancini. Everything pertaining to him seems to have been removed from the files, including where he was transferred to back in May of last year.'

Bykers sat back in his chair and regarded Jimmy thoughtfully. The silence was punctuated by rainwater dripping into the bucket.

'There's more to this than you're telling me, isn't there, Sergeant?'

Jimmy had a decision to make. Pretending had never been one of his strong points.

'Yessir.'

He was now suspecting that he could lose one or more of his stripes after this, but he also believed Lily's story and felt honour-bound to help. 'I believe there have been one or two unusual coincidences recently, sir. One is that Sergeant Randle left very quickly after the rumour about him abducting a boy. He also left without taking his furniture or leaving a forwarding address.'

'Sergeant Randle left without leaving a forwarding address because he didn't have one at the time,' said Bykers sharply. 'He was also mentally affected by the cowardly attack on him, which is why he was given his discharge papers.'

'According to records we still haven't got a forwarding address for him, sir.'

'And why do you find this a problem, Sergeant?'

'I find it curious, sir.'

'In what way?'

'Well, sir, the rumour about Sergeant Randle was connected to another rumour about Major Mancini buying the abducted boy from Randle.'

'This would be the boy called Michael Robinson.'

'Sir.'

'Which is the real reason why you were checking on Mancini's records.'

'Yessir,' admitted Jimmy.

'So Mancini was this mysterious Italian, was he?'

334

Jimmy paused, then admitted, 'Yessir. I just found it odd that the two men who are at the heart of these rumours have both disappeared without trace, sir. On top of which, Sergeant Randle had access to the camp files, so he could have removed Mancini's records.'

'Sergeant. Is this a personal crusade of yours, or is there an ulterior motive?'

'I don't understand, sir.'

'Are you in contact with the missing boy's mother?'

'She came here a few weeks ago with a friend of mine, Charlie Cleghorn. He was stationed here for a short while, sir.'

'Ah, yes. I remember Private Cleghorn. Came to help out as an interpreter, didn't he?'

'Yessir. We both came together, sir'

'And he's in league with the boy's mother?'

'They're friends, sir. He's convinced her story is the truth and she's convinced that Sergeant Randle is the person who took her son . . . sir.'

Bykers picked up a fountain pen and twirled it between his fingers, expertly. 'And what about you, Sergeant? Are you convinced?'

'I just thought you needed to know the whole story, sir.'

The major put down his pen and stroked his moustache, thinking it could be a blessing that Randle been discharged and had disappeared without trace. Similar with Mancini, whom he had never liked. It would be better for the army for the whole thing to go away, but this man standing in front of him wasn't the type to let it go away. All the seniority of rank in the world wouldn't scare this man into not doing what he thought was right. The officer allowed time to pass as he thought of the least painful solution. The water dripped into the bucket; Jimmy stood rigidly to attention, as he hadn't been given permission to stand at ease, which he found a bit disconcerting. He was uncomfortable; not sure he'd done the right thing; his khaki uniform heavy with rainwater; his eyes focused on the wall just above Major Bykers' head, where the photo of Mrs Bykers hung. *Drip, drip, drip.* The major arrived at a decision.

'The original crime, Sergeant – the abduction of the boy – is a civilian matter. I believe the Leeds police are dealing with this, are they not, Sergeant?'

'Yessir. A Sergeant Bannister.'

'Then we must not hamper their investigations by interfering. I'll alert Sergeant Bannister to everything you've told me. He may wish to come over here and interview you. In the meantime I want you to keep all this under your hat. Do not go spreading it around the camp.'

'Yessir.'

'Is there anything else, Sergeant?'

'No, sir. Thank you, sir.'

'Very good. Dismissed.'

Jimmy did a smart about turn and marched out into the rain before breaking into a run to get back to the camp office before he was completely saturated.

Bykers sat at his desk for several minutes, mulling over the best way to proceed. He came to the conclusion that it would be better if this matter didn't proceed at all but that wasn't his decision to make. He picked up

336

the phone and asked the telephonist to put him through to the Leeds City police.

'This is Major Bykers of Eden camp. I wish to speak with someone connected with the disappearance of the boy, Michael Robinson.'

Chapter 54

They were in Mary Cleghorn's house, sitting in the comfortable living room. Mary, who had effortlessly assumed the role of grandma, had the sleeping Christopher in her arms. Lily looked on approvingly, wishing Michael was here as well. Her missing boy was never more than an inch away from her thoughts. Even in her dreams, Michael was always there.

Charlie glanced at her and knew he was in love with her but he also knew he'd be wasting his time making any sort of overtures while her son was missing. She got on with her life under Dee's vigilant guidance. They worked the markets three days a week while Mary looked after Christopher, and the other four days were devoted to Christopher and to their search for Michael.

A week had gone by since Jimmy's talk with Major Bykers, during which time Lily had been hopeful that Bannister might have got in touch with Jimmy to pursue the missing records angle, not to mention Randle doing an overnight bunk and leaving no forwarding address. It had seemed to all four of them, including Jimmy, to be such a good line of enquiry that they were amazed it hadn't been followed up. Charlie guessed the army would prefer this story to go away. A child abduction carried out by a British soldier under the pay of a former Italian POW wouldn't look good in the national press. Dee suspected the police might like it to go away as well, in view of the what the law had done to Lily. Both agreed it was a cover-up. That morning Lily had rung Bannister.

'I know about Sergeant Randle doing a bunk and about this Major Mancini, who's said to have paid Randle to abduct my son for him, disappearing off the face of the earth after having his records removed from the camp. What are you doing about it, Detective Sergeant Bannister?'

'My superior discussed this with the camp command-ing officer and they decided that these events are probably not linked, and individually are not as unusual as it might seem. Records do get lost and Sergeant Randle was under severe mental stress.'

'And you believe that, do you?'

Bannister made no reply. Lily went on. 'I find it strange that you didn't bother to have a word with Sergeant Dunkersley who brought these matters to his CO's attention.' Lily's voice now had a sharp edge to it. 'He certainly thinks it's all very odd – and he's much more involved with the camp records than his CO.'

'I'm sorry, Mrs Robinson, but we can't devote police resources to investigating baseless rumours, which is all these are. We have people working on your cases all the time. As soon as we hear anything we'll let you know.'

'In other words, the army want to cover it up,' said Lily, with ice in her voice. 'And you don't want the truth to come out after the way you've treated me. Tell you what, never mind, Sergeant. Don't bother. We'll find my boys ourselves!'

It had been Lily's idea to meet at Mary's and to put their collective heads together and plan the next move. It was there that Mary revealed news that came as something of a shock to them, especially to Charlie.

'I've been having a word with your father, Charlie, about this Italian chap.'

'Mum, you haven't told him about Christopher, have you?'

'Of course I haven't, although your dad'd sooner chop his right arm off than get you into any trouble. He obviously knows you're helping Lily, and he doesn't approve. He thinks you should leave it to the police.'

'Yes, I'm aware of that, Mum. So, what were you talking about?'

Mary went quiet for a few seconds as one would before revealing a piece of delicate information. 'Well, I mentioned that this Italian chap might have had help from British fascists who had avoided being interned.' She stopped there, as if worried about what to say next.

'Right,' said Charlie, 'and . . . ?'

'And the reason I mentioned it, was to see if he might be able to help.'

'Help? In what way could Dad help?'

Mary lowered her eyes under the curious gazes from the others. She smiled down at Christopher, then lifted him up to her face and kissed his forehead. Her love for him couldn't have been any more had she been his real grandmother. When Mary looked up at them again, her lips had tightened as if she was steeling herself for what she had to say next. She turned her attention to Charlie.

'Many years ago, your dad was a member of the British Union of Fascists – in fact he was one of their Black Shirts for four years.'

'What?'

'I'm afraid so.'

'My dad a fascist? No, Never!'

Mary continued, her voice quiet. 'Your dad was totally convinced that Oswald Mosley was right. He took me to a meeting once. Mosley was amazingly charismatic. Brilliant speaker, but there again so was Hitler.' She looked at Lily and Dee. 'We lived in London back then, which is why Charlie never fully acquired the Yorkshire accent.'

'Did he convince you?' Lily asked.

Mary shook her head. 'No, not for a second, but I could see why he had so many followers. Tom and I argued about it night and day. It didn't do our marriage much good.'

'Mum,' said Charlie, 'how come I never knew about this?'

'Because we never told you. To be honest, your dad and I were never really suited. We got married because . . .'

'Because of me,' Charlie said. 'I had worked it out.'

Lily and Dee were now listening with interest, with both of them having married for the same reason. There was now a common bond between the three of them.

'Yes, I thought you might,' Mary said. 'Don't get me

wrong. Tom Cleghorn's a good man. In fact it's probably because of him that I never remarried. I kept comparing other men to him and they didn't come up to scratch. The trouble was, neither did your dad. This fascist nonsense was the last straw. I left him in 1933, a year after he joined.'

'So,' said Charlie, struggling to take this in. 'How long was he a member? How come he wasn't interned in 1939?'

'Tom left them well before then – in 1936. There was a big march in London that was opposed by communists, Jews and Irish dockers. A massive fight broke out and your dad apparently had a sort of road to Damascus moment. He ended up ripping off his black shirt and siding with the communists – typical Tom Cleghorn – he didn't like the way things were going. He was arrested and ended up in a cell full of Jewish blokes. Good job he didn't have his shirt on.'

She smiled at the memory. 'You and I were living here by then, with your grandma and granddad.'

She looked at Lily and Dee and added, 'They both died in 1939, within three months of each other.'

'I'm sorry to hear that,' said Lily.

'Oh, don't be. Mum died first. Dad was no good without her – they had a beautiful marriage.' She twinkled at Lily. 'Some people do, you know. They left me with this house and quite a lot of money.'

'Dad always reckoned he'd married above his station,' put in Charlie. 'Mum was privately educated, Dad was just a working-class charmer. Although he now runs a very profitable business.'

His mother frowned. 'Demolition wasn't exactly the career I had mapped out for you. You could have been head of languages at one of the top public schools. Still could for that matter.'

'I think I have a working-class soul, Mum,' grinned Charlie.

'You were telling us about Charlie's dad,' said Dee, eager to know where this story was going.'

'Yes, of course. I read about the riots in the paper and knew Tom would be involved. The papers called it the Battle of Cable Street. The next thing I knew he was knocking on our door.'

'What? He wanted to come back to you?'

'Not specifically – I think he knew as well as I that we weren't really suited. He took life far too seriously. Still does for that matter.'

'Do you get on with him OK?' said Lily.

'Oh, yes. You've heard the old saying, "Absence makes the heart grow fonder" – in our case it's distance.'

'You were telling us about his fascist connections,' said Dee, impatient that this story kept going off track.

'Oh, yes. Well, Tom wanted a clean break from his life down in London. He left the British Union of Fascists and decided to come and live in Leeds to be near his boy. He asked if we could put him up for a few days while he got himself fixed up with somewhere to live.'

'I remember that,' said Charlie. 'I wanted him to stay. Dad said it wouldn't be a good idea but, if I wanted, I could go and work for him when he got his new demolition business up and running.'

'You said you'd mentioned to him about this Italian chap being a fascist,' said Dee.

'I did, yes. I mentioned that it was highly likely that he'd been helped by local people with fascist sympathies.' She looked at them, one by one. 'He told me about a Yorkshire farmer who lives in a place called Thorpe Newton, which isn't far from Malton. He reckons this farmer's a died-in-the-wool fascist.'

'And Dad knows him, does he?'

'He met him just once at a party rally in London about ten years ago,' said Mary, smiling at a memory. 'It was the name Thorpe Newton that stuck in Tom's mind. Apparently Tom had two best pals at school, Edwin Thorpe and Tommy Newton. They got up to a lot of mischief together and the names Thorpe, Newton and Cleghorn were often linked by their teachers when investigating misdemeanours.'

'Did the man's name stick there as well?' asked Dee hopefully.

'I'm afraid not. Tom reckons it's a family farm and the man'll still be farming there. I've looked Thorpe Newton up on a map and it's only a small village just off the A64. There can't be too many farms near there.'

'If he's a member of the BUF he'll have been interned, surely,' said Charlie.

'Not necessarily, according to your dad. Plenty of them escaped the net and with this man being a farmer it's doubtful they'll have looked too hard at him. On top of which it's more than likely he'll have kept his politics secret from his neighbours. Two hundred miles away in London he could shout his rubbish as loud as he liked, but it'd have got him into no end of trouble in a small village in Yorkshire.'

'Do we know what this man looks like?' Lily asked, feeling her excitement mounting. It seemed that the door to Michael's whereabouts had creaked open another inch.

'Yes, he's apparently a very big man. Needed a hair-cut, red face, big nose, well over six feet – six foot six maybe, with a build to suit. Probably in his forties by now. Liked his drink and after a couple of pints he was quite intimidating, according to Tom. Not a man you'd want to get on the wrong side of.'

'Oh, great,' said Lily, knowing what Charlie was like.

Charlie was smiling. He was glad his dad had come through with something useful. He hadn't given up hope of them getting back together.

'Well,' he said. 'If he's not the one who was helping Mancini he probably knows who was. There can't be too many fascists around that area. It's just a question of persuading him to tell us what he knows.'

The three women exchanged glances. All of them aware of Charlie's capabilities, and the punishment if he was caught.

'Tread carefully, Charlie,' warned Mary.

'Don't worry, Mum. I know what I'm doing.'

Two of the women were already worrying.

Chapter 55

A phone call to Jimmy confirmed that a lot of German prisoners were working on farms in the Thorpe Newton area, as had the Italians, but it was unlikely that Mancini would have worked there, with him being an officer.

'I wouldn't have expected him to work there,' said Charlie. 'In fact I wouldn't expect they wanted to be seen together. Someone might have put two and two together and taken a closer look at the farmer. Are there any pubs in the Thorpe Newton area where this bloke might do his drinking? I gather he likes a drink.'

'There's only one pub in Thorpe Newton, the Star and Garter. I've had a few pints in there myself. Yeah, quite a few farmers get in. It might be an idea to call in and ask the landlord if he knows anyone who fits that description, but you'll have to do your own asking, Charlie. This thing's nearly cost me my stripes.'

'Sorry about that, mate. Star and Garter at Thorpe Newton, do you say? Must try and remember that.'

Thorpe Newton was half a mile off the A64, just a few miles east of Malton. Charlie took Lily there in his van, leaving Dee to work her stall and Mary looking after

Christopher. The road took them though the centre of York, a city Lily had only ever passed through, on a couple of coach trips to the coast with Larry. She persuaded Charlie to stop there for a while so she could take a look around. They drove past the Knavesmire – York racecourse – now a POW camp, then he took the van into the city centre and parked. Lily linked his arm as he showed her the Shambles, York Minster and Clifford's Tower, inside which, in 1170, a hundred and fifty Jews were burned to death by the anti-semitic citizens of York. As Charlie told her the story Lily nodded, as if understanding the plight of the Jews.

'I kind of know what it's like to be ostracised from society,' she said, looking up at the tower perched on top of a high mound. 'Maybe my neighbours would have tried to burn my house down, if I'd still been living in it.'

Charlie put an arm round her and she leaned into him. To both of them it felt right, but to Lily it also felt like betrayal of her dead husband and her missing son. She gave a short laugh.

'Or am I being paranoid?'

'Dunno,' said Charlie, still holding her to him. 'People do things they regret when it's too late.'

'Like sending Michael off with two people I hardly knew?'

'Lily, I didn't mean that.'

Her shoulders slumped. 'I know,' she said. 'I'm sorry. It's just on my mind every minute of every day.'

'Which is why I'm trying to do something about it. We need to get Michael back so that you can get on with your life.'

She looked up at him and smiled. 'And then what? What do you have in mind for my life, Mr Cleghorn?'

Was she offering him a way to open up about his feelings for her? He was painfully aware of the turmoil boiling deep within her. That might confuse her; even turn her against him if he made any sort of advances.

'I want whatever you want, Lily. It's important to me that you get your happiness back.'

'Charlie. I think that's the nicest thing anyone's ever said to me.'

Anyone? Would that include Larry? Charlie hoped so but didn't say it.

They went to a café by the River Ouse for lunch. So far it had been the best day Lily had had since Larry went away. There was colour back in her cheeks and a spark about her that Charlie hadn't seen before but he reckoned it had always been there; suppressed by the horrors of her recent life.

They both had roast beef and Yorkshire pudding – a rare delight in those days of rationing. Charlie suspected he might have a tough time ahead of him that afternoon and he'd always hated going into battle on an empty stomach. If this farmer did indeed know anything at all about the Italian officer and Lily's son, Charlie was prepared to do whatever it took to extract from this man every piece of information he had. It was with this thought in mind that he wondered at the wisdom in bringing Lily along.

She'd insisted; that's why she was here. And there was no way he could have told her she couldn't come lest she witnessed a side of him she might not like. After they'd both cleared their plates he looked at her and said, 'Lily, what we're about to do might take some sort of force from me.'

'I suspected it might,' she said.

'Does this bother you?'

'It will if you get hurt, Charlie.'

'Hopefully it won't come to that, but I want you to bear in mind one thing. If it comes to any sort of confrontation it's not Charlie Cleghorn you'll be seeing, it'll be me putting on my psycho act. It took me a while to perfect it, and I know it's scary, but it's just an act, nothing more.'

'Really? Are you a good actor?'

'In the army it was part of my job to get information out of people. I was quite good at it.'

Lily thought about the information he'd got from Randle. 'Yes, I imagine that's true.'

'But it's just an act . . . to get Michael back.'

Lily got up to go, feeling that her enjoyment of this day was going to take a turn for the worse.

Chapter 56

The Star and Garter was an old coaching inn situated right in the middle of Thorpe Newton. Over the one hundred and seventy-five years of its existence it had changed its name three times to keep up with modern trends. Fifteen years previously it had been called the Eagle but the new, and present, landlord thought a double-barrelled name might have a bit more class. Charlie and Lily arrived at half past five, just as it was opening for evening trade. Charlie had planned it thus. He wanted an empty pub to give him a chance to chat to the landlord without interference from customers. The pub was empty apart from one local who had managed to beat them through the door. Charlie ordered a pint of John Smith's for him and a brandy for Lily. The landlord was an amiable chap, happy to have a bit of unexpected custom, and quite chatty.

'You don't sound as if yer from round 'ere.'

'I'm originally from London,' said Charlie. 'I was stationed in Eden camp for a while and I thought I'd call back to see a few old pals.'

'We don't get too many in here from the camp. One or two of the officers, but they've got their own transport.'

'Unlike us squaddies,' grinned Charlie. 'Anyway, I'm out of it now and I've got my own limousine – that's if you call a Morris Eight van a limousine.'

This raised a smile from the landlord as he placed Charlie's pint on the bar and pressed a brandy glass into an optic.

'I actually knew a bloke from round here,' Charlie went on. 'Met him in a pub in Malton. I think he had a farm. Great big bloke, six foot six . . . trying to remember his name.'

'Charlie, you're useless at names,' chipped in Lily.

'I am not!' protested Charlie. 'Give me a second, I'll remember it.'

'A second?' said Lily. 'I could give you an hour, you wouldn't remember it.'

The landlord was grinning at this banter as he placed the brandy on the bar. 'That'll be two and threepence,' he said, then added, 'I'm the same for forgettin' names. Only yesterday I was tryin' ter remember the name o' that bloke who was in *Gone With The Wind*. The more yer try ter remember the more yer mind goes blank.'

'Clark Gable,' said Lily.

'That's right – no, I did remember but only after I stopped tryin'.

Charlie handed him half a crown and told him to keep the change, then added, to Lily. 'I'll remember that bloke's name if it kills me.' He took a sip of his drink and looked at the landlord. 'Big fella, needed a haircut, red face, big nose – you must know him. He likes a drink. He's got a farm near Thorpe Newton, at least he had two years ago.'

The lone customer, who'd been listening to the conversation, called out, 'Sounds like Bert Pinkney ter me.'

'Aye,' grinned the landlord. 'It'll be Bert. He's the only one farming round here what fits that description.'

Charlie held up a delighted finger. 'Bert! That's his name' He turned to Lily. 'Told you I'd remember.'

'You didn't remember,' said Lily jabbing a thumb over her shoulder at the customer. 'It was that gentleman who told you.'

'You're splitting hairs again.' Charlie grinned, then to the landlord he said, 'Does he drink in here? I know he likes a drink.'

'He likes too many drinks, that's his trouble. I've lost count of the number of times I've barred him fer causin' trouble.' He scratched his head. 'In fact I don't know whether or not he's barred right now.'

The customer called out again. 'Yer missis barred him last Sat'day. Told him not ter bother comin' back. Hey! She's got some bloody bottle has your Doris.'

Charlie pulled a face and said, 'Oh dear. Does he live far away? I might pop in and see him.'

'What on earth do you want to see him for?' said Lily. 'He doesn't sound like someone I'd like to meet.'

'Well, as a matter of fact,' said Charlie, 'he owes me five bob I took off him at darts. He didn't have it on him at the time and he told me he'd be back the following week to pay me, but I got transferred. He's bound to remember once he sees me.'

'Is that why you brought me here?' said Lily, in mock protest. 'To track down five flipping bob a bloke owes you?'

'No, I've only just remembered. Five bob's five bob. I might not be round here again.'

The landlord and the customer were grinning at each other. 'If you turn left out o' the car park,' the landlord said, 'his farm's half a mile on yer right. Yer can't miss it. It's called Beckwater Farm.' He leaned over the bar and spoke to Charlie confidentially so that the customer couldn't hear. 'Look, I don't know how well yer know him but, I'd be careful.' He tapped his temple with a forefinger. 'He blows hot and cold does Bert – if yer know what I mean. Personally, I'd forget about that five bob.'

'Right,' said Charlie. 'He did strike me as being a bit, aggressive.'

'Oh, he can be a lot aggressive, can Bert.' The landlord leaned even closer. 'There's a rumour that he used ter be in Mosley's mob. Yer know what I'm sayin'?'

'I think I do, yes. Thanks for the warning. Does he live alone?'

'He's got a lad as big as him, and he used to have a foreign bloke stayin' there. Greek refugee, he told me. I never saw him but there's them as did. Why he'd take a refugee in, God only knows. Mebbe a bit o' cheap labour or mebbe there's some good in him what I don't know about. There's nowt as queer as folk, is there?'

'Is the Greek still there?'

'No, he left a few months back, accordin' ter Bert. Hey, I should leave well alone if I were you.'

Chapter 57

'That Greek refugee might be Mancini,' said Lily, after they'd got back in the van. 'How would anyone round here know the difference between a Greek accent and an Italian accent?'

'That's what I was thinking,' said Charlie. 'In any event, Bert's definitely our man. By the way, well done for joining in back there. I think we gave a convincing performance.'

'I might have been a bit more convincing had you warned me what you were going to say.'

'How did I know what I was going to say? I was just playing it by ear.'

'Why couldn't you just give the landlord the bloke's description and ask if he knew him?'

'Because,' said Charlie, 'these villages are very parochial. A stranger comes in the local pub and starts after asking about one of the neighbours, their very first reaction is suspicion. He might have told us, he might not, but either way he might well have been on the phone to this Bert Pinkney the minute we left.'

'That's if Bert Pinkney's got a phone.'

'That's a risk I wasn't prepared to take. I didn't want

Bert to be expecting me. Forewarned is forearmed and all that.'

'I don't think the landlord has any great love for Bert – I doubt if he'd have warned him.'

'We know that now.'

'This is more stuff you learned in the army? Blimey, Charlie! The army's made you paranoid.'

Charlie pressed the starter. 'Paranoid, but still alive, Lily.'

He was smiling inwardly. The exchange had pleased him. They were talking like a couple who owed each other explanations. *A proper couple*. As they approached Beckwater Farm he changed his mindset to prepare for confrontation, perhaps physical. He'd come more prepared than Lily knew about. He hadn't told her everything.

'I'm going to assume the Greek is Mancini.' He said it as much to himself as to Lily.

'OK,' she said, not knowing the implications of what he'd decided.

There was a driveway to the farm which stood about a hundred yards from the road. Charlie turned in and drove slowly, taking in deep, controlling breaths. Lily looked at him and decided not to disturb what was going on in his mind. Whatever it was, it was for her benefit. It was to get Michael back.

'Charlie,' she murmured. 'Whatever you do, I'm with you all the way.'

He nodded without looking at her and got out of the van. She got out as well. Whatever happened next he wasn't in this on his own.

The door was large and heavy, no doubt like its

owner. It had no bell or knocker so Charlie rapped on it as loudly as his knuckles would stand. He heard bad-tempered grumbling from within and winked at Lily.

'I think I've aroused the denizens.'

The door was opened by a giant of a man dressed in capacious corduroy trousers held up by a broad leather belt that served the dual purpose of keeping his huge stomach in check. Braces, obviously held in reserve for additional trouser support, hung down by his thighs. He had the red face and big nose that Mary had described, plus the unkempt hair. His general attitude wasn't welcoming to these strangers at his door. Charlie smiled and held out a hand of greeting, which was ignored.

'Good afternoon, Mr Pinkney – Charlie Cleghorn.'

Pinkney looked beyond him to the van and read the lettering. His voice was broad Yorkshire and harsh. 'We don't want nowt demolishin', so bugger off!'

Charlie maintained his smile. 'We're not here on company business, Mr Pinkney, we're here to discuss a mutual friend of ours. May we come in?'

Pinkney instinctively stood to one side as Charlie pushed past him into the farmhouse, closely followed by Lily. The door opened into a large room, maybe twenty feet square. It was an unattractive room furnished with heavy furniture. A smell of sweat, stale beer and cigarette smoke hung in the air. There was a long, wooden table littered with dirty crockery, empty beer bottles and a sleeping dog. Several chairs were scattered around, some wooden, some upholstered. None of them looked all that comfortable. A crackling radio was playing music and in one of the chairs was a younger man, probably the same size as Pinkney. He was drinking beer from a bottle, reading a newspaper and paying no attention to the new arrivals.

'So,' said Pinkney, 'who's this mutual friend?'

'Major Mancini,' said Charlie brightly. Lily was wondering if he was taking the right approach.

'Never heard of him.'

'Oh, I think you have. He stayed here for quite a while after he did a bunk from Eden camp. You told everyone he was a Greek refugee.'

Lily could see Pinkney's eyes bulging with rage. The son had put his paper down and had got to his feet. Charlie nodded at him. 'You'll be Bert's son, will you?' He held out a hand. 'Charlie Cleghorn.'

His hand was ignored. The son said nothing but the look on his face told Charlie he wasn't welcome in this room. Lily was now comparing the size of these two giants to Charlie, who was a good six feet tall and athletically built, but a dwarf compared to these men who must each have weighed at least eighteen stone. Their combined weight was three times that of Charlie.

Pinkney stepped right into Charlie's face and growled at him. 'Are yer callin' me a liar?' He pushed Charlie with a huge hand. Charlie staggered backwards but didn't react. ' 'Cos if yer are I'll break yer bloody neck and hers as well.'

He looked at Lily and gave a frightening grin full of rotten teeth. The son was grinning as well. His teeth showed promise of ending up like his dad's. 'In fact,' smirked Pinkney, 'we might have a bit o' fun wi' this one's body afore we break her neck.'

'Mancini abducted a small child, no doubt with your assistance,' Charlie went on. His manner was eminently reasonable, to Lily's amazement. These two men were threatening to do heaven knows what to her and he was being polite to them. Pinkney reached out and placed a hand on her breasts. She reacted by slapping him hard across the face. He roared with laughter. 'By God, yer'll definitely pay fer that with yer body, girl!' He began to unbuckle his belt. 'The coppers can't touch me. Yer trespassin' in my house. I can do what I like wi' yer.'

'I don't think so,' she said uncertainly. Charlie was saying or doing nothing to help her situation. Jesus! she thought. Have I got him wrong. Is he a coward?

Bert was sniggering in anticipation. 'Well, I don't give a toss what yer think – Ezra, strip the woman naked fer yer father's pleasure, I'll leave enough fer you ter pleasure yersen after I've done with her.'

Ezra gave a menacing snigger then stepped forward and lunged at Lily. Charlie brought an arm up and jabbed his elbow into Ezra's face with extreme, bone-breaking force. Lily heard the bone snapping and stepped away from the spraying blood. In the blink of an eye Charlie jabbed his elbow again, this time breaking several of Ezra's teeth. Blood ran down Ezra's face and he screamed with pain. Charlie's voice was still the voice of reason as he turned his attention to Pinkney. From somewhere he'd produced a pistol and was holding it against the big man's left eye.

'You see, Mr Pinkney, I'm doing my level best to be reasonable here and you're not helping me. You're not helping me at all.' He moved the gun slightly to one side and pulled the trigger. The report was deafening, more so to Pinkney as the bullet took away part of his ear before embedding itself in a door. The man screamed with pain and rage and threw a violent fist at Charlie.

Charlie ducked under the punch at the same time as sticking the gun in his pocket. He hooked the big man's flailing arm under his right arm then, with his left hand took hold of Pinkney's wrist and and bent it back to breaking point causing the farmer to howl in even more agony.

Ezra, still in pain with his broken nose and teeth, had now taken note of what was happening to his father. He stepped towards Charlie who held on to Bert's wrist with his left hand, easily avoided Ezra's flailing punch and swung his right hand in a well-practised, back-handed chop to the side of Ezra's neck, landing his blow smack on the carotid artery. It was the most effective weapon in his armoury: a karate blow he'd perfected during his time in Italy. If expertly delivered, it would render the biggest of men unconscious without noise, or blood. Ezra collapsed to the floor like a puppet with its strings cut.

Charlie's voice was still calm but had now taken on a manic tone. His grip on Pinkney's wrist had the big man bent almost double. 'Right, Mr Pinkney. Can we talk sense now or do you enjoy pain? Tell you what, why don't I break a few fingers to make you more cooperative?'

With that he took a grip on Pinkney's left thumb and snapped it backwards with a sickening crack. Pinkney yelled with this new pain that now obscured the pain from his ear.

'Will that do it, Mr Pinkney, or would you like me to carry on? You've got nine more fingers to go at before I start on your arms and legs – or shall I remove your manhood?' He took out his gun again, held it against Pinkney's groin and pulled the trigger. The bullet didn't touch anything but Pinkey felt the heat of it in his private parts. He lifted Pinkney's head up with the barrel of the gun and stared into his face. Charlie's eyes had widened into those of a madman. Lily was pleased he'd forewarned her about this act.

'Damn! Missed!' said Charlie. He let go of Pinkney's hand and pointed the gun directly between the stricken farmer's legs. He closed one eye to take aim. Pinkney was moaning in pain from his damaged ear and broken thumb. He sank to his knees.

'I'll call t' police, yer know.'

'Be my guest,' said Charlie, hefting the gun in his right hand. 'Call them and tell them you're a member of the British Union of Fascists who's been helping an Italian prisoner of war to abduct a British child. In fact you harboured the man under the guise of a Greek refugee. How long do you think they'll lock you up for?'

Pinkney gave this some thought, then looked down at his unconscious son. 'Is he all right?'

'For the time being, Mr Pinkney. If I don't get what I want from you I'll kill you both and bury you on your farm. From what I hear not too many people will come looking for you. But before then I'll do my best to persuade you to do the right thing.' He reached down and grabbed one of Pinkney's hands, gripping his middle finger and pulling it back.

360

'ALL RIGHT!' roared Pinkney. He had tears of pain streaming down his face, mingling with the blood dripping from his ear. 'Leave me alone. What d'yer want ter know?'

'Good,' said Charlie. 'We're beginning to understand each other.'

He said nothing more for a while. He allowed the room to fall into a silence, broken only by Pinkney's moaning and his son's noisy breathing. He looked at Lily. 'Could you lock the door then go to the window and check we're not having any visitors?' He then returned his attention to Pinkney.

'Right, Mr Pinkney. It's time for you to try and save your miserable hide and that of your boy. I want you to tell me everything you know about Mancini. And I mean everything, from the beginning. From how you first met him. And if I think you're lying I'll start breaking fingers again.'

'I met him when he came ter work here,' Pinkney began.

'He was an officer,' screamed Charlie. 'Officers weren't forced to work.'

'He only came here now and again at first,' said Pinkney quickly, hiding his hands behind his back to keep his fingers away from this madman. 'He told t' camp guards he liked t' exercise. He knew about me from an organisation called Fascists Abroad.'

Charlie switched off his unbalanced rage. '*Fascisti all'Estero*,' he said, in a perfect Italian accent. And you're a member of the BUF.'

'*Was* a member,' groaned Pinkney, holding his

broken hand to his damaged ear. Had he not been so vile to her earlier Lily would have felt sorry for him. 'They got banned back in '40.'

'When the Italians were moved from Eden camp,' said Charlie, 'he destroyed his camp records and came to stay with you.'

Pinkney gave a painful nod.

'And you told everyone he was a Greek refugee and nobody questioned it, not even the police?'

Pinkney managed a laugh. 'Mancini had money being sent to him. He gave t' coppers back-handers ter keep quiet. With t' war in Italy bein' over they thought nowt of it.'

'How did he get hold of the money?'

'I picked it up fer him. It were sent over to a London bank belongin' ter some business man or other, never knew his name.'

'Another BUF man?'

Pinknet grimaced and moaned in pain before answering. 'Prob'ly, aye. There's still a lot about yer know. Mancini married into a wealthy family. They had money in Swiss banks what they transferred over here. I used ter go ter London ter pick it up, as and when it were needed. I gave it ter Mancini. It made his life a damn sight sweeter in that camp.'

'I bet it made your life a bit sweeter, too.'

'He gave me a few quid fer me trouble, yeah.'

'One day last April you were sent to pick up two thousand pounds. Did you know what this was for?'

'Last April? Aye. No idea what it were for, not at first. It were a rush job. Randle rang up early one mornin'

362

askin' ter speak to Mancini. After he put t' phone down Mancini asked me ter get mesen down ter London that same day and bring a parcel back that night. I've no idea what were in it. I thought it might be money.'

'Would that have been back in April?' asked Lily.

Pinkney looked up at her, 'Back end of April – aye.'

Charlie looked at Lily. 'My guess is it'll have been the same day as Randle and his wife came to see you. They'll have been banking on getting Michael from you that day and they'll have told Mancini to have the money ready when they dropped the boy off. He must have held on to Michael overnight to give Mancini time to get the money together.' He turned back to Pinkney who was alternately nursing his broken thumb and tenderly fingering his damaged ear to check the extent of the damage.

'Go on,' Charlie ordered.

'Well, it were well past midnight when I got back here. My lad had ter pick me up from York station. Randle turned up early that same mornin'. That's when Mancini told me he'd decided to leave.'

'Did Randle have a small boy in the car?' Charlie asked.

Lily was now listening intently for the first definite confirmation that her son was alive.

Pinkney clammed shut, believing he'd now said too much. Charlie reached round Pinkey's back and took hold of his middle finger once again. 'I'll count to three,' he said, coldly, bending the finger back to breaking point.

'One, two, thr—'

'All right! I saw a kid in the car.'

Lily suddenly burst into tears. Her boy was alive. Pinkney continued: 'Only fer a few minutes. He were in the back o' Randle's car, fast asleep. I asked Mancini who he was. He told me he were an orphan who were goin' to a better life. That's all I know about him.'

Lily screamed at him. 'He's my son. Randle stole him from me and you helped – you vile bastard!'

'What do you think the police will make of all this?' said Charlie. 'How long do you think you'll get? My guess is twenty years fer you and ten for the lad if he's helped you harbour Mancini, which is not punishment enough – but I know what is punishment enough!' With a deranged grin he took his gun out and stuck it in Pinkney's face.

'Charlie, don't!' shouted Lily, genuinely alarmed.

Her concern convinced Pinkney that Charlie wasn't bluffing. If she thought this madman was about to pull the trigger maybe he was in more trouble than he thought. 'Jesus!' He shouted, holding out his arms in supplication. 'Please, don't shoot me. I've told yer everythin' I know.'

'No you haven't,' said Charlie, lowering the gun, his voice icy with feigned madness. 'You haven't told us where he is now.'

Pinkney hung his head in relief. 'To be honest, I think he could be back in Italy. I heard Randle and Mancini talking about going to London to meet the London connection.'

'And the London connection somehow smuggled them over to Italy?' said Charlie. 'How the hell would that work?'

'I don't know,' said Pinkney miserably. 'I know money makes most things work in this world and Mancini had stacks of that. My guess is that Mancini stayed in London until the war was finally over and his contacts somehow bought him and the boy a passage to Venice.'

'Venice?' said Lily. 'Oh my God! Is that where my boy is?'

Pinkney looked at her and shrugged. 'All I know is that's where Mancini lived.'

'I want his address, you fat, slimy bastard!' said Charlie, holding the gun to Pinkney's head once more. He sounded frighteningly unbalanced once again. Pinkney looked beseechingly at Lily. 'Call him off, will yer, luv?'

'Just give us Mancini's address in Venice,' she said, pretending to be a bit unbalanced herself now. She was about to learn exactly where her boy was.

Pinkney inclined his head towards a distressed-looking chest of drawers. 'There's an envelope with his address on it in t' top drawer over there. He were gonna post it, but he never got round to it. I think he took t' letter with him.'

Lily went over to the drawer, inside which was a jumble of items. She found the envelope with an Italian address and handed it to Charlie. The envelope was empty. He read the address. 'Palazzo Cominelli. Sestiere di Dorsoduro. Four-oh-eight-one. Venezia, Italia.'

'Do you know Venice?' Lily asked.

'No,' said Charlie. 'I never got over there, but it was still under German occupation until April this year.'

'It was April when Michael was taken.'

'I know,' said Charlie, looking down at the men on the floor. Ezra was stirring, Bert was moaning.

He stuffed the envelope in his pocket. 'OK, gentlemen. We won't mention this discussion to the police if you don't. If I need any more information from you I'll be back and I trust you'll be more hospitable.' He looked at Lily. 'They didn't even offer us a cup of tea.'

Charlie gave Pinkney a wide-eyed manic stare. 'Mr Pinkney. You probably think I'm an unreasonable man but if you try to get word of our visit to Mr Mancini or to the police I will know and I will come back here and show you just how unreasonable I can be. Do I make myself clear?' His voice rose to frenzied proportions towards the end of this. Once again Lily was glad he'd warned her about his act, which was very impressive.

'I should take him seriously,' she said to Pinkney. 'You've caught him in a good mood today. He can go a bit too far when he's crossed.' She looked at the dog, still asleep under the table. 'Good guard dog you've got, by the way.'

Pinkney closed his eyes to shut out the pain in his ear and fingers. Ezra's eyes were open and he was feeling the pain from his broken nose and broken teeth once again.

Lily breathed out a long sigh as they drove out of the farmyard. 'Whew! That was something of an experience, Charlie.'

'You think I went over the top, don't you?'

'I don't know. You were a bit scary. I suppose I wondered if it might have been possible to use less violence.'

366

'Oh, it's definitely possible, given time. By time I mean days, sometimes weeks. I didn't have that luxury. I had to convince the Pinkneys that I was prepared to kill them, if need be. I also had to inflict fear and unbearable pain to get Bert to talk quickly and truthfully. I didn't inflict too much lasting damage, apart from his ear – and that was only cosmetic. Broken fingers and noses heal fairly quickly. I knew it'd look scary, which is why I warned you.'

'When we first went in there, why did you let them bully us? Why didn't you go straight for them?'

'Because I needed to prove to myself – and to you – that they deserved what I was going to do to them. If they'd been all reasonable and pleasant I couldn't have done it, even if they refused to tell me what I wanted to know.' Charlie pulled a face. 'Actually, I hate having to do that. I thought that was all in the past.'

'Being Superman's quite a handy skill to have,' she said.

'It's not too good for peace of mind, knowing I'm capable of stuff like that. I'd rather never have to do it again but, if I need to, to get Michael back, I will.'

'So, what do we do now?'

'Well we can't tell Bannister I've just scared the truth out of Bert Pinkney. I'd get locked up for assault.'

'Right then, Mr Cleghorn. I assume you know the way to Venice.'

'Head for the Alps and turn left, you can't miss it.'

Chapter 58

Mary had a map of Europe spread across her kitchen table. Around it sat the four of them: Mary, Lily, Charlie and Dee. A thought struck Charlie. He looked up at Lily.

'You'll need to get a passport – that might take a while.'

Lily looked at him through disapproving eyes. 'So, you thought a poor, back-street girl like me wouldn't have a passport? I've had one since my Larry got big ideas of going over to Norway for a family holiday. Getting a passport was as far as we got. Michael's on my passport as well.'

Charlie held up his hands in apology. He looked at Dee, who said, 'I've been around Europe a bit myself, Charlie,' she said. 'My passport's not out of date yet, even if I am.'

'OK,' said Charlie. 'Immediate problem solved. Three to go, four to come back. Problem number two is how to get there. Do we fly, do we go by train – or do we go in my van or on our bikes?'

'I think you can cancel three of them out,' said Mary. 'Van and motorbike – lack of comfort for a thousand-mile journey, and flying would cost a fortune right now.'

'Train it is then,' said Charlie.

'How do we get across the Channel?' Lily asked.

'Ferry from Folkestone,' said Charlie.

'To where?' said Lily, poring over the map. 'Calais?'

'I think Calais's out of action for civilians right now, but I know we can get to Ostend.'

All four of them examined the map, Mary ran a finger from Ostend to Venice, tracking railway routes. 'Ostend to Paris, Paris to Milan, Milan to Venice,' she said. 'You should still be able to get a through train from Paris if the war hasn't messed things up.'

'Still?' said Charlie. 'Mum, have you actually been to Venice?'

'Yes, I have. I spent a whole summer there when I was twenty-two. I was just out of university and was offered a job as an English tutor in a Venice summer school. I got to live in a marvellous apartment overlooking the Grand Canal. Then I came home and met your father. Talk about the sublime to the ridiculous – sorry, Charlie. I didn't mean that.'

'Oh, yes, you did,' said Charlie, grinning.

'Talking about my ex-husband, how about cost? Can you afford it or shall we bully Tom for the money?'

The four of them looked at each other. 'I'm OK for money,' said Lily. 'I still haven't drawn any of my war-widow's pension.'

'I can pay my way,' said Charlie.'

'I'll give Henry Smithson a ring,' said Dee. 'He works on the *Craven Herald*,' she explained to Mary. 'I've given him first dabs at an exclusive on this story. Now that it's coming to a head I think they can get their hands into their pockets and pay our expenses. If not, I'm OK for money.'

'That's it, then,' said Charlie. 'We go by train and we don't have to worry Dad.' He pushed the envelope with the address written on it over to his mother. 'What are we to make of this address?'

Mary examined it carefully. 'Well, the very word *palazzo* means we're looking for a really high-class residence.'

'Yeah, I figured that,' said Charlie. 'The direct translation is palace.'

'Dorsoduro,' said Mary, 'tells me it's in Venice itself and not on mainland Venice, which means it could be a devil to find without directions, despite having an address.'

'What's Dorsoduro?' Lily asked.

'It's a *sestiere*,' said Mary. 'It means area. There are six of them in Venice: I lived in one called San Marco when I was there.'

'Pity you can't come with us,' said Dee.

'It's a question of where I'll be most use. Here looking after Christopher or showing you round Venice.'

'Here, looking after Christopher,' said Lily, who had grown to know and trust Mary.

It transpired that Henry Smithson had now retired from the *Craven Herald* but he was prepared to take a gamble on what might well be a sensational exclusive. Out of his own pocket he'd funded them to the tune of £200 for the trip.

They each took only a rucksack containing whatever they thought might be necessary for a trip of unknown duration. The journey to Venice would take them approximately four days. The trip to Folkestone alone took seven hours including four train changes. Lily said she didn't mind. Every hour was an hour nearer to her son. Dee had planned the route which included an overnight in Folkestone, one in Paris and maybe one in Milan if they couldn't get a through train to Venice.

Lily didn't speak a single word from Ostend to Paris. She was sitting opposite Charlie who watched her with some concern. She seemed to be sinking into a deep depression. Much rested on this journey. She was thinking about her previous disappointments and about how she'd cope if Michael wasn't there at the end of it.

Charlie watched her intently. She had a handkerchief clasped in her hand with which she kept wiping away tears. He could almost read her thoughts. If she was like this now she'd be a wreck when they got to Venice. He reached across and took her hand.

'Lily, you really need to be strong right now.'

'I know. It's just that?—'

'You don't have to explain. I know. When we get to Paris we'll do something to take your mind off it for a couple of hours. Buck you up a bit. You need it.'

'OK, thanks, Charlie.'

'I think I've got the very thing,' said Dee, sitting next to her.

Her very thing was a visit to the Moulin Rouge where Edith Piaf was topping the bill with her latest lover, Yves Montand. It was the latter whom Dee wanted to see in the flesh, and Lily got the impression when he came on stage that, as far as Auntie Dee was concerned, the more flesh the better. The diminutive Piaf sang her latest recording, 'La Vie en Rose,' to raucous applause from the forty or so American servicemen in the audience, who went on to heckle Yves Montand to the point where he almost left the stage.

Dee got up from her chair and walked over to where the Americans were sitting. On the way she picked up a carafe of red wine from a passing waiter and tipped it over the head of the biggest and noisest American. He sprang to his feet with his fists at the ready, but not ready enough. Dee pushed him with all of her might, sending him back into his seat and then to the floor, to loud laughter from his comrades. Dee addressed them all.

'The audience paid good money to listen to this man sing, not listen to you lot howl like a bunch of brainless baboons. Just shut up or clear off!'

The rest of the audience burst into spontaneous applause. Yves Montand blew her a kiss and gave her a gracious bow as she sat back down. Lily leaned over to Charlie and said, 'And I thought you were good at the rough stuff.'

'There's always someone better,' said Charlie, pleased that Lily seemed to have enjoyed Dee's contribution to the entertainment.

Yves sang his latest recording, 'Battling Joe,' without taking his eyes off Dee. Nor did she take her eyes off him. The Americans sat through the rest of the show in sullen silence. A bottle of champagne arrived at their table.

'*Avec les compliments de Mademoiselle Piaf,*' announced the waiter.

They all looked up and spotted Edith Piaf standing there in the wings in her black dress, smiling across at them as she waited to rejoin Yves on stage.

'You'd think she'd be jealous,' said Dee. 'After all, her bloke's just sung to me. She's got to feel threatened, surely.'

Lily and Charlie laughed. It was by far the best night Lily had had since Michael disappeared. She looked at her two friends and felt revitalised by their strength and their friendship. Tomorrow they were due to board a train that would take them straight through to Venice; straight to within walking distance of where her boy was.

Chapter 59

The distance from Paris to Venice by train is 670 miles, which worked out at a fourteen-hour journey which began at six-thirty in the morning. It was dark when they arrived in Santa Lucia station after crossing from the Venice mainland via the two-miles-long Ponte delle Libertà bridge. They all alighted and looked around, disoriented.

'Anybody got any ideas?' said Charlie.

'Follow the crowd,' said Lily. 'They'll all be heading into town.'

They followed the other departing passengers, many of whom wore army uniforms, British, American and New Zealand. Within two minutes they found themselves beside the Grand Canal. A few gondolas were about and the occasional water taxi. The water reflected the lights from the canal side buildings which were as beautiful as they were old. After another five minutes walk, which took them across two bridges, they came to the Hotel Calabria which looked a bit dishevelled and therefore cheap. They went inside and found an unmanned reception desk. Charlie rang a bell and a young man appeared, dressed more as a gondolier than a receptionist.

'*Avete una stanza libera?*' said Charlie.

'How many rooms?' said the young man in English.

'Two – how did you know I was English?' said Charlie. 'Is my Italian that bad?'

'Your Italian is perfect. I hear you talking before I came in.'

'*Quanta si paga per notte?*' asked Charlie, who felt a need to practise his Italian – or maybe he felt a need to impress Lily.

'Three thousand lira for double room, two thousand for single,' said the young man, who wanted to practise his English.

'What?' exclaimed Dee. 'That's extortionate!'

'Do you take English money?' said Charlie. 'We haven't had time to change to lira.'

'Certainly. That will be one pound and ten shillings sterling each night for the double, one pound for single. This will include, of course, breakfast.'

'Ah,' said Dee.

'For an extra five shillings per person I can give you two rooms overlooking Grand Canal.'

'We'll take those,' said Charlie. '*Per favore, mi svegli domane alle sette e mezzo.*'

'Seven thirty – just you, sir?'

'Just me. I'll wake the ladies.'

'Ah, the ladies are to share the double room?'

'Yes, they are. *Chiave per favore.*'

'Certainly, sir,' said the young man taking two keys off hooks behind the desk. 'Your rooms are 208 and 209, both on the first floor. You each have a balcony overlooking the canal.'

'*Grazie*,' said Charlie.
'*Grazie*,' said Lily and Dee simultaneously.

Charlie lay on his bed wondering what the hell he was doing here. He wasn't even sure if Lily was interested in him. She definitely liked him well enough, but during the months he'd known her they'd never kissed or even whispered the odd sweet nothing to one another. It was, without question, up to her to make the first move. The last thing a recently widowed woman with a missing child needed was to be staving off the advances of an unwelcome admirer. He opened the full-length window and stepped out on to the narrow balcony where there was a single wooden chair in which he sat and looked out over the Grand Canal.

Directly opposite was a beautiful building which he assumed would be a *palazzo*. Square in shape, baroque in style, it emerged from the water without a pavement in front of it, as did most of the canalside buildings. It was four storeys high with the top two storeys being the most important, judging from the height of the windows. They each had a set of five windows which had to be at least fifteen feet high, surmounted by what he would call Gothic arches, but no doubt the Venetian architect would have had an Italian name for them. From one of the windows was draped an Italian flag and Charlie guessed it had been there since April when the city was liberated by New Zealand forces. At water level was a portico with five arches, providing an unloading area for boats. In front of the portico was a line of vertical wooden poles, sticking out of the water, painted red and white like barber's poles. These were moorings for the gondolas. The whole façade was illuminated by flood-lights shooting upwards and giving the building an enchanting air, but no more enchanting then the rest of the buildings emerging from the Grand Canal.

'It's beautiful, isn't it?'

He turned his head and looked up at Lily who was out on the next door balcony, standing not four feet away from him. 'It's kind of indescribable,' said Charlie, getting to his feet and leaning again the shared balcony rail.

They both look at the canal in silence. Then Lily said, 'Charlie, have you ever lost a fight?'

'What?'

'Well, you seem kind of invincible.'

Charlie smiled. 'In my life I've probably lost more than I've won.'

'You could have fooled me.'

'I went to a tough school and got bullied a lot, with me being skinny. I didn't know how to fight until my dad heard about what was happening at school and came round to where I was living with Mum and set up a mini gym in a shed in the back garden. I had a punch bag, a speed ball, all sorts of weights, boxing gloves, practise gloves – and a sparring partner – my dad. He taught me how to box.'

'Did the bullying stop then?'

'Not immediately. It took me a while to get the confidence to fight back. Then one day, it was a Monday – dinner-money day, this big kid called Buster Ackroyd told me to give him my dinner money. He pushed his face right into mine so I could feel the spit coming out of his mouth. I nutted him on his nose.'

'Did you dad teach you that?'

'No. It was more instinct than anything else. He was so close I just nutted him to get him away from me. His nose started bleeding and he yelled like a baby. Somebody shouted "fight" like they do in playgrounds and all the kids gathered round in a circle. He was a lot bigger than me but as soon as I squared up to him it was obvious he didn't know much about boxing. That was the moment I got the confidence to fight back. I knew I could beat him. In fact, at that moment, I thought I could beat anyone in the school. I was a skinny twelve year old, he was a big fat thirteen year old and I beat him fair and square. That was the first and last playground fight I ever had.'

'All the bullies left you alone?'

'Yeah, but I didn't leave them alone. I made a point of getting my dinner money back off every one of them who'd stolen it from me.' He smiled. 'It was an amazing feeling.'

'Are you ever scared of anything?'

'I spent four months undercover, terrified that the German SS would find me out. Yeah, I know all about being scared.'

Lily looked over the canal. A gondola glided by. It had a light on the back and two passengers on board being serenaded by the gondolier, no doubt hoping for a thousand–lira tip. Charlie looked down at the romantic scene below, then up at Lily.

'Do you fancy a ride in a gondola?' he said casually.

It could hardly be classed as an advance – just a ride

in a boat, with an Italian in a striped shirt *singing romantic songs to them*. Hmm, maybe it *was* an advance. *Don't push it, Charlie*. She didn't answer. It was as if she hadn't heard him.

'Charlie, I'm scared,' she said eventually.

He understood. 'Yeah, I imagine you are. You're probably within a mile of Michael but you don't know what's going to happen tomorrow.'

'I don't even know if he'll remember much about me, if anything. It's been over seven months and he's still only four. I doubt if he'll remember his dad at all. These people he's with, they're rich, aren't they, which means they're important. It means Michael's been living in a Venetian palace for seven months and I'm going to bring him home to a back-to-back in Leeds. Surely we can't just march in and snatch him from under their noses. For all we know they might have us all locked up.'

'Lily, I think you've been letting your imagination run away with you. This is a civilised country now. Mussolini's dead. The Germans have gone. It's full of Allied soldiers. I've still got my old army accreditation with me – including my Military Medal. If Michael's here, and I think he is, he's not stopping here. You have my word on that.'

'Thanks, Charlie.'

Charlie looked out at the canal, hoping he hadn't just made a promise he couldn't keep, thereby destroying the faith she had in him. When he turned round she'd gone back inside. He sighed and sat down again, wondering what tomorrow might bring.

Chapter 60

Breakfast consisted of freshly baked pastries, fresh fruit and coffee. Charlie was tucking into it when Lily and Dee came down.

'Sleep OK?' he asked.

'Like a log,' said Dee.

'I got about two hours,' said Lily.

'Here, have some of this coffee, it'll brighten you up.'

The young man who booked them in the previous night came to the table. He was wearing a black and white striped T-shirt.

'This is Gianni,' said Charlie. 'He's a general dogs-body when he's not a gondolier.'

'How wonderful,' said Dee. 'Maybe you can take us to where we need to go in your gondola.'

'Maybe I can. Where is it you wish to be?'

Charlie took out the envelope he'd brought from Pinkney's farm and read out the address.

Gianni hesitated for a moment, then said, 'This is very fine *palazzo*. You know Signore Cominelli?'

'Not personally, no. But we need to pay him a visit.'

'You do? He's very important man. He once was the Mayor of Venezia, you know. They are very old family.

Maybe one thousand years old. There have been Cominelli senators in Venice for hundreds of years – right back to time of Casanova and your Lord Byron and Canaletto and—'

'Are they very rich?' Dee interrupted.

'Oh yes. Very rich people. The Cominelli family own many *palazzi* in Venezia and many businesses.'

'So,' said Charlie. You could take us to this address in your gondola?'

'It will be my pleasure, Signore Charlie.'

After Gianni left Lily said, 'According to Brenda this Mancini bloke couldn't have children and he wanted a son to take home to his wife after the war. I'm guessing he did it to ingratiate himself with her family. A son to continue the Cominelli family line – my son.'

'Bloody hell!' said Dee. 'I've heard soldiers like to bring souvenirs home but that's taking it too far.'

Chapter 61

Under other circumstances the gondola trip down the Grand Canal would have been enjoyable. It was a bright day in early December and the temperature was probably in the mid-forties, cold enough for them all to have their coats wrapped round them. But it was a silent journey, with Gianni picking up on the fact that their visit to the Cominelli family was not to be a joyous occasion. He didn't envy them their visit. Crossing swords with powerful families was a dangerous occupation in Venezia.

After twenty minutes Gianni pointed to a fabulous *palazzo* to their right. The one Charlie had been admiring the night before paled into insignificance beside this one. 'That is Palazzo Cominelli. I will have to put you off down there on landing stage.'

'How do we get in the *palazzo* without getting wet?' Charlie asked.

Gianni laughed at this Englishman's joke. 'I will give you the directions to get in from street. I would warn you that the Cominellis are very private family. They may not let you in their home too easily.'

'I think they might,' said Charlie, who had a plan of sorts.

382

'Okey dokey, Mr Charlie.'

Gianni took the gondola another few hundred yards down the canal and brought it in to a small, wooden landing stage, then leaped off and tied his craft to a plain mooring pole. The three of them followed him on to dry land. They were at the side of one of the many small canals that ran at right angles to the Grand Canal. Gianni now gave them directions.

'You are now about three hundred metres from Palazzo Cominelli. This is as near as I can bring you. From here you walk down this pathway then turn right over bridge and down street in front of you. You will come to canal where you turn right and then left over another bridge.' He paused for thought before continuing. 'Then you turn right for ten metres and left over bridge, down another street in front of you where you will see school and church? After the church is garden and after this is Palazzo Cominelli. You will not mistake it. Is beautiful and very enormous. The cost of this is one thousand lira.'

'Here, keep the change.' Charlie stuck a pound note in Gianni's hand and thanked him for his help.

Lily's heart was pounding as they walked alongside the canal towards the first bridge. Moored at the side of the canal was a boat full of fruit and vegetables with a canvas canopy over it. An old Venetian woman dressed in dark clothing was buying fruit and a gondola was gliding by on the way to the Grand Canal. A dog trotted along the path on the opposite side of the canal, followed by two small children, presumably on their way to school. It was a place without wheels; a place without cars or buses or trams; a place of decrepit magnificence, built on wooden piles hammered into a hundred islands a thousand years ago. All the buildings were three to six storeys high to squeeze as much floor space as possible on to the limited ground area. The streets were high and narrow and largely shaded from the sun. It was a city of lavish, unashamed beauty but with an air of timeless tranquility about it. Everything seemed so ordinary to its inhabitants, but there was nothing ordinary about this day or about this place to Lily. The whole damned world was as abnormal as it could get.

They crossed the stone bridge and headed up a very narrow street, at the end of which was another canal where they turned right and then left over another bridge. A man in a motor boat with a dog at the bow was passing under the bridge. He was dressed in a business suit and had a briefcase on board. Charlie guessed the dog was there to guard the boat while the man was at his business. Every building was a work of decaying beauty. Delicately carved religious statues occupied alcoves in walls and from the stone rainwater gutters at the tops of buildings, weatherbeaten gargoyles leered down on them, as though delighted at their hopeless quest. The breathtaking texture, the fading colours, the plant life growing from the walls all added to the unique atmosphere of this strange and splendid city on the sea.

'Right for ten metres, then left over another bridge,' Dee reminded him.

'Then down the street in front of us,' added Charlie, who had safely memorised Gianni's directions. The street beyond this bridge was wider. There was a shop selling beautiful Murano glass, a clothes shop, a tobacco shop, a restaurant and a school, outside which many young children were milling. Lily looked at them and wondered if this was the school to which her son would be going. In England he'd have started Quarry Mount junior school school back in September. This looked to be a good school, better than Quarry Mount. Then a thought struck her. Maybe Michael had started school. Maybe he was one of these children. She held up a staying hand.

'Could we stop for a minute?'

Charlie and Dee looked at each other, then at the children whose ages ranged from five upwards. They both understood. They both scanned the young faces, having only a photograph to go on. Charlie saw one young boy whom he thought might be Michael.

'The boy by the wall, standing facing us.'

Lily shook her head. There were only half a dozen boys young enough to have been Michael. He wasn't here. They moved on. Beyond the school stood a large church beside a public garden and beyond the garden a large *palazzo*, enclosed by an eight-foot-high wall. Set in the wall was an iron gate and beside it, painted on to the stone, the faded number 4081. Beyond the gate was a garden which, Charlie guessed, would be very beautiful in the summer. The garden was enclosed on three sides by the *palazzo*. At the side of the gate a rope dangled, attached to a bell on top of the wall. He pulled on the rope and set the bell jangling. Dee said, 'I'll be off then.'

'You've got the note?' said Charlie.

Dee took a piece of paper from her pocket and

showed it to him. 'I hope you write good Italian as well as speak it,' she said.

'Like a native,' said Charlie.

'Don't forget to speak English in there.'

'I know exactly what to do, bossyboots. It's my plan, remember?'

He said it with a smile to ease the tension she was obviously feeling. Dee nodded, then turned and went on her way. Charlie watched her go. Her part in this was of the utmost importance. Lily had said nothing. Her heart was too near her mouth for speech. A woman who looked to be some sort of servant came to the gate. She asked if she could help them.

'Posso aiutarvi?'

'Major Mancini,' said Charlie politely, in English. 'We're looking for Major Mancini.'

The woman stared at him, suspiciously, for a while, before turning and leaving them at the gate. 'Do you think she's gone to get him?' asked Lily. 'She didn't look too helpful to me.'

They waited a few minutes, then Charlie rang the bell again. The old woman reappeared. He was polite once more.

'Major Mancini *per favore.*'

The woman left. Lily said, 'You spoke Italian.'

'Most English tourists know the odd phrase. I said it in an English accent. I wish I'd changed some money now. I could have bribed her. We'll have to find one of those money-changing places later.'

A few more minutes later Charlie was about to ring the bell for a third time when a man came to the gate.

He was dressed in civilian clothes but looked about right for a major, and about the right age to fit Brenda's description of Mancini – mid-forties.

'Major Mancini, I presume,' said Charlie brightly.

'Who are you?'

'I'm here to represent Mr Bert Pinkney with whom you stayed for a while.'

'I beg your pardon?'

'Bert Pinkney. You stayed on his farm in Yorkshire. He used to pick up money for you from London.'

The horrified look on Mancini's face told both Charlie and Lily that this was the man who'd taken Michael. Horrified that someone from his past had tracked him down here.

'I do not know this Bert Pinkney.'

'Oh, I think you do, Major. You know Bert and his son Ezra – oh, and Sergeant Bernard Randle, of course. I'm just a messenger, Major. I've come all this way to deliver you a message from good old Bert.'

'What message?'

'I don't want to give you this message with iron bars between us, Major. Would you let us in please so that we can have a civilised talk?'

Mancini looked at Lily. 'And who is this woman?'

'She's with me, Major, that's all you need to know. I've also had instructions from Bert Pinkney to go to the *carabinieri* if you give me problems. So, can I come in, please? It's for the best.'

'What is it you're after: money?'

'Could be, Major. It should be worth lots of money for me to keep quiet about what you got up to in

England. The British police are currently looking for the missing boy and they don't take too kindly to Italians who reward our hospitality by stealing our children. Imagine how such a disgrace would besmirch the Cominelli family name. But there's no need for the police to know, is there?'

Mancini gave an angry frown and took a key from his pocket. He opened the gate to let them in.

'Don't lock the gate,' said Charlie. 'We'll be letting ourselves out.'

Mancini led them through the garden to a covered courtyard beyond, in which was a round table and six chairs. At the end of the courtyard a balcony led into the main building. Lily looked up at the balcony in the vain hope of seeing Michael. The Italian sat down without making any gesture for Charlie and Lily to do likewise. They both sat down without being invited.

'How much do you want?' asked Mancini.

'First we want to see Michael,' said Lily. 'We want to see that no harm has come to him.'

'Why would harm have come to him? You cannot see him. I will not have him distressed like this.'

Charlie got to his feet, as did Lily. 'In that case we have no further business to discuss,' said Charlie. 'Come on, Lily. We'll discuss it all with the *carabinieri*. They can contact the British police about the missing boy, who's obviously here.'

They headed back to the gate and were almost there when Mancini called them back. Lily breathed a sigh of relief that their bluff hadn't been called.

'I will call Michele.'

Lily's heart leaped. As they turned a woman appeared. She was around the same age as Mancini and carried an air of refined beauty that came with great privilege and wealth.

'Who are these people?' she asked Mancini in Italian.

'These people come from England to ask about Michele. They helped me bring him over here.'

The woman gave them a serene smile and beckoned for them to sit down. 'And you wish to see our son?' she said in perfect English.

My son? Her words Lily grated with Lily. Charlie spoke for them both. 'Yes, we'd love to see him.'

'Then you shall.'

Charlie looked at Mancini, who was trying to appear unconcerned. Lily's heart was pounding as Signora Mancini got up and rang a bell at the side of the court-yard to summon the maid who appeared almost before the bell had stopped pealing. She asked the maid to bring Michele.

What seemed to Lily to be an age passed before she heard a door open behind her. Charlie was sitting opposite her and saw the boy first. 'Michael,' he said. 'How are you?'

'We call him Michele now,' said Signora Mancini.

Lily drew in a deep breath and stared at Charlie, knowing her son was standing behind her and not daring to look round at him. Frightened that he might not know who she was. Frightened that he might not want to be taken away from this luxury. She heard Michael speak and she recognised his voice. It was most definitely her son.

'I don't know who you are,' Michael said to Charlie.

'No, but you know who this lady is don't you, Michael?' Charlie nodded at Lily, urging her to look round.

Lily slowly turned. Her eyes were glistening with tears. Not ten feet away from her was Michael. She'd found him.

'Hello, Michael,' she said gently.

He looked slightly older, taller, slightly less of a child, but he looked well cared for. He was beautifully dressed in a sailor suit that looked to have been tailored for him. He stared at Lily for a long moment, then turned his attention to Mancini's wife – his new mother. Lily's heart almost stopped with shock. He didn't know her. Her eyes flooded. She could hardly catch her breath. Charlie got to his feet and smiled at the boy.

'You know who this lady is don't you, Michael?'

Michael gave a slight nod, then looked at the ground sullenly. Then he spoke. Not quite the words his mother might have been longing for, but good enough words all the same. Words that told her that her son still knew exactly who he was and who she was and to whom he rightfully belonged.

'Why did you send me away?'

'He didn't send you away,' said Mancini's wife, who'd got hold of the wrong end of the stick. 'He helped you to come and live with us.'

'Michael wasn't talking to Charlie,' said Lily quietly. 'He was talking to me.'

Signora Mancini looked at Michael, then at Lily. The boy was looking at his mother with a reproachful look on his face.

'Who is this woman?' said Mancini, now concerned.

'Take a guess,' said Charlie, watching the unfolding reunion with a smile on his face.

Lily went over and knelt in front of her son, hugging him to her. Eventually Michael's arms came round her and hugged her back. The Mancinis looked on in horror as Lily spoke to Michael. Lily could hardly see him through her tears.

'That nasty man who took you in his car tricked me,' she said. 'Then he gave you to these people for money. I didn't send you away. You were stolen from me.'

She wasn't certain how much Michael remembered. She just hoped she was jogging what memory he had.

'He was going to take me to feed the horses,' Michael remembered.

'Yes, that's right! He was, my darling, but he was telling lies.'

'Can I come with you? I don't like it here. They all talk funny and there's no one to play with.'

The blood was draining from Signora Mancini's face. Tears of horror and despair were streaming down her cheeks. These people had come to take her son away. This beautiful boy brought to her by her husband. Her lying, deceitful husband whose face was puce with rage.

'What the hell is this?' he fumed, in Italian.

'It's my way of reuniting a mother with her son,' said Charlie, also in Italian.

'Mother?' screamed Mancini's wife. 'You told me he was an orphan!'

'I was told he was an orphan,' protested Mancini.

'He was abducted from his mother by a friend of your

husband,' said Charlie evenly. 'Either way, you two are in a lot of trouble.'

Two young men appeared, possibly called to the scene by the maid. 'Get rid of them!' screamed Mancini.

The two men approached Charlie. Lily turned her son round so that she could see the action but Michael couldn't. Through her tears all she saw was a blur of arms and fists, culminating in the two men ending up on the floor, no threat to anyone, and Charlie scarcely out of breath.

Two older people arrived. A man and a woman. Lily guessed them to be Mancini's in-laws, the Cominellis. The rich people who sent him money. Mancini began talking fast in Italian.

'These people came here trying to extort money out of me. They say unless I give them three million lira they're going to report me to the authorities for bringing Michael here illegally.'

The older couple glared at Charlie and at Lily, who was still hugging her son. Not knowing what was being said, Charlie spoke to them in Italian.

'That woman is the boy's mother. Major Mancini had him abducted from his home in England. We haven't come for money. We've come to take the boy home to England where he belongs.'

Three more men arrived. Charlie wondered where they were all coming from. Were they part of the Cominelli family or were they hired guards? These men looked more capable than the other two, who might well have been family members, and Charlie had serious doubts about handling the three newcomers. Mancini decided to join in. Lily watched as the four of them surrounded Charlie. There had to be a limit to his capabilities and these odds looked to be stretching things.

Charlie decided to compartmentalise his problem. One thing at a time. Mancini first. He knew the major was behind him and, by watching the eyes of one of the men in front, he could pretty much tell where. He spun round with his right arm stretched out and took Mancini down with his favourite chop to the neck. The major knew nothing about it.

Charlie felt one of the men behind him take him in a stranglehold, choking him. Lily screamed at the man to stop. Michael turned and saw this man who had arrived with his mother being beaten up. Lily looked at Cominelli, who was watching the fight with interest, and she realised that it would save his treasured reputation if Charlie didn't come out of this alive. And if Charlie didn't nor would she. Nor was Signora Cominelli showing any sign of stopping the fight. These people were prepared for her and Charlie to die rather than have their family name besmirched. Mancini's wife was shivering with shock. Lily clung to Michael, not knowing what to do for the best.

Charlie was kicking his legs as one man held him in a stranglehold and the other two punched him viciously about the head. Some of Charlie's kicks were hitting their mark and one of the men doubled over in pain. Cominelli made a slight movement with his head which directed the injured man to approach Lily and take his revenge out on her. She stared at the approaching thug in abject desolation. She'd found her boy but at what cost? She kissed Michael's head, knowing he was going to be snatched away from her at any second. A loud voice from over her shoulder shouted for all this to stop.

'Basta!'

Lily looked up to see that all the action had stopped. The three men were all slowly raising their hands. Charlie had dropped to the floor with blood dripping from his face. She looked around to see three men in uniform pointing guns at the Italian thugs. The two that Charlie had taken down were stirring. Mancini was still out cold. Dee was standing behind the three men in uniform. The *carabinieri*.

'Are you OK, Lily?' she called out.

'I am, Charlie isn't, though.'

Cominelli started speaking in Italian to the *carabinieri*.

'You know who I am.'

'Yes, sir, we know who you are.'

'Then I want these two people locked up for trespassing on my property and attempting to blackmail my son-in-law.'

'He's lying,' said Charlie, also in Italian. 'We came here to take that boy back to England from where he was abducted by him.' He pointed to Mancini, then he looked at Lily who was still hugging Michael.

'She's the boy's mother, as you can tell.' He took a piece of paper from his pocket. 'If you don't believe me contact the British police. They've been searching for the boy for months.'

The paper had Bannister's contact details. 'You can either telephone this British policeman or if that's not possible from over here you can contact him by teleprinter.'

'Telephone is possible,' said one of the *carabinieri* after checking with his colleagues, who had both nodded.

'They lie!' screamed Signora Cominelli. 'She isn't his mother. My daughter is the boy's mother.'

'Show them your passport, Lily,' said Charlie.

Lily, who had understood none of the conversation until Charlie asked her this, let go of Michael for the first time and opened her bag. She took out her passport that also had Michael's photograph and details on it and handed it to a *carabiniere* without saying a word. He looked at the photograph and then at Michael before passing it to his colleagues.

'This woman appears to be the boy's mother,' he announced. 'I want everyone here to come to the station where we can sort all this out.' He looked at Cominelli. 'I assume, sir, that there is a telephone in your house.'

Cominelli scowled. His family reputation was ruined. Mancini began to come round. As he tried to sit up, his wife, who was ashen-faced and in floods of tears, suddenly flung herself at him. Kicking, screaming, gouging and biting. One of the *carabinieri* pulled her away, her legs still flailing, trying to get at her husband.

Mancini's face was white with shock and rage. His eyes widened and his hands quivered. He picked up a fruit knife from where it lay next to a bowl of fruit on the garden table and darted across to where Michael was standing, just a yard away from Lily and completely perplexed by what was happening. Mancini swept the boy up with his left arm and, with his right hand, held the knife to Michael's throat. He backed away. The look on his face was that of an unbalanced man. He was grinning and staring all around. In the space of a few minutes his life had crumbled to ashes. Everything he held dear had been taken away from him. The shock of it all left him feeling he had nothing left to live for. He was shouting at the *carabinieri* with wild-eyed madness.

'Now what are you going to do? Do you think you can get to me before I kill the boy?' He spoke Italian. Lily didn't understand.

'What's he saying, Charlie?'

Charlie couldn't think of a reply. Mancini could. He now spoke English.

'I'm going to kill the boy before anyone of you can get to me.'

'No!' screamed Lily. 'Please, he hasn't done anything to you.'

'Hasn't done anything? Do you know what I had to go through to get him here, just so I could satisfy that bitch of a wife of mine and her arrogant parents. It's not even my fault we can't have children ourselves. It's that barren bitch who's the problem.'

'How dare you!' yelled Cominelli. 'There's nothing wrong with my daughter.'

Mancini laughed maniacally. 'Nothing wrong with her? I've got a daughter over in England that proves there's nothing wrong with me.'

'*Voi bastardi*!' screamed his wife.

None of the *carabinieri* dared fire for fear of hitting the boy. Michael, having now learned his fate, was crying with terror. Lily was fighting the impulse to rush this madman and rescue her son, but she knew that such a move might prompt him to plunge the knife into

Michael's throat. Charlie was sitting on the floor, dripping blood but with his eyes firmly on Mancini, who was standing ten feet away from him and liable to kill the boy at any second. The Italian drew his knife arm away in readiness to plunge it into the boy's neck. He didn't care what happened to him, he was that most dangerous of men – one with nothing to lose.

All eyes were on the knife in Mancini's white-knuckled hand. The Cominellis were unconcerned about the outcome. If the boy died, so be it. He was not their grandchild any more. Their daughter was weeping with shock and despair. The son she had longed for was no longer her son and now the man who had lied to her about him was about to kill him.

Charlie was weighing up the options. The pain from his injuries was forgotten by the stress of the situation, but he *was* weaker. The blows he'd taken would slow him down, he knew that. Under normal circumstance he could cover the distance between him and Mancini in two seconds, exploding like a greyhound from a trap. If he screamed as he pounced Mancini would be unnerved, if only for a second or two, which was all the time he needed. With no time to spare he put his plan into action.

His scream was bloodcurdling. It was a madman's scream he'd practised before, and he knew it worked. He was within a yard of Mancini when the Italian turned the knife round and slashed at Charlie, ripping it into him. Charlie stumbled and fell to the ground with blood pumping from his chest. He twitched about, face down, for several seconds then lay still.

Lily screamed and moved towards Charlie but Mancini shouted at her to stay back. He was once again holding the knife at Michael's throat. His face cracked in a wide, manic grin.

'See? I kill your man. What have I got to lose by killing the boy?'

Dee approached Mancini from behind. As the Italian drew the knife back to stab Michael, she reached round him and grabbed his wrist, twisting it until he dropped the knife. Then she forced his arm downwards and backwards until she heard a bone snap. Mancini cried out in agony. Michael struggled free. One of the *carabinieri* shouted at Mancini to get to the ground. Dee didn't understand the order but she helped Mancini comply, with a kick to his back. Lily ran to Michael, then still holding her son, knelt down by Charlie, who wasn't moving a muscle. She looked up at Dee.

'My God! He's dead, Auntie Dee. He's killed Charlie!'

A *carabiniere* stood over Mancini and pointed a pistol at his head. Another took Lily and Michael away from Charlie, as a third one knelt down to check Charlie for life signs.

For several seconds there was a strange stillness and silence in the garden, as if no one quite knew what to do next. Mancini's head was bobbing up and down, partly from pain, partly from rage, but mainly from despair. As if he realised the irreversible hopelessness of his situation he exploded into life. Using his good arm to bat the pistol away from the *carabiniere* standing over him he picked up the knife and flung himself in the direction of Lily and Michael to exact one last piece of retribution from these people who had destroyed him. He was within two feet of Lily, who was cowering with her eyes shut tight, when two guns fired in unison, sending him to the ground, dead. Lily opened her eyes and looked at the dead Italian, then beyond him at the prone body of Charlie, lying in a pool of blood.

She clung to Michael and wept.

Chapter 62

'Come in . . . Ah, John.'

DI Foster looked up from his desk as Sergeant Bannister knocked and came into his office.

'What is it?'

'We've just had a teleprinter message from Venice, sir. The *carabinieri* – it's the Italian police.'

'I know what the *carabinieri* is, John. Please don't tell me this is about this bloody Robinson woman and her stupid ideas about her boy being abducted by an Italian soldier.'

'That's pretty much it, sir.'

He handed the detective inspector a rolled-up scroll of paper which the inspector unravelled and read.

'Hmm . . . It's not very good English, but it seems she's found her son over there.'

'Yessir. It seems that her story was true . . . sir.'

Foster nodded as he read on. 'Her son was abducted and sold to an Italian officer called Mancini. Mrs Robinson and the Maguire woman and Mr Cleghorn tracked the boy to Venice.'

He looked up at Bannister. 'Venice? How the hell did they manage that?'

'Without any help from us . . . sir.'

'That's because neither we nor the courts nor anyone believed her story, Sergeant. Jesus! This puts the law in a very bad light – us in particular.'

'That's true sir, but it's good that she got her boy back.'

'It's not good for us, Sergeant. No doubt she'll make a big thing about this to the papers.'

'I think it's a strong possibility, sir. There's one other thing, sir, if you read on.'

'What's that?'

'The report said that Mr Cleghorn was fatally wounded by Mancini and that Mancini was shot dead by the *carabinieri*.'

Chapter 63

A week later. Millgarth Police Station, Leeds.
'I have an appointment with Detective Sergeant Bannister.'

The desk sergeant didn't look up from the ledger he was poring over, which Lily thought was very rude.

'My name is Lilian Robinson. Did you hear what I said, Sergeant?'

The sergeant now looked up. It was a name he recognised. A name that had done the police no favours. A name that was currently in the newspapers. Henry Smithson had written the story and had sold an exclusive to the *Daily Mail*. The story had told of how no one had believed war widow Lily Robinson. It told of how many people thought she'd murdered her missing son and hidden the body. It told of how her neighbours had blamed her, bullied her, and two of them had lied to get her in trouble with the courts. In a sub-heading, Perseverance Street had been given the title *The Street of Shame*. It told of how her dead husband's family took her newborn baby from her and had left the boy alone outside a shop from where he'd been stolen. Even the police had had their doubts about Lily and had half-heartedly investigated Michael's disappearance while all

402

the time believing Lily had killed him. It told of her dreadful treatment at the hands of Dr Freeman after being sent by the court to Ecclestone House Hospital. Freeman was now in Armley jail, Leeds, awaiting trial. It told of the Randles who had abducted Michael pretending to be someone else and of Major Mancini and the Cominelli family in Venice and the stabbing of war hero Charlie.

It was a story that brought shame down on the heads of many people, all of whom had been named in the article, including Hilda Muscroft and Vera Pilkington – a condition demanded by Lily before she gave the story to Henry.

The only person who escaped castigation by the article was DS Bannister and this was only because Lily still needed him on her side. Within half a minute of asking for him, Bannister was at the desk. He glanced behind her to see if any reporters were tagging along. He saw only Dee, who had read his mind.

'We lost the reporters in the market,' she said.

'Right . . . good. You got back from Venice OK then?'

'Yesterday,' said Lily. 'The RAF flew us all back.'

'Good, now my inspector would like a word with you.'

Lily shook her head. 'Tell your inspector he's six months too late wanting a word with me. I only want to talk to you, Sergeant Bannister – no one else. You're the most senior man the police ever assigned to my case.'

'Well, you'd better come through.'

He led them through into an informal interview

room furnished with comfortable chairs and a coffee table. 'Can I get you anything to drink? Tea, coffee?'

'No, thanks. I just want to know what's happening about Randle.'

'Well, we picked up Mr and Mrs Randle in Bournemouth where they were about to open up a boarding house. They're both being held on remand in separate prisons. Bernard Randle's in Armley.'

'How long do you think they'll get?'

'Child abduction? Selling a British child to an enemy of the crown? We're thinking ten years minimum, possibly life.'

'What about the Cominellis?'

'The whole family's being held in a Venice prison, including Mrs Mancini and various thugs who attacked Mr Cleghorn. Could be they'll need you and Mrs Maguire to go over there and testify.'

Bannister allowed a few seconds to pass before he changed the subject. 'How was Michael treated when he was over there?'

'Well enough, but considering the murderous pig he would have for a father, who knows how long that might have lasted?'

'I was sorry to hear about Mr Cleghorn.'

'He saved Michael's life, as did this lady here.' She inclined her head towards Dee, who was standing behind her.

Bannister nodded, then said, 'Lily, we're pulling out all the stops in the search for Christopher.'

'No need,' said Lily, fixing the detective sergeant with an innocent stare. 'We found him ourselves, which

404

is really why we wanted to see you. Someone left him in his pram outside Auntie Dee's house this morning. Didn't they, Auntie Dee?'

'Right outside my front door, seven o'clock this very morning,' confirmed Dee. 'We were still in bed. Knock comes on the door. I went down, and there he was, in his pram. In good health. Not a mark on him. I had a good look around. No one about.'

Bannister held Lily's gaze, not believing this for one moment. 'Did they really? You must be overjoyed.'

'Ecstatic,' said Lily. 'He's outside the station right now, being looked after by Charlie's mum. Do you want to see him?'

Bannister sat back in his chair. He was guessing that Charlie might have had a hand in Christopher's disappearance, which would make Lily an accessory. This was an investigation that could only further damage the police. Lily could guess what was going through Bannister's mind.

'You haven't come out of this too badly, have you, Sergeant? That was my doing. I told the reporter to go easy on you.'

Bannister shook his head and got to his feet. 'I'm delighted you've got Christopher back. I'd better take a look at the child . . . then I'll have a word with my superiors. Advise that the case be closed. Whoever took him wasted a hell of a lot of police time.'

'Well, the police didn't waste too much time looking for Michael, did they?' said Lily. 'So, it kind of balances things out, wouldn't you say?'

Chapter 64

'Stop here please would you, driver?'

The taxi pulled up near the end of Perseverance Street. Lily and Michael got out and the taxi driver helped her to put Christopher in a pram. Lily held out two half-crowns to pay the fare.

'No charge, Mrs Robinson. I know who you are. It was an honour to bring you here. Something to tell 'em about back at the office.'

Lily smiled. 'Thank you, but I must insist. If you won't take it as my fare take it as a tip.'

It was a cold but bright Saturday, three days from Christmas, the first time she'd been back to Perseverance Street since returning from Italy. There'd be children playing in the street, maybe the odd adult standing in a doorway talking to a neighbour. A normal Saturday for them. Not for Lily. It had been a long time since she'd had a normal day. She pushed the pram along the stone-flagged pavement and turned the corner into her street. A telegraph boy cycled past her on his creaking red bike, whistling loudly. Lily recognised him as the same boy who'd delivered the bad news about Larry. She smiled as she watched him pedal down the street. The end of the war must have made his job easier, but she knew it wasn't all good news. Not all the men were coming home, and not all the men who did come home were coming back to the same wives they'd left behind. Many wives had been doing war work instead of housework and had developed an independence they were disinclined to relinquish. Infidelities were being exposed, marriages were breaking down. But these men were better off than the men who had no homes to come home to, just piles of rubble. And even these men were better off than the men who had no homes or wives and families to come home to. Families killed by the Luftwaffe. Then there were the men who came back with heads full of the horrors of war and not wishing to share these horrors with anyone. They would cope by not talking about what they'd seen. It had been a bad time for a lot of people. In many ways Lily had got off lightly. It was her way of looking at things. She was still alive. Her boys were still alive. As she thought these thoughts her mind dwelt on Charlie. A group of children were playing rounders, including Harry Bridges, the boy who threw the brick through her window. As she walked past him she stopped and called out.

'Harry Bridges. Why did you break my window?'

There was no anger in her voice. Just a woman being curious, wanting an answer to a simple question.

Harry was eleven years old. Old enough to throw bricks through windows but too young to know why. The game stopped. All the children were looking at Lily, not knowing what to do. They all knew her story. It had been in the papers. They all knew what their parents had been saying about her killing Michael, but there he was. Alive and grinning at them.

'That brick you threw just missed my baby.' She held out her thumb and finger to indicate the narrowness of Christopher's escape. 'Might have killed him, you know.'

Harry said nothing. A door opened and Harry's mother appeared. She looked at her son, then at Lily.

'I was just telling Harry how he nearly hit my Christopher with that brick he threw through my window. Still, I don't suppose it was all his idea.'

'I never told him to do that,' blustered Mrs Bridges.

'Yer did, Mam,' said Harry.

Lily looked at her and smiled. 'You weren't the only one, Mrs Bridges. It was a really hard time for me. Just when I really needed my neighbours you all turned on me.'

Her few quiet words were far more effective than any blistering verbal attack she could have launched on the woman. She walked on as a severely chastened Mrs Bridges ushered her son into the house. Albert Pilkington was on his way to the lavatories, newspaper under his arm. He stopped as Lily approached. Embarrassed, he wiped a hand across his mouth then frowned and looked down at the ground, mumbling.

'I'm proper sorry fer what I did, lass.'

'For what *you* did? What was it you did, Albert?'

'For what I *didn't* do, more like. I didn't tell t' bobbies what really happened when you had that do with Hilda and she tripped and banged her head. Me keepin' me gob shut got you locked up. Any road I've been down ter t' cop shop and given 'em a proper statement. It were just like it said in t' paper. I told 'em Hilda lied. I told 'em Vera lied as well.'

'Does Vera know?'

He nodded. 'We had coppers round at our 'ouse and Hilda's ter take new statements. They were talkin' about perjury or summat – but I just think they wanted ter frighten 'em. I don't think t' coppers came out o' this too well.'

'None of us did, Albert. I bet Vera's making your life a misery.'

'She's been doin' that fer years, love, but I feel a bit better about meself. The coppers told me it were bit late to help you, but it might help you if yer want ter claim some compensation.'

'I might just do that, Albert. Mainly, I just want to forget about it.'

'This street's been havin' a right bad time since folk round here read about us in t' papers. We've all been ostri . . . er.'

'Ostracised.'

'Mind you, we deserve it. Vera and Hilda daren't show their faces. They're both livin' like flippin' hermits. It might help if yer came back ter live in yer old house.'

'Sorry, I won't be doing that, Albert.'

'I can't say I blame yer, lass. Anyroad, best o' luck.'

'Thanks, Albert.'

Curtains twitched as she moved on down the street. Guilty curtains. Lily felt a mixture of triumph and sadness – sadness that people had been all too eager to get hold of the wrong end of the stick. She blamed it mainly on

Hilda. For a couple of seconds she stopped and looked across at Hilda's house. She gave the Muscroft window a shake of her head knowing Hilda would be looking back at her from behind her net curtains. Then she took out her key and opened the door to number 13. An unlucky house if you believed in that sort of thing, which Lily didn't. Her luck had been determined by the likes of Adolf Hitler and an evil couple who had called themselves the Oldroyds, and it had not been helped by neighbours who had been too ready to believe the worst of her.

She opened the door and laughed as Michael raced past her, running round the house from room to room shouting at everything he recognised. She pulled the pram up into the house. Christopher was fast asleep so she left him there, sat down and lit a cigarette. It was only then that she began to feel that the nightmare was finally over. She'd got her boys back, justice had been done.

Her thoughts went to Charlie and why he'd made no advances towards her. What would she have done if he had? Maybe if they'd got together romantically things might have turned out differently. A car pulled up outside. She looked through the window and went immediately to the door. Mary was getting out of her car.

'I rang Dee. She said you'd be coming over here this afternoon so I've brought him, straight from hospital.'

'What? He's been discharged? I thought he'd be in for another week.'

The front passenger door opened. Charlie got out and leaned on the roof of the car.

'Had the stitches out yesterday afternoon. Never felt better in my life.'

'Can you walk without help?' Lily asked him.

'With my trusty stick, you bet. The quack thinks I'll make a full recovery in two months.'

Mary corrected him. 'He actually said four.'

Charlie took a walking stick from the car and made his way over to Lily. 'Am I invited in?'

'Of course. Mary, would you like to come in fo—'

'No, no. I must be on my way. I'll leave you lot to it.'

Inside the house Lily sat down. Charlie stuck his free hand in his pockets and went over to the window.

'Charlie, come over here and sit down.'

'I'm sick of sitting down and lying down. I want to get myself mobile as soon as poss.'

'Is it over, Charlie?' she said. 'Is it really all over?'

'Bar the shouting, yeah. Oh, I phoned Jimmy this morning — Brenda's broken it off with her Brylcreem Boy.'

'What? the RAF officer? That didn't last long. She should make a play for Jimmy if she's got any sense.'

'Do you like Jimmy?'

'I do, yes.'

'Maybe *you* should make a play for him.'

It was a clumsy thing to say and he regretted it the moment it came out. Lily made no attempt to comment. Charlie tried to repair the damage.

'Too soon after Larry, eh?'

Still no comment. All that day he been summoning up the courage to ask her out on a proper date, but he was scared of her rejection. He'd been scared of many things in his life but none more so than rejection by Lily. Still looking out of the window he said, 'You know, I've been thinking. It's time you started enjoying life again.'

'I've already started – thanks to you and Auntie Dee.'

'Right, yeah. I was actually wondering if you fancied a night out with me.' His heart was thumping, anticipating her saying something about how she hadn't got over Larry's death yet.'

'Like a date, you mean?'

'Well, I was just thinking of a night out. Maybe the pictures and fish and chips afterwards. There's *Captain Kidd* on at the Odeon. I know Mum would babysit.'

'It's only eight months since Larry died.'

It sounded as though she was turning down his invitation. He gave a disappointed grimace which she couldn't see because he still had his back to her. He watched Hilda Muscroft emerge from her house and hurry down the street with her head down and arms folded across her front.

'I was wrong about Michael not really remembering Larry,' Lily went on. 'He doesn't remember much, but he has some good memories of his daddy. I certainly won't forget him, although I don't want his parents anywhere near my boys after what they did to me.'

'Don't blame you,' Charlie said. 'By the way, Sergeant Bannister rang me up to talk about what was happening in Venice. Hey! Did you know he'd got a teleprinter message saying I was fatally wounded? I think something was lost in the translation there. Mind you, it felt a bit fatal at the time. Hell of a scar I've got. Fourteen inches long, ninety stitches. The surgeons in that Venice hospital did beautiful work according to the people down at Leeds Infirmary. Any deeper and it'd sliced through the old ticker and the teleprinter would have been correct.'

'Charlie, I don't even want to think about that. We all thought you were dead until that man in the boat ambulance told us he'd found a pulse. Even then it was two days before the hospital told us you were out of danger.'

'I'm told you stayed with me all through the first night.'

'Somebody had to. You saved Michael's life.'

'I knew you were there, you know.'

'You didn't say anything.'

'No, I decided to devote what little energy I had to staying alive. Sorry if I seemed a bit rude.'

'You're forgiven.'

'Thank you. Bannister also mentioned that Godfrey's in serious trouble with the police for selling black-market meat. He was at it in a big way – could end up doing time, apparently.'

'Oh, dear,' said Lily. 'I must write and tell them they're not allowed to see my boys ever again. I don't want their sort bringing shame on my family.'

'There's something else that might cheer you up,' Charlie said. 'The coppers have made Godfrey write a list of all his black-market customers. He knows he's got to cooperate otherwise a judge'll come down on him like a ton of bricks. Apparently several of his fellow magistrates were on the list, including the one who sent you to the nuthouse – a bloke called Iredale.'

'You don't have to remind me. I remember him well.'

'I don't think he'll be sitting on the bench for much longer.'

'I reckon Godfrey persuaded Iredale to have me sent away so he could get his hands on Christopher.'

'It'd do no harm to mention that to the cops,' said Charlie. 'If Godfrey's singing he might as well do his whole repertoire. You never know, they might end up as cell mates.'

Lily laughed. 'Now that's too good a chance to miss. The other inmates'll love 'em.'

Charlie was still looking out of the window. His conversation was on one subject, his mind on another: he couldn't understand why he was so nervous about asking Lily out on a date. He'd dated plenty of girls before, but never one who might break his heart by turning him down.

'I can't remember the last time I went to the pictures.'

'Could you manage it?'

'What, sitting in a seat for a couple of hours, why not?' He paused then added. 'I don't suppose Larry would mind you going to the pictures with a friend.' He said it as casually as he could.

'Charlie,' she said, quietly, looking at the back of his head. 'Is that what you are – just a friend?'

His heart quickened. 'Lily,' he said, turning to her, leaning heavily on his stick. 'I'll be whatever you want me to be.'

She left it for several seconds before saying, 'Actually, I don't know.'

'More than just a friend,' he said. 'A lot more if you like.'

Their eyes met. Lily was frowning as she tried to make sense of her feelings for him. Her emotions had been in a turmoil for a long time now and she wasn't entirely sure of what she felt about anything, or anyone, except her boys. They were the only certainties in her life – or were they? Was there another certainty, staring her in the face? She knew how devastated she'd felt when she thought he was dead. But was that love, or just pity for a wonderful friend who'd died to save her son's life?

'Charlie, there's only one thing I can think of that would make us a lot more than just friends.'

'That'll be it, then.'

'Charlie, do you mean . . . 'til death us do part and all that?'

He didn't respond. He could read the signs. Reading the signs had kept him alive in Italy more than once. Rejection loomed. Lily looked up at him and remembered all the risks he'd taken on her behalf. She remembered the pangs of jealousy she'd felt when she thought Brenda was making a play for him. She remembered the time he'd put his hand on her shoulder after her confrontation in Leeds market with Hilda. It had been just what she needed. It had felt unbelievably welcome. Strong, comforting and undemanding – just a hand, but it had done all that. And he'd just proposed to her – at least that's what it had sounded like.

'Oh, by the way,' remembered Charlie, changing the subject once again, to postpone the inevitable rejection, 'I've been asked to go to Venice as soon as I'm well enough, to give evidence at the trial of the Italian guys who were trying to beat me to death. Apparently they've

415

all been charged with my attempted murder. The *carabinieri* are key witnesses but I'm told I'll be asked to appear in court as well. They'd like you to go as well if you're up to it, all expenses pa—'

There was a loud knock on the door. Charlie gave a mild curse under his breath He'd been carefully working his way round to a critical moment, which was about to be disturbed. It was a special knock that Michael, who was upstairs, remembered with a huge grin. He raced down and answered it. Tony Lafferty, scruffy and snotty as ever, stood on the doorstep. His mother stood beside him. Lily followed her son to the door.

'Mrs Lafferty, how are you?'

'Better than I would be if it weren't for you. I've just come ter tell yer that I'll pay yer back as soon as I can.'

She was around the same age as Lily but there the similarity ended. Irene Lafferty was a short, stubby woman with wild hair and a ruddy face. Her teeth looked to be on their last legs, awaiting the dentist's pliers, to be replaced by a set of dentures, should she ever be able to afford them. Maybe when this free health service the new Labour government were talking about got started. Lily noticed that Tony was wearing newish boots and a half-decent Fair Isle pullover and he wasn't looking quite so emaciated. Her money seemed have been well used.

'It won't be necessary, Mrs Lafferty. It was a gift to thank you for not believing I killed Michael. You were the only one round here who didn't. It meant a lot to me.'

Mrs Lafferty looked down at her son. 'I suppose Buggerlugs told yer that, did he?'

416

Lily confirmed that Buggerlugs had indeed told her.

'Well it were right. I never did believe such a thing. My lad's felt the weight of my hand on his backside more than once, but that's all. Yer can't do away with yer own, can yer?' She gave Lily a cracked smile and added, 'I was wonderin' what that note meant.'

The note accompanying the money had said, simply, *Thank you for believing in me.*

'Anyroad, I don't s'pose we'll be seein' too much of yer from now on. I don't know if yer've heard but my Wally buggered off wi' some French tart. Never came home.'

'Oh dear. I'm sorry to hear that.'

'Yeah. Left us high and bloody dry with no money fer rent nor nowt. And by the way, don't think I'm lookin' fer another handout, 'cos I'm not. I haven't sunk to beggin' – not yet.'

'I didn't think for a minute—'

'Your brass helped me a lot. New boots fer Buggerlugs and I paid off some back rent, but we're still behind. T' landlord wants us out next week if I can't pay me arrears. God knows where we'll live.'

'Mam, can I play out, with Tony?' asked Michael.

Lily hesitated as the realisation of normality hit her. She looked down at her son who was still not five years old and yet had been through so much. How could she let him out of her sight to play with the likes of Tony Rafferty? Then she thought of the pampered life he'd just left and she was grateful he'd totally forgotten that life, to the extent that he was happy to play with Tony Rafferty on the cobbles of Perseverance Street.

'Play where I can see you through the window, and put your coat back on.'

Michael grabbed his coat and charged out of the house.

'Can't say as I blame yer fer not wantin' him out of yer sight,' said Mrs Lafferty, craning her neck to see who else was inside the house. If it was a man she wouldn't blame Lily, not one bit. She wouldn't say no to a new man herself. Lily suddenly felt immense pity for this woman who was a bit rough and ready but had probably never done anyone any harm.

'Do you have any idea where you'll be living?'

'Norra clue. I expect we'll end up in some bed and breakfast dump. One thing I do know. The buggers aren't gonna take my Tony off me. Not for summat what's not my fault.'

Her next words seemed to tumble out of Lily's mouth of their own accord. It was as if she lost control of her voice. Charlie heard what she said and stiffened in surprise, hoping she knew what she was doing.

'Mrs Lafferty. I'm not staying on here. You can live in this house if you like and pay me whatever rent you can afford.'

Mrs Lafferty stared at her as if she couldn't believe her ears.

'What?'

'You and Tony can stay here.'

'We can't . . . can we?'

'Yes you can. I'm leaving most of the furniture as well. It's all quite good stuff.'

'Quite good? Buggerlugs reckons it's like a palace. Are yer sure about all this, Mrs Robinson?'

418

'Absolutely sure. You can move in tomorrow if you like. When I leave here this afternoon I'm gone for good. Too many bad memories of the neighbours – that doesn't include you, of course.'

Tears had now filled Mrs Lafferty's eyes. She clamped her hand to her mouth. Her voice was tremulous. 'Bloody hell, Mrs Robinson. I've never known no one do nowt like this for anyone. It's like a bloody dream come true. I can pay some rent, yer know. I can gerra job on t' school dinners and do a bit o' cleanin'. It all adds up.'

'I'm sure you can manage.' Lily took a key from the door lock and gave it to the weeping woman. 'Look, take this key. Come back tomorrow and have a look round. The place might need a bit of a clean. I'll be staying with my auntie in Bradford. I'll leave you her address and phone number. We'll sort out all the details later.'

Mrs Lafferty was frozen to the spot, her shoulders shaking with emotion. All her worries had been suddenly lifted from her shoulders. She turned to go, then she turned back, still not believing this was happening. Lily read her thoughts.

'It's OK, Mrs Lafferty. I mean what I say. The house is yours to live in.'

'For how long?'

'Until you get back on your feet.'

'That could take years.'

'Then you'll be staying here for years.'

The woman nodded, then turned to go again and hurried off down the street. Charlie joined Lily at the door. 'Who was that?' he asked.

'Just a woman on hard times. There's a lot of them around.'

'One less by the sound of it.'

'I hope so.'

Lily looked out at her son who was busy telling Tony his unbelievable story. She took Charlie's hand without taking her eyes off Michael.

'How is he?' Charlie asked.

'Amazing. They're so resilient at that age. We had a little talk about what went on that day in Venice and his life with the Cominellis. To tell the truth he got a bit bored so I took him to the pictures. He's never mentioned it since. Charlie, did you just propose to me?'

'What?'

She turned her head and looked at him. 'I said, did you just propose to me?'

'Well, it was kind of conditional. I mean, it wasn't a proposal if you're going to turn me down. I couldn't handle that.'

'Charlie, that'll make me Lily Cleghorn. Not much of a ring to it – Lily Cleghorn. Before I married Larry my maiden name was Windsor – Lilian Marie Windsor. I could have married a prince with a name like that, and you want me to be Lily Cleghorn? I thought you liked me.'

'It never did me any harm.'

'Ah, Cleghorn's the most beautiful name in the world when you put Charlie in front of it, but Lily Cleghorn . . . now that'd take some getting used to. Anyway, what's this about an all-expenses-paid trip to Venice?'

'Well, we could fly to Paris and take the Orient Express through to Venice. It's running again, so understand. We'd have to spend a few hours in court at some stage, but we could stay in Venice for a good week, all paid for by the Italians. I've kind of arranged it. My mother would look after Michael and Christopher.'

'You seem to have it all organised – almost as if it were a honeymoon.'

'Well,' Charlie admitted, with courage he didn't realise he possessed, 'that certainly crossed my mind.' He grasped the shaft of his stick in both hands and went down on one knee. He took a deep breath and came right out with it.

'For God's sake, Lilian Marie Robinson or Windsor or whatever your flipping name is, will you marry me?'

'Hmm. Can we go on a gondola and be serenaded by the gondolier?'

'If it'll help you say yes.'

'Do you love me, Charlie?'

He got back to his feet. 'Of course I love you. If I didn't love you would I be quaking in my boots afraid you might turn me down? Do you love me?'

'Charlie, I think I fell in love with you some time ago only I daren't admit it to myself.'

He breathed out an immense sigh of happiness and relief, moved away a lock of hair that had fallen over her left eye and kissed her forehead. 'So, we're agreed that we're in love?'

'It seems so.'

'And you really want to marry me?'

'Yes, Charlie. I really want to marry you.'

He let his stick go and put both arms round her, kissing her with as much passion as his injured body would

421

allow. Lily responded in like fashion. It was a kiss that swept away all the bad stuff that had happened to her over the past eight months. A kiss that told her the future with this lovely man was going to be a bright future, full of love and laughter. He suddenly drew back from her. Lily was concerned that their embrace had hurt his chest.

'Charlie, are you in pain?'

'A bit, but all in a good cause.' He fumbled in his pocket. 'I've been wanting to give you this ring for months.'

She laughed with delight when he opened a small box.

'Oh, Charlie! Are you sure it's a real diamond?'

'If it's not,' he said, sliding the ring on to her finger, 'some woman in Leeds market's done me out of four quid.'

Acknowledgments

To my wife's late mother Lilian who, in her youth, lived on Perseverance Street, although the inhabitants back then were far nicer than some of the people I've invented in this book.

Do you love historical fiction?

**Want the chance to hear news about your favourite
authors (and the chance to win free books)?**

Mary Balogh

Charlotte Betts

Jessica Blair

Frances Brody

Gaelen Foley

Elizabeth Hoyt

Eloisa James

Lisa Kleypas

Stephanie Laurens

Claire Lorrimer

Amanda Quick

Julia Quinn

Ken McCoy

Then visit the Piatkus website and blog
www.piatkus.co.uk | www.piatkusbooks.net

And follow us on Facebook and Twitter
www.facebook.com/piatkusfiction | www.twitter.com/piatkusbooks

piatkus